ADVANCE REVIEW COPY

NOT FOR SALE, HIRE OR LOAN

The Sufi Storyteller

Faiqa Mansab

NEEM TREE
PRESS
An imprint of Unbound

ADVANCE REVIEW COPY
NOT FOR SALE, HIRE OR LOAN

The Sufi Storyteller
by Faiqa Mansab

HB • 9781915584526 • £16.99/$27.95 • 320pp
UK & Europe: 20 March 2025
USA & RoW: 25 March 2025

PB • 9781915584250 • £9.99/$17.95 • 320pp
UK & Europe: 5 March 2026
USA & RoW: 2 June 2026

Distributed in the UK and Europe by PGUK/Macmillan
and in the USA & RoW by Consortium/Ingram

#TheSufiStoryteller @FaiqaMansab

Neem Tree Press, an imprint of Unbound

Sales: Gemma@unbound.com
Publicity: Rina@unbound.com

www.unbound.com

For my brilliant, brave son, Ahmad Nabi Noor Jehangir (N.N. Jehangir). You are the strongest, kindest and the most gentle man I have ever known. You will always be my anchor and my North Star. You are forever in my heart, my son. I love you, always and forever.
Till we meet again, meri jan.

786

"Sufi stories are not merely a tale told but a reality lived."
The Sufis by Idries Shah

BOOK ONE

The Beginning of the End

ONE

Halfway into her first semester teaching "Sufi Stories and their Literary Alchemy BA427", Layla Rashid discovered a dead body in the library. She knew then that she hadn't run far enough or well enough from her past.

The day began as it usually did with no helpful warnings of impending disaster.

A short stop at the café before work, five days a week. A tall chai-latte with cinnamon, and the table by the window. Sultan out of the pet-carrier for that brief time, and in her lap. Her hand in his silky black pelt, comforting them both. She, nibbling at her lemon muffin. He, judging with a golden stare.

Layla's days followed each other in disciplined monotony like ducklings in a neat little row. Keeping to a severe albeit fulfilling routine left no time for anything else. She had moved here eight months ago and had built a somewhat new routine for her brand-new life. Layla found routine enriching; it so often slipped into ritual. Routine and ritual had helped her construct her life, day by day, for thirty-two years.

Build your house with straw and sticks and the big bad wolf—people's opinions, your own insecurities, a million other things—would blow your house down all too easily. But build your house, brick by brick, with routine, unearthing your true self as you negotiate with yourself and your life, honouring the trivial as you go along, and you imbue it with the protective magic of identity. And Layla had painstakingly done exactly that.

She was content.

She took another sip of her chai-latte. Almost content. There was no denying that something had finally blown her house down. She had found the old woman's picture eight months ago. That had been the catalyst for her move. Would it matter though? Would her quest end at last? But then, Layla believed every experience was useful. Even pain and failure.

Especially, pain and failure.

The library, which doubled as her office, was in a separate block from the university and only five minutes away from the café. Students hardly ever came to this building—a neglected archive with no electronic keys.

Most days she came half an hour early to avoid the rush hour. She often sat outside in the quad, enjoying the musical psithurism of the leafy tall trees, poplars, oak, maple, the Ohio buckeye, so beautiful and so different from the sparse landscape she'd grown up with in that horrid place. She remembered things in flashes—pictures, sometimes a sound or smell. Vegetation had been minimal there, just stunted barely-green bush, except for the hills of deodar forests which she remembered seeing only once. And here, there was hardly a rush hour in the small university town. The rush-hour mentality was a relic from her New York days.

It was a chilly silver-blue morning of late September. She put the pet carrier down and inserted the old-fashioned key into the lock. It stuck in the out-of-date lock and took a few minutes of precious time before it turned. Not the best day for it to happen. She hadn't slept well, thanks to her recurrent dreams, and she was already running late according to the schedule she'd set for herself.

She opened the door and stepped in. It was the noisome air that struck her first, alerted her senses to everything else that was unfamiliar. She was a creature of habit because it meant safety. Even the slightest of changes sent alarm bells ringing inside her head. There was something in the air, a different smell than the usual dusty-book smell she loved. It was more than the musty odour of the library. It was almost recognizable; almost familiar. She turned the lights on and put her bag and Sultan's heavy carrier on her desk. He growled in the back of his throat, adding to her mounting unease.

Her eyes snagged on the splash of red on the floor. It was a plush crimson velvet cloak. At first, Layla was afraid it was blood. But there was no blood. Just the red cloak.

And the dead woman on the floor.

Heart hammering in her chest and her throat tight, Layla stared at the still, porcelain face of the woman. Empty blue eyes stared at the ceiling. Lips, drained of colour, slightly open, as if her mouth had just begun to form a scream Layla could not hear.

The stillness was eerie. The silence, sinister.

She stared at the corpse. A dead woman on the floor of her library. The woman was pretty. She was also petite; anyone could have carried her easily inside in the thick of night.

Her breath congealed in her chest. Layla rested her hands on the desk for support. Stories might emerge from reality, but reality emerged from stories too. She did not remember much of her past, but she remembered enough to know that if it ever caught up with her, she would be in trouble. The kind of trouble that was staring her in the face. The cold, acrid stench of the room made her gag. The woman was naked and spread-eagled in an obscene, vulnerable fashion. The smell in Layla's nostrils was her own rancid fear, not just the heavy curdling of dead blood.

Layla's legs wobbled. She grabbed the back of her chair and sank into it. She turned again towards the body on the floor. There was a bluish tinge to the face of the woman. The red cloak was too bright in contrast, too reminiscent of life to be attached to something dead. It drew her attention repeatedly. Its vivid colour belied the coldness of death. *Was it murder? Was she looking at a murdered woman?*

She got up with a start, turned to run, to flee the scene and let someone else deal with the responsibility, the attention of being the one to find a dead body.

But she didn't.

Instead, she stepped closer to the dead woman on the floor. There were bruises on her throat, a dark line visible from beneath the fold of the cloak. *Had the dead woman been strangled with its strings?* The hood lay half buried under her head, golden hair parted and curled, the slightly darker roots visible.

Something stirred in her memory. Something she had seen? A movie? A picture? Then, just as quickly, vanished like a swift-footed animal into a neural black-hole of shock. This naked, dead body had plucked the memory of the other naked, dead woman she had seen on another campus, just a few months earlier, and superimposed itself on all other thought. This was not the first young woman's dead body she had seen.

That first time, Layla had been in the middle of changing jobs. At the time, she had barely registered the murder. She had been too busy thinking of the practicalities of her move and her reasons for doing so. She had considered the murder an unfortunate incident on campus, a bit of sad news at the periphery of her life. Something that had happened at a place that was already a past she was leaving behind.

And now this.

She stepped away from the dead body and called the police.

TWO

By the time the police arrived, there was already a crowd outside. Layla had informed her dean and the news had spread. The library was sealed by the police. The yellow tape made it seem like a movie set, rather than something that would actually happen in a small university town in rural America. Students stood in small groups near the yellow tape. Fear and excitement hung around them like miasma, murky with dark whispers and cigarette smoke. Layla's colleagues expressed their concern for her by filling her nervous hands with Styrofoam cups of coffee. She nodded and murmured, but her mind was stuck on the tune of her fears.

The police had walked Layla to a side office and had gone through the formalities of questioning "the member of the public that had first discovered the body" as soon as they had secured the area. Back outside, she stood with the crowd as forensics photographed the scene, took swabs and whatever else they did.

Who was she? The murdered woman? Layla overheard one of the policemen tell another that a woman had been reported missing only three days before. *Was it her?* The dead body was put in a black body bag. She saw it wheeled away on a stretcher.

She squeezed her eyes shut.

Stories had taught Layla the shape of the world. The puissant world of storytelling and its laws, their innate intuitive knowledge, their warp and weft, had not just been her scholarly pursuit but the totality of her life. No one knew better than her that the beginnings of stories were rarely ever the onset of things, and as a historian of stories and their roots, she recognized the beginning of a story when she saw one.

Her eyes flew open. She saw the maple trees around her, their verdant green only half visible as the leaves had already changed colour to yellow and shades of russet. But her thoughts flew elsewhere from the beauty of early autumn in mid-west America. Just that morning, she had been thinking of rituals and routine. Murder was as far from routine as was possible. But long ago, it had been ritual—sacrifice, and propitiation.

The fact that this was the second dead body she had seen that year, terrified her. *Both women? Both naked? What did it mean?*

Her mind—moulded and informed by the rich, diverse storytelling traditions of the world, blending myth, history, and folklore—used stories, their tropes and archetypes, as ciphers to navigate the world. Numbers were a language. She knew rituals and prayers were coded in odd numbers, in threes or sevens. Significant things happened in odd numbers. In the mythopoeic oeuvre of the world, odd numbers were associated with light, with goodness, and even numbers with the infinite and the dark. Virgil was known to have said that the deity is pleased with odd numbers. Shakespeare wrote that there was divinity in odd numbers. In Islamic mysticism, odd numbers are important: "Verily God is an odd number and loves the odd number".

Yet murder—a dark horrid act—also occurred in odd numbers. In mythopoeic traditions odd numbers did refer to magic and light. Yet, evil magic and murderers had appropriated odd numbers too. *What did this inversion mean? If there were two bodies, might there be another?* Someone touched her shoulder. Layla looked up and gave a small smile, taking the cup of tea offered, the sympathetic words, the curious questioning glances. She had done everything she could to not attract attention. So why was the body in her library?

She could no longer allow that first murder in January, at Belmont university to remain in the past. This could not be a coincidence.

Coincidence was a concept Layla did not subscribe to, because coincidence was a marker in stories urging the protagonist and the reader to scrutinize the situation more closely. Coincidence hinted at parallel truths, inter-connectivity, histories and clues that may have been forgotten by the protagonist, but were vital to the story, and their own survival.

In stories, coincidence was never truly a fluke. If something happened twice, there was a pattern.

Something terrible had happened now. She had ignored it the first time and another woman had been murdered because she had not paid attention.

A definite and dark pattern was beginning to reveal itself to Layla and her breath clotted in her throat, choking her.

THREE

Layla was used to waking up early to harvest the stillness of dawn, when the Universe was silent, listening. She felt an affinity with the cosmos then. The vast silence around her was an extension of her own. Dawn was also the traditional time for Layla to supplicate.

She woke up in a sweat that morning, her heart still thudding from a nightmare. One she had been having since she was nine years old. But ever since the murder in the library three days ago, the nightmare seemed to be a rather more persistent haunting. It left her agitated. Like always, in the dream she had been a child; terrified, seeking approval, devastated. Despite her efforts, she couldn't quite make out what the tall, teary-eyed woman whispered to her. She had strained to hear. She had cried, not in fear but at her own helplessness. If only she could understand the woman, then she'd have her answer.

She threw her bedcovers off.

The murder had shaken her. That was all. *Surely it had nothing to do with her?* She had been trying to convince herself of that for the last three days.

Layla swung her legs down the side of her bed, head in her trembling hands. She reached for the bottle on her nightstand and took a gulp of water. Sultan purred and moved his lithe body against her back. She quickly scooped him in her arms. He protested but she put her face against his warmth. She'd found her one-eared black cat ten years ago in Lahore, when he was still a kitten, abandoned and starving. Now Layla was his pet, and he was an exacting master.

"Go back to sleep," she kissed her velvety cat. "I'm okay."

Sultan twitched his tail and took her advice for once, burrowing into the covers.

If Layla had still been teaching her "Dreams and Stories 101" class, she would have told her students that in some cultures, dreams were deemed a supernatural temporal space, a subconscious, automatic psychic realm. Dreams emerged from a site where nature and its secrets could neither be enhanced nor perverted. And what was the most ancient symbol of nature?

Yes, indeed. Mother.

The schism that separated her scholar's mind from the wounded part of her selfhood usually kicked in on its own, and she could feel it grinding awake, efficiently putting up the fences, disconnecting the feral child of her dreams from the domain of the capable scholar. She put the bottle back on the table, still sitting in the dark, trying to get her heart to slow down, separating the dream from reality.

Layla got up and went to the bathroom. She did her ablutions quickly, as quietly as possible. Silence had been instilled in her long ago. Splashing cold water on her hot face, her arms. Washing her feet. She wrapped a scarf around her head and stood facing Mecca, somewhere in the north-east, unseen and invisible to her, like the God she worshipped. The one she questioned every day, a hundred different ways. She began praying. With her heart in her mouth, and her forehead still glistening with sweat, she became an ardent supplicant. Her heartbeat slowed down beneath her open palms resting on her chest.

Wasn't sleep called the little death, a gateway to a new dimension of time and space, to a new realm? The only space where dream world and reality collided and became one whole was at the junction of a story. Sufi stories often blossomed in just such a fluctuating realm of dream and reality, like the world of *Alice in Wonderland*. Sufi stories often had an episodic, unfinished sense of structure and form, because such stories were a representation of the human being—fragmented, in the process of becoming, and therefore transforming and changing.

Like her life. Like her identity. She had a sudden urge to hug Sultan's warm little body to her cold heart.

Layla prostrated.

She shook her head, concentrating on the Arabic words, their meaning. Irreverent thoughts intruded upon her pious devotion like ants crawling on an open pot of honey, blackening the pristine gold, rendering its sweetness bitter, inedible. There was little conviction in her prayers at times. No miracle had strengthened her crumbling faith. Layla turned her covered head to the right shoulder first then the left, and raised her hands for a supplementary prayer, her forehead still creased.

She had waited for a miracle, a sign, a hint, for nearly twenty-three years about her birth mother. Had she finally got one eight months ago?

The familiar pain struck like a viper, whenever she thought of her birth mother, and dominated all other thought.

How could she have abandoned me?

A sibilant whisper, dream memory, or life memory, she did not know, tugged her mind like an old familiar song, "Sshh, silent and strong. You have to be silent and strong like a mountain... with your roots so deep into the ground no storm can break you, nothing can move you."

She was still trying to find the happy ending of her abandoned story. Hadn't she spent enough of her life hiding in universities and libraries, and the kitchen in her adoptive mother Hasina's house, studying and learning, and trying to piece together the mystery of her own life? Where had it got her?

Her heart leaped in response, as she thought of how, after twenty-three years, she had finally found a clue. She had followed a woman into this underfunded university, leaving her big city university behind. She had been following the woman for a few months now, but she was still unsure, still afraid.

Layla, an expert on parsing stories, had found the beginning of her own story at last. Or so she believed, and she did not want to end that hunch too quickly and find out that she mistaken. But how did the murdered bodies of the two women fit? Were they really connected to each other, to her? Or was it her innate fear making connections?

She got up and folded her scarf, putting it away along with thoughts of her birth mother and murder. She walked towards the window of her studio-flat and peered out. It still surprised her that this slender backstreet in a university town in the

Midwest, USA, should remind her of Lahore. Or maybe she looked for clues of Lahore wherever she found herself, to keep the memory of Khayyam close. So close, she could smell him.

The tiny café across the narrow alley was aglow with warm yellow light. Every morning, when it was still dark, a young man, grumpy with sleep, arrived on his bike. He pushed a few buttons and the café groaned and stirred into reluctant life. Layla unlatched the window, opened it a sliver and inhaled the bitter-sweet fragrance of coffee. Magic must smell like this. She felt the joy curl up in her heart like a twirl of steam over a cup. The smell of coffee was comfort. That was the smell she remembered from twenty-three years ago, when she and her birth mother had entered the American Consulate in that far-off city she remembered only as a smell. Only then, Layla hadn't known what the strong, inviting fragrance was, except that it had been the smell of safety, surely, else why had her mother sobbed with relief?

Layla turned away from the window but left it open for Sultan. He might choose to stay that day. She usually put a pet basket on the floor and gave him a choice. If he got in, she could take him with her and stay as long as she liked at the library. If he didn't, and chose to stay back at home, she had to leave his bowls full and return early to feed him.

She put on her standard uniform of blue jeans and loose white top, her curly brown hair with the generous sprinkling of grey that had come too soon, hung loose over her shoulders. People often commented on her grey hair. That she looked distinguished, or that she was too young for it and should get her hair dyed, everyone else did. Or that she was not actually thirty-two at all, but much older. When would people learn to not comment on a woman's appearance? It was her choice, damn it! But she never said it. She tried to disappear in crowds, wore neutral colours and chose solitude. Over the course of her life, she had bound herself so tightly in regret and fear, there was no room left for living. She was like an ancient mummy, wrapped in bandages of caution, embalmed in broken memories, so that no one knew who she was underneath. Not least herself.

At thirty-two, she was considered too young by academics to be given the deference half of them thought she deserved. Her first book had been about the history of fables and their Sufi roots. Her second, the history of women's storytelling techniques and their canon. Her third book was about the intersectionality of Sufi storytelling and folktales from around the world. Two more had come out one after another. She had made a name for herself already. She threw her keys into her leather bag, put on her sneakers, itching to get her first cup of coffee for the day.

She put the pet carrier down and called out to the cat. "Sultan."

He slunk past her legs, rubbing himself archly on both, entwining around her ankles in a figure of eight and then pattered towards the couch.

"Fine," she said and poured cat food and water in his bowls. "I'd rather not work long today either. I'll be back by three with some tuna for you."

She walked to the university. It gave her time to compose her various selves. There were so many little parts of her, all broken and fragile, and they made her whole in a tessellated sort of way. This part of her that was Professor Layla Rashid was a capable woman. But the frightened little girl continued to survive in the sub fusc corners of her adult consciousness, still trying to mine memories she knew lurked behind the mist of amnesia.

FOUR

Layla preferred the reveille classes no one wanted. Starting her day early kept her days tightly reined in, just the way she liked. It was second nature to her, this craving for invisibility but she had no recollection where this instinct emanated from. She just knew that it was important because one false step could unravel the punctiliously woven tapestry of normal and hard-won inconspicuousness. Well-believed lies were planted in time. Dress the part, look the part and people accepted what you represented. One's hidden reality was immaterial. Only what was visible on the outside mattered. No one could tell how practiced it was, or how precious the mask was to her. And she was very good at hiding.

"Good morning," Layla said, facing her small class of undergraduates. Then threw the question into the air, like a ball to be caught, "Why do we read stories?"

"Is it true you found a dead body in your office?"

Layla shut her eyes in defeat. Of course. How could she have thought she'd be able to avoid the gruesome interest? The little goblins would want nothing else.

"Yes, it's true."

"Was it someone you know?"

"Why was it in your office? Will you be arrested?"

"Have the police found anything yet?"

"Why your office?"

She raised her hand. There was silence.

"You're asking me for a story I cannot tell. Simply because I don't know the whole of it. Yet. Yes, I found an unfortunate woman who had been killed. Yes, the body was in my office slash library. That is all we know. Why, who, when…these are questions for law enforcement. And if we are to learn how to excavate facts from fiction, and truth from both, then we need to go back to my question: why do we yearn for stories?"

The buzz made her smile…almost. Her tribe might be miniscule, but they belonged together, although thankfully, only for an hour a day, three days a week. She raised an eyebrow and the corner of her nude lips in a half-smile of encouragement. The murder had shaken them all of course. But she squared her shoulders and tried to keep her thoughts on her class.

"Come on. I'm not looking for wisdom and truth with a capital 'T'. Least of all from my undergrads."

There was a smattering of laughter.

"Just opinion. I know you all have one…too many."

Gul, a young woman, possibly from Uzbekistan, in a bright patterned hijab that matched her blouse, responded. "Empathy? We feel understood when we read stories to which we can relate."

"Absolutely!" Layla nodded. "Because there are so many reasons, right? In fact, there can be opposing reasons. Stories are birthed from people, their experiences, culture, limitations and imagination. There are plenty of reasons why we love stories."

Another student, John, tall and lanky with messy blond hair, raised his hand. "Stories help us make sense of our own experiences, the world and our own psyche even, like in myths… and even fairytales."

Smiling broadly Layla, nodded. All memory of excoriating dreams forgotten, and their spurious questions larruped out of her mind by the magic of stories.

"Wonderful! Someone's read Bettelheim, at last. Well done! Stories can be heuristic in that sense. Stories anchor us. They spin a web of familiarity and comfort and rock us to sleep. But webs are traditionally…traps."

They looked at her in surprise. Her smile widened. This was the fun part.

"Some stories fit into one another, the first leading to the next making a chain like a string of pearls. Each one is precious and complete on its own but when strung together they emerge as a beautiful whole. A sequence of tales offers deeper insights than a single story might. Do any examples come to mind?"

Gul raised her hand again. "Mullah Nasruddin stories."

Layla smiled. "Ah, my favourite. Yes, absolutely. Did you know *Don Quixote* is said to be inspired by the Mullah? Yes, look it up. Nasruddin is the quintessential Wise Fool, a remarkable figure found in Sufi stories, often known as Teaching stories, who himself comes across as someone naïve and foolish but instructs others through his ostensive foolishness. The Sufi Master Idries Shah archived many Mullah Nasruddin stories. One goes like this. The Mullah came to the local teashop one day looking particularly smug, and a regular customer, who was in a bad mood, asked, 'What're you so happy about?' The Mullah said, 'If you had made a whole tribe of bloodthirsty cannibals run, you'd be smug about it too.' Everyone gasped. 'What did you do?' asked the man. 'What do you think I did? I ran and they all ran after me.'"

Those who'd been listening laughed.

Another student, Maria, dark-eyed and serious, joined the discussion. "There are other examples of such nesting stories. Russian folktales. *The Arabian Nights*, or *A Thousand and One Nights*. A story within a story is also called *mise en abyme*?"

"Very good," said Layla. "*Mise en abyme* is a concept in the plastic arts of an image within an image. The same image which appears infinitely. This is the concept that is used to tell a story within a story, play within play, like in *Hamlet*. It presupposes multiple narratives, often hierarchical, and the Jungian concept of mirroring and identity are frequently connected to it, especially when reading tales within Sufi traditions. The mirroring can be of the hidden self or the future image of self as a desirable goal. The stories of the Mullah, *A Thousand and One Nights, The Conference of the Birds*, the *Shahnameh,* and several others—including stories by Italo Calvino and Jostein Gaarder—demonstrate this concept."

Layla had discussed the same with Khayyam, long ago. A century ago, it seemed. How he'd revelled in the connections she made, explaining influences, confluence and contrasts. Sometimes she thought she'd made him up. Maybe he wasn't real at all. Ten years was a long time to keep a memory alive.

"About the teaching story," said Gul, "I don't understand how that is possible? How can millions of readers learn the same lessons from a story? People are from different cultures. What I see, John will not—I believe *cannot* see—say, in the stories of Mullah Nasruddin because he is an American city dweller. I know why donkeys feature in so many of the Mullah's tales because these are stories largely from the Middle East and Asia where donkeys are beasts of burden and often treated cruelly, and so it's a trope of helplessness, but to John the donkey is almost an exotic animal."

Layla laughed. Gul had successfully brought her back to the present.

"Hey," said John only half-seriously, "what I see may be different, but it has equal value!"

"Yes, of course," Gul was impatient at the interruption, "But if we're talking of Sufi storytelling traditions and searching for meaning, how can you possibly know what the story means if you're not familiar with its traditions, its morality, its jokes and humour?"

"Ah, Gul," Layla asked. "Are you the one who wants to do her thesis on Sufi storytelling traditions?"

"Yes," beamed the girl.

"You're obviously passionate about the subject. That's good. You're well-informed. But you misunderstood me. The reader's identity does not matter to the story. The story, however, matters to the identity of the reader."

"Got it," said Gul. "That makes sense now. The story is the catalyst but not for all readers. It is a catalyst only if allowed to be by the reader's state of mind and self-awareness."

"Absolutely right," said Layla, smiling. "Some stories were once sacred and the same ones become profane later, in a different political climate. There are recensions and expurgations to make them palatable for shifting regimes and cultures. Don't forget Foucault, who said that we are all constructs, and Marx, who identified capitalism as the most dominant structure of all. The reader's state of mind is thus a product of their own political climate, and also their personal level of growth. Can they break those social conditionings, or will they fall into old traps?"

Layla had been leaning against her desk, facing her class. She turned away, fumbling with her papers on the desk, suddenly thinking of her nightmares. Nobody broke away from cultural traps and those who did hurt their loved ones in the process. Hadn't she been abandoned by the person who was supposed to love and protect her the most? The world was still selling feminist princesses to the gullible. Universities were just another fish market where knowledge and information were interchangeable, and wisdom remained rare. One had merely to know what to sell and how to sell it.

She gathered herself together and turned back around to face the students again. Her hands flurried as if to get rid of invisible flies. Her mask was back in place.

She brought Sufi mythology into the disquisition, "There's an old Sufi legend about there being a Pole, the Universal Man, or Perfect Man, the world's spiritual leader. There are four pillars who support him and together they serve the world. And often save it too. They don't seek attention and always remain secret. Knowledge is passed to them and through them. They are the Axis Mundi. There are five such people in every era and they serve humanity and their spiritual well-being. Of course, this is Sufi mythology, but if true even at the most mundane level, doesn't it make one wonder how much of this knowledge is encapsulated in Sufi stories?"

Some of them were furiously taking notes, Gul and John among them. Others were staring into space, or scrolling through their phones. Layla was just grateful for the office space and the treasure trove of books, and the annals at her disposal for research. Teaching was a necessary evil.

"Are they always men?" Gul asked frowning.

"I doubt it. But it is a legend, and we cannot know. When I first began to study stories," Layla said, "I wondered how they were preserved and how they migrated across borders and boundaries, and who were these people making sure they were passed on? Stories change their face but the bones remain. Sufi tradition says we take from the story what we will, according to our own stage of spiritual and mental development. Storytellers linked spiritual development to personal growth. What other links did they make?"

Her mind reeled, and she faltered, struck dumb by the vision of a pair of green eyes. Were the words memory that had quickened on her tongue?

Gul looked up. "I don't understand? You're talking of what Idries Shah refers to as 'teaching stories'?"

"Not just those. Sufi stories cannot be bound. Not within books nor within rigid frameworks. That's why they were oral for so long. They change and morph. Sufi stories are efflorescent in nature and often turn up as fairytales, fables, and even jokes. Sufi stories do not die. They escape the norms of storytelling. Coruscate with wisdom, they will leak out even from the confines of time and culture, as have *The Arabian Nights*, the *Conference of Birds*, stories of Zal, Rustam and Sohrab from the *Shahnameh*. They regenerate tale after tale for hundreds of years, as old beliefs and old wives' tales and songs. Why? How?"

Layla touched the rectangular carnelian at her throat, inscribed with protective verses from the Quran.

"Sufi stories have been called talismans by some," she said, "and I agree. I feel the very text of a Sufi story is apotropaic, a magic spell against the vagaries of life and human baseness. They guard us against the evil of untruths, even though most stories wear the garb of fiction to roam the earth."

She wore two pendants and many bracelets, talismans all, which she had collected over the years, from Turkey, Iran, Pakistan and India. From the shrines of saints and from vendors who'd inscribed special words for her on semi-precious stones. Khayyam had given her the very first one. Her talismans were armour against hurt, despair, abandonment. Her tattoos too. When people asked her about them, as they invariably did, she told them her body was a sacred site, and that she had tattoos from different stages of her life to mark their passage.

"That was amazing. Prof, are you...I mean, are you a Sufi?" asked John.

"Sadly, no," said Layla.

There was laughter. Students often mistook her for one because she taught Sufi stories and their traditions. And because of her talismans and loose tunics.

"So, what you're saying is that each story imparts a different meaning to a different person?" asked another girl.

"Yes, absolutely. All good stories do, no matter their origin, don't they?" said Layla.

"So, if Sufi stories are all that, why do you refer often to Greek myths and Western literature?" asked Maria.

Layla should have suppressed her irritation. "Just because I am teaching the history and tradition of Sufi stories, I am not denying other canons. When I refer to other rich cultures and traditions, I am acknowledging and referring to the amalgamation of ancient traditions, their influence over each other through translations, through trade and through travel. Sufi influences are rich in Aesop. Some say she was Greek, others that she was African. It is also believed that Aesop wasn't one person at one specific time. Who can say? But the possibilities are endless in story. Western literature did not happen in a vacuum. The world was not always as small as it is now, but stories have a way of reaching places they are meant to, for people who need them." People like her, who didn't feel so broken in the world of stories. She had only been able to locate herself in the geographies of unfamiliar cities, within the narrow streets of university towns, to feel secure in the cold dampness of unfamiliar weather. She preferred large, bustling cities. Cities with their noise and people meant safety.

And yet here she was in this little town following someone into the past. Or despair. Or maybe they were the same.

"Can you explain?" asked Gul.

Layla nodded, "For example, the story of the scorpion going across the river on the back of a frog, a turtle, an eel and even a trout, seems to have found universal appeal. Which canon can truly claim it? It is widely acknowledged as an Aesop fable. It is also quoted by Idries Shah as a Sufi tale. Stories will never be a victim to the world's bias and prejudice. They travel where they will and find a home where they're needed. The polarization of the world through religion and colour has never been able to defeat or curb stories. It never will."

"Can you tell us the story?" called someone from the back row.

"The story is famous but for those who don't know it, it goes like this," said Layla. "The scorpion asked the frog to help it cross the river. 'I'll climb on your back,' it said. 'You'll sting me,' said the frog. The scorpion said, 'Why would I? Then we'd both drown.' The logic was faultless, and the frog agreed. Midway across the river, the scorpion stung the frog. 'Why did you do that?' The dying frog was stunned at the betrayal. 'I was helping you. I was kind to you.'

" 'Why are you blaming me for my nature?' asked the scorpion. 'It's your nature to help and be kind. And mine to sting. Why do you think your nature is morally better and not mine?' " Layla watched her students for reactions. "What do you make of this story?"

Gul said, "The story is about free will and nature. Choice seems to be the lesson here or at least one of them. Choices make us who we are and not obedience to nature or culture or whatever."

"Excellent!" Layla said concluding her class.

When they left, Layla gathered her books in a leather tote bag she had bought from Lahore ten years ago, when she'd come home with a bruised heart and a bagful of memories. Leather was cheap in South Asia and she liked natural materials. Natural fabrics lasted longer. Even her clothes, faded now, were all made from cotton or wool. She saved her teacher's salary for travel, searching Asiatic lands for what she had lost. One time she had bought a Turkish carpet she'd fallen in love with at an old, dusty shop. She'd had to dip into her savings. The following year she had been unable to travel. She still prized that carpet, which was even now the centre piece in her flat.

She entered the empty library, now clear for use again. The police had taken what evidence they could glean from it. Row upon row of wooden shelves groaned under the weight of books, and the small section of temperature-controlled manuscripts, letters and diaries of an obscure local writer. On the left at the entrance was a notice board that always drew Layla's attention. A poster offering a talk on storytelling. She stared at the woman in the poster.

Mira Heshmat's eyes were fierce. This was the woman she had been following for months. She had attended every single one of Mira's talks, no matter where it was held. She had even caught trains and planes to get there. And yet she had not had the courage to approach her, let alone speak with her.

Mira Heshmat reminded Layla of the woman in her dreams. Layla believed Mira was her birth mother.

FIVE

Mourning and grief were not the same. One could stop mourning, but grief was a hollow darkness that carved its home in the heart. Grief permeated the cells of one's skin, and bones and teeth. It ate one up, one nibble at a time. Slowly, painfully.

Layla had lived with just such a grief ever since her birth mother had abandoned her.

And she had not yet been able to muster the courage to seek out Mira and confront her. Instead, she called up Hasina, her adoptive mother, to tell her she would visit over the weekend. To herself, Layla made the excuse that she wasn't running away from facing Mira, and she wasn't afraid to hear the truth and be disappointed. She was merely waiting for the right time to speak with Mira.

In any case, Hasina needed her attention. There was an unspoken rule between them. Never more than six months of absence. It was already six months since they had last met, and she would soon begin supervision for dissertations, making it impossible to go to Chicago to visit Ma.

"Salam, Layla," Hasina's calm, soft voice was bright with pleasure. "So glad to hear from you! It has been six months and ten days since your last visit."

Layla had had no intention of telling Ma about the murder but as soon as she heard her voice, something changed. That rock solid heart she was so complacent about thudded uncomfortably loud.

"Ma, there's been a murder here."

Layla heard the sharply drawn breath.

"Are you okay?" Ma asked.

All Layla wanted to hear was that she had nothing to worry about. It was a horrid coincidence. It could happen.

"Yes. It…the body was in my library. I found it. I called the police. But I—" Layla hadn't told Hasina about the previous murder. Needless worry, she'd thought at the time. Now she was babbling about this one and it was all too complicated. She was afraid, Layla realized. And the fear was rooted in the beginning of the pattern she could almost discern. But why worry Ma? And over the phone! She took a deep breath, infused her voice with false brightness, "just thought I'd let you in on the excitement on campus."

Surely there was nothing to worry about! She was being silly. So what if her heart jumped in her throat at every loud noise?

The disappointed silence at the other end was a reprimand and Layla cursed herself for underestimating her adoptive mother's intelligence and her scruples.

"Sorry, Ma," she said quickly.

"Be safe, my darling. And do not treat death with flippancy. It is not right, nor respectful."

"Love you, Ma. Will call again soon."

"As if I'd believe that after all these years. My luck can't be changing this fast, scary though it is, this phone call. Very scary. I thought this was a small, boring university. Are you sure you wouldn't like to come home for a while? I'm not getting any younger you know."

"Could've fooled me."

The chuckle warmed Layla and she smiled. What a reward.

"Get on with you. Keep me in the loop. Don't go out late at night. And come for a visit."

"I think I will. That is why I called. I will be coming over next Friday as I have Monday off."

Ma's happiness at her acceptance of the invitation was evident in the way she discussed three different menus in the span of two minutes on the phone, all of which, Layla knew, would be discarded for a fourth.

Layla moved on light feet after she put away her phone. Now that she'd made plans to visit, Layla couldn't wait for the days to pass and on Friday she took the train to Chicago. She took a taxi from the train-station and bought a bunch of flowers on the way, chocolate, and some traditional sweets from the Bengali shop at the corner. Sultan sat staring at her in the carrier.

"Just a few minutes," she coaxed.

He blinked and stretched.

"I am not mean. I disagree strongly," she said with a smile.

Sultan yawned. Or was that a laugh disguised as a yawn?

When they reached her Ma's place, Layla put her stuff on the doorstep and let Sultan out first. Outside, hawthorn grew in abundance. The house was old stone and bricks. Sitting in some apartment or other she had rented for the duration, she would yearn for these stone walls, the tiny sun-room, and the simple life of her childhood. She and Ma loved this little house that smelled of mint and turmeric and roasted fennel. Healing herbs all of them. It also smelled of stories. There was a musty odour attached to all the books she had left here. The variety of scents made for a rich intoxicating personal history.

Sultan stretched and padded towards the door. She let them both in with her own set of keys and heard the gaggle of voices, recognising one immediately. Those raspy, tobacco-abused vocal cords couldn't sound comforting to anyone but Layla. Munia was their neighbour. There couldn't be a celebration in anybody's home on the street, especially not at Hasina's, without Munia. She was a permanent party fixture, the proverbial fairy godmother no one forgot despite her bluntness. Yes, Munia's voice meant comfort.

"Now behave," she warned Sultan. Ignoring her, he padded into the kitchen.

For Hasina, the kitchen was home. Little orphan Layla had adapted so happily to her new surroundings all those years ago because along with cooking, stories had been—and continued to be—a big part of their lives.

The faint aroma of spices from the previous night permeated the air. A comforting reminder of the magic conjured in the kitchen. Ma used to say a kitchen that didn't smell wasn't a clean kitchen but a dead one. Smell, she believed, wasn't always a bad thing.

"People use spices as carelessly as words," she'd say, "with little idea of where they should actually go."

Remembering her Ma's gnomic pronouncements brought a smile to her face.

"Some people actually put garam masala as seasoning in vegetables. Some temper split chickpeas with garlic." Ma's lips would tremble with horror and then give in to laughter.

"Sultan!" she heard Ma exclaim with love. Sultan purred. He preferred Ma to her of course. He was an intelligent cat. She and Ma had had a very serious conversation about the possibility of Sultan being an abandoned djinn child. He was silky black and had an ear missing as if there had never been one. Thick fur had grown on that missing piece of ear but when she'd found him on the thirteenth of June, there had been a pinkish bald patch but no blood or scar.

The aunties were all making a fuss of him. She didn't recognize the other voices immediately, but when she caught a few intonations, she was able to put names and faces to them. Aunty Sheila, Aunty Coco, and Aunty Helen; there were some new ones too. She put her bag on the foyer table and walked briskly to the living room. Ma had knocked down the wall that separated the kitchen from the living room. From the large windows, she could see the silver maple and green elms, leaves rustling in the breeze.

Munia stood in the archway smiling. Her arms outstretched for a hug. Layla fell into the embrace. How often had she seen Ma and Munia having tea together every morning in this kitchen? She would join them occasionally. Mostly, it was just the two of them—Hasina and flamboyant Munia—sipping fragrant tea and exchanging recipes, stories and gossip. Sometimes Layla would make the tea. Water boiled with three green cardamoms, a stick of cinnamon and a sliver of ginger. They liked their tea strong; no new-fangled brands would do. They bought their tea leaves from the Bengali shop at the corner. There was nothing more satisfying, nothing more comforting than a daily tea ritual with an old friend.

"Layla!" Hasina hurried towards her with open arms. "We've been waiting for you. Doesn't the room look great? Come, meet everyone."

Layla hugged Munia, and the other Aunties. There were a couple of new faces, and she shook hands with them. Ma poured milk in Sultan's special saucer. It was Windsor.

"Dye your hair, darling," said Munia, ruffling Layla's grey strands gently.

"Look at you!" exclaimed Aunty Coco.

"How are you?" asked Aunty Helen.

The house smelled of mint and healing stories. The heady fragrance of mustard seeds reminded her of adventure stories; black peppercorns gave courage to heroes stuck in peril; rose water for a dash of romance, and star anise for magic.

Hasina squeezed her shoulder, "Would you like to rest for now?"

"No," she said quickly. "I see some new faces." Ma wanted to protect her from her people-anxiety but Layla hadn't seen her mother and her friends in a long time and she tried to fight the anxiety.

"Diba, Tara, Nicole, Rashmi, Haya…"

The words swirled around her.

"…started a cooking club…"

"…she saved my life with this…."

Layla's shoulders eased and she smiled. A cooking club! Only Hasina could devote so much time to others. Layla un-entangled herself from the conversation, resisting the urge to hide, and moved to another group.

"I'll rinse and wash, chop and cut, Ma. I'll be your sous chef." That had been a running joke in their house. Layla could cook but she never really did.

Layla entered the kitchen to join the rest of them, following the sounds of happy, blustery movements, footfalls scraping, shuffling, clicking. Even sounds not heard for months could be so familiar. Layla recognized the aroma of the traditional thirteen spices ground and mixed, their strong scent caught in her throat, and she coughed. The reaction was familiar. Layla's happiest memories of Ma were her laughter, her soft wrinkly skin and the scent of spices. The aromas wafting in this house were a mix of a thousand South Asian nights and days;

of powdered spices and heat; of water and roses; of earth and petrichor; of cinnamon and saffron.

When she was young, in an attempt to entice her into the kitchen, Ma would often say, "You know, some people like stories that dwell on horror, others like those that dwell on love. The art of storytelling is the same as the art of cooking. You need to have the right ingredients for what you're cooking, and you have to measure the ingredients required. You mess up one quantity of even a single ingredient, too much or too little, and you've failed. Word by word, spice by spice, you add and layer until you create a piece of beauty."

"What is that smile? What are you thinking of?" Munia slid up to her. Sultan had happily taken up his favourite seat at the kitchen windowsill.

Layla chuckled. "Food and Ma, and of you both having morning tea."

"You were such an eavesdropper," Munia smiled with affection.

Laughing, Layla began pounding the pestle against the stone to crush the dry spices. Dark brown cinnamon, green cardamom, black pepper corns, mahogany cloves, mustard seeds. The sound was oddly soothing–rough, not hollow, a full and meaningful sound of friction; stone against stone, rubbing, crushing, and breaking down the dry spices into a homogenous powder.

"Sometimes," said Hasina, coming towards Layla, "a dish needs seasoning that is already mixed and infused like ground garam masala, especially for certain meat dishes. It doesn't do to throw them in as separate wholes in everything, just as it wouldn't do to grind them for everything. Imagine pulao with ground garam masala seasoning instead of whole spices."

Ma was particular about spices just as Layla was about stories. She nudged Layla away and took over the crushing. Layla reached for the small heap of vegetables. The tangy, citrusy fragrance of fresh limes was a happy smell redolent with memories: peeling lemon and lime rinds with Ma in the golden warm winter sun; her hands cold and stiff as she sorted the rinds in separate bowls; Ma expertly peeling thin ribbons of rinds from green limes, yellow lemons and tangy oranges.

"What are these for?" Layla would ask.

"Zarda. The sweet yellow rice you love so much."

That brought her back to the present. "What are we having for dessert?"

Hasina's nut-brown eyes shone as she gazed at her daughter. "Zarda, of course. But also, gulab jamun."

Grinning, Layla took the cinnamon sticks Munia offered and sniffed. A slightly dusty and bitter-sweet scent. She offered them to Aunty Helen.

"Beautiful, aren't they?" said Aunty Helen. "Aunty Coco's niece got them from Sri Lanka last month. We've been using them a lot."

Layla inhaled the infusion of aromata suspended in the kitchen. She spotted a white china bowl of the spicy-hot green chilies.

"Did you see the new boy at the Bengali shop the other day?" Aunty Coco asked Aunty Trish. "He was refreshing the dry mixed herbs by running his hands through them."

"Imbecile," Hasina said. "Mixing spices already ruins them but most buyers wouldn't know that and suffer the consequences. When their cooked meat has a stale, dull odor rather than the fresh pungent aroma of garam masala it should have, they won't even know why."

Aside from the alluring aroma of spices, Hasina's home often smelled of incense, usually jasmine or sandalwood. But the spices in the kitchen and the dining room were striking. Layla had learned to recognize them early—garlic, ginger, sage, lemongrass.

Layla understood why Hasina couldn't ever talk about her home before she came to the U.S. Ma's memories had been smothered by the violence, the hurt and the betrayal she had endured. She had lived with many such painful memories and had internalized them and kept them locked up. She tried to be strong and to be there for everyone, to heal and to feed. Food was healing. The more effort you put into cooking the more healing it held within its taste, packed into its nutrients. Ma's hurts had been deep; wounds gouged on the soul by parents never heal. Layla understood that perfectly; she had a similarly painful inheritance. She'd learned of Hasina's forced marriage, the abuse, the divorce, and the loss of support from her own family, only when she had grown up and finally understood the snatches of conversations she'd heard growing up.

"I almost forgot," said Ma. She took a big piece of fish out of a bowl where it had been resting and popped it in the oven. "For Sultan. I'll just grill it. He'll love it."

Cool breeze wafted through the open window. Layla found Hasina watching her and plastered a smile on her face, hoping the shadow of those earlier memories was not visible on her face.

"No wonder he loves you more. I just feed him cat food."

Hasina kissed her cheek and moved away with a smile, leaving behind the scent of jasmine and fennel.

"Fine weather," said a woman whose name she hadn't caught.

Layla surveyed the splashes of colour on the counter—brinjal, tomatoes, red chilies, green chilies, papaya, and a small bundle of mint tied with a tough blade of grass. She picked it up and buried her face in its sweet, fresh fragrance.

"Mint is cooling you know," Ma would apply the crushed leaves on Layla's burnt finger when she was little. Even now Layla felt its healing icy sting as it sucked away the heat and the hurt.

"I'm sorry, Layla," Ma had held her hand gently once upon a time. "I should have warned you not to touch the wok. Karahi is best served in the wok it's made in, and I put it on the table without telling you."

"I was hungry. It smelled divine," she had said, still new from the orphanage, still afraid she'd be kicked out of this lovely new home. And she had remembered from another life, from another mother-daughter relationship, that words mattered.

"I know. I'm sorry," Ma had taken her in her warm embrace.

The scent of the fabric conditioner on Ma's sweater had been infused with other smells. Cayenne, cumin, coriander.

She'd been unused to hugs, the physical touch of love. Even in that previous life, which may have included a mother, that tall, painfully thin woman, long before the orphanage, there had been little or no physical touch.

She put the bundle of mint back on the table and sidled towards the other end of the table. Aroma was the strongest link with memories. It made the memory more real, visceral, clear. So many of hers were linked with cooking and stories and mothers.

Another flurry of warm breeze brought with it a waft of fennel and paprika. Layla turned her head and sniffed. Cumin. Always use with potatoes for its digestive properties. What else could she detect? She took another deep breath. Cardamom! Green was fragrant even when uncooked. Used in tea, dessert and korma or biryani. Black cardamom was fragrant only when cooked and its smokiness enhanced other flavours. Used in rice, dhal, and curries.

"Why do you smell of roses?" she'd asked Hasina, crinkling her nose when they had been travelling to Ma's home from the orphanage that first time.

"My Ma made me drink milk boiled in rose petals, cardamom and khoya. And seven almonds. I just never got out of the habit. I drink it every night. So, I cooked a batch for us both before coming to get you."

She had asked, "Why seven almonds? And I hate roses."

"We don't say hate. It is a negative word. A bad word. We say dislike. Okay? As for the almonds, when cooking, every ingredient is measured. One ingredient a tad too much, or too little, upsets the balance and ruins the perfect result. Each ingredient in the recipe is there for a reason. If anything is out of joint, the whole dish will be ruined. Numbers and quantity are crucial to cooking."

"Just like in stories!" the little Layla had exclaimed.

"Aren't you the clever one!" Hasina had patted her head. "Yes, just like in stories. You need a hero, a villain, and a higher purpose. If the goal of the hero is selfish, who cares whether or not she or he achieves it? But if it is something selfless, even if it is just for one person, then it is a higher goal and is much more valuable. What if there was no wicked witch in a story?"

Layla's mind had taken her back to the past, to a time before the orphanage. "There's always a wicked someone. Witches got a bad name because they were women."

Hasina had hugged her then but revealed many years later that she'd been won over in that moment and that Layla had become her daughter forever. Layla did not tell her that the words were learned from another mother.

Hasina whispered to her while the others chatted, "Have you heard from Khayyam by any chance?"

Startled, Layla glanced at Ma. She was speechless for a moment. Just a few days ago, she had been thinking of Khayyam too.

"I was just curious. We haven't heard from him in so long."

Ma ambled away towards her friends and her cooking, leaving Layla in a turmoil of forgotten emotions. Thinking of Khayyam made all her regrets buzz like hornets inside her head.

She slipped away from the kitchen and went up to her small room, still neat and clean, kept ready for her by Ma. Layla smiled at the small sandalwood box on her chest of drawers. This box had been her doorway into a new life. She opened it reverently. There it was, the old tan leather, dark as mahogany in some places. The ratty string that tied it. She unfurled the leather and looked at the yellowed thick paper, the edges curled, the unmatched pages, some smooth and others rough, filled with stories, charcoal illustrations that still symbolized comfort. She hugged it and put it on the bed beside her. She'd missed it and she wanted to be able to show it to Mira when she was ready. The book of her childhood.

Layla's unusual perspicacity sprang from her deep study of the histories of stories. She deconstructed them, identified patterns, connections, codes and symbols hidden deep within their very fabric. It was all because of this book she now held in her hands. A roughhewn, handwritten book with chiaroscuro-like drawings. It had helped her navigate life and even people because the reflections of stories were found clearly in both.

She always unknotted life and people in the light of her immense knowledge of stories.

When she turned, Sultan was in the doorway, watching her with those big soulful eyes. He mewed and tiptoed towards her. She was surprised when he showed any vulnerability. His honey-golden eyes seemed to show emotion only at moments like these.

"I didn't abandon you," she smiled. "Come here."

He jumped into her lap. She cuddled him, burying her face in his thick soft black fur. She whispered, "Just here to collect this. That's all." He wriggled. She hung on to him. He pressed his paws into her thighs and wriggled again.

"Fine." She let go. He jumped off her and waited behind the open door. She could see his tail.

"Let's go."

When she went back downstairs, Sultan vanished, and Hasina was speaking about cooking. She loved to hear Ma speak about food, it was like poetry. She walked in beaming.

"For me, food is a kind of language, and it implies knowledge, culture, wisdom, beauty and love. Just like any language, you can use it lightly, with no respect and without paying any attention to it, but then it's a poor shadow of what it is supposed to be. If you don't pay attention to it and you just throw things together, sure you'd have something to eat but that's not enough. Cook with the right intentions. Cook to nourish and nurture."

Layla smiled affectionately as she listened to her mother. It was good to be home.

SIX

On her way back from Hasina's, having lived with the noise and fragrant food she associated with Lahore, Layla felt a physical homesickness for Khayyam. The aroma of cumin, mustard seeds and ginger, of sheep fat sizzling on hot coals, and the occasional whiff of the garbage that managed to elbow its way into the melee of odours, reminded her of Lahore. It hadn't helped that Ma spoke of him often. Especially recalling their time in Lahore when they had gone to look for her birth mother. Hasina had one connection in Lahore. Khayyam. She knew him because she had known his mother. He had been their chauffeur and private investigator and guide and friend, all rolled into one. Hasina had done a lot of humanitarian work in her life, she still did. Khayyam and children like him, had been what kept Hasina going. The walled city of Lahore had a lot of orphans, women who were abused or were victims of trafficking, domestic violence. Hasina had tried to help them any way she could. Even after she had immigrated to the USA, she had kept in touch. And so when they visited Lahore, they had been met by Khayyam at the airport.

Briefly, ten years ago, Khayyam had begun to mean home to Layla. She remembered every detail of their encounter vividly, as if it were this very morning that she had traversed the streets of old Lahore with his warm laugh nestled in her ear, and the weight and warmth of his arms around her.

She remembered the narrow street bright with naked bulbs and busy with pedestrians, motorbikes and rickshaws that jostled each other. A sliver of a street separated Khayyam's flat which doubled as his studio, from the dimly lit rooms of the most sought-after women of the red-light area of Lahore. Young women dressed in finery, their long hair adorned with roses and jhumka flowers, posed at open windows. Several balconies overlooked the clatter of the noisy street. Rooms clambered over each other with lopsided, gravity-defying tenacity. As families grew, buildings seemed to breed along with them in haphazard disarray. Crowded and chaotic though it was, there was charm in multiplicity, growth and imbalance.

Ten years ago in June, Layla had gone to Lahore with Hasina to look for her birth mother and had found Khayyam, instead. How she'd loved his old, abandoned mansion! He had inherited it from his mother after she died and had locked it up. He had a love-hate relationship with it. He couldn't live in it, but he had shown it to her with some pride. Most homes she had seen in the old walled city of Lahore were a colourful map of mismatched floors patched with marble slabs and stone tiles, nicked from the restorations of the Lahore Fort, the mausoleum of Mughal Emperor Jahangir and the Wazir Khan Mosque. Decades on, room by room, his mansion too had become a narrative of multiple revolutions, simultaneous histories, opposing arts and a synthesis of splendour and elegance.

The velvety beat of the tabla and the soulful strains of the sitar, which Khayyam remembered so fondly from his neglected childhood, had been replaced with the latest Bollywood songs. She was fascinated by both. Khayyam had played the sitar and the tabla for her often, and she'd tucked her heart away somewhere in the mellifluous sitar strains of Raag Darbari and the velvety tabla rhythms of Raag Malkauns. The magic had been interrupted by the sudden volley of obscenities mingled with raucous laughter, intruding in staccato bursts, and had clashed with the soft music.

She had gone to his studio where he lived and worked, just one week after they had met, when he had had his first solo exhibition, and had been fascinated. His friendly, almost exclusively female neighbours were keen to engage with the men watching them with such interest. A woman's rich laughter had drifted on the air. An older prostitute sharing a laugh with her younger colleagues, helping them embellish their bodies and hair with perfumes and flowers. And Layla had wondered out loud, how could a woman with the life she'd led, be happy? But laughter wasn't happiness. Not really.

Khayyam had often told her about his childhood. How he had lived in the ruins of that old mansion with the Old Man and the three Old Women, and his mother. Only much later had he learned to recognize them as his grandfather and his wives. Only one of the wives had given the Old Man a child—his mother. They'd long forgotten which one of the wives was the biological mother and so they'd lived, a cranky old man and his wives, much like the mansion, in defiance. She remembered the tone of his voice when he'd told her. His voice had been thick with moisture, like a cloud ready to rain.

She remembered his descriptions like a favourite story.

The mansion he'd lived in as a child was a warren of rooms that stumbled into each other, crumbling into history, forgotten gradually. They'd wandered into it at night and at daytime. She remembered their moon-soft kisses, and their sun-soaked laughter. The old walls wept when it rained, and the old timbers in the roof creaked and trembled and she'd whispered in awe that it was beautiful. Yellowed paint peeled off in layers and hung like un-shed skin on walls and ceilings. They'd watched mould stains and peeled-paint-patches for shapes like people watched the sky and clouds.

By the time he was ten, he'd told her with such pride, he knew all the secret passageways in and out of the sprawling mansion. He knew which windows opened their kaleidoscopic colours at his touch and which were stuck fast. He had discovered everything there was to discover in the old house, but the past was full of unfamiliar stories. One in particular, haunted him. It wore no face, but he called it father.

No wonder they had connected. Their stories were so similar.

The low boundary wall of Khayyam's mansion had toppled drunkenly into the tiny wild garden, and was propped up by two trees, old austere sentinels. Stray dogs and cats often wandered in through the wrought-iron gates that were always open. The small brick courtyard had been bitten into by the gates and they'd stood in a death grip for years. Every monsoon, the driveway won a quarter of an inch of ground and the gate found comfort in dragging the pillar down with it.

She had such obscure memories of her own childhood. She had hung on to his every vivid description, lapped up every visit to the old mansion now abandoned, but still his. He had left that house as soon as he was able and had moved to the old Fine Arts University, he'd said. It had still been too close for comfort. He had only taken her there to show it to her. To share a fragment of his past that was like his backbone. But she had fallen in love, and they visited it every day. The neighbourhood was heavily populated with the poor and the wretched of the earth and Khayyam's mansion had been the biggest, most dilapidated house in the neighbourhood. But it was just as ill-reputed as the rest of the vicinity.

The mansion, for those who knew where to find it, was situated within the secret past of a city older than memory. She could find it still if she ever went back. Parts of the city's past lay within reach, behind the main thoroughfares in old, cobbled streets, hovels that grew around decrepit mansions and havelis, the dried baths of the Mughals, the forgotten mosques of the Khiljis and the mausoleums of kings from seven different dynasties, which even the old city of Lahore only half remembered begrudgingly.

The cab driver honked loudly, and she was pulled back to the present. Stuck in traffic in Chicago. She had left in plenty of time to catch the train. She would get there in time. She settled back and closed her eyes. Khayyam's habit of rubbing his fingertips together absently. It had so irritated her. He'd laughed it off, said almost in apology, that the rough paint stains on his fingertips was part of his identity. Paint reminded him of who he was and that his destiny lay in the colours and textures of paint and canvas.

She was still surprised at how quickly they'd fallen for each other. How hard. In just two weeks. Hasina had been with her in Lahore, but she didn't even remember her presence. All she recalled was Khayyam. It brought a smile to her face now.

People knew of the past much as they did of poetry and dreams: half-remembered, partially understood, often misinterpreted, she thought, looking out of her cab window. She and Khayyam had survived on the threshold of past and present, on the liminal of real and imagined, in the shadows, within the borders of dreams and myths. Just like a forgotten tale. A story.

Maybe their grief and their losses were what had drawn them to each other. She'd never thought about it before. He had been obsessed with finding his father. And she, with finding her mother. He rarely talked about the woman who had birthed him, and she never mentioned her father. They were both trying to forget one parent and find the other.

They talked about their dreams, their art, their love. They never spoke about the future. Did he also know that there wouldn't be any? She hadn't quite known it. She still didn't. Because secretly, she was still in love with him after all this time.

She had loved everything about him, his city, his home, his art. The champa flowers, chameli buds, the topaz summer dawns of Lahore. How she'd made him see the wonder of the place again. And then she'd left him, as everyone always did, he had said. Her eyes welled up, and she bit her lip to control this sudden, unfamiliar sensation. She hardly ever cried.

His past was not a happy place. Neither was hers. He wished he could erase it all. And she? She was not sure she believed in erasure. The past made people who they were, shaped them and honed them. She believed in the story of a life.

Khayyam had been standing by the window looking out when she had entered his studio with, she now realized, her heart on her sleeve. It must have been obvious to him. But then, he wasn't much older or more experienced than her. Maybe it hadn't been that obvious to him. They had been inseparable for five days, yearning and not touching. She had been too young to be cautious about her first love.

It was his first solo exhibition at only twenty-three. The studio in his flat in the old walled city was teeming with art aficionados and wannabes of the Lahori glitterati, wealthy men accompanied by women dripping diamonds and toting designer bags that cost more than the year's salaries of their cooks and maids. They all looked the same at first glance. The women with hair dyed in honey blonde tones, expensively cut and coiffed, wore the latest in western fashion, all de rigueur at night parties in Karachi and Lahore.

"*Jani*, I've bought two already! They'll look fabulous in the study, no?"

"They'll look fabulous in your drawing room, Niggi. The colour scheme is very similar. You have no eye for such details, sweetie."

"*Jani*, don't be silly, I can't have nudes just anywhere in the house. My mother-in-law lives with us. She'd have a heart attack."

"Then hang them in her room."

The women tittered as they gossiped. The men bandied ribald jokes and guffawed uproariously. Khayyam chatted politely with those who sought him out for pictures or to rekindle a vague acquaintance.

The street below his first-floor studio was lined with food stalls and kiosks, lively as ever. The touristy residents of Gulberg and other posh localities, sporting jeans and discomfort, were instantly distinguishable from the regular patrons, overweight, moustachioed men in shalwar kameez born and bred there in the red-light districts. Their grandfathers had been born there, they claimed loudly for the benefits of the rich touristy citizens of a city they shared but did not ever mingle with, save perhaps for this one place. They called the serving boys cheerfully by name and threw friendly insults at them ensuring they were served dinner quickly. Their loquacious chatter punctuated with laughter was littered with inventive obscenities. Layla was fascinated.

The dented, rickety, metal tables, crowded together cheek by jowl, were too small for the stainless-steel platters piled with mutton chops and chicken karahi. The noise and sense of community comforted Khayyam, he said, but it also called to mind Paris, Prague, London, New York. These grand cities of the first world had their dirty little streets too, like Rio too, where life was cheaper than art supplies. He was beginning to miss those streets and those lonely nights, he'd complained. The crowd loved his stories almost as much as his paintings.

She had become a sort of talisman for him, he'd said later, his compass even. Was he making a mistake? He'd asked only in jest, but she had wondered ad infinitum since then. Ad nauseum. He'd thought of her as his destiny. His obsession with her was embarrassing to him, surreal for her.

He'd been surprised to see her there without Ma. His umber eyes had been on her when she'd turned and given him a smile, a rare thing for her, even then. He'd claimed later that was the moment he'd fallen in love. Lies of course. He hadn't fallen in love with her till he'd shown her his mother's portrait and seen her reaction to it. That was when he had fallen in love because all his barriers had come crashing down. Or so she liked to believe.

SEVEN

Despite the traffic and the radio in the cab, it was difficult to hold back the tidal wave of memories. She could almost smell the sharp turpentine and the linseed oil paints of Khayyam's studio, which had been swarming with people eager to tell him how much they admired his work and keen to chat with him about art and in doing so let him know how cultured they were compared to others. Because it wasn't about identity but identity in comparison to others. Someone made an inane remark about a painting, and he answered mechanically in the enigmatic parlance expected from artists, about inspiration, artistic temperament, and the mysteries of creation.

He'd followed her as she went around the studio standing before each painting for long moments while he had expatiated on technique and subject. Both of them not much older than the young art students thronging the studio.

One of them had asked her own mother tentatively, "Mama…er, is it okay if we wave to those girls?"

Her eyes were on the young prostitutes across the street. It was a daring act for an over-protected young girl that would make her feel good about herself because she'd have given the gift of acknowledgement to a fallen woman. Layla didn't hear what the mother said but couldn't help thinking that his use of this neighbourhood as backdrop was rather clever. After all, he owed his mystique in a large part to it.

Then Layla had asked him, gesturing towards the sex-workers, "How old do you think those girls are?"

He'd shrugged and answered, "Teenagers mostly."

"They look older."

"It's because they've seen too much."

"Haven't we all?"

"How old are you exactly?" he'd mocked, grinning.

"Older than I look," she'd parried. She'd said almost as an afterthought, "I'll take one painting. I can afford one."

She'd taken much more than the painting.

Given back quite a bit too…

They'd watched in silence as one of the prostitutes disappeared through a door with a middle-aged man who wore his guilt lightly and his desperation far too openly.

"What's his story do you think?"

Khayyam had shrugged. "The same as everyone else's I suppose."

He had added wryly, "My mother used to say men who come here are seeking what they've lost to their women at home."

"I'm not sure I understand."

"Their mothers emasculate them, and their wives demonize them."

She'd cracked up with laughter.

She smiled now at the memory, but his smile had faltered before it had formed fully.

Even then, that familiar murmur, the buzz that travelled with him everywhere, had risen in pitch and volume and become audible. The echo of a whisper he'd first heard when he was five, he said, and had been echoing in his ears ever since.

"His mother was a prostitute, you know. All of his paintings depict this area and these women."

"Seriously? How sad."

"Wasn't he in South America since like, forever?"

"Is she still alive? The mother, I mean?"

"I don't know. Why's that important?"

"Well…he's so well-known and respected now. I guess it would've made her happy…"

Youth was so romantic. Everything was a tragedy. All whores were victims and all bastards made good. But some whores were more equal than others. And as always, every time he heard those whispers he heard the silence too, where the unasked all-important question resounded. Silence that to him was as loud as the voluble branding he'd received all his life. Who was his father, they asked? Or wasn't that important because his mother was a whore?

Layla remembered his pain like her own. It was her own. She knew him like she knew herself.

Although no one asked, he'd been obsessed with the question until he'd finally put a face to that phantom, the shadow that had darkened his life and blocked the light with its far-reaching stretch. He'd managed to trace him before Layla had left Lahore. His father, it turned out, was a bigger whore than his mother had ever been, and Khayyam had been too ashamed of that tenuous connection to respectability. His mother may have sold her body, but his father had profited from robbing the weak, the poor and the powerless. If he'd wanted to be melodramatic and Faustian, he'd have said his father had sold his soul. His mother had been an honest whore.

It was nothing more than trickery and smokescreens in the end. The lost boys of the night, the scavengers and the predators who roamed the city and dwelt in their own darkness, all ended up as victims of these upright citizens. They were all the same under their masks, some worse, some better at camouflaging their darkness than these creatures born of dark destinies born to die on the garbage heap. And these others, people like his father, were born to watch and wince in momentary sympathy. Then, they moved to the next spectacle, the next novelty.

There was such darkness in Khayyam. It had frightened her. But it also fascinated her, drew her to him. He had become almost violent when he had found out about his father. But before that, on that first night, they had connected due to their hurt.

"That's a nice look for the man of the hour," Layla had whispered when she'd found him sitting alone in a dark corner later, watching the throngs of people with a scowl.

He'd made an effort to smile and had said on an impulse, "Let me show you something." He'd led her towards the back wall of the studio.

"Solo exhibition at twenty-three? You're already famous and rich."

"Almost famous…and not at all rich."

She'd linked her arm through his, in mocking disbelief.

She paid the cab driver and pulled her bag behind her, into the beautiful Union Station. She had always loved architecture, art of any sort really. Slowly, she walked towards her train, still thinking of Khayyam. He'd worked with museums since then, she knew, and had had exhibitions all over the world, one in New York only six years ago. He hadn't ever tried to find her, and she wished he had tried. He would never have, she knew, he was too stubborn and hurt. Or maybe he had forgotten her, she had feared. And it was only she who was carrying the torch for him still.

The night of his exhibition he'd shown her the portrait of his mother that first day she had come. He'd put his dreams to sleep on canvas after canvas, crystallized in a vice of colour and form. Some had emerged as twisted nightmares, others as singed vestiges of shattered hopes.

That painting was both.

Like the woman, the painting had exacted much from him. Layla could almost feel the weight and texture of the palette knife as if it were she who had mixed and smeared, brushed and stroked paint on canvas in a frenzy of ecstasy and despair, until the woman emerged out of its blankness in the arms of a man, a faceless lover. Those dark eyes stared back forever following him, unforgiving, uninterested, the eyes of a stranger. Only they weren't the eyes of a stranger. Worse. They were the eyes of a mother not interested in her child. He wasn't merely a painter; he was voyeur and conspirator, sinner and judge, plunderer and saviour.

"Is this your mother?" Layla had asked; it didn't matter to her who his mother was and what she did. With her, he had confessed later, he hadn't felt the burning shame that he had with others about his lineage because for Layla it really didn't matter. Mothers could be sinners too. They were the worst sinners. She and Khayyam both knew the secret ugly truth.

She'd stepped up to the canvas to study it more closely. Women had exclaimed, men had ogled and grinned. She hadn't been taken aback at all. As if painting one's mother in the nude in the arms of a paramour was a perfectly acceptable thing to do. She hadn't been constrained by the culture of any land, as if she were a wild thing; her mind not a slave to anything, any mores, any norms, but free, he'd said later.

"It is beautiful, certainly."

"But?"

She'd smiled but she was sad. "You're hurting like me. That makes me sad. You've been so helpful in the last week. And I can't help you at all."

"You did. You have."

She'd frowned. She hadn't believed him.

"It's one of your best, I think."

"Yeah, it's more than I thought it would be."

She understood him the way she understood stories. And when he talked, she realized that most of all perhaps, he was seeker and agnostic. In his anger and hurt he'd believed at the time he was stripping his mother down to her reality. But possibly it was his own reality that he was baring. Or had they become so inextricably intertwined he couldn't tell the difference?

A part of him had put his mother on a pedestal once. Only it hadn't been the whole of her. And here she was again, the first woman he'd loved, the woman he couldn't forget, couldn't denounce, and couldn't forgive. Neither his pedestal nor his easel appeared to hold any significance.

That night he had led her to the window again and told her that, once, a window like this one had been his escape to sounds other than those that came from his mother's room: the low voice that she had only ever used with those men, the tinkling laughter, then the long silences, or those other sounds he hadn't then understood. He'd tried to block out all that with sights, smells, and sounds of life that had assaulted his senses from this window. It had provided a vantage point from where he'd observed the incredible vista into which he'd been born and condemned to repeat, or perhaps inspired to apotheosize? He knew the beauty and the brutality, the charm and the crassness of this small sliver of humanity intimately; and he suffered with it, for it, and he hated it, even as he loved it.

They stood together, in silence in the wake of his words.

Their eyes rested on a boy, barely ten, his clothes torn and stained, watching a table of feasting men with an unwavering gaze. Without warm clothing and oblivious to the cold he moved between two pillars outside the awning of the ramshackle restaurant. Layla didn't have to lean forward to know that the boy wore no shoes. One of the men at the table, sporting a lush moustache, noticed the boy swallow hungrily as his mouth watered. Gold chains glinted around the man's thick neck. Big gold rings twinkled on his fleshy fingers; his moustache twitched as he murmured to his companions, making them explode with raucous laughter. With his eyes still on the boy, the man picked up a chop, took quick chunky bites to leave as little meat as possible on the bone, and then flung it across.

The boy darted forward. A stray cat sprang at the discarded bone with a yowl, simultaneously.

The men roared as the boy wrestled over the bone with the cat.

Shame was hot in Khayyam's eyes, revulsion bitter in his mouth as he vented it in colourful languages. All three that he was fluent in but only loud enough for her to hear. The casual pity he'd felt for street children in Brazil had brought no shame or anger. This was home. This was his life and his city. He was as helpless here as he'd been for those strangers, his brothers in luck if not in blood.

She loved his sensitivity, his desire to help strangers, his facility with languages.

Triumphant, but scratched and bedraggled, the boy gnawed at the bone hungrily. Heedless to the laughter and the pity, he chewed the bone bare. Nothing existed but the scraps he'd won in a battle he'd have forgotten by morning, because it wasn't unfamiliar or remarkable. A cat today, a boy tomorrow, a shadow in the thick of night, each day was a different battle, and who knew how many scars he'd suffer until finally, he'd be stripped of anything remotely childlike, long before he ceased to be a child.

Khayyam had taken one last look at the rich thug who'd thrown the bone.

"Such people don't deserve to live," he'd cursed.

She had patted his shoulder, tried to calm him down.

Guests and hangers on began to leave in twos and threes. Khayyam turned his back to the window and faced the room again. Something inside him crowed when people bought his art, but he wanted to snatch the paintings back from them. It was like giving away pieces of himself. She felt his visceral reactions and was taken aback at the violence that lay just beneath his epidermis, oozing out of his pores. The proud new owners of his paintings smirked from their lofty positions of wealth. They, the purveyors of wealth, could do this for him, buy his art. They bought, therefore his art existed. The condescension pierced his soul and every transaction violating his being and his body was the subtext for her to read. Was it the pain of creation that made it so worthwhile? Or was it the other way around?

It had always been like this. Layla stood before the nude of an aging prostitute who'd been kind to him growing up. He'd captured her as she was; hanging flesh, wrinkles, misery and all. But he'd also managed to transfuse in some measure her fierce and indefatigable spirit on to the canvas.

"This is magnificent, Khayyam." Layla had been riveted by the painting.

"She was magnificent." That was the painting she had decided to buy. He'd been happy to have her buy it. At a discount.

Doubt flickered in his eyes. He had been about to say something but had refrained. She could tell.

Thinking back to that time over the chasm of years, she acknowledged, she had confounded him the same way his birthplace did. Before they'd parted, he had said he couldn't determine what drained him more, his love for them, that city or her, or the terrible anger they induced in him. They held him captive, but neither his love nor his art was enough to hold them. They eluded him, his vision and his dreams, mocking his desire to claim or own them, he'd said.

A small dark shape detached itself from the wall and cautiously poked at her hand. It was a kitten black as the night outside. One of its ears had been torn off.

"It is a stray I rescued today," he had said.

"Well, it is mine now," she'd replied. "Do you mind?"

"Of course not. What will you call him?"

She had thought a bit and then replied, "Sultan."

A dog barked, bringing their attention back to the street. The boy lay curled up in a corner with a skinny dog. Two strays…three, if she were to count herself, the eternal stray. Some women of the night, older and less attractive were perched on the windowsills and combing their hair as they eyed the few stragglers still eating *kebabs* and *tikkas* and enjoying the dangerous aftereffects of homemade liquor, which could just as easily kill as intoxicate.

The wood panelled windows began to close one by one, as if the city were shutting her out. The metallic smell of cold hung in the air. The street had disgorged its human burden back out from the welcoming arms of the women who provided a simulacrum of love.

The boy stirred in his sleep, shivered and snuggled closer to the mangy dog. Layla picked up the small black kitten and hugged it close. The street harboured only the wretched and the rejects of society who slept on the pavement every night. The women on the street were like animals for the men of the city, mounted and slaughtered at will. These streets had new-borns in its refuse bins or abandoned in plastic bags where hungry dogs found them. No one commented on it anymore. Those who survived lived to die another day.

The trains hooted, chugged. She found hers and climbed in. She put the luggage in the overhead carrier and sat down, choosing the last seat that no one ever wanted so she would not be disturbed. She sat down and closed her eyes. She remembered vividly the way Khayyam had stood in the shadowed room, a hand on the window-frame, an arched brow, a slight smile teasing at the corner of his mouth, ready to sprint across his face. She'd pushed back the fears and doubts.

A drunken man had belted out the snatch of a song on the street. She'd put her head on his shoulder and together they'd looked out from the window to the dark street below. He had taken her face in his hands and his bedroom eyes were on her. He had run his fingers through her short cap of curly hair and smiled, fingering her hair.

He had dropped his hands to his sides and asked again, "Layla, are you sure? Do you really…"

That had been enough. At least then. Later, they'd had so many harsh conversations too. In such a short while. And she remembered them all.

"You and I are young stories. We are who we are. There is no mystery. In some years, we will be layered and subtle. But now, right now, we're just hormones and optimism."

That wasn't true and perhaps she'd known it even then. But she'd spun a version of them both for that night to keep it simple. Maybe she was right, maybe he couldn't respect women. How could he, growing up the way he had? A woman's body was both sacred and profane. His mother had given herself too easily to men, and some women gave themselves as if it was the most momentous decision of their lives, as if that was all that mattered.

Maybe, it hadn't mattered to her. She realised he'd expected her to at least try and blackmail him into marriage. She hadn't. That had shocked him, even disillusioned him a little. She may have been right about one thing. He wanted to save someone, even if he failed every time he tried.

Time was a great healer, they said. Time could also be irrelevant. And there she had been standing so close, her face lifted to his, her hands on his chest; he almost made her forget everything else.

She'd come back to his studio of her own free will. Those few times. Ten years ago. Had it really been that long?

That last night together she had said almost flippantly, "Someday, you might paint me."

They'd been in bed. He hadn't looked at her. Just said with a smile playing on his lips.

"I have a small flat in Rio. That part of the city's quite similar to home…the vibrant chaos, the smells, the noise. Sometimes, I close my eyes and imagine I am back here." Kissing the top of her head he said, "You'd like it there."

"I wish my life were this simple and I could just vanish somewhere with you. But I cannot."

"Why?"

How many times had he asked over their last week?

She'd looked at him kindly as if he were an errant child, "You know what, Khayyam? I don't think it's my life you want to rewrite."

The smoke had curled from the end of his cigarette in the still night; its acrid smell permeated the room. Everything was familiar: the room, the pain and the endless night ahead. He'd wanted to put her on a pedestal. Only it hadn't been the whole of her. She was the first woman he'd loved who didn't see him as part of a tainted world.

Time truly was irrelevant. It made no difference at all. She'd worried the scab for ten years; she'd scratched and watched it ooze and bleed and had welcomed the pain, because this way, it remained alive. At least like this, she had the memory of something that hadn't hurt, that had nurtured hope in her once.

EIGHT

Later, much later, when she had reached her university apartment, she slept for two days straight to recover from exhaustion and memories of heartbreak. When she finally felt her head was securely screwed back on her shoulders, she tightly locked away all the memories of Khayyam and Lahore back into their box.

The fear that had slept in the shade of happy trysts with Ma, resurfaced. There had been a murder. There had been two, in fact.

She brought out her records to find the calling card the detective in the Belmont University case had given everyone during the murder investigation. She'd put it off long enough. She was an organized woman: files, labels, stickers, markers, the works. She was a woman with a plan; the kind of woman who always had a timetable and charts and blueprints, and little notecards. Life was chaotic and messy without them. Her mind was messy without them. Goals couldn't be achieved without the careful, step by step planning that led to success. She was disciplined. She was focused. She'd had to be to survive since she was a child.

Her lost mother had instilled the discipline in her, all too well. Any small failure was the end of the world. There was always an alphabet to learn in some language or other, along with a story. She'd sensed even as a child that she was some sort of trophy for her birth mother. Layla's earliest memories of her were of her mother's fear; her soft skin and the fragrance of roses and something saltine which she later identified as turmeric. Those were the memories that still haunted her. She had recognized the smell at Hasina's, and it had repelled her initially because a vague memory of unhappiness was attached to it. She hadn't remembered what it was, just that it made her unhappy.

She looked at Detective James Lance's card in her hand and decided to wait. It was too early to surmise anything. Sultan jumped into her lap out of nowhere.

"Oh, you little darling!" she laughed, hugging him. Finally some love from the great Sultan! He purred and rubbed his dear little face to hers. She put the card back in its folder. When Sultan offered free love, she took it without questions and interruption. That lasted for about three minutes.

Days passed and Layla heard no news. No arrests. No suspects. She resisted calling the Detective but after a week of suspense with no further news or progress on the case except loads of speculation and sensation amongst the students and faculty, she made the call. Had they, may be arrested someone for the previous murder? There was something niggling at her, and she needed to make sure there was nothing to her sense of foreboding.

When someone picked up the phone at the other end, she said, "Hello, Detective Lance, this is Layla Rashid. I was the professor of cultural history at the Belmont University earlier this year. There was a murder if you recall, a girl with ash on her body…"

"How may I help you?"

"I…I was curious…did you find anything? Did you find the murderer?"

There was a pause at the other end.

"It was a murder, Professor." The detective's voice was curt. "It is slightly more complicated than reading a book and marking papers. These things take time. There were no fingerprints. There were no witnesses. How do you propose we solve the case? All this was in the newspapers. Why do you ask?"

"I…I am sorry. I didn't mean to…I was curious." She would not volunteer information at this time. "Sorry to have taken your time," she said and cut the line.

It was nothing. There was no connection. Or he would have said something. A weight lifted off of her.

But then, why hadn't they caught anyone? Why were there no suspects?

There was only one thing to do. She looked at the pamphlet she'd taken from the notice board in the library earlier. Mira Heshmat's talk was that evening. She hadn't missed any of her lectures since she had first seen her photograph and wasn't about to now. Especially now. She needed to be in storyland to feel safe.

NINE

"Welcome sisters, to the fireside of storytelling. And brothers too. For stories are important to us all."

The local community hall was packed, and the lights dimmed. A spotlight focused on Mira Heshmat ensconced in a black armchair looking out at the audience from the middle of the small stage. A walking stick resting against the armchair. Bluish lights from phones indicated that many in the audience were recording the session. In the darkened hall where only stories reigned supreme, Layla could almost forget the dead body she'd found in the library. Almost.

"Like the fireside, storytelling is also a metaphor. As is story itself. The oldest metaphor there is."

Long silver hair fell in waves over the woman's shoulders. She was dressed in an ankle-length white dress and wore several strings of beads around her neck. Moonstone-studded silver rings caught the light when she moved her hands as she talked and gestured. A silk scarf was draped around her throat and hung down her front, dip dyed in different shades of blue. Mira was obviously someone who understood the importance of stage presence.

"Sufi stories are embedded with life lessons. They bring to the surface what is hidden, what is secret. Story is communal when shared orally. While writing, it is a lonelier art." She paused for effect and for the idea to sink in. "Story develops fully and has most impact when it is shared, when it is discussed and mined for meaning, symbolism and subtext, as when you write papers, reviews, discuss them in book clubs, have class discussions, and even if just two people talk about it, though they may not be like-minded. In fact, in my experience, and I have seventy years' worth of it, difference is essential. But there must be one commonality. Just one." The audience hung on to her words as she looked around slowly. "All must be seekers of Truth!"

Layla glanced around and found that Mira had the room in thrall. People were mesmerized. As was she; every time she came to Mira Heshmat's talks she was spellbound. She forgot her hopes and fears about her birth mother and what she suspected Mira to be and even now, she watched the Storyteller with awe and reverence. She forgot everything but the magic Mira wove on stage.

Looking around at the audience similarly awestruck, Layla noticed a man two rows down, sitting on her right. He looked tall, even while sitting. He was thin with greying hair and the lines on his face as he turned his face sideways to look at the audience, likely a testament more to suffering than age. He must be closer to her own age. Mid to early thirties. Professor Reza.

He had joined their university just this semester. He was attractive and also brilliant. They had never met but she had read his books. There was a delicious touch of mystery about him. Rumours that he had vanished for years to learn Angkor secrets and emerged with a new book and the lean lithe body of an Angkor god. Or maybe he'd always had that. His books on religious myth and archetypes had made him a sudden, albeit reluctant, celebrity in the academic world, as had his meteoric rise in academic circles. He had always favoured big universities and his appointment was a surprise to many. The university was so grateful for having him they bent over backwards to accommodate him and there was resentment amongst other academics. Rumour had it that he was being paid even more than the President herself.

Layla turned her attention back to the stage. Like everyone else, she was eager only to hear the Master storyteller speak.

"Stories set the quiet, the lost, the confused, the misfit and the inner self, the subterranean self, the hidden self, into motion. We have all heard about the call to adventure, have we not? Stories can be that call. Stories can be the candle that light the dark cave in which our frightened child-self hides."

Layla's heart jumped to her throat and her breathing became shallow. The storyteller hit too close to home. She watched Mira's face for anything familiar, an expression, a quirk. Nothing. She listened to her voice closely. Was there any inflection that would trigger a memory? But Mira was just a familiar stranger. Layla knew her like she knew celebrities. And yet she felt she could not give up pursuing Mira. Or her hunch. Was this a sick comfort? A mirage of hope against the harshness of not knowing?

"Stories can show us the way when life does not. Stories can lead us back to ourselves when life has drawn us away. But I do not speak of all stories. I do not speak of all seekers, either. I speak of deeper stories that are old as time. They touch our spirit selves, like fairy tales do. They reflect back to us our archetypes, such as the Wise Fool, Old Wise Man or Woman, or the good-hearted ingénue, that are perhaps hidden from us, perhaps waiting to be recognized. Such stories are allegorical and metaphorical and unfold in layers. They only use language we are willing to understand, regardless of the language of the story itself."

Those were the best kind. Those were the stories that helped shape psyche and intellect.

"Do you understand?" Mira asked. "The story may be in English or Farsi or Russian, the message is beyond language. A story in Farsi, written and shared by a Persian speaker and received by a native of the language, may still not be enough to convey the message. Because one must be open to receiving the message. It is about being ready to receive the transmission left for us ages ago within the story.

"We recognize such stories. They may wear the garb of myth, folktale, fairytale, song, poem or novel. We recognize them immediately because something within us awakens and dances to their rhythm."

Mira's words took Layla to another place and time and her heart swelled with love and longing. Storyland was home. Hiraeth, the longing for something, was embedded in the soul of all the people here, the acute desiderium for stories, and that had brought them all together. She looked around again. People were smiling. They felt it too, the magic of words spun just right. The woman on the stage paused. Placed on her right was a small table with a bottle and a glass. She took her time to pour the water. She did not hurry, as if it were a ritual.

Mira took a sip of water. Swallowed. This she repeated, thrice. Three swallows of water. Numbers were important. Water was cleansing. Water was ritual. Three was a magical number.

"Such stories," Mira continued, "have hidden insights and messages. Such stories warn you not to trust appearances. They caution us that if we don't trust our own instincts, we endanger not just ourselves but all other stories connected with ours, our families, friends and communities. And when we, the hero, because each one of us is the hero of our stories, when we endanger ourselves, we put our communities in danger."

The discomfort in the audience was palpable.

A young man spoke out, "What if we are not heroes? Not everyone is a hero."

There was a nervous titter in the audience.

Mira's laugh was rich and deep, "Aha! But you my friend are already the hero. You have a voice!"

This time the laughter was more confident and accompanied by a smattering of applause.

"But seriously, if you are not the hero of your own story, you my dear, need stories most of all."

When she ended her regaling of mesmerising stories, the audience rose *en masse* to applaud. The woman bowed her head slightly, held her hand together, waved, put her right hand on her chest in acknowledgement, executing the three globally recognized gestures of thanks and then exited the stage to her right', with the help of a walking stick.

Layla moved towards the door with the others and caught up with Professor Reza. "Hello, Professor Reza!"

His sable grey eyes registered shock at being recognized. He was all grey: a long grey overcoat, a lighter grey sweater, grey corduroy trousers. *Was he trying to be invisible?*

"I am Professor Layla Rashid of cultural history and oral traditions at the university. I joined last year."

"Hello Professor…er," he paused eyeing her curiously.

"Layla, please."

His eyes twinkled and he laughed. "Professor of cultural history and oral traditions? I think you are much more than that, Layla."

She inclined her head, smiling, "Are you walking back to the university?"

He beamed, "Yes. What an interesting talk! Is this your first time listening to the Grand Dame of Storytelling?"

"No," said Layla. Was there a hint of jealousy in his voice? Rebuke? "I've heard her speak before."

She felt like a thief admitting it. No one knew why she was such a devotee.

"She doesn't write books. One would've thought she would cash in on the popularity," he said.

Again, Layla heard a hidden undercurrent of something. Envy?

"Somebody asked her once and she said she believed in the oral traditions of storytelling and that she wanted to keep those traditions alive. If she wrote about it, she would feel she was selling out."

"Remarkable, isn't it, to have such scruples in this day and age?"

Disbelief and wonder were evident in what was intended as a laugh but came out like a snort.

They left the theatre slowly to be able to talk and get the first bit of information about each other out of the way.

"You studied in Turkey and India?" she asked.

"Yes. I was born in Turkey and my education has been mostly Asian."

She nodded, "I can see that in your writing. I have to say I am a fan. I love your books. You write like a storyteller."

He stiffened.

"I meant it as a compliment," she said quickly.

He smiled coolly, "I know. I just don't think it is a compliment, I'm sorry. I am an academic. I have worked very hard to get where I am. I don't pull stuff out of my head and pretend it is real."

A twinge of regret. This was not a kindred spirit. She hadn't been mistaken about the undercurrents in his voice or the inflections of dismissal she had noticed earlier.

"I really am sorry to have offended you, Reza."

He nodded in acknowledgement, a wry smile. "No harm done."

"So why religious mythology?" she changed the subject.

His smile was nice though perfunctory.

"I am an agnostic, just to be clear. I think only someone who doesn't believe in anything can really interpret these ancient and overwhelming narratives of religion. Especially the Abrahamic traditions. They're the most popular and the most widespread. They're also rather misogynistic and patriarchal. All three claim to have the same God, but He is different in all three mythologies. The God of vengeance in Judean tradition. God of forgiveness in Christian tradition, and God of righteousness in the Islamic."

Layla said, "I hope you're working on something new. I have read all three of your books."

"I have read all five of yours. You're very prolific."

Layla laughed, "You have? I thought you didn't like stories."

"I like your books because you don't tell stories. They're not fiction and imagination. They take stories apart. They demystify them like a detective lining up clues."

"But they're about fiction, stories and old folktales, the where and how of them. I write their histories, go to their roots because I love stories."

"Or maybe you write to find the fallacies in them?" he asked smiling.

She was startled. "Hmm. Interesting thought. There are those too, of course. But I've seen that when we forage through stories and their beginnings, we often find that like multiple beginnings, they have multiple endings. I find that fascinating and also a little intimidating."

"See, that's precisely why I hate stories and fiction. I read your books because you take the mystery out of them and crush it with logic."

Layla gasped and said coolly, "God, I hope not."

Reza laughed, "God?"

Layla did not respond. Reza had shown her a side of her work she had not seen, and it shook her bearings. Was she not serving stories then? Was she destroying them? He had a point, she had to admit.

They chatted companionably until they reached the crossing and Reza turned towards the university accommodation for professors.

"Well, Layla, this conversation has been far more entertaining than that Mira Heshmat's talk. I hope to see you soon. Good night."

Layla bid him goodnight and couldn't help thinking about him with a smile on her lips. Few men were as good-looking and as erudite as Reza. She had liked him. Too much, too soon perhaps, and that made her want to be cautious. By nature, she had been distrusting all her life and had to push herself to be less paranoid. However, where male strangers were concerned, she allowed herself to be paranoid.

She turned towards her flat. She liked the hustle and bustle of the town centre where she lived. It was only a little more expensive than the university flat she could have got but had refused because she liked the night noises of the town centre. She liked the distant crowds. They helped her disappear, become invisible whenever she liked.

Unlike the dead girl in the library.

The memory of the murder crashed upon her consciousness like a bolt of lightning. She shuddered and began to jog towards her flat, fear suddenly gripped her. She locked the door behind her and put a chair in front of it. She drew her heavy curtains. And even then, she stayed awake for a long time staring at the locked door and the window.

TEN

Then a week later, her phone rang, and Khayyam was at the other end.

The past collided with the present—a present, rather inopportunely and regrettably already knotted and tangled with threads and patterns from the past.

"Hello? Layla? This is Khayyam…er from Lahore?"

She was speechless for a moment.

"Have you forgotten me?" he laughed. She knew the subtext of that laugh—nervous and bit affronted.

"No. Of course not. I know, Khayyam! It's just that I didn't expect your call. I…I'd been thinking of you."

Another coincidence? So soon on the heels of the first?

But Khayyam's voice, warm and deep and familiar was like a comfort read or a beloved song.

"I'm here. I wanted to see you. I was wondering if we could meet."

"Here? You're in Illinois?"

"I'm near your university. Can you see me today?"

"Yes. Yes, of course."

Her face was hot. Her eyes too bright in the mirror.

She rushed out of the flat and hurried towards, the café near the university. He must have dealt with his past or at least enough to want to leave it behind to have contacted her now after all this time? She had believed once that she loved him. He'd certainly believed he loved her. But they'd been young and raw. She was a different woman now. Wasn't she?

She asked herself that all the way to the café.

The cold air was clean and refreshing. There was a lake on the way, the centre of all summer activities and for skating in winter. Having such a large body of water close by made the air smell of it. There was a flash of memory. A stone-dark cave, the dank smell of water. At times she could recall the geography of the mountainous wastelands where she'd grown up, and yet she couldn't recall the topography of her birth mother's face. She remembered only those green eyes, and how terribly unhappy they were.

She remembered every conversation she'd had with Khayyam ten years ago but memories of that earlier time, that other place, came in snatches. A past where her birth mother had been so miserable, and Layla had always been afraid. Her voice a frightened whisper, lest someone hear them. She remembered the cold, the dry winds, and the cloyingly sweet fragrance of roses. Later, when Ma had taken her under her wing, psychologists had suggested that she'd shut down a lot of her memories—dissociative amnesia; that her anxiety was rooted in that childhood fear and trauma.

Ten years ago, Khayyam had been surprised, and relieved when he'd discerned, she wasn't interested in flowers and chocolates. It had been a whirlwind romance. If that was the word at all to use for what they'd had. What they'd been. Almost. No, not almost, but rather, for a time.

She came out to the Main Road of the town, crossed it and turned left. The smell of coffee told her she had another left to take and there was the café. It was usually full of university students and staff.

Layla spotted Khayyam at a table for two outside. All the feelings she had put in a little box named Khayyam and locked somewhere in the subterranean recesses of her brain, came rushing out. That wavy brown hair set in the Hollywood style of Clarke Gable and those dreamy umber eyes!

She waved. He got up, tall like a Chinar tree, a grin brightening his otherwise serious face. A carnival song on a gloomy day, that grin. He kissed her on her cheeks and held her close for a moment. She clung to him. Her deep, contented sigh was involuntary, and she breathed in his aftershave, his clean soapy smell, and his signature cologne. He pulled away first. Her laugh came out as a nervous snicker. He smiled. The same, slightly lop-sided charming smile. The secret stars hiding in his eyes had come alight with that smile. But when she looked for them in his eyes now, she couldn't find them.

Khayyam looked her over with a broad grin. "You haven't changed."

The breeze carrying the delicious fragrance of coffee was already chilly. Autumn would soon be in full swing. The trees, mostly maple, were bursts of russet and yellow turning to brown.

"After all these years that's what you have to say?" Layla smiled. That was the expected reaction to such a remark. You haven't aged. You haven't changed. She *had* changed. And he had too. Hope had abandoned his eyes. Khayyam's eyes seemed bleak. A stranger's eyes. His had never been this tired, had always been alight with the magic of hope. Something she had only ever found in stories.

"What can I say?" Khayyam smiled wryly. "I thought you liked status quo."

And there it was—the first pinprick. She hadn't wanted more. Not then. He had. Back then.

"Well, you have changed a little," she said and her heart dipped a little. It seemed true already.

"I always wanted to. I was always too busy running from myself."

"I tried to keep in touch," she reminded him softly. And there it was, that pinch of hurt. He hadn't responded.

"It's true. You tried thrice." The underlying sadness in his voice was new. It had used to be rage.

"That's thrice more than you," she said, still searching his face. It had more planes and angles. Those rugged cheekbones seemed sharper than before. The jawline squarer.

"I always knew I'd find you when it was time."

Her heart leaped like a hare in March. "Time for what?"

"To find you," he said softly.

Did he still fancy himself in love with her then? Layla felt her mouth begin to widen in a smile and pulled it back. Caution ran in her veins like blood. Was she still wary of commitment? She wasn't sure. She was nothing more than a yearning for her birth mother and the love of stories she'd inherited from her. She'd drowned in the waves of trauma and fear long ago. Who was she now, but a shade? All her desires and needs were reduced to a single question: where is my mother?

"Where are you staying?" she asked. The box was pulling all the runaway feelings back into itself. Soon it would lock itself again. For good perhaps this time? It had taken Khayyam ten years to get over her last rejection.

His eyes flickered, "With a friend."

A woman. Of course. How silly of her to think that because she'd lived like a monk, he had chosen the same. She got the distinct feeling he didn't want her to ask any more questions.

"I didn't know you had any other friends here," she smiled. Keep it light.

He laughed, "I do though."

A young student waiting tables as a part-time gig came over for their orders. Layla ordered avocado and prawn salad, and Khayyam ordered a beef burger with extra chips.

"Hungry, are we?" she asked smiling. He was a Lahori foodie.

"You've no idea. What I wouldn't give for Hasina's mutton leg roast right now! I know I only had it once in Lahore, but boy do I miss it."

"Come home with me this weekend. I'm going. Going again, I should say. I visited only two weeks ago after half a year and I'd like to go sooner this time. And Ma would love to meet you."

The truth was she wanted to go back because she felt unsettled. And she had forgotten to bring her childhood book back with her. She needed to show it to Mira.

"Like you have to ask," he said with a grin. He seemed to be relaxing around her gradually. "What are you doing these days?"

"Teaching. Writing."

"Anything about that other matter?" he made a move with his hand, as if he wanted to touch her hand, lying just inches away from his, on the table. But the twitch of his hand stilled. And he moved his hand to lift his coffee cup.

She recalled the warmth of his hand. No one had ever made her feel the way he had. But that had been a long time ago. And he had wanted so much more than she was willing to give at the time. Did he still? And what about her? Was she still wary of love and sharing her half-life with someone? Khayyam, she corrected herself. Not someone, him.

She shrugged in response to his question. She was suddenly unable to speak.

This time he took her hand without thinking, squeezed it in a comforting gesture.

"I shouldn't have asked."

"Don't worry about it. Anyway, on to the missing piece of your life that I know nothing about. Tell all," she said lightly, changing the tone of the conversation.

"I became a pirate."

She laughed, "Try again."

Laughter was such a gift. She got it rarely. But she had laughed a lot ten years ago in the weeks that she had been with him. They had laughed a lot.

Khayyam shrugged, "I travelled. Central Asia mostly. Twenty universities and not one would have me on tenure track. I didn't give up though. I did odd jobs, private collectors and museums mostly, backpacked wherever I wanted. I became a nomad. The grants helped."

"Not too far a cry from a pirate then."

They both smiled.

"Your turn," he said.

"You know already."

His eyes full of sympathy, he nodded. "I'm so very sorry we couldn't find your mother. And then you…ah, left so suddenly."

The silences in their conversations had never been awkward. She felt the pressure of this silence. The ballooning of it between them. She felt her heart sink with apprehension.

Then he said with a smile, "We did what you said we should with our lives though. I painted. You wrote. We are adults now more than we were back then. No?"

Her relief was short-lived. There was an edge to his voice.

She nodded, "I know. I was ready to move on from my search and I did for a while. I tried to stay in touch but you were still…"

TEN

That awkward pause again.

"Sulking?" he furnished with the quirk of an eyebrow. That was new too. A rather pirate-like gesture, she thought.

"I guess," she said, looking at him, her head slightly to the side. Was he still upset? Was she? He had moved on like she'd asked him. He'd painted, won awards, made a name for himself. Why did she feel let down then?

"Shouldn't I have?" he laughed, but there was that undertone again. A brittle sound.

Layla looked away. Thank God. Shame was quick to follow the relief. How cruel of her to reject him ten years ago and be happy that he had been hurting all these years. Just like her. Cruel and unnecessary…he had wanted to be in her life, not the other way around. She could have…but this was foolish. *Stop.*

Meeting him after all this time suddenly made her feel old. She questioned her motives then of refusing him, three times, and now she felt as if it was a mistake. Was it? Or was this just something she would think for a few days, till she discovered something annoying about him which she hadn't remembered, or he had developed since she last saw him?

"Painting teaches one a few tricks in detection. Some canvases take detective work, some reveal themselves slowly, others drop a hint and keep you guessing, and just, you know…" he made a fist and clenched his teeth. "You know? That frustration, the niggling, dark messy thing that latches onto your heart and won't let go?"

"No." Layla shook her hand. "Not really. I love stories and writing about them, their theories and their history but this gut-wrenching frustration is something I've never experienced. Not yet anyway."

"You're a stoic. You never did allow your emotions to cloud your judgment or decisions. Even in art."

There was a bitter trace to the words that permeated the air between them. He had been furious then. He had believed she should be as clear about them "belonging together" as he was, and she just wasn't a romantic. She didn't even belong to herself. She still didn't. She belonged to the quest of finding her mother.

"I don't know if it was stoicism or something else entirely." She rolled her eyes, and smiled to lighten the rising simmering tension. The past found a way to grip the present in a vice of its own tempers.

A gust of wind on the sidewalk did a quick waltz with the fallen autumn-coloured leaves. Then it was gone leaving behind the magical rustle of dry leaves and smell of winter's promise.

Then he said lightly, "Maybe this frustration comes with creating something. You still haven't stepped foot into writing fiction. You will. Then you'll see."

She shrugged, smiling. But didn't contradict him.

"It's like taking wrong turns," he said referring to the discussion of painting. Then pointed a finger at her, "You don't allow yourself to accept that there are wrong turns."

"No. I make them right even if they were wrong initially. What about you? Taken any wrong turns lately?"

"Oh, I take wrong turns all the time. I try to move on and not waste my time mourning the mistakes I've made. But a stroke on a canvas that isn't right? I abandon those I cannot fix. Which happens more often than I care to admit. Or if there is something that has led me to more than I'd bargained for, then…I let it be. For another time. Another version of me to finish it—a future me in five or ten years or never. Who can say?"

"Have you ever gone back to any canvas?" Layla asked.

"Just once. But I had to abandon it again."

"Why?"

He looked up at her, and then away, with a small smile, a frown, his voice oozed regret, "I didn't know my subject well enough. I don't think my subject knew herself well enough either. We were young. She was hurting. She still is and I can't do a damn thing about it."

Layla couldn't hold his gaze, but he didn't look away this time. She didn't know what to say. He was right. Her gaze flickered and dropped.

He picked up his coffee cup.

TEN

"You side stepped the question," he asked. He lifted his cup for a sip, his eyes visible over the rim, "You said 'for a while'? Did you pursue your search then?"

"Yes, I did. That's why I'm here actually. Because a woman, who I think is my mother, is here. I am following her, trying to be close to her. I am not even sure it's her. Late last year, I discovered her almost by accident and so here I am now. I tracked her for a bit and then got a job here because she is here."

His movement frozen, his eyes on her keen, serious, he queried, "You haven't asked her yet? Or met her?"

Layla shook her head.

"Why not?" he was incredulous.

It was hard to admit. "I just haven't had the courage."

He watched her in silence till she squirmed in her seat, "Fine, fine. I'll get in touch with her. I will."

She laughed. His presence was bolstering, she had to admit.

He nodded, satisfied. Then he looked at his watch and whistled. "Where did the time go? It's five already. I have to go to a job interview."

"Are you planning on staying?"

He shrugged, "I'm flexible."

She nodded, confused now. He was staying? She blabbed, "This was…fun."

"Yeah," Khayyam smiled.

Genuinely moved at his happiness, she whispered, "What else is new?"

They walked towards the crossing.

"I sold the mansion. I let go. Not just of the mansion either. It was time."

She thought heartbreak was the same every time. She'd had enough experience. But this time it was more subtle, like a clean knife cut, and yet she knew she would live with the pain for the rest of her life.

She nodded, "Must've been hard." Her heart had become a heavy dead thing inside her chest. Oh, it hurt. She'd thought it couldn't anymore.

The sun had long dipped from the sky. It was that in-between time when light was faded and weak, but it was not dark enough to put lights on. But it would be soon. And the street would be alight and look pretty and festive.

Khayyam shrugged, "Yeah. I'm at peace. All my angst goes into my paintings now, nothing left over."

Layla nodded. "I used to be so certain back then. I miss that about me."

Khayyam smiled.

"You remember how we met in Lahore?" Layla asked. Why was she saying this? Had Khayyam's abandoned hope found home in her broken heart? "And then when we went to the American Embassy?"

"Yes. They didn't say anything about your mother. Even though we went back there with the portraits you had me draw of her from memory. We searched at every university, shrines, and even homeless shelters. I remember everything."

Layla said slowly,

"I guess it's like your paintings. What I remembered was no longer true or real. The face you painted didn't exist. When you talked about your canvases being riddles, that's a bit like memory, and a bit like stories too, they have only half the meaning, the other half is in the reader's gaze. Although I've never noticed the similarities before. I always thought plastic arts were stagnant and not changeable but stories grow organically, and are reproduced and retold, and so they change. But now I think I see the similitude in the creation of the arts."

Khayyam said, after a pause, "Do you regret the past?"

She couldn't answer that without breaking apart into a million pieces. Deliberately misunderstanding him, she said, "I've found her only recently. I moved here because of her. But I am not sure who it is I have found."

She had planned to tell him about the murder. At least the recent one. But she didn't want his attention distracted from her. Or was it something else? Was it that same intense fear that had quelled the topic from arising with Reza the other day?

They were the last ones remaining. The café staff were cleaning tables and they put their pretty fairy lights on and the smell of roasting coffee had vanished. Everything seemed to have stopped around them, waiting. Even the breeze had stilled. The air was suddenly frosty. Darkness nibbled at the edges of the horizon.

She'd pulled away now from answering the question he'd asked. Because the truth was that she did regret the past.

ELEVEN

The world continued to spin despite the murders of women and children, whether in universities, first-world immigrant cages or capitalist war zones. It still surprised Layla that it went on spinning; that it didn't shudder in disgust and just give up. She was in her office, waiting for Gul. She randomly moved a few books from where they were peacefully shelved, to another one for no reason but to occupy her hands and her mind. She would regret that later when her mind was back to being orderly again.

Layla was looking forward to driving with Khayyam to Ma's for the weekend. She had ceased to question Khayyam's return. She couldn't even remember her misgivings.

But first she had to have this short meeting with Gul. That was her last duty of the day and then she'd meet Khayyam in front of the office building. He'd hired a car and they'd make a road trip of it. When Gul knocked, Layla took a moment to gather her thoughts and sat down.

"Come in," she called. She was looking forward to an intelligent academic discussion with an exceptionally bright student.

Sultan yawned and stretched in the corner.

"Hi Professor Rashid. Thanks for seeing me." She saw Sultan. "Awwww."

"Hello Gul. Have a seat." But Gul went straight to Sultan, who allowed her to stroke him. "I'm happy to discuss your dissertation with you. I've read your submission about Sufi storytelling symbols, and I like your enthusiasm."

Gul made a face, "It wasn't any good?"

"You've started well," Layla said. "The introduction is well-written and focused. You could talk more about storytellers not always inventing their material, rather retelling and reinventing beloved tales or traditional tales. Storytellers changed their stories to fit the new orthodox or to escape it."

Sultan jumped onto the desk. There was a patch of sunlight there. He curled up and Layla stroked him.

Gul had been scribbling madly. She looked up when Layla paused. "But the audience? The reader? They were aware the changes were outside their control and must have resented those changed stories, no? Stories that are propaganda or mouthpieces of power, they're sterile? You say that in your book."

Smiling Layla said, "First of all, you're assuming the audience would notice the changes. Not everyone did and these changes occurred slowly, over time. In olden times conquests were bloody and common. And yes, stories can be sterile. What makes them sterile? And we are talking about Sufi tales specifically. How did they survive the ages?"

Layla paused to give Gul a chance to speak but continued when she didn't. "Those who remembered became storytellers by night to children and grandchildren, in caravanserais, by lonely campfires in the desert. So, you'll find them as poetry, in ritual, in history which is part story, in religious stories and under many insouciant tales, there will be secret codes recognizable only to those who are in the know. There are other values attached to Sufi stories I've discussed with you before."

"Yes, I read about that in your book where you said Sufi stories add meaning and value to our lives and that they have talismanic powers. I didn't quite get that, even in class that day when you mentioned it."

Layla smiled, and said, "A talisman is an inscribed object. Anything especially crafted and inscribed with words from the Quran, in order to protect, is a talisman. In olden times gemstones were expressly mined for such purposes for rich merchants, or rulers. Old stones, or stones that had been in the hands of sellers for too long, were not used for fear that they had been corrupted by random energies. There are many stories where special gemstones are carved under the full moon, the equinox, or an eclipse, while rituals of chanting and purification are performed. But it is always the words that make an ordinary stone into a talisman. Sufi Stories, because they are constituted of special words, are therefore themselves talismans. They have the potential to guide and protect from harm, as Cautionary Tales do. Stories are evidence that words are magic. Words have power. They invoke change and action, even in others. Words are the real magic, extant magic."

Gul beamed, "According to Sufi beliefs, human beings are connected to God through their souls and Sufi Teaching Stories are the catalysts that trigger the awakening of the soul. The Quran has so many Teaching Stories."

"Yes, indeed. Their form, content and style have a heuristic effect," Layla smiled. "But I am not sure if Scriptural stories should be included in your thesis, though your point is valid of course. Think about it. You could divide your thesis into chapters according to theories you have read and want to expound or stories you're studying. Have you thought that far yet?"

Gul shook her head, looking worried.

"Well, there is still time," Layla reassured. "You've picked a topic close to my heart and I will try hard not to spoon-feed you too much. It is your thesis after all."

"Do please…I love hearing you speak about it. I've learnt your books almost by heart."

"Sufi stories are a blessing, for those who are ready to benefit from them, and who possess a level of personal growth essential for that internal change to occur. Scriptural stories are just that."

Gul scribbled furiously to keep pace.

"Remember that a Sufi story has a strong connection with time and its passage. In Sufi and alchemical traditions, knowledge is shared in a manner that different layers of meaning are revealed at different times. At first reading, *The Conference of Birds* is about birds looking for their king, and that is a metaphor for finding inner strength. But as you grow older, you begin to see how each story is about a human condition, and some of those birds don't make it to the end. Is the great mystic Fariduddin Attar telling us that some characteristics in us are bound to lead to failure and cannot be escaped? Such questions are still debated amongst scholars."

Hadn't her own journey taught her that? And what of Khayyam and his journey? Yet here they were again, exactly where they'd started and looking at each other anew, seeing with fresh eyes and prior knowledge.

Gul frowned. "But that's true of many stories, even Western ones."

"Yes. But only the really good ones, the ones we call 'true' stories in Sufi parlance, will have this quality. When we speak of Sufi stories, we must understand that stories and traditions travel, migrate, cross-pollinate. Western canon, folktales, and fairytales have borrowed from Sufi traditions. Shakespeare has many Sufi leitmotifs and subtexts and so do Jostein Gaarder, Ibsen, Cervantes, Calvino, Borges and others. When you read their texts, you can see the similarities in themes and the core of the text. Stories are never static. If they are, they die. Stories come in all shapes and sizes."

"Even as jokes," said Gul.

"Indeed. The Sufi story isn't always easy to understand, unless it is a joke, and sometimes not even then. Sufis believe that deep intuition is actually a guide to deep knowledge and Sufi stories are used like spiritual exercises to gain access to that deep, often hidden, wisdom. A popular Sufi joke about Mullah Nasruddin is that the Mullah was throwing handfuls of crumbs around his house.

"'What are you doing?' a passerby asked.

"'Keeping tigers away,' the Mullah replied.

"The passerby laughed. 'There are no tigers here, Mullah.'

"'Effective, isn't it?' the Mullah said."

Gul laughed and continued to take notes.

"Sufi stories were deliberately resistant to being deciphered because only those who were truly worthy pondered over an enigma to seek the truth. Sufi storytellers had a symbol of storytelling: the walnut. The hard shell of form and structure, held within it the kernel of meaning."

Layla rose abruptly. The image of a dead woman smeared with ash and frost, in a small frozen garden hit her with the force of a punch. She saw it as clearly as if she'd seen it yesterday. Only she hadn't, she'd seen it in early January, the beginning of that year. The woman had been holding a walnut in her right hand. It had seemed so strange to her then, when she'd seen the pictures that were circulated on the internet. She'd noticed it immediately. The embossed brown shell, frosted over in the palm of the dead girl; her fingers unfurled, black tipped with frostbite and sparkling with ice crystals. No one else was too bothered about it. They were concerned about the murder. The dead girl. But now Layla recollected with dawning fear. She must talk to Detective James Lance. *Did it mean something more? Or was it another coincidence?*

"I'm sorry I must go, Gul."

"Thank you, Professor. This was so useful and I am so grateful. I have to see Professor Reza now. I'm getting his books autographed by him." The girl looked radiant. Reza had that effect on young women. *Women of any age* whispered a little voice.

"I'm going that way too." She was afraid of walking alone in broad daylight in her own campus. "Just let me put Sultan in his carrier."

"Oh, I'm so glad," Gul responded with relief. "Ever since the murder, I try not to go alone. Even in daytime. All the girls try not to. It's so surreal and so unfair that girls have to be even more careful than before."

"Yes, that's very true. It really is unfair," Layla said. Women murdered, women afraid, was an ancient theme.

Gul started talking about someone she knew, who had done something…Layla paid little attention to Gul's chatter as they walked to the university together.

*Sufi stories are words of power. They are ritualistic and symbolic. Sufi stories are…*Her mind was in a loop, stuck on that image of the murdered woman holding a walnut. *Stories. Power.*

She caught a glimpse of a man in uniform, a police officer walking by. The investigation was still on and that meant a lot of police officers on campus. There was fear and an obscene denial in the air.

Power. Words and symbols of power.

Sufi stories were about rituals and symbols. Storytelling is the rite, the words the passage which open up to change. Walnuts were a symbol of the covert message, the secret. The story within the story, the hidden meaning, appearance versus reality.

And the dead girl with a walnut in her hand? The dead girl with ash smeared on her body?

"Layla!"

Her head whipped up. The sun shone bright and cheerful. The street was lined with tall elms and sugar maple trees. Their top branches swayed and waved in the chilly breeze.

Reza was walking towards them. Gul beamed.

"Hello Reza," said Layla, with more equanimity than she felt.

Reza laughed. "So good to see you. Ah, Gul. My one and only fan!"

"Certainly not only, Professor, but definitely your most ardent fan," Gul said.

"Don't let me keep you. I have to catch up with an old friend." Layla made to move away.

"What's the rush? Join us for a cup of tea. Gul wants a personalized note from me. I'd love to catch up with the brightest professor and her star pupil."

With her thoughts still elsewhere, Layla couldn't find a polite enough reason to decline. Was she really thinking rationally? *Did the walnut even mean anything? She was overthinking, surely?* She shrugged and with a too-bright smile followed Gul inside.

Reza's office was airy and light. Layla felt a veritable assault of endorphins. One of the more unfamiliar hormones. Sultan scratched at the carrier.

"What a handsome creature! Do let him out," said Reza.

"Meet Sultan," she said, setting him free. He promptly ran to Reza's outstretched hands.

"Nice office," she commented taking in the richly woven Turkish carpet that perfectly complemented the wood panelled walls. She was surprised at how friendly Sultan was with Reza, and he was usually so recalcitrant. But he was a cat after all. He was his own master and his moods a mystery. "I have a beautiful carpet at home too. One of my prized possessions."

"How wonderful to know we share such similar tastes. Sit, ladies. I'll make us some tea. Turkish. The best."

Sultan was now stretched in the sunniest spot of the room. Layla looked around and spotted her own books. She had been looking for them. She was a little embarrassed at the thrill of pleasure. His bookshelves were crammed with all sorts of books, fairy tales, folktales, a variety of genres from history and war to fiction and philosophy.

"Eclectic collection," she remarked.

"Just a few favourites," he said with a wink.

"Professor Reza is interested in Sufi stories," Gul said. "He asked a lot of good questions the last time we met, and I'm incorporating many of the points he raised in my thesis."

Layla sensed a strange frisson in the air. Reza's face was in shadow. "Indeed."

What a cold response. Layla fought the urge to make up to Gul for his lack of warmth to compensate for that awkward moment. But she fought her own urges to comfort others. Where did they come from? She had a flash of memory. Mountains, children and a tall woman, tears running down her cheeks.

Reza brought tea in beautiful Turkish glasses. "How is the dissertation going?"

Gul demurred, "Er…um…okay I guess."

Layla tried to smile. She had been raised to contain natural impulses, to control her emotions, to be unreadable. Even after so many years, she had to consciously display emotion. Sometimes, when it had been bottled too long, she was afraid it might slip out at the wrong moment, at the wrong place.

"I'm sure you're doing great."

Layla looked around again. "It really is a beautiful office."

Reza smiled, "Thank you. I'm sure you've heard the stories of how I vanished for years in Angkor. That basket is from there." He waved his hand dismissively. "I was studying with the monks. They wove baskets all day. It was part of their meditation. I must admit, it helped control thoughts and thinking patterns. It got me thinking about your books on weaving. Everyone agrees spinning thread and weaving cloth were once religious practices used to teach the cycles of life and death, birth and re-birth, the Greeks used it. Romans, Egyptians. These were ways to learn about the inward journeys and about inviting growth through the process of actually seeing and building with one's hands."

He leaned forward with his charming smile and said slowly, "But you claim that the initial weavers were women as were the first storytellers." He looked into her eyes, still smiling. "Forgive me for asking but isn't that a bit far-fetched? I mean 'only women' were weavers and storytellers? I mean I could've claimed 'only men' in Angkor but I didn't."

Layla had heard this question so often; she almost had an automatic response: "I never said all women and only women. I researched for years and present the evidence in my books—it was *mostly* women because weaving was and still is 'woman work', as are cooking and housework in most cultures. Storytelling has also been and is still one of the primary means of bonding with children. As parenting was 'woman work' in many cultures for the longest time, telling stories was how mothers and grandmothers communicated with and disciplined their children."

"Sure, sure," Reza looked a little red-faced.

There was tension in the air. As a child Layla had learned to read her environment. The changing emotional needs of her mother and her own childish heart had made her sensitive to the undercurrents. Reza was upset about something.

"Maybe you're right," he said. "Your books were very well-received. They've made an impact. I'm just curious. I don't know. I mean I don't consider weaving and storytelling such world-changing discoveries, as say, the wheel."

Layla laughed with him. She understood such people even though they were so different from her. She'd always tried to find herself within the pages of books, between the lines, within various languages. She had started to write for the same reason. Her birth mother had taught her to read but Layla had surrounded herself with books out of choice. Books were her totems, her talismans. Books made her feel safe. But men like Reza got lost easily when their comfortable worlds were challenged with new ideas. For him books were a means to an end. Books were the clothes he dressed himself in to "seem" cultured, intellectual. They were not his bread and butter. They were not part of him. She'd thought better of him.

"I don't mean to belittle your work," he said, looking unhappy. A little too dramatically unhappy, as if he were trying to act on stage about being sad. And just by saying it implied that he did think nothing of it. But she knew that he admired her work, so she took him at face value.

"Of course not," she said. He needed to be excused from any responsibility of misogyny and racism or anything that was politically incorrect. Political correctness was a term indecent people had invented when they were forced to be decent to people different from themselves. Her heart felt a twinge of distress. She had so wanted to like him, and this conversation was making it impossible. At least for now. And this was something new with Reza. Even so, something drew her to him, maybe it was academia, or their preferred loneliness, but she felt an instinctual connection. Almost like she had with Khayyam. An instant recognition of someone dear. She had never seen him with a woman. He was always alone. He seemed so easily likeable. And yet. That innate caution, or paranoia, pulled her back.

"Sufi stories have no single author," she said.

His face now showed concern, as if to imply she was floundering. Layla had no time for him if he was this narrow-minded, but there was a quiet student listening to this exchange. A young woman who needed to see a woman speaking up, defending her work and defending what was hers.

"They are altered and passed on from generation to generation, like rare woven shawls, carpets and rugs. Like cloth, stories are woven, embroidered, changed and enhanced. They are handed down generation to generation."

Gul jumped in. "Also, you know, stories are misremembered and adapted, sometimes because of censorship, and we are seeing a resurgence of that with books being banned around the world. Just as a thread might be dropped in stitching or a pattern lost or even threads cut with scissors. Stories are alchemy happening before our very eyes. They are the process of alchemy. If they don't change, they're not true stories. I mean, True, with a capital T. Writing was so rare in ancient times. Illustrations in weaving and cut-work were common. In fact, Ann Bergen says that weaving was the feminine semiotic."

Layla glanced at Gul proudly.

Reza was amused. "You have quite the protégée here. How is fiction true? Convince me."

"I really don't have the time nor the inclination, Professor," Layla laughed. "I do have to leave now. I will see you, Gul. It was really nice chatting with you both."

Reza said, as he got up, "I hope I have not offended you in any way?"

"Not at all," Layla said politely.

"I can convince you, Professor Reza," Gul said as they stood up, and Layla stopped to listen. "Princess Rukhsar in the old Persian folktale, who used weaving to trick her enemy and also to unmask the truth of her rape, is a great example of story revealing truth. Spinning the yarn and spinning a tale are the same because of this tradition of storytelling. There are plenty such. Princess Rukhsar sends a cloak woven by her in a forest far away to her mother. The mother 'reads' the story woven into the cloth and learns the truth of her daughter's rape, how her tongue was cut out to prevent her from speaking the name of the culprit, her new stepfather the king, and how Rukhsar was exiled by him to cover his crime. The Queen had been told that Rukhsar had run away with a secret lover. But when the cloak comes as a present for the new Queen's coronation, the truth comes out. This kind of story is about Truth always coming out, no matter how much the villain may want to hide it. Three things cannot long be hidden: the sun, the moon and the truth, says Buddhist teaching. An Urdu version says, perfume and love cannot long be hidden."

"Brilliantly done, Gul. This is how the secret feminine semiotic works, as Bergen says, it is a code, written by a woman and deciphered by another," Layla nodded at her student with encouragement. "Perfume is also said to have been invented by a woman in Mesopotamia four thousand years ago.'

Gul beamed. "Professor Rashid…I think I know exactly what I want to do. I'd like to focus on the carpet as a symbol of storytelling in Sufi stories. I could write about weaving as a dynamic metaphor for storytelling in Sufi stories as in *The Arabian Nights*."

"That's brilliant, Gul," said Layla. "Feel free to come and see the one in my flat. I love it because it has many of the Sufi symbols like the hoopoe and rose."

"So glad to have been such a catalyst in your career, Gul," Reza said.

"Just like a man to take credit where none is due," Layla said laughing so that he wouldn't take offense. "I'll see you both after reading week."

TWELVE

She smelled dry sand when she walked out, Sultan in her arms, and his carrier empty in her hand. They were cleaning the roads. The dry leaves and dried mud whirled into the rotating brush-wheels. It made her think of her past and that other place. The dry barren mountains and the desert that surrounded the barren mountains.

The desert wasn't a merely a physical place. You carried it within you. Just like your past. It was who you were. It blew into your eyes and your throat and your mouth. It settled inside the cavities of your nose. It made your blood gritty and your skin rough. It never quite washed out of your pores no matter how damp the city you hid yourself in, the desert stayed with you. People often forgot the cold desert of dry mountain lands. Desert meant the ochre fine grain of hot countries to most people. She knew better.

Her mood lifted when she saw Khayyam lounging against his rented Cadillac in the parking lot of the university. The ground was littered with autumn-coloured leaves. The air smelled of the pristine cold of autumn. The ground was wet with the slush of melted snow and mud. Once winter came the snow would be inches deep. Layla did not look forward to that. She did not like snow.

Khayyam lifted his hand in greeting. Ever since he had come back into her life…come back, she corrected herself. Not necessarily into her life. She bit her lip. He was a wanderer. He said, a wanderer was someone who was looking for something the nature of which was unknown to him. He'd say that gaining meant losing as well, that gaining wasn't necessarily owning.

But when Khayyam had appeared in her line of vision, her heart had lurched. Ten years could change a lot. But not this apparently. His hold on her heart was permanent. But he had let go. He had sold the mansion even. Who was he now? Certainly not the tortured young man obsessed with finding a father who had abandoned him, a father who didn't want to be found. Though Khayyam had.

When relationships shed their skins, as theirs had, and when relationships disappeared without a trace, as theirs had…did they sometimes reappear in a different form? Had they found each other again or someone else? He hadn't fallen into her bed yet. It had been so easy and natural last time. She hadn't pushed this time. Perhaps they were both afraid of repeating past mistakes. Or perhaps, he didn't have any residual left-over feelings like she did.

"Hey," he called. "What kept you?"

"Students and fellow tutors," she smiled.

He lifted Sultan from her. Sultan purred. Khayyam grinned.

"He loves me," Khayyam said kissing Sultan on the top of the earless side of his head.

"Don't be too sure," she said. Was she jealous of her own cat? She was disgusted with herself.

Laughing, he gave Sultan back to her, and reluctantly she put him in his carrier and at the back of the car.

He hadn't said anything about them since his return. A few friendly kisses and hugs were all he could spare her now. She'd figured once she found her mother she'd go back to Lahore, to Khayyam and his old mansion, full of rooms, antiques and secrets. *Had she lost him forever?* The question grated. Why was she thinking like a Victorian damsel?

"What's with the thunderous look?" Khayyam leaned to peck on her cheek.

"What thunderous look?" she offered her cheek, breathing his scent in. Cardamom and tobacco.

"Something wrong?" he asked.

"No, not really."

"You seem tense," he said.

She shrugged. Reza had shaken her a bit with his rudeness. How could well-educated men still harbour such misogyny was incomprehensible to her.

"I'm fine."

They got into the rental car. Khayyam was driving. It would take them a day to reach Ma's house. A week off and they'd be spending it as a family after ages. They'd got snacks.

"Look at that," she pointed at a bird in flight. "That's a kestrel."

From the road they could see forests of maple, and hackberry and white pine rolling away till the eye could see.

Khayyam looked at the black speck, "How can you tell?"

"I've enjoyed bird-watching all my life. As a child I used to watch the skies for hours."

"And where was this? You hardly ever talk about your childhood. I don't even know where you grew up? I mean I know it was America, but where?"

Layla was quiet for some time. "Actually, I was born somewhere else. I came to the U.S when I was nine."

"Really? Where were you born?"

Layla turned away.

"I don't like talking about that period of my life."

Khayyam said quickly, "No problem. I understand."

They drove in silence for a while. She spotted a flash of fire in the trees. Was it a cardinal?

Khayyam said, "I was reading something, and it made me think of you—something about a mind observing itself." He glanced at her. "If engaged in observation, what would it be observing? If it were all engaged in being mind, what would do the observing?"

She nodded smiling, "You were reading Al-Ghazali, the great Sufi Master, mathematician, rhetorician, philosopher."

He smiled, "She knows all."

Then asked her to light a cigarette for him. She took a long drag and passed it to him, "Filthy habit."

He laughed, "Tell me about it."

She'd said the same to him ten years ago. "I did. Long ago."

He laughed and did not take the bait.

It seemed so long ago.

"I've been meaning to tell you," said Khayyam. "When I read your books, I painted for days without stopping. You know, when the first two came out? I read them together. What struck me most, from the second one especially, was when you talk about stories being the weave of fate and how the art of weaving was women's work for centuries, as was storytelling. You wrote about Sufi Stories being the penetrable opening in the weaving of culture and history, of Sufi stories, women's stories, themselves being the very warp and weft of fate and time."

"I remember."

Layla could hear the wonder in his voice. She had been thinking of her own life and her mother's too when she'd written that. She was surprised they were talking about this after Reza had mentioned the same thing only that morning.

"Yeah, you said Sufi stories could sometimes be agents of social cohesion but sometimes, they are the trick of the Trickster. They are the law of surprise in a world trapped in systems, structures, and social constraints of class, gender, marriage, motherhood, masculinity, patriarchy, and so forth. That blew my mind. Because…I guess, I'm a victim of patriarchy too. That book opened up something in me. I did a series of paintings after that."

Poplar trees whizzed by. It was a long journey. Khayyam said he'd rather drive than travel by train. She knew he liked speed.

"I know, I saw them, they're in the Museum of Modern Art in New York."

"You saw them?" He sounded surprised but also pleased.

"Of course. You received the MacArthur grant after that series. But you only came to the opening and then vanished. Caused quite a stir in the art world. You became even more of a critics' darling."

He laughed, shrugged, "I went back to Rio."

That was six years ago. Layla had gone home after touring his exhibition and had been making herself a cup of tea. The cup had slipped to the floor with a resounding crash as if her hand were suddenly lifeless. She'd trembled with the force of an unknown emotion that had appeared from nowhere and gripped her in a gut-wrenching fury of passion. She'd cried for hours.

"Thank you for saying that, Khayyam. Your paintings opened up something in me too. I especially liked the one with the old woman and the little girl. The old woman is weaving her loom, but her face is turned away towards the child. The girl looks entranced as if she is listening to a story, a magical story. The old woman's lips are parted, as if she is speaking. You used the colours of alchemy in stark shades—white, red and black."

Layla identified with both the old woman and the child. In a culture where fashion and slimness and youth meant sexiness, Layla was beginning to wear her age like an invisibility cloak. In a culture where grey hair meant old, and old was synonymous with irrelevant, she was already beginning to fade into the margins for others. She had grown up amongst old women and never had friends her own age except briefly. Khayyam for a two weeks in her twenties and then silence from him for a decade. Those she thought of as friends were mostly older than her. Ageing was a gift, especially in a world that put a premium on youth and so she was happy with her grey strands. She understood older people well. That was why she and Ma had got along so well.

Layla chided herself, she was only in her early thirties. She should not be calling that aging. She was young. Just felt old because of her experiences. Nothing to do with grey hair and age. One had to fight hard the internalized misogynistic codes. She was young, she told herself again, even if she felt like an exile from her own youth.

"So, you really did see them." He sounded pleased. "That one wasn't just because of the book though."

"I know," Layla said quietly. She hadn't told him much back then, but she had told him about the stories her birth-mother had shared. Just enough for him to understand the bond that had existed and then been severed so brutally. The last painting in the series showed the girl as a young woman, now weaving a carpet which was half-finished with alphabets from different languages falling in a heap at her feet from the loom. It looked as if the carpet was disintegrating from thread into broken words. A crumbling world.

That hadn't upset her at all. Her words did not fall broken into heaps, unless she intended them to. When we talk of stories, what we like, what comforts us, what disturbs us, we are talking of ourselves as much as the story. In fairytales, folktales, myths, and other such stories innocence is the key that opens the door through which the protagonist can escape. In Sufi stories, as in life, innocence must be swallowed, eaten up by knowledge and experience to access escape.

But the painting, together with his reticence now, did manage to pierce the walls of protection that she'd built around herself. How could she not, with the life she'd lived?

Khayyam reached over and squeezed her hand. And words tumbled out of her, like old bricks crumbling out of a disintegrating wall.

"Living as an adopted child is living a lie, telling yourself every day that your life is good, it is normal, yet knowing full well that it isn't. It's like living in two worlds simultaneously. The real one of truth—abandonment and adoption. And the imaginary world where you hope to find your mother and she tells you that it was all a mistake. That she didn't mean to abandon you at all."

She turned and smiled, squeezed his hand back. Ten years was a long time. Yet she hadn't given up on finding her birth mother in twenty-three. Ten years was nothing.

THIRTEEN

Layla and Khayyam spent almost the entire week-long vacation in the kitchen with Hasina, who had been delighted to see Khayyam again. The three of them chatted long into the night. It was soon obvious that despite the opportunity, Khayyam was in no hurry to rekindle their romance. And Layla wasn't sure what she wanted from one minute to the next. She oscillated between utter yearning and absolute terror at being accepted. Or rejected. She had had enough of that to last her a lifetime.

Again, Khayyam and all of Layla's adopted aunties were in her large, airy kitchen and Hasina was conducting her cooking class with her signature panache. The two windows in the kitchen were open to the sun's warming rays and the air was fragrant and not at all oppressive despite the steaming pots and pans.

"Those who understand this language," said Hasina, "who speak it, know that their table is their pride, their grace, their raison d'etre. It is a reflection of their creativity. Food is a universal language like music or math, if you want to be prosaic about it. There's a Persian saying, *pehle tuaam, baad uz kalaam*. Food before conversation, because food is a way of communication and one that is universally understood. In olden times, important decisions were discussed over dinner by rajahs and noblemen. We celebrate with food. We mourn by bringing food to the aggrieved. Food is language."

Khayyam stood at the black granite counter, cutting crunchy fresh cucumbers into paper-thin slices. He was enjoying himself and it showed. Sultan lurked around Khayyam, and he fed him stolen bits of minced meat.

"It's the intimacy of food," Munia said with a faraway look. "I like what you said Hasina. Food is expression, an intimate exchange so subtle we miss the esoteric pattern of sharing a whole history, culture, racial identity on the one hand, and the personal, individual connection on the other. We've lost the understanding of food as an art."

"True." Aunty Coco munched a cucumber slice. "I have heard you say it often enough. Food is an integral part of one's identity."

"Yes," Hasina moved the chopped fresh coriander to the side and rinsed the knife. "It reflects the bounty of Allah, the Universe. Food is a blessing, a miracle that has to be appreciated spiritually." She opened her box of spices and put a teaspoon each of cumin and red chilli powder on a small, patterned china plate.

Khayyam put the cucumbers to one side and began slicing a carrot. "On that note, food should also not be wasted. It's criminal. It's the worst kind of ingratitude."

Layla knew he was thinking of the street children in Lahore and Rio.

She said, "I was surprised to discover how important food is in most stories, even if it is just three pomegranate seeds. I guess it's because food is the one thing in culture that embodies the best of it, and translates into its language, its art, its history. Every recipe has a story if we listen carefully."

Khayyam had finished chopping the salad and Layla helped him plate it. Their fingers touched, retreated, touched again. They smiled in the sun-lit kitchen like a domesticated couple. Layla sprinkled a bit of pink Himalayan salt on it, added dried rose petals and pomegranate seeds.

"You're so right about that, Layla," said Hasina. "I'm sure we all have stories related to food."

"I do," said Aunty Sheila. "My mother-in-law was a doctor and there I was, scouring the city for just the right cuts of meat, the right variety of mustard leaves. You see, for me, planning the menu was part of a ritual of looking after my family. It had to be the best food—according to the season, and of course their health demands. She used to get microwavable food and be done. Then I met Hasina. What is it...twenty-five years ago now? She said I should accept the differences between us, my mother-in-law and I, like I accept the amalgamation of spices, some are sour, some sweet, some sharp, some mellow and together they make a good meal. People are like that. A family is made up of different combinations. Learn to enjoy it. That bit of advice really cooled down a lot of unnecessary drama in my life."

Everyone had a story of Hasina and how she'd counselled them. Her mother was more than a brilliant chef. She was a friend, a therapist, a guide. Clucking the compliments away she brought the conversation back to food.

"If only speech, like oil, was tempered first," said Hasina. They all sniggered. Hasina was a maestro at work. She chopped and stirred, cooked and talked. And Layla was reminded strongly of why she had chosen her next semester topic to be food.

"No cooking is refined if the oil used is not tempered properly. And no communication either if thought and speech are raw. Every recipe is different but for most savoury dishes oil is tempered with dry spices like cardamom, bay leaves, nutmeg and my favourite, garlic. Then it is strained and used for cooking. I'm surprised at people who buy bottled oil and use it as is. They don't temper it before cooking."

They were making biryani too that day at Khayyam's ardent request. Layla measured the rice in a bowl. Cooked with meat, nuts, potatoes and lots of spices, most South Asian and Central Asian people loved this rice dish and so of course there were countless variations of it. Just like fairytales. Food, a Sufi Sheikh had said, was a well-told story, for just as food did, a story satiated a hungry man.

"Cooking on 'dum' or slow cooking brings out the taste of ingredients at different temperatures." Hasina put a large smooth oval shaped stone on a pristine white cloth, wrapped the stone in it and put it onto the flat lid of the cooking pot. The small black knob that should have been in the middle of the lid was missing, so the stone sat plump on the lid. "Meat, as you all know, tastes best cooked slow, that way all the flavours blend and fuse with each other to enrich the taste and aroma."

"Thank you for that. I've never really done slow cooking yet," said Khayyam.

Hasina turned twinkling eyes at him. "Yet?"

"I cook a lot," admitted Khayyam. "Quite complicated recipes too. Tomorrow, I'll make you a few Brazilian recipes I love."

Hasina said, "That will be truly wonderful. I'd love to take a break from cooking. And don't worry about slow cooking, you will learn. You watch and listen and taste. And when you start slow cooking, you'll see the difference. For now, get a feel of the things we use and the temperatures we cook at. Have you ever ground garlic, ginger or dry spices in a mortar and pestle?"

Hasina gestured to these important kitchen tools.

"Er…no. We have machines now," offered Khayyam.

Hasina clucked with contempt. "Convenience in cooking has stripped it of all flavour. Machines are not the same as a stone. The minerals in the stone add to the taste you see. I use clay pots to cook meat, but I use the convenience of non-stick pots for rice. Convenience should be chosen carefully to avoid compromising the quality of the experience."

Khayyam nodded and grinned, "Do you mind if I take notes?"

Hasina chuckled. "No, I don't mind but I'd rather you listened and observed. When we listen, and see and smell, that's longer lasting than notes on paper. Tell me why?"

Khayyam looked at the pots and pans, the vegetables and spices. "Taking notes would engage one sense only: aural." He smiled at Hasina. "But with a live demo I get to engage all the other senses as well. If I'm not concentrating on taking notes I will hear, and see, and smell. Cooking really is an art."

Hasina beamed and spread her hands. "There you have it. And now, it's time to check the biriyani." She lifted the stone wrapped in now damp cloth and put it aside on a large ancient, polished-to-a-shine copper tray she had brought with her from India all those years ago. She lifted the lid with a brightly-coloured cloth. The aroma was piquant and intense.

Layla's mouth watered. "Oh, my God the fragrance is absolutely divine! It's the spices. Fiery, potent…but there's something else, like perfume. Mmm."

"Take a look, Layla."

Hasina beamed with a faint air of pride.

Layla peeped into the fragrant pot with its medley of colour. White rice grains jostled yellow and red ones—the long delicate grains tumescent with flavour, and golden-brown pieces of chicken, glistening round red-chillies, slivers of lemon rind and small sultanas added to the riot of colour and added even more flavour and texture.

"It's so beautiful," whispered Layla in awe. "It's like *The Arabian Nights*…this is what it must smell like, look like. This is what Scheherazade and Prince Shehryar ate, surely."

Hasina scooped up a spoonful, blew on it to cool it, and offered it to Layla.

Layla accepted the offering almost reverently. "Mmm… wow…there's something…mmm…unfamiliar," she swallowed. "Delicious, but unfamiliar."

"Yes, probably the touch of khoya, the concentrated milk granules I usually add to biryani. It enriches the flavour of meat. You've forgotten everything."

"I really feel I should be writing the ingredients down," Khayyam dipped into the rice with a spoon. "At least those, if not all these wonderful aphorisms you keep dropping like pearls of wisdom. God, this is beautiful as well as delicious."

Hasina didn't respond till she'd put the lid back on the cooking pot. "Time, I feel, is the ingredient most precious in all recipes. Slow cooking works on food just as the passage of time balances a relationship. Ingredients or circumstance, heat or struggle, pressure or stress, they all work together in harmony or opposition to create something new, to make it the best it can be."

Khayyam and Layla had made a long makeshift table on the other end of the room so that they could all sit together. Even with the wall down, it was cozy with twelve of them, including the ladies of the cooking class. But the windows let in plenty of light, making the room lively.

"Tell me about your new job, Layla?" said Aunty Coco, once they were seated.

"It's good. Quiet. Just the way I like it," she said quickly, the perfumes of rich food made her mouth water. Sultan slunk by her chair and sat down, expectantly.

"Writing anything new?" asked Khayyam.

She hesitated. It was hard to confess she was writing a novel. It seemed almost pompous. Reluctantly, she admitted, "Yes, I am. I'm trying something different. It's fiction but it involves a lot of research."

She smuggled Sultan a piece of meat.

"Oh, sounds intriguing, Layla, tell us more."

"I don't like to discuss my books till I'm done, Aunty Coco. I feel the energy is sort of vanquished if I do. It's just a feeling I have. And this one, this book's particularly close to my heart. I've never done fiction before. Didn't think it would be this fun. Or this hard."

She was grateful no one said they'd always wanted to write a book too but never had the time.

"Fiction?" Khayyam quirked an eyebrow. "That's new. You'd resisted long enough. I've always said you were a born storyteller."

"Thank you." Then she turned to Hasina and said, "This is delicious, Ma."

"Of course, it is," said Munia. "What else is it going to be when your Ma cooks?"

"Talking of food…and stories," Layla lifted the platter of rice and helped herself. "Guess what my next course is going to be, Ma? Food and the Abrahamic Scriptures. It came out of my latest book about women in the three monotheistic religions. You wouldn't believe how many stories start or end with food as miracle or strategy."

"That sounds amazing, Layla. Were you thinking of Judith and Salome?" said Khayyam. The plate before him was piled high with food and he was dipping into the gravy and rice with his fingers. She watched him enjoy a bite. Food was sensuous too.

Layla said brightly, "I might as well practice part of my first lecture notes. And yes, those two come to mind immediately, don't they? But there are other stories too. Hints even." They all made enthusiastic noises she said, "There are so many stories in the Old and New Testaments that revolve around celebrations and executions simultaneously. Food and women are central to many Biblical stories. Women are shown to use food to seduce, kill and conquer. Jael, Judith, Esther killed their enemies—all men, by the way—during or after a feast. Food was used for seduction, for parley and for friendship. It was used to either swing favour of kings, generals and prophets or lull the enemy before murdering them." Layla glanced at the women around the table, briefly allowing her eyes to settle on her mother with a grin. "I don't know where I got the idea from, Ma, but I wanted to explore the cultural connections between food and sexuality, friendship and betrayals linked with food in literary and sacred history."

"Yes, I wonder where," Coco laughed. Others joined in on the obvious joke that it was from her Ma.

"Salome and Delilah were on the 'other' side of the historian's perspectives, so they're written as villains and viragos. Hope you're changing that?" Munia said, helping herself to some red and green chilli chutney sitting in tiny silver bowls side by side. "They were rad. History just isn't fair to us women."

"You're bringing history into new perspective with stories. I like that." Hasina looked so proud of her daughter. "Even in the *Arabian Nights* there is a lot about food. There are many examples of food in the Quran as metaphors or analogies. Food is a central concept in religion, not least as sacrifice. Another hit on your hands, I'd say."

Layla smiled at the compliments and the input of useful ideas. Ma picked up the mountains of thinly cut cucumbers, radishes, onions, tomatoes for a green salad. The medley of green, purple and red looked so pretty. Layla wanted to take a picture with her phone but resisted the urge.

"Absolutely, Ma. Cain and Abel offered food as sacrifice. In that way, the very first murder in the world was linked indirectly to food. And food, sexuality and death have been portrayed as an Oriental fantasy in many Western stories over the years, but people forget that food itself is treated as a strong ritualistic object in the Bible and the Quran. It is a very old and important symbol, and as in Eid-ul-Adha, it is used as celebration and for comfort."

"The Last Supper," Khayyam said thoughtfully. "I never thought about it like that. But Maybe Leonardo da Vinci did. Wish I knew if he thought of it that way. I'll have to look at it again. Fancy going to Rome with me?"

He looked at Layla with a smile. She laughed. There it was then. Good. She felt she might be giving off a sparkle.

"Remember also the relationship between eating and nurturing." Hasina passed the platter of rice to Coco. "And nurturing is identified with women."

"Exactly. Food is perceived as a gift by God. In the Quran, Zachariah asks Mary where she gets her food from every day. That is the first sign of her extreme piety. Allah sent her heavenly food according to the Quran. Food is a sacred gift. Wouldn't you agree? Like manna was for the Jewish people," said Layla.

"Layla, you make me feel so much better," said Aunty Sheila. "I'm not the only one who loves food, then."

They all laughed, and Layla had another point for her project: shared laughter over shared food. "No, Aunty Sheila, it isn't just you," she said. "It is often centripetal even to faith stories."

Khayyam's gaze was warm on her. She realized she was happy. In this moment, she was happy.

FOURTEEN

Layla waited by the duck pond in the local park for Mira Heshmat. She sat under a large oak, an old sentinel of the park. A warbler sang somewhere. It was a sunny but chilly day. She wore her coat and scarf and held on to the book of her childhood. She had requested a meeting two days after Mira's talk. Mira was due to give a lecture at Layla's university in a few days, and she could have met her there, but she couldn't wait any more. And she wanted privacy. There were so many questions she wanted to ask Mira.

Deliberately, she looked around. She was wary of walking into the past. So, she catalogued the present. Street cafes. Teenagers kissing. Cyclists. The town was pretty. Tourists swarmed it in the summer. She watched cyclists enjoying the day. Families having picnics.

But she couldn't help it. The past was always there, sucking her back into itself. Layla didn't remember much of the time before that dark night when her birth mother had abandoned her at the orphanage in a little town in Delaware. All she remembered was the dank smell and her own sobs.

"Don't leave me," she had repeated in all the languages she knew. Surely, her mother knew she was a good girl and that she had learned everything she'd wanted her to learn. And there was a great deal her mother had wanted her to learn. She had spent twenty odd years wondering why that was. Why'd she wanted to teach her all these languages? Seven languages to call her mother, and then...abandonment.

She remembered every small detail her mother had taught her. But not much else.

Was Mira that woman?

For years, she had gone to sleep reading the stories, handwritten and illustrated in secret by her mother. Those stories had been the warm embrace of her lost mother and it was those stories that had moulded her and made her who she was. Was Mira her mother? If Layla asked, would Mira admit it?

She had discovered Mira's picture in a newspaper in October last year. It was a picture of the detective who had solved a serial killer case and behind him, in the picture almost out of the frame, stood Mira. The caption said, a storyteller had helped the detective crack the case. That was how she'd found her in a small town, half the country away.

Seeing Mira's picture like that had stunned Layla. Pulled the ground from beneath her feet. She'd felt vertigo. And then she'd gone and done what she would never have done if she were in her senses. She'd resigned her lucrative job and won a reputation for being eccentric. But it would be worth it. If Mira was who Layla thought she was. It was all worth it.

The cooing of a mourning dove, probably taking a rest between buildings, pulled her back to the present. It was a beautiful park, embellished with redbuds, hickory, and white oak. She could hear birds tittering and cooing often.

Layla thought she'd start by telling Mira about the two murders and ask her for help. It would be a way to engage with her. After all, Layla had found this body and had been present at the other university too, where another young woman had been murdered. She still felt a frisson of unease at the thought.

Her phone rang. It was Detective Lance. "Hello, Detective Lance."

"Hi there, Professor. Any reason you didn't tell me about the murder when you called? That is why you called isn't it?"

Layla winced. She should have told him. "Yes. I figured you'd get a more accurate report from your colleagues."

He grunted.

"You know how it looks, right? You were there and now here. Again."

Layla knew exactly what it looked like.

"I think you know it wasn't me, Detective. But I agree there are no coincidences. I was at both universities. I'd like to know what that means as much as you. Or if it means anything at all?"

He let his breath out at the other end as if he'd been holding it. "Anything you can think of that might help?"

"I...I'm not sure what you mean?"

"Any crazy ex-boyfriends that might be following you to get your attention?"

"No." No boyfriends at all. She was a double PhD at the age of thirty-two. She had slept with random strangers when she'd wanted, been in a couple of pseudo-serious relationships that had fizzled out. Nothing to see there.

Khayyam didn't count as a boyfriend. Not at all. The endearments he called her, and the cardamom on his breath crept into her memory. No, Khayyam didn't count as a boyfriend. He gazed at her and gauged her emotions, her fear and embarrassment, and calmed her with a wink and a smile; he cut cucumbers in her mother's kitchen as if he'd been doing that all his life. No, he didn't count as a boyfriend.

And why was he asking about her boyfriends? This was not about her. Her heart fell to the bottom of her stomach. Let this not be about her, she prayed.

"Any idea who it might be?"

"No," she said. *You?* She wanted to ask.

"We'd like to see you at the station at noon tomorrow."

"You're here?" she asked surprised. So, there was a connection. He wouldn't be here if there wasn't.

"Yes. I am liaising with the other detectives on this case. See you tomorrow. Have a good day, Professor."

"You too, Detective Lance."

"And Professor? Don't go anywhere without telling us, will you?"

"I'm not going anywhere."

"Good."

She put the phone away. She would know more by evening. If the murderer had found her twice to spook her, he'd succeeded. But why? She knew in her gut this was linked to her. It was too much of a coincidence. She just had to figure out how and why.

Layla kept going back to the list in her head. It was a short, neat little list.

1. The body
2. The cloak
3. The other murder

There was a loud squawk. A crow. Scavengers. Portends of magic and evil. She looked up. There it was. One perched right above her head on the lovely oak. Her gaze dropped back down and she saw Mira ambling towards her. Her straight back and tall frame belied her age. She was almost seventy and carried herself well. The breeze played with her shiny silver hair blowing it around her face and away from it giving her an ethereal look. Her heralds should be swans, not crows, thought Layla, despite the stick she used to walk.

"Hello, Layla. It is really nice to meet you. Thank you for reaching out. I've been waiting for this."

"Hello, Ms. Heshmat. Thank you for coming."

Layla's nerves were taut. *Waiting?*

"Call me, Mira."

"Thank you. I…you said waiting," said Layla.

Mira said, "Yes. You've followed my talks for months now."

"How did you know that?" The skin on Layla's arms pocked and she had to suppress a shiver.

"I usually go through the final lists. They're not very big gatherings a lot of the time. Storytelling should be intimate even when it is communal. And so, after a few times, some names stick out. Like yours. Faces too."

Layla let her breath out slowly. Her shoulders relaxed. *That was all, was it?*

Mira's presence made Layla doubt her intuition. Her notions seemed so foolish, so melodramatic. All her life she had told herself that one day she would find her mother even though she did not know her name. No one had addressed her mother by name at that other place. She had only heard it once when her mother had said it to give her own identity as proof at the American embassy. Layla had not been paying attention then. She did not remember it at all.

She searched Mira's face. She searched each wrinkle, each amber speck in the green eyes. A black wind blew through her barren heart, its coldness brought tears to her eyes. She blinked hard trying not to let the tears drop but she had learned to fashion her tears into something more useful long ago, as a child.

Mira watched her with those knowing wise eyes. "The deepest work of our souls is often the most difficult. It is painful. Do not be afraid. The more you face your pain, the stronger you will be. Tell me what ails you."

"You seem to know other people's tales just by looking at them."

Mira nodded. "But a tale is known by telling it."

Yes, yes, she supposed it was and in telling it there was both power and vulnerability. Was she strong enough to be vulnerable? She decided to test herself.

"I was left at an orphanage by my mother. I know she had a reason for it. I just cannot remember what it was. I was nine. I don't remember her face. I remember her eyes, full of promise and love. Only her eyes. And her stories. She told me so many.

"My favourite book is still the one she wrote herself. She wrote each story by hand, and each in a different language." She extended her hand to Mira, book in it. "Here it is. This is the one. It's old and tattered now but I treasure it. I know all the seven tales by heart. I became a polyglot and a historian of tales because of that book."

Mira took the book. There was a strange expression on her face. Fear, and revulsion but also sadness. She gave the book back without opening it. Quickly, as if it was too heavy for her.

"I was at the orphanage for less than a year," Layla continued, taking the book back. If it had been her mother, would she have taken it lovingly? She did not know.

"Then I was adopted by Ma. She's a wonderful cook, and a sort of storyteller herself. She is hard-working and made me work hard. I was smart and got scholarships but there were no friends, no boyfriends, just work. I learned that single-minded devotion to my plans from my birth-mother."

"You learned well," Mira said in a quiet, strangled voice.

Layla waited for her to say something else. Something more. Something Layla needed to hear.

Instead, she said, "There is more." Mira was watching her closely.

"Yes," said Layla. "But even that is just half the story."

Mira smiled, "Tell me."

Layla was not going to ask the woman if she was her mother. Maybe she was not after all. Wouldn't she have said so herself by now if she were? Layla had bared her heart, and Mira hadn't admitted she was her mother with a hug and a teary smile. Layla's face became warm. What a fool she'd been.

"I don't know why I'm telling you all this. I had a feeling, had hoped, you might be able to help because you've done this before. You must've heard about the murder already. The body was in my library. I say mine because it doubles as my office."

Layla showed Mira the pictures and Mira's expression changed, her eyes turned dark and her face lost colour.

"I'm sorry."

"Thank you. I found the body. No one goes to the archives except for me and my two postgraduate assistants. She…the body, I mean…The woman wore a red cloak only. The other murder happened earlier this year. I was leaving the previous university. I had accepted this new job in December. The murder took place on my last day there in early January. That was also a woman about my age, perhaps a little younger. My friend and I had been walking home. The body was in our front yard. I had moved from there already. I was picking up a few things from my old room. That murdered girl was also naked. She had ash rubbed on her face, hands and feet."

Mira stared into nothing for a long moment, then she took a deep breath and announced, "We need tea. You live close by, don't you? Let's go."

"How do you know where I live?" Layla was taken aback.

"There is much to talk about. We should go."

Mira really was eccentric.

The walk was short and quiet. They hustled from the park to the main road which led to the small alley where her flat was and so they reached it within seven minutes. Mira looked around when they entered the flat, "Pretty. Sparse."

"Please make yourself comfortable. I'll get the tea. Lemon? Milk?"

"Just honey, if you have it."

They were soon comfortably ensconced on the sofa with the tea on the centre table. Layla adjusted a cushion behind her and turned to Mira expectantly. "Your turn."

"Indeed, it is." Mira took a sip of her tea. "I teach with stories. You know that already. I have seen the pictures of the murdered woman in the library. When you showed me the pictures, the red cloak reminded me of a story. A story long distorted by male storytellers. Little Red Riding Hood. But I will tell you the true story and that should help us understand. Or it might confuse us further. Either way, the true story must be told because eventually, truth is the only path to any answers."

FIFTEEN

"There was an Old Woman, who lived alone in the forest. The Old Woman had not approved of the man her daughter loved and wanted to marry and so the daughter had distanced herself from her mother in anger. The Old Woman saw him for what he was—the kind of man who preys on young women. But the daughter had not listened. She married him and they had a daughter. The man then abandoned his young family and disappeared.

"The daughter, angry and ashamed, shored her anger against her own mother.

"The Old Woman found joy in her young granddaughter who visited once a month. Every day, the Old Woman did her gardening and sold her plants in the village. She lived alone in her house at the place and in the time where the spirit of the wild and the woman become one.

"Years passed, and the granddaughter turned thirteen. The Old Woman knew the Wolf would come one day soon now. It was destined. She was not afraid.

"The Old Woman was the culmination of a journey and the land of trees and the wild where she lived was old and ancient, sustained by the laws of mysticism. One day, she heard a knock on her door and heard the panting of the Wolf.

"'Who is it?' she asked.

"The Wolf replied, 'It is I, and it is time.'

"The Old Woman opened the door, and the Wolf opened its jaws wide, and wider still, until the Old Woman could walk into them. When she was inside, the Wolf snapped its jaws shut.

"'What if the girl is not ready?' asked the Wolf.

"The Old Woman replied from inside his stomach, the place of change and rebirth, the melting pot where what is eaten, is transformed, where alchemy happens. 'The girl is ready. I gave her the red cloak of the initiate last season.'

"Satisfied, the Wolf waited.

"The girl soon knocked on the cottage door.

"'Who is it?' the voice that answered was of both the Old Woman and the Wolf.

"'It is I, Little Red,' the girl said.

"'Come in, Little Red,' said the Wolf.

"As soon as Little Red saw the Wolf she cried, 'You are the Wolf I saw on the path. Where is my grandmother?'

"The Wolf looked deep into the eyes of Little Red, its yellow eyes steady and calm. 'Where do you think, Little Red?'

"The girl looked around and her gaze fell upon an axe in the corner. It was made from the ash tree, the tree of magic, and the blade was of iron that breaks all magic, her grandmother had often told her. She put her basket down and lifted the axe.

"The Wolf stood still and let Little Red swing her axe at him.

"The Old Woman emerged from the Wolf's bones and the Wolf spirit, born anew.

"'Grandmother,' said Little Red. 'You look so different. What great ears you have.'

"The Old woman replied, 'All the better to hear you with, Little Red, and I bequeath them to you.'

"All at once Little Red heard all the stories she had never heard, all the lies she had not known, and learned the truth that had been hidden from her about herself.

"Little Red noticed her grandmother's eyes had turned yellow like those of the Wolf.

"'Grandmother, what strange eyes you have.'

"'All the better to see you with and I bequeath the sight to you.'

"And Little Red began to see how cruelly the world treated her sisters and her. She began to see the patterns that had been changed in stories to fit the narrative that served those who would wound her, and her sisters.

"Little Red noticed her grandmother's teeth, sharp and strong.

"'Grandmother, what great teeth you have.'

"'All the better to eat the traps that bind me, and I bequeath them to you.'

"The grandmother hugged her, 'You are more than you were before. You are now Keeper of the Truth. Within you lives the spirit of the wild wolf who is Woman. You have her ears, her eyes, her teeth, her snarl and her spirit. Use them well, Little Red and don't lose them because many will want you to kill it, lock it up, shun it and starve it, so that they can control your power.'

"The Old Woman left the house and disappeared into the woods. Little Red caught a glimpse of the swish of a tail. When Little Red had crossed the woods, she looked back one last time and saw a pair of yellow eyes looking back.

"Little Red smiled."

SIXTEEN

"I have never heard this version before."

Strength seemed to course through Layla's body, and then came to rest in her heart, like something sinewy curling up there to nest. A healing story did that.

Mira smiled, "These are old tales, often called Old Wives' Tales to discredit their power, or called folktales and fairytales for the same reason, because the implication is that what comes from the imagination and the mouths of women for children must not be anything of value. Yet these stories have been appropriated by male storytellers. From the sixteenth century onwards, Charles Perrault, Hans Christian Anderson, the Grimm Brothers, and others became famous thanks to fairytales. They were essentially teaching stories that ancient cultures used to guide young children and for different stages of life and rites of passage. But self-stylized civilized men changed them so much that they lost their magic, their true meaning. But I preach to the choir."

The acknowledgment warmed her.

"Thank you for that. And you are right about the stories being manipulated. It was so common, so widespread that it never registered until perhaps the twentieth century when women began to write about it. This still continues, even though more and more women are rewriting history and stories. We discount the importance and influence of stories actually. Stories make generations. Stories make us."

Mira sipped her tea and nodded.

"Indeed. Most such tales are about the power of women and their psyche. Men changed the stories and the roles of women so that was the way women began to perceive themselves. That was the beginning of control: how they were repeatedly perceived, written about, spoken about, portrayed, painted, and sung about. You see? An old healer became a witch, a wild benevolent female spirit became an androgynous angel, or helpful faery or animals. Power was taken away from female characters and female imagination. This is how women's teaching stories, their canon, their tales of wisdom, death, rebirth and transformation were lost. These old tales were retold to exclude the feminine power, their mystique and their various avatars. It was all ever about fear and power."

Layla stared at her.

"I grew up with stories. I know their value. My mother knew so many. She never told me anything like this story and she knew a lot of stories."

"Your mother told you the bare bones of the stories so that when it was time, you could add the flesh and the skin and the tendon, and infuse them with the blood of truth. The Old Woman in the story transformed and apotheosized, walked out of the story. But in the new versions the storyteller was a man and did not want to tell the story of a powerful woman, especially an older woman. Power is not female in the tales written by men. Especially not an Old Woman, who cannot be sexualized or infantilized by men for their pleasure. The male storyteller wanted to tell the story of a little girl who disobeyed a patriarchal agent, the mother. The girl is almost eaten by a wolf, reminiscent of ancient wisdom of womanhood and so a creature that scared the male storyteller, and then the girl is saved by a brawny man, written into the modern version of the story. But now we know that is not the true story but a cover story."

"The stories themselves are the proof. And yet it is so hard to believe that such hate was practiced against women for so long and went unchecked. I mean, it still does."

Layla couldn't believe that the woman she had been following since last autumn, was finally sitting so close to her. She listened to the intonations of her voice. She compared it to the dreams and the whispers she'd heard since she was nine but there was nothing. Mira sat on her bright yellow window seat cushions and Layla listened, as star-struck as she always was when listening to Mira Heshmat.

"I am a seeker of truth and thus a seeker of stories. I have spent my entire life collecting stories of women. My lifework has taken me deep into the intuitive and the psychic to the erasure of women and their stories. I do not speak lightly of this matter. And what more proof do you need? Pick up stories written by men and see. Pick up history books. Women who are portrayed as heroes, Catherine the Great, Elizabeth I, are women who were either sexualized or portrayed with traits identified as masculine. Where are the women with their own power? Where are the stories of Princesses Rukhsar, and Badura and the others? And yes, there are always exceptions. And there are male allies. I do not deny that."

Those green eyes questioned her, encouraged her. "Women and a few men have only recently started to point this out. Only a few decades," said Mira. "The injustice however has been perpetrated for millennia."

Layla was drawn to her, yet she was certain that Mira was hiding something. According to Sufi teachings, Truth was revealed at the right time. If it was revealed before its time, it became dangerous. Revealed too late, it was useless or toxic. She would have to be patient.

"How does this new version of Little Red help us with the murder?" asked Layla. She did not want to think about what Mira might be hiding from her. Certainly it could not be Layla's relationship with her, not after everything they had said?

"It doesn't. Not yet. But we cannot understand unless we have the truth of the tale. The Old Woman is the Crone. Little Red is the Maiden; the food she brings to her grandmother is the symbol of life and youth."

"But the grandmother dies. The Wolf eats her."

"The Wolf did not kill her. The Wolf *swallowed* her. The Old Woman walked into the Wolf's mouth willingly. You see, in the ancient tradition this is a resurrection story, a miracle, a tale of the soul and the cyclical nature of the universe. Told correctly, it is about the psyche and archetypes, not about preventing girls from wandering into forests. The Wolf in this story is not male nor does it symbolize patriarchy. It symbolizes the often rejected deep feminine, as it is shown to be rejected by the mother, the daughter of the Old Woman.

"There is no huntsman, Little Red is supposed to kill the Wolf with the iron axe because iron is also symbolic of purity of the soul, as is the wood of the ash tree from which the handle of the axe is made. They are both metaphors for power that is linked with women, magic and the goddess Ishtar, as old manuscripts show."

"I get it." Layla nodded. "The red cloak on the murdered woman and the dead woman are a hint at the fairytale of Little Red Riding Hood. The day I saw the body, the cloak reminded me of something, but I couldn't connect the two at the time. What we need to know is why the dead body in the library was made to indicate that particular fairytale? And why she was spread so grotesquely, as if she was having sex with someone invisible."

Mira said nothing.

Layla's mind raced. Western canon or Western fairytales at least, were merging with Eastern storytelling canon and making a production of murder. Why? Fairytales and Sufi symbols? There was the walnut...but what else? Maybe she was wrong. Maybe it was just murder. But was it a serial killer? Murders of women. Women's bodies were a site of inflicting violence; at least that was something on which all canons seemed to agree.

"I don't know. The body was made to look overtly sexualized whereas the original story is a miracle story about breathing life into an ailing relationship," Mira said thoughtfully. "But few are familiar with it. The murderer presented the victim as Little Red, who has lost her way, been devoured by the big bad wolf of the fairytale. I'm glad you agree with my conjecture."

"I think it's more than just conjecture. You also said the story is about ailing relationships?" Layla frowned. "Whose ailing relationship?"

"The Old Woman is the archetype for wisdom, for the soul. She is the archivist of the deep forgotten often rejected female instinct. She lives in the woods alone because her daughter left her after the old Woman opposed the union with an unworthy man. The daughter loves the Old Woman still, which is why she sends her food, the symbol of nourishment and youth and the token of her love, but she herself does not come to see her. She feels that staying away is the correct path for them. She was wrong. She is ashamed. She should have faced her shame, embraced her truth. She didn't and that ailing relationship between mother and daughter endangered them all."

Mira became pale and paused. She rose and took an agitated turn around the room.

Layla put a hand to her throat and swallowed as if to remove a constriction. Who was Mira talking about? The room was suddenly depleted of oxygen. "Who do you mean?" she whispered.

Mira's eyes widened. "No." Her voice was heavy. "It cannot be. No one knows."

Layla's eyes were wide with fear. "What don't they know?"

"What if I am wrong?" Mira put her hand to her face, her expression tense. "What if the murderer knows the original tales? You have published many books on the history of women and storytelling. What if he knows the true tales?"

"What are you saying?" Layla was confused. "Obviously, anyone could have read my books, but I have not written about this story. I'd never even heard it before now."

"Yes, yes," Mira sounded relieved. "Of course, you haven't. No, you are right. It couldn't possibly be about—no."

Layla became alarmed at Mira's nervous laugh and taut body. She was still agitated.

Mira turned to her suddenly. "I must see the pictures of the first murder. That should shed some light on this."

"You know the Detective in charge," said Layla.

"Then I must go now. We will meet again." She gave her a quick hug, and left, the stick more painfully apparent than before, as if in her agitation, her legs almost failed her.

Layla stood at the door alone for a long time after Mira had left. Hope was such a cruel thing. It came and nestled in your heart and dug its talons in its soft warm flesh. She steeled her heart. Sometimes it took minutes, mere seconds even to do so and other times it took weeks, months, years to submit the bleeding heart into obeisance.

She did not know the fragrance of this woman. Her hair did not smell of roses nor did her skin smell of honey and lemon.

But that embrace, that intimate embrace from a near stranger was too familiar. It unravelled her. Layla curled into a ball on her sofa and let the dark winds blow in her heart, but their chill brought no tears to her eyes.

SEVENTEEN

Layla had been avoiding the library since the murder and only went there for student tutorials. The fears connected to the unfinished story that had started there, kept her from it. It had been a scrap of a story. Now after Mira's re-telling it became a labyrinth.

Mira.

The murder.

The story.

The words buzzed in her head like hornets.

Stories were powerful. Those that began with no end in sight were the most dangerous. They threatened to suck you in. She had to see the patterns. She had to solve the covert codes. She had to separate the doxa from the canon. If not, who knew where the labyrinthine clues would take her?

She stopped at the café for her morning chai-latte and lemon muffin. As she sipped her tea, she gazed absently at the passers-by from her table facing the street. The narrow streets and the sidewalks of the town were now lined with piles of fallen maple leaves in shades of bronze, rust and crimson. People bundled up in light jackets, coats and scarves bustled about, a riot of colours. Soon it would be winter. Another two weeks and it would start snowing in earnest and people would hide behind balaclavas, mittens and Cheshire coats.

Her own clothing was modest by comparison. Black jeans, black long sweater and a black peacoat she'd had for more years than she cared to count. All very sensible and serviceable.

Someone outside took a double turn and smiled at her. It took her a few seconds to focus on the handsome man in a grey sweater and grey Sherpa jacket smiling at her. Reza. She waved. He tilted his head and raised an eyebrow, pointing at her. She nodded, smiling.

He was at her table a moment later. "Hello, Layla. Good to see you."

He put his bag down and pecked her on the cheek.

"Chai-latte?" he peered into her cup.

She laughed, "Yes. I love it."

"You and me both. I'll go get one."

"Discovered the body, did you?" He joined her with his cup a few minutes later.

"I did."

"Peter told me just this morning that it was you. He was impressed with your equanimity, he said by the way. But man! You find a dead body in a dead town and you don't tell me?"

"A dead town," she murmured.

"Yeah, tell me about it, should've shaken things up a bit. But no."

Layla gave him a quizzical look.

"Then why did you take this job? I mean if you don't like small towns?"

He looked blank for a second then he said airily, "Well, I thought it would be a nice change of pace. I had just come out of a messy break-up."

"Yeah." She wrapped her fingers around the cup. "That would do it."

"Well, this isn't a dead town now, obviously! Murder?" he shook his head, sipped his tea. He looked miserable. "They're not paying me enough for this."

Layla laughed, "More than what they're paying the rest of us, if rumours are to be believed."

"Well..." he smiled, embarrassed. "You write a book that changes the way you look at a dead civilization and suddenly you're a celebrity!"

Layla laughed. Oh no! He was making her like him again. She had the insane desire to tell him everything, to unburden herself and allow him to comfort her.

"Reza, strangely enough..."

"Yes?" he leaned forward.

His eagerness stalled her. Caution was too ingrained in her bones. "I don't know if I should..."

"Oh, come on!"

Why not? She had told Mira. The Detective knew. Why couldn't she tell Reza? "Okay, but don't freak out. I'm trying not to…and this is a secret. I think."

"I hate secrets." He looked serious.

"I'm telling you anyway." Layla's lips twisted. "Strangely enough, this was not my first time seeing a murder on campus."

"You're kidding?" His eyes looked at her sharply from over his cup. He frowned.

She would have felt the same. He probably thought she was making it up, or that she was crazy.

"Nope. No kidding. Last year, I was at the University of Belmont. There was a murder just around the time I was moving."

"What a coincidence." His voice had suddenly dropped a decibel.

She took a sip taking her time to respond. "Was it though?"

He raised his eyebrows. "You can't possibly think it isn't? That would mean that it was connected to y—"

He stopped, looking uncomfortable.

"You can say it. I've been thinking the same."

He leaned forward, "Good God, Layla, that's nuts. But why? Do you have money? Are you an heiress? Why would anyone be after you? This is crazy."

"I'm no heiress," she laughed. She felt better already. Sharing bad news did lighten the burden.

"You were at both places. It's too much of a coincidence," he said watching her solemnly.

She shrugged. "I don't know what else to think. But that was my reaction exactly."

"Do you have anyone here? Anyone you can talk to? Friends? Family?" He looked suitably intrigued and scared.

"Just Ma. She lives in Chicago."

"Ah. Another converging place for us immigrants."

"Yes. She loves it there. She's got a lot of friends for neighbours now. The community is strong there."

"You love her," he sounded surprised.

Layla chuckled, "Of course I do. She's Ma. I'm adopted, you know, but she's my mother."

Reza smiled. It lit up his face. He was such a handsome man.

"I'm sure you loved your mother too. Don't we all?" she asked.

"She died when I was eighteen."

"I'm so sorry."

"Thank you. I migrated soon after her death."

She rested her hand on his arm gently. He was quiet. She watched as he rotated his cup in his hand, regret and loss reflected on his face. She looked away. It was as if she'd intruded on a private moment. Faces, eyes especially, couldn't keep secrets as well as we thought.

"Are you okay, Reza?"

He smiled wryly, "Just thinking. Sometimes I feel I've lived in this country too long. My identity is all tangled and mutated. I don't have anyone I'd call friends. Wherever I've lived, people around me have only ever known a single culture and called one place home—except for Angkor, of course. Cambodia is beautiful, but the hectares of Angkor temple are like a slice of Eden. Quiet, isolated and the nearest villages are all so primitive and friendly. I loved it there.

"I hail from multicultural, contrapuntal, pluralistic cultures of Central Asia. I've lived like a nomad in so many countries I feel I belong everywhere and all of these rich cultures that are a part of me are mine too. The borders of my Self have been dismantled so many times I am a patchwork of identities. I don't understand the rigidities of American identities. I've never felt at home here. Have you?"

Layla was surprised he was sharing so much. But she was grateful. He had successfully taken her mind off the murders for a few minutes. She squeezed his hand. "Thank you. That's exactly how I feel too. But I do love it here. This is home."

"Good for you. Maybe you can help change my mind." His smile was charming, and Layla couldn't look away. His eyes on hers were warm and friendly.

Her phone rang, startling them both.

"Uh, I'm sorry I have to take this."

Reza took a sip of his chai-latte and shrugged.

"Detective Lance," she said when she held the phone to her ear.

"Professor? We need you to come in as soon as possible."

"You said noon?" It was only eight thirty.

"There has been a development. How soon can you be here?"

"Give me ten," she said.

"Just come as soon as you can. We have something you need to see."

"Sure," she stared at the phone.

"What is it?"

"They want me downtown."

"Why? Is it about the murder?"

"Yes, it must be. What else could it be?"

"Would you like me to come with you?"

"Thank you," she smiled with gratitude and a little pleasure, "That's kind of you, but no need."

"All right then. Let me know if you need anything."

She walked across the street and stopped. She thought of turning back and accepting Reza's offer. He was still sitting where she'd left him, drinking his tea, watching the sun begin its slow descent on the horizon. She'd been drawn to him since the first day she'd met him. He was so very handsome, so suave. Yet there was something about him that sent alarm bells ringing in her head.

And now Khayyam was back. Sufi stories often came back full circle, representing unity and cohesion so lacking in life, but so important to spiritual well-being.

Soon she reached the easily detectable small square building, red brick and unassuming. She went inside and asked for Detective Lance.

A tall African-American man came forward, "Professor Layla Rashid. I'm James Lance."

"Hi, Detective."

"Please come with me."

He took her to a smaller room at the back and when he opened the door, she stopped dead in her tracks.

Mira was sitting there.

EIGHTEEN

The detective made the introductions. Layla nodded and said hello, and Mira smiled back, greeting her politely. Neither of them acknowledged prior acquaintanceship. Layla sat down.

"Mira is here because of this." He pointed at a piece of paper on the table. "You know why you're here?"

"No," said Layla.

He looked at Mira. "You tell her."

Mira nodded. "About ten years ago there was a serial killer the police couldn't find. I was following the story in the papers. Detective Lance was the investigating officer. I called him to offer my help. I thought I could see a pattern after reading about the murders—something beneath the obvious patterns of a serial killer. I think the detective accepted because he was curious to see what I would do. I was famous, after all. It became a habit. Sometimes he'd call me for advice. To see things, he felt, that I could see, and they couldn't. All unofficial of course."

"Yes. I saw a picture of you with the cops in a newspaper last year. That's how I knew there was something that connected you to murder and crime, that's why I wanted to talk to you. I read that story. I recognized you even in that grainy black and white picture and you almost out of the frame."

"What does this have to do with me?" Even though Layla knew there had to be a link.

Mira hadn't been at the last university where the murder had been committed, but Layla had been. She was part of the pattern.

"I'm getting to it," said Mira gently. "I must admit to using gerontocracy on the detective to get on the case that first time. When the good detective shared the pictures of the dead bodies, my suspicions were confirmed. We narrowed down the suspects to two men. The murderer was caught the next day."

"And I've been a fan ever since," said Detective Lance.

Mira's short laugh was a hoarse sound, rusty with age and disuse.

"You are here, professor," Detective Lance looked at Layla, "because Mira requested it. And she isn't here just because she is one hell of a detective. She is here because of this."

He slipped the piece of paper he'd pointed to earlier towards Layla.

"We found it on the body. In the pocket of the cloak."

He put a transparent, sealed evidence bag before them. It had a piece of paper inside.

Layla peered at the words. *Mira Heshmat, find me. The answer is stories.*

Relief flooded Layla. All the niggling fear of coincidences evaporated. The net of the pattern that had been tightening around her vanished. She wasn't used to being inside the pattern, much less being part of it. She was the one who looked at patterns, analysed them, deconstructed them, pulled them apart to demystify the story so everyone could understand and learn.

"This isn't about me at all. Why am I here? Do I need a lawyer?" Layla wanted to run as far away as possible from all this and from Mira. She was so relieved all her fears were baseless. She unclenched her hands slowly.

"No, you don't need a lawyer. Yet. You're forgetting both murders took place at your university," Detective Lance said. "Mira has very kindly offered her assistance. She requested that you should be included in our investigation team."

"Look, Detective Lance," Layla said irritably, "I really don't think—"

"This isn't a request, Professor," the detective sounded stern. "You could easily be a suspect and you should jump at the chance to help us prove you're innocent. Mira said you would be an asset in this investigation."

"Mira said?" Layla scoffed.

Being part of the pattern hadn't totally blinded her. She knew there were patterns hidden beneath the ones that were obvious. Stories helped readers develop the desire for a higher consciousness. There was something hidden still, and she was keen to find out.

Lance said, "Look Professor. I don't claim to know you, but I know Mira. She helped solve the last murder and identify that serial killer. Without her, we might not have caught him before he killed another woman. If she says she needs you, I trust her."

But why? And she recalled what Mira had said in her flat about someone knowing. But knowing what? And she became fearful again. Her instinct was to flee. She got up.

"I think this is all a big misunderstanding."

"No it isn't. Sit, please," said Detective Lance.

"But I have nothing to do with this!"

"Please Sche-Layla, please."

Layla froze. She turned to look at Mira. What had she almost called her? There was only one person…only one woman who would call her Scheherzade. She stared at Mira, her heart in her mouth.

"Mullah Nasruddin walked into a shop one day," Layla said softly. "The owner came forward to serve him. First things first, said the Mullah. Did you see me enter your shop? Surprised, the shopkeeper said simply, of course. The Mullah asked, have you ever seen me before? No, came the reply. Then how do you know it is *me*?"

The Detective looked at Mira with a grin, "It is her, isn't it?"

"May I have a moment with Layla, James?" Mira said, unsmiling.

"Don't take too long, we have work to do." He closed the door behind him.

Mira leaned forward and said quickly, before Layla could formulate another thought. "Layla, you are in danger."

She was not surprised Mira thought so. Layla had feared it. Reza had feared it and not said it. And he didn't even know much about her. And Mira was pretending she had not just almost called her by her other name.

Of course she was in danger, but why was Mira saying it? What made her think so? What else did she know?

"From whom?" asked Layla. She did not mention Mira's slip. She was truly afraid now of what she might say in response.

"I don't know yet. But…I know you are in danger. And it is because of our shared past."

Layla froze. She felt sick. How do you know it is me? *How do you know—*

Mira, still looking calm, confessed, "This is about us. This is clearly about us. My sacrifice did nothing. I did not stay away far enough. I tried. You know I did. I changed your name, even though I almost let slip the first one just now. And I changed mine too. And still, here we are in the thick of murders. Someone knows."

"What are you saying?" Layla whispered. *How do you know it is me?*

"You know." said Mira softly. "You know who I am to you. Do you think I did not see you when you came to hear me speak? I looked for you in the audience every time. All my talks were for you, to give you the next steps of the initiation."

"What initiation?" Layla cried. What was happening? She felt like Alice when she had gone through the looking glass. Everything felt wrong. Crazy. Yet the logic of the illogical was undeniable.

Mira waved her hand. It was an agitated gesture. "How could anyone know? I was so careful. Did you tell anyone what you suspected about me?"

An icy shiver slithered up Layla's spine. Her mind became a cold foggy and fearful place. A dark foreboding seeped into her bones and she was being pushed into a small tight space. This was not happening. Mira had asked her in the park what ailed her. Layla had told her the whole story of her abandonment. And even then, Mira hadn't…

"This is the most ridiculous thing I have ever heard." Layla jumped to her feet. "What are you talking about? You're not really saying anything at all, are you?" She sounded incoherent even to her own ears. "You must be—"

"Crazy?" asked Mira. She looked sad. "Have stories taught you nothing? Has your name, your true name, taught you nothing?"

"How dare you?"

Mira came forward to gently lay her hand on Layla's. "You know who I am, don't you, Scheherazade?"

There it was! Layla gasped for air.

"Yes, my darling, magic girl. I am your mother and you have always known it."

Layla couldn't move. The dream. The woman with long white hair stood before Layla. She was whispering in her ear and Layla couldn't hear a thing.

"I don't understand." Layla shook her head.

Was she dreaming? Was she awake? No, this was real. Yes, she had had such strong suspicions. But now she was full of doubt. Too many coincidences too soon. The lost mother did not just turn up. A new mother or mother figure did…in all the old stories. Mira Heshmat said not to trust the tales she'd grown up with because they were all lies. Everything was a lie.

Stories did not lie. The laws of story were being broken.

She couldn't cope.

Her breath came out wheezing. The loss of innocence isn't a single step. It is a long painful journey of growth and rebirth.

Sufi stories often revealed the two centres of a human being, the conscious and the subconscious, through their own dual structures. There is always an outer story and the inner secret story that is revealed at the end to show the truth. The outer story is like our own known reality, what we believe to be true, and it is a prison and a lie. The hidden truth is the real story, and it also represents the subconscious nature of a person. Getting to that esoteric truth and the subconscious, which is free from dogma, was the goal of the Sufi storyteller. Such stories revealed the censorship society built in our minds so insidiously most people do not even realize that they are there. The conscious is a prison of dogmatic beliefs imposed by society, customs, culture and the subconscious is free from all that.

Selfhood was found in this liminal world of bardo, a space of possibility.

Layla was in bardo—the in-between world where the boundaries between dream and reality had ceased to exist. She stared at the woman who had haunted her dreams for so long.

"I don't understand. How can you be my mother? Where have you been? Why did you leave me after everything we'd been through? For years you taught me stories, language, symbols, patterns, to watch for what was hidden. Prepared me for escape." Her voice broke. "And when we finally escaped that hell, you abandoned me."

"No, I did not abandon you. I left you, to protect you," Mira stretched out her hand to touch her. Layla flinched.

Mira withdrew her hand.

"What do you remember?" she asked gently.

"Enough."

"Or not nearly enough," said Mira.

Hope had turned to ashes in her mouth. Layla was cold; she wrapped her arms around herself.

Mira's voice, when she spoke again, had changed and softened. It was warm, honey and comfort. "It is time to fill the gaps then," said Mira. "I will tell you the missing pieces."

NINETEEN

"Stop!" Layla cried. "I don't want to hear it!"

Detective Lance opened the door. "Is everything alright?"

"Yes. Just give us a moment more," Mira said with a tight smile.

He left with a long look at Mira.

"You're my mother." Layla stared at Mira. "You just announce it as if it is part of a story? I asked you…in the park. I told you about being abandoned and how I felt. And you didn't say anything. You had tea in my flat and told me a fairytale."

A strange grief was beginning to wrap itself around Layla like a too-heavy robe. This was not how she'd imagined this scene. And she'd imagined it every day since she was nine. She had not imagined such pragmatic planning from her birth mother. She had not allowed for murder overwhelming everything else. She had never imagined grief at finding her birth mother. She had always imagined, despite logic reasoning saying otherwise, that her mother would be a mirror of her own wounded self. Instead, she'd found a strong woman with no regrets, or not nearly enough to assuage Layla's grief.

"A stranger brought me up, and I brought myself up with books and stories because you abandoned me. I love Ma, yes but you…I can't even look at you."

Mira opened her mouth. Made a strangled sound.

"What are you afraid to say? That you didn't want me?"

Mira shut her eyes, as if in pain. So, it was true. She hadn't wanted her; it was that simple.

"I…"

Layla raised her hand. In protest, or defence, or just because she couldn't hear why. She steeled herself; willed herself to gather up the broken pieces again.

She asked, "Why do you think these murder are linked to me?"

"Beginnings are important. This is not where the tale begins."

Layla laughed. It was short. Bitter. Like a slap.

Mira winced. "Please, Scheherazade."

"That is not my name," Layla mimicked Mira's tone. It was instinct. Like falling into an old pattern. She shook her head in confusion. She did feel some grim satisfaction when she heard the bitterness in her voice. "My name is Layla. You named me again. But this second naming was a kindness. I always hated the other one."

Mira nodded. "Your first is too strong a name, after all. If you reject it, it will do more harm than good to call you by it. So, Layla it is."

Layla tried to calm herself as if she were in class, engaged in an interesting debate with a student. Her tone and inflection changed, and she felt more in control.

"Why did you burden me with it in the first place? The wretched creature who told stories for a thousand and one nights but was never able to tell her own story? She has the voice and she uses it to articulate every damned story except her own. What did she endure? She bore the Sultan three sons he didn't even know existed till the very end of the tale. In the bargain, she gave her sister to the Sultan's brother, and although she speaks, it is never of her own torment, her own trauma. Why did you name me after such a victim?"

"You were my talisman, my magic bean, my spell to break me out of prison. She may be all that you say but she is more than that. She is the Trickster who won the game she was playing. We don't hear from her because we see her weaving the web of tales, through which she changes the Sultan's mind, her own destiny, and that of many others. All the stories are hers, even if they are not. She is an archetype of victim, hero, trickster. She is woman."

The knell of truth had been rung. Layla heard it and knew it. She knew the truth of stories like she knew herself.

Sufi stories use a complex narrative structure to convey deeper truths. They tell a story within a story, which represents the layers of human consciousness—the outer story is like our conscious mind and the inner story is like our subconscious. By unfolding the inner story, the reader's perception is dramatically changed, much like discovering a hidden insight or like finding the soft kernel in a hard shell of a nut. This technique is used to bridge the gap between our surface understanding and deeper awareness, allowing the reader to grasp profound truths that were previously unrecognized.

Mira was right. The circle had to be completed.

It was time to fill the gaps trauma had gouged out in her memory.

Layla looked Mira square in the eye. The truth was Layla didn't know what to feel. She wanted Mira to tell her story so Layla could sort out her emotions. She was happy she had found Mira. She had been right. She had found her mother. She was also enraged.

"I recall very little," Layla said. "I barely remembered your face. Just your eyes. They call it trauma induced amnesia or dissociative amnesia."

Mira stood up as if to hug Layla.

"No," Layla put out a hand. "I'm not ready yet for that. But I will hear your story."

Mira sank back into the chair and took a moment to gather herself.

"I had to leave you at the orphanage in Detroit because the CIA was after me. Do you remember our second escape? It was easier. It did not take me thirteen years. Just three days. We escaped at the supermarket. We took the bus. I vanished into a big city first. Then I went to smaller ones to throw them off. But we didn't stay long. I wanted them to lose the trail. After that I took you to a small town because small communities look after each other better. I left you there right outside the orphanage while you slept. There was a small patch of grass in front, azaleas grew in pots, and there was a small yellow light at the corner of the small building. I covered you with a coat and left. It started to rain."

Mira's face crumpled as she wept. A dark satisfaction blossomed in Layla's heart. She made no effort to soothe or comfort her. Mira stared at her with compassion, with understanding.

Every reader, every recipient of a tale feels differently. How the story is told, made a difference.

"I am waiting," Layla's eyes were too bright, her chin wobbly. "The great storyteller is among us. She must tell her tale. Let me get comfortable so I can enjoy the show."

"You are too fine a storyteller, and woman, to be this way," said Mira.

Layla felt immense gratification at the undertones of a whine. Guilt?

"This is who I am, Mira—an abandoned child in a woman's body," Layla's smile was cold.

"You do not know yourself yet. But you will. You will. And now, hear my tale as I lived it, not as you saw me live it."

BOOK TWO

The Beginning

ONE

Some stories you walk into, unaware that they are traps. They weave their web of words paralyzing you with wonder; words that seep into your blood and become plasma in your veins. They never let you go. They make you their home.

I walked into a story one day.

Not all stories begin at the beginning. I find often that the beginning reveals itself when the story is ending. No story is ever so simple as to be just itself. Every story floats on the surface of an endless ocean, and we see glimpses of hidden treasures—depths and layers reveal themselves in shafts of light and the dance of waves. A good storyteller spins a new tale every time she tells it. Sometimes, when I lose the magic of the telling, I stop mid-tale. I serve the tale as much as those who've come to listen.

Born before we know ourselves renders that first beginning false, nascent, and ignorant. I've had years to think about the beginning of this one, and I don't know which beginning to choose. Heroic stories don't tell you about the small irritants or the physical discomfort of the protagonist. If they did, the heroes would be less heroic. They'd be too human, too petty. Fighting physical discomforts isn't as gallant and valiant as fighting a powerful foe. Petty discomforts chip away at any sense of heroism one might have harboured, even subconsciously. If I ever had any, such notions slipped away from me unnoticed. When you have to squat to defecate with a dozen others, inhaling not just the mephitic stink of your own waste but also the feculent dross of others, there isn't much left for you to do but accept yourself as unremarkable, ordinary. Definitely unworthy as the subject of stories and songs.

Beginnings are difficult to determine. The beginning of my story more than most, because there are so many of them. And endings are equally problematic. Happy endings are justly scorned by literary intellectuals because they're misrepresentations of the world. Life has but one ending and it is death. And who would call that a happy one?

Kamli said I was born a Trickster, with my pale skin, green eyes and black hair and a soul that absorbed all kinds of tales. She was a storyteller long before I was baptized into their arcana. She came from a long line of story givers and was the one who planted the seed of story in me.

Did my story begin when I became a storyteller? I think not. Long before I became one, I was listening, and seeing and thinking, and all of that made me, and so my story had already commenced years before.

But I think perhaps it began when I went to Afghanistan.

TWO

I didn't even realize we were being kidnapped.

We were covering an assignment in Afghanistan, and that day we'd been scouting the brown hills populated with an occasional acacia tree, where control was disputed between three countries. Juniper trees grew on the far hillside. Shadow and light played hide and seek on the hills. It was summer and the air when it blew would sometimes embrace one warmly and others, quite coolly. Occasionally we would spot a golden eagle far overhead hunting for prey.

We had just done an interview with one of the elders of the Hakkani tribe rumoured to be close to the Taliban, and we were walking past a hill. The village had been a few miles behind us, and we thought to enjoy the sunny June day as we began the hour or so's walk back to our truck. Then they came, a group of men from the road before us on foot, all in traditional black shalwar kameez. They surrounded us quickly. All of them had huge guns. But we were American journalists, we had immunity. Or so we believed.

My cameraman and technician knew some Dari, but I knew instantly the men surrounding us were Pashtun.

"*Salam Aleichem*. I am from the U.S.A. We are American citizens. I am here to make a documentary with my team about your beautiful country." I used Pashto I had learned from my father. It would drive my mother mad because she couldn't understand when Dad and I used our secret language. My father had stopped going into the field years ago, before I even started, but I had learned a great deal from him. And I learned that I loved languages and the ancient secrets they guarded within their forgotten oral and archival traditions. That talent got me the job I never thought I would have. I became a war correspondent.

I was thirty-four at the time. I felt I was invincible. I had got this assignment because I was a veteran journalist, and I knew the dangers.

As I spoke to the group, their leader was watching me. I felt a passing pleasure at the attention of a handsome man. I knew he was the leader because he said something to the rest of the men and their bodies shifted, became immediately cautious and less openly hostile.

"You know Pashto?" he seemed pleased. "Then you must be familiar with our customs. We cannot have guests and not show them proper hospitality. We would like you all to have dinner with us."

He was a very beautiful man. Also in his mid-thirties perhaps? I was a worldly woman. He had lived all his life in these mountains with goats and toxic masculinity. I felt I must be an intriguing novelty to him.

I would later rage at my naiveté.

"I'm not sure that's such a good idea. It's already late," said Cyril, my cameraman cautioning us.

Though it was late afternoon, the sun still shone in the sky. But night came suddenly in the hills. We knew that. We had come to Afghanistan for the first time, but we had already been there for a week.

The Pashtun man extended his hand, "I'm Gulraiz, the chief's son. You are our honoured guests. Please follow me."

It wasn't a suggestion. Nobody moved.

He smiled and gestured at the surroundings. Barren mountains surrounded the greener hills we stood amongst. The hills were dressed in sanober pine trees and dappled sunlight.

"All this," he said, "is ours. No army, no government. It's us. Just us."

It was a threat.

I shrugged. I wasn't afraid. I was an American citizen.

"How can we say no?" I said. Cyril shook his head. He was afraid. Shawn nodded and we all followed.

We were herded into a line with Gulraiz leading us. We started climbing.

He said, "I like your hijab.'

I thanked him. I was wearing a dupatta on my head, a loose tunic top and jeans. My trainers were practical.

We were so busy listening to Gulraiz's chatter we never had a chance. We lost count of the turns, the colour of the hills we had left far behind, any familiar landmarks, as we were led so cleverly up the winding paths of the mountains that even if we'd wanted to, we couldn't have run far. The mountains, barren and dusty, were covered in fine sard coloured sand. On one side was the undulating brown desert dotted with cacti. As we walked, the sun dipped behind the hills. It became suddenly dark, and a smattering of the men switched on torches, although the moon was so big and so close there was plenty of light.

Finally, we arrived at a small plateau nestled between two mountain peaks, perhaps after walking for an hour or little more. It was a settlement of rough clay-brick houses. A few stunted cypress trees stood like exclamation marks near the houses. Some fifteen or twenty of them surrounded by inhospitable destitute mountains pockmarked with dark caves that seemed like tiny open maws. We could see the lights, oil lamps in windows and outside doors. Children stopped their games—they all sat in huddles, playing with marbles and plastic toys, and turned to look at us with curious eyes, lamp lights flickering across their shadowy faces. Men, toting AK47s and Kalashnikovs seemed like looming shadows, also turned towards us.

Gulraiz spoke rapidly so I barely caught a few stray words. Dinner, meat, behave. Women? Men? I couldn't tell.

"You must know our customs. Your friends must stay here. They are men and outsiders, and we protect our women. You will meet my mother and sisters. When the dinner is prepared, we will eat together."

"My friends too," I said with firmness.

"Of course." He laughed, "You think they will go hungry?"

I could sense the tension in the women's quarters as soon as I entered. It was a small room, lit with lamps and a round metal fireplace in the centre. Vibrantly dressed, the eight or ten women huddled in twos and threes as if against the cold, their bright clothes with glinting mirrors and little bells were at odds with their sudden reticence at my entry. They floor was padded with woollen mats and woven jute rugs. Large round pillows, embroidered, and embellished with tiny bells, mirrors and shiny beads adorned the room. It was a warm room, a feminine room even. Yet, I shuddered. The nights were much cooler in the mountains, even in June. I was cold, I told myself.

Gulraiz said something and a woman got up and came towards me with a small smile.

"Welcome. I am Firdous," she said. She was in her late fifties perhaps. Her handsome face was lined, but her striking blue eyes were sharp, and icy.

Gulraiz said something to her to the effect of, no need to hide. Her smile was maternal, but tinged with a kind of jealous pride. She didn't say anything else though. I didn't understand Gulraiz's comment until much later when I realized she was his first wife and actually much older than him.

Dinner was lavish. Rice, rich with flavours and vegetables and nuts. Meat thick with gravy and spices. I ate with relish and gave compliments to the women. Firdous's eyes were on me and Gulraiz talked with ease. I made the mistake of relaxing in the warmth of such cosy intimacy. Only half-way through did I think to ask where my friends were because I knew that men not related to women were not asked into their company. Gulraiz was bestowing an honor on me by having me eat with his family, especially the women.

"It is late. Your friends had a hearty meal and were tired and have gone to sleep already. Why don't you also rest and you can meet them for breakfast?" said Gulraiz.

I nodded, because what else could I do? Or that is the story I have been telling myself these past years. When morning came, Firdous gave me breakfast while the other women watched me, some with a touch of fear, some with hints of pity but all of them with hostility. They were all strikingly beautiful, from ages fifteen to seventy. They wore long, loose frocks, brightly coloured and embellished with bells, and shiny gold and silver embroidery and other colours. Everything was very bright, except the burqas they wore to go out, which were white, sky blue or black.

I tried to make conversation with Firdous, as she seemed to be the matriarch and the one who could speak to me, as others had made no effort the previous night. Not even when I had asked questions. Stupid questions, I see now. What did they do all day? What kind of food did they cook? Everything was subject to their husbands. They were subjects. And I became one too. For the longest time.

By nightfall I was afraid. The small room had no windows, a low ceiling and a narrow double-slatted wooden door. It was not painted, or even finished wood. There was no furniture, except a small wooden, roughly hewn table. The floor was covered in cotton wool filled mattresses, then covered with hand embroidered sheets. And baguette shaped cushions. Everybody sat on the floor, ate there, and slept there. Later I would learn their yearly patterns of embroidering everything, from their own clothes to bedsheets, tablecloths, which they called *jadol tokar* or *dastarkhawan*.

"I want to see my friends," I said to Firdous, who was clearly the figure of authority among the women.

She shook her head. I got up and opened the door. There were two men with guns outside. They pointed their guns at me and yelled, "Go inside! Inside!"

Frightened, I jumped back, and they shut the door from the outside.

I yelled at the women.

"Help me! What have they done to my friends? Are they still alive? What kind of monsters are you?"

I went on like that for hours until I lay down exhausted. Only a frail old woman came over to lay a hand of comfort. "Patience, dear one," she whispered.

Firdous angrily told her off and she receded into the background where the others were huddled together watching the spectacle. My eyes remained on the woman I would later know as Kamli, my friend. She wore her red hair long and loose, a shocking contrast against her nutmeg-coloured wrinkly skin.

Her eyes were hidden within folds of skin so that it seemed as if she was always smiling.

"Who are you?" I asked. "What's happening?"

Kamli came forward again and began to dance.

The women laughed.

Kamli whirled and clapped and sang in Persian, "What I am, you will be. I am. You. Will. Be."

She was mad. I jerked back when she came near me.

"What do you want from me?" I screamed. "Who are you?"

She was suddenly in my face.

"Wrong questions, beget wrong answers," she whispered.

Someone pulled her away. She continued to sing and whirled herself out of the door.

Then they left me and locked me in behind them. I could hear cats yowling and dogs barking all night. Strangely, these people who would imprison strangers were very kind to animals. They believed it a sin to kill a helpless creature. They did not kill animals unless hunting, and they ate what they hunted. Cats and dogs abounded. Mostly strays. And now, their barking and their yowling lulled me to sleep at night.

No feast was offered that night, no politeness showered on me.

I didn't understand that I was already a prisoner. I thought I would be released because I was American, even if I was a mixed race American. I would not be toyed with because such things happened in movies and books, and I covered such stories on the news. How could this be happening to me?

I was an American citizen. I had a big, bad life. I lived in the biggest, baddest city of the world—New York. I broke war stories to the world. I didn't need to build a house of bricks and mortar because I was what they built the house against. Who was drawing this circle around me, pushing my big, bad life into a small box? Why was my larger-than-life identity being broken and beaten into this tiny space nestled amidst unnamed mountains no one cared about? I was in the wrong story. I wasn't Cinderella or Sleeping Beauty. I was no princess, and no dragon would imprison me in a tower or a mud-house. I would rescue myself.

After an unsettled night I awoke the next morning with my head pounding. I thought I was alone in the room until I looked around and saw Gulraiz watching me, cradling a long staff in his hands, smiling as if he were visiting an old friend.

THREE

"Firdous tells me you've been asking about your friends. They have left. They were in a hurry to get back. My men have escorted them out of the tribal area."

Lies, whispered the fear coiling around me like a python.

"You killed them," I choked. "They're dead."

His face darkened, "You are calling me a liar? How dare you speak to the next tribal chief like this?"

The python within released me. I was breaking apart at the seams. *Shawn and Cyril.*

"Does the present chief know you have an American citizen as a hostage?" I asked in what I thought was a reasonable voice. "That you have killed two other Americans? Does he know? Do you know what will happen to your pathetic little tribe? You'll be chief of ashes, you pig!"

His face changed colour. "Pig? You called me pig?" he loomed over me. "Do you know what that means to us? My people?"

Names and words mattered to him when they were about him. And yet he had killed two men. Taken their lives. That did not seem to matter to him.

"Look Gulraiz, it is extremely dangerous for you to do this. And it will cost your father and your whole tribe if you continue down this path. But we can still make this right. Trust me. Just let me go. Everything will be alright."

I sat down beside him and spoke in a soothing voice, "I will speak with my government. I will ask them to pardon you."

Not on your life, you filthy bastard. Fear the American drones that I will rain on you!

His eyes were fiery and proud. "You think me a fool? You think because I don't wear a suit, I don't speak your language, I am an idiot?"

I protested, albeit weakly. I did think him lacking basic human qualities, and he had proved me correct, hadn't he? Did he think of me as not quite human?

"Look at this," he cut me short. He showed me the staff. "Take it in your hands. Feel it." He shoved it in my hand. It was a beautiful staff as tall as a man, made of mahogany with silver caps at both ends. The top cap was twelve inches, carved with markhors, lapwings, birds and roses. The tip of the stick was a smaller version of the same cap, also silver, about four inches. "This was my grandfather's. It is made from a tree that grew in his enemy's house. One night he went to his enemy's house with a couple of men. He cut down the tree with an axe. Cut it right down, while the man cowered inside. My grandfather had it lugged away with a tractor and broke the wooden gates of the enemy's house as he pulled the great sheesham with his trolley-tractor. It was a very old and very large tree. The enemy had great pride in it. My grandfather had the wood treated and made into this staff. The artisan worked day and night. It took a whole year and a day for this staff to be carved and polished. During that time his enemy tried to kill him many times. They did not succeed. Isn't this beautiful?"

"It is exquisite. It shows how great your family is and how old. You must be proud."

Flattery would get me my freedom, perhaps?

"This staff you hold so lovingly in your beautiful, delicate hands has killed one hundred and twenty-one men."

My hands trembled, and the staff almost fell from my hands. He grabbed it and stroked it lovingly.

"It has never fallen from our hands. A staff on the ground indicates defeat and shame. After forty days and forty nights of this staff being made, when the tribes had all learned this man had been emasculated by my grandfather, when the stories had reached the farthest tribes, and when that eunuch of a man had been shamed to my grandfather's satisfaction, then my grandfather went to his enemy's house with this staff and with it, he beat the enemy to death. People still tell the story. There were seventy gashes on his head alone they say."

A hundred and twenty-one. A year and a day. Seventy.

Numbers symbolize magical properties, they represent power and meaning. To know a number is to understand its manifest magic and meaning, with all its powers. The contrast of an odd number with an even number invokes mysticism; it is a marriage of the impossible. A hundred and twenty is a blessing in some cultures. A hundred and twenty-one, its opposite, a curse in others. In ancient folktales, a year and a day was required for the toughest magic to come to fruition. A synthesis of differences was required to make a whole, seven and zero, to make seventy. It thus becomes a number of mystique and with the metaphysical reference to seventy *hurs* as reward after death for good men.

My mind wandered away from the truth that was beginning to stare into my eyes. Numbness was insulating me from pain and a part of me had begun to accept my fate. I averted my eyes from that great Firebird called truth.

I gathered some vestige of courage and put my hand on his. "Gulraiz, you are a civilized man—"

He laughed.

"You people think being civilized means being Western. Or something to be happy about? America is civilized in your eyes? What they did in Japan and Vietnam, was that civilized? What they have done here in Afghanistan and Iraq, is that civilized? What they do to their own people because their skin colour is different?"

He waited for my response. I was supposed to deny his comments but couldn't. What he said was true and I had never seen myself as anything but on the side of civilization.

"See? You think it is and we think it is not. What we do in our own countries and tribes is not your business. You are drunk on your imperialistic powers and aims. And if you are going to wander in our lands as if you own them…well, we will have to retaliate."

"You can't punish me for my country's actions."

"How have I punished you? I have fed you, spared your life, brought you home to my women, you call that punishment? You don't know anything."

I hadn't eaten anything for twenty-four hours. I hadn't even had any water. I was beginning to feel the hunger and thirst of my animal body. My mind was shutting down and instinct was taking over. I could feel my mind slipping away and the canny, slyness of instinct taking over.

"I feel faint," I whispered. "I haven't eaten in hours, Gulraiz. Why are you treating me this way?"

"If you promise to do as I say, I will send someone with food. Do you promise?"

I nodded on a sob.

"Good. We will talk after."

Firdous entered with a jug of water and food laden on a tray. Two cats followed her in. They were probably strays that followed the smell of food. Or maybe they were hers. I stretched a trembling hand towards one, but it slipped away, mewling. The smell of food made me nauseous and she made me lie down.

She put some rice in a plate and encouraged me to eat it. "Slowly, now."

I took a small hesitant portion and when it stayed down, I took in another bite. She added more to my plate as she saw me devouring the delicious rice and gravy. My mind in that moment was blank. There was only the food.

When I had finished, she poured water from the jug.

"Have a sip of water," she offered me the glass.

Satiated now and exhausted from all that had occurred since my arrival, I began to feel drowsy.

"Gulraiz wants to marry you. The maulana will come now and ask you. Say yes three times, okay?"

My head was heavy. Someone was laughing. Firdous was watching me. *Who was laughing?* I looked blearily around the laughter increased. I hiccupped and the laughter stopped. I blinked stupidly at the floor. *It had been me! I had been laughing.* And there it was again!

The rest of the evening was a blur. Firdous sat by my side. An old man came in and I said yes each time because Firdous whispered in my ear to do so. I remember being in a dark room, Firdous helping me slip out of my clothes and getting me into bed. I remember waking up in the dark with a heaving man on top of me; I remember trying to push him away and his angry command: "Stop it!"

There are so many stories like mine. Newspapers are full of them. This is not new in the steady stream of news. But it was new to me.

I was drugged.

I was forced into marriage.

I was raped.

Nothing earth shattering. It happens all the time to women all over the world. But this was my story, and in my story it had never happened before. Until then all those other stories had been one dimensional for me.

FOUR

I had no way to tell the time. Where were my things? My little backpack that carried my wallet, passport, watch, the diamond studs that had belonged to my mother, the gold chain with my grandmother's jade pendant, everything was gone. I'd been wearing locally bought jeans and a white embroidered top and had covered my dark brown hair with a scarf. It hadn't saved me that day. Nothing did. Not the colour of skin, not my passport and not the hijab. Not one of the patriarchy-approved symbols for good women saved me. Not one of the symbols of the Western civilization saved me. Nothing saved me that day.

Rape is a word that might inflict horror, but the word is not enough to hold its own meaning. It's too small. It is just not enough. There is so much one feels. Violated. Abused. Helpless. Angry. Dirty. Less than other people. There is shame. Guilt. Rage at being a woman. Rage at being helpless. Rage. So much of it. My very being had been stolen from me.

He stole from me. Gulraiz first captured me and stole my freedom; he raped me and stole my image of myself from me. I began to look at myself differently. My life choices became wrong and stupid. I became stupid in my eyes. "If only I hadn't" became a regular sentence in my internal dialogue. My story changed because he chose to violate my body. I would learn that "if only I had" was not the right way to think, and that shamed me too. How could I blame myself for even a second? That is what rape does. But finally, I would decide that I was not going to allow those words to ever enter my mind again. I was not responsible for what a man had chosen to do.

"How is this fair?" became a familiar question.

"Do not do this, Gulraiz," I had warned him. "I am not the woman you think I am." My words smacked of arrogance to me later. What had I meant? That other women may be weak, but

I am not? Other women may be easily imprisoned, but I would not be so easy to tame? There is a Sufi saying, no man will die before committing the sin he blamed his fellows of committing. It is hubris to judge others because judgment is His alone. And He is always watching.

"And how are you different?" Gulraiz laughed, "Do you not have soft breasts and a warm cunt?"

"You will regret this!" I shouted.

Stupid, blind words. I waited desperately to be rescued. Sometimes I thought I heard helicopters. Years later, I would find out that indeed people had come looking but the whole village had denied my existence or even seeing me. Initially the hunt for me had been urgent. The helicopters I imagined I heard had been real. They looked daily for four weeks. Then every few days and then finally they stopped looking. But I was kept locked up even then. My screams were not heard by anyone but the guards outside my door. No one ever found me.

He violated me almost every day. I lost count. How should I tell of my pain? Do such words exist? Words don't convey pain. They wouldn't express my humiliation and helplessness; the constant ache and hurt. How unclean I felt. When I raged or cried, he became even more violent. Initially, it was slaps and punches then one day he broke my arm. As I shrank away in pain, he told me about how the world was looking for me and my companions. It was big news he said and laughed.

"You are important, a journalist, an American woman! They keep you on the news. Helicopters come again and again. Army comes from across the borders! They keep asking, every few months. But no one will find you because I won't let them. Those that can be bribed I will pay and those that can't, I will kill. But you are my trophy. No one has an American white wife."

But I am not white, I yelled. But he paid no heed. I looked white enough and that was all that mattered to him.

As time passed, I began to understand him and his triggers. It frightened me that I understood his silence, his expressions and his body language. When he wanted to punish me, he broke a bone or caused muscle damage and would banish me to a cave. I began to think of it as my cave of punishments. The eerie echoes of water dripping somewhere deep in the ear canals of this cave, at the mouth of which was a halo of light. I would watch it and promise myself, *I will get out of here. One day, I will get out of this place.* It was a promise I would make every day for many years.

Kamli would come and see me often in my cave of punishments. Often ten or so cats followed her. She fed them. Even if it meant giving them her own food and going hungry herself. From her role as healer, she became friend and companion. She was a tall woman, and thin as a reed with her bright henna dyed hair.

"Gulraiz thinks she is a witch with that long red hair," Firdous often said, "Unnatural bitch. I don't know why you tolerate her."

Kamli told me she was the keeper of stories, secrets and wisdom. She became my teacher, my fairy godmother. My brain conjured that image and a spurious laugh extruded blood from my broken nose. Gulraiz had knocked me unconscious, and I had a broken nose. I was back in the cave of punishments. I lifted my head, still throbbing with pain, and tilted it sideways. In the low aqueous light, I spotted the piece of yellowed cloth, next to my head and put it to my nose to staunch the flow of blood. The cloth smelled of turmeric. Mildly spicy. The orange-yellow stain on the cloth made sense suddenly. The muslin cloth had been soaked in turmeric paste and rose oil. The perfume was neither pleasant nor reassuring. It smelled of far-away lands and sickness.

Kamli must have visited me. She must have told me a story, wasted on me as I was unconscious. When had that ever stopped her? She knew stories would become our secret language. They were as much for her, as for me—two grown women exchanging stories to survive.

Kamli's hoarse whisper soon became familiar, "Turmeric is anti-inflammatory and rose oil is antiseptic. It will help with the physical pain. For the pain of the heart and the soul, I have a story. Or several. Each one for what ails you."

I had recoiled in fear from the thin bent old woman with her vacant eyes when she had first started hovering around me protectively and muttering nonsense words when I was captured. Words I did not hear initially. I did not even try to hear her.

When she visited me in my solitary confinement, she sat at the mouth of the cave, mumbling, whispering. I would cry and scream till my throat was rough and aching. In the silence that followed her words would begin to make sense. She was telling stories. Under her breath there was always a story unfurling like the delicate green finger of a vine, which, if I wanted, I could hold onto and follow out of the labyrinth of the monstrous reality I found myself in, and track it into myth, or legend, or laughter.

"A man stopped Mullah Nasruddin." she clasped her hands at bent knees as she leaned against the wall of the cave at the entrance. "As the Mullah was walking away looking busy and important, the man asked, "What day is it?" The Mullah was incensed. "How should I know? I am a stranger in these parts and cannot know what days of the week you have here. Out of my way!"

I chuckled. She was pleased. I knew the story was for me. I was the stranger in the land.

Long ago, in another land and another life it seemed, I had grown up on a staple supply of stories. My father, my mother and my grandmother, had all told me tales from their countries, in their languages. I had always been captivated by storytellers and stories. There is androgyny and a natural flux in the art of storytelling. My family seemed so far away, but somehow stories had found me. And now, Kamli's tales and the memory of my childhood ones kept me going. They coalesced and crystallized to become a raft for me in the sea of uncertainty and fear.

"They call you mad," I whispered, afraid I was holding on to something fragile that would drown. One of the cats often sat in my lap. It was a nondescript, white and black cat that curled up with me whenever I was in the cave. "That's what Kamli means, isn't it?" I stroked the cat I had named Snow.

"I called myself that. It's a disguise," she winked and cackled.

My pain had made me churlish. She was crazy. "Why do you tell me stories? I am not a child." Snow jumped away from me.

My hoarse query reached her old, and I had presumed deaf, ears.

"Stories are for those who are hurting," She had a loud hoarse voice. She smoked the hookah as she spun stories about her travels. She carried it with her. A small hookah, with a long snaky pipe and a small silver stomach. "Stories for those who seek more than they see, more than they are told they can be."

She crawled inside the mouth of the cave and beckoned. It was night outside. The silvery light seemed magical and otherworldly to me. The moon was full and a chicore partridge cried against the lapis sky. We sat side by side in the dirt at the mouth of a cave that opened over a cliff and nibbled the two dry figs she produced from somewhere. Down below hurtled a river, its flow a fast furious gush of white. The gurgling noise of the water was strangely soothing, despite being so loud.

I can never forget the whiff of freedom she brought with her. She would waltz into my hut or cave from the open mountain paths as if the boundary between harsh wilderness and doors held no significance. Whereas for me, the mountains, the desert at the foot of the mountains was unknown and forbidden unless I was with a man, usually Gulraiz. I wanted to be like her even if I managed to escape because boundaries for women are drawn everywhere. I wanted to be like her; a wild woman, who could cross any boundaries and who had innumerable stories to tell.

"I am a storyteller," she declared often with pride. "I have collected stories on my travels. I have mined them from within me, my old female underworld, the female collective subconscious, repressed and oppressed for thousands of years, claimed by men, colonized by religion and cult, and I have gathered them from the silence of deserts, from the wild animals of the jungle." She turned a wry smile at me. "Even concrete ones."

Gradually, she started talking about herself, looking back into memory. At those times, she would speak haltingly as if every word was precious, weighed just right, before it was uttered.

"A storyteller is born with the nose to smell stories, a keen sense for story and humour, to have the ear to hear the whispers of the wind, to listen to the stillness of summer and to recall the dead cold of winter, to recognize the heart of many stories. Courage, yes." She looked at my latest injuries and then into my eyes. "Listen now, dear one. Listen and learn."

Kamli slathered an herbal paste on my bruised and swollen skin, "We understand stories, you and I. We understand them so well, we don't see people. We see lecher, monster, guide, lover, hero and villain. Who really knows anyone? A human being will never be the same from one incident to another…from one stage of life to another. When we see them next, they become someone else and in that moment that story changes forever and begins anew."

At night I would hear the koel, cuckoos or the bulbul, the nightingale. Such pretty sounds and yet I hated their songs and their freedom, their ability to fly away.

"Will you help me escape?" I whimpered. Surely, that was the only kindness I needed. For me that was all that mattered.

Kamli continued as if I hadn't spoken. "People who don't know themselves are the ones who make the best stories because they are in the process of becoming. When we are on the journey of becoming, we are in transition. That means feeding the soul with love, solitude and growth. When we feed the soul, it heals the darkness and the wounds of the hidden self, and each soul requires different ways of healing."

"I don't care about healing." I thought she was of no help. How wrong I was, I soon realized.

"You should. You must. Listen to the whispers, still the mind."

I closed my eyes and her soothing voice, to me at least, lulled the pain somewhat.

"Ancient tales are about deeper truths. A difficult lesson is revealed only through artful storytelling. A revelation of wisdom or experience through story makes a better story. Do you want to learn?"

I was a reluctant listener and yet I remember every word. Though I didn't forget for a single moment that I was a prisoner.

How could I? I learned to live within the framework of that awareness, to live one day at a time, feeling the pulse of the devious trust I was building with my captors. I would have to learn to read the pulse of these people and gain knowledge of their weak defences. One day I would escape.

This "one day" was hope, it was the dream, and it was the lifetime I lived to reach tomorrow so I could live it all over again.

The navy sky was embellished with unfamiliar stars, the moon, a spotlight like a Cyclops's eye.

"I will go home to my country, my bustling city, my tiny apartment. I don't belong here," I whispered. "That big white moon staring down at us from over the crest of an unfamiliar mountain, is not my moon. Mine is small, often a pale dirty yellow haze, thanks to pollution. This silence? I have never encountered it in my life not even when I covered stories in the desert. Working with a team involved chatter, laughter, drinking and jokes. I was a guest there and so there was music and tales of bravado, as is usual with the people of the desert. I don't recognize this silence."

Kamli watched me with wise eyes, her fingers laced around her knees. I touched the earth. "The ground feels hot. When I look outside the window back at home, the ground is white with snow and my window is frosty cold. I must go home, Kamli."

She spat out the hard bit of dried fig that formed a ring just inside the fleshy bit. That told me it was stale. "You think this was always my home? I wasn't born here but I keep coming back. They think I am a Malang. Do you know what that is?"

I nodded. A Malang was a mystic, a holy person. Female Malang were rare; they were considered mad but not dangerous.

"Good. You understand. I always come back here. I was waiting for something. Now I know what."

My heart jolted. "What?" My mouth was dry. What was she saying? What had she been waiting for? She concentrated on chewing her fig, as if it was the most delicious thing under the moon.

"What happened to you to make you like this?" I asked.

"I am not mad. Just different. I chose. That is enough to make them think I am mad. I did not conform. I was once a young girl set to marry. But I did not. I began to travel. I have collected stories on my journeys, mined them from within me, the old female underworld, the female collective intuitive treasure-lode. That is why they call me mad."

When I lay in pain, which was often, I listened to her soft rhythmic words as she put rosehip oil on my swollen feet where I had been beaten with a wooden stick to discourage escape. Sweet and pungent the smell of roses was an oppressive fragrance. They were constantly afraid I would escape even though I had had no chance yet to do so. But their fear gave me hope.

"A story is not a finished or a dead thing. It is a living organism, and it grows and reproduces. It travels across boundaries crossing oceans and even time. A single tale is the mother of many in the hands of a true poet and craftswoman because a master storyteller lives in the caves of her secret self, and births her own language for each telling. She eats pain and drinks patience. She nibbles on hope and sips grace."

The cave was lit dimly with the reflection of water and glow worms. Sometimes, they gathered on the ceiling of the cave like stars. "You will see in winter," she said.

"No. I will not," I screamed. "I will not be here in winter." My eyes streamed hot, helpless tears and my heart seared and burned.

*

When I saw the glow-worms in winter, they really did look like stars. I had never seen stars growing up. Who does in the city? I had lived in the biggest city in the world. New York. They named it twice, it was so spectacular. New York, New York. I hummed under my breath in the cool lonely cave, and Kamli moistened my forehead with a wet cloth.

"You still don't believe in stories?" she sounded disappointed. "You should. We live in stories. Do you think you stepped into the wrong one? No. No. We never do. They are unfamiliar and feel wrong but they are ours, shaping us, melding us into better versions of ourselves or just new versions. We call it growth. Others call it change. Metamorphosis."

Had I changed? I must have. But had I grown, become a better version of myself? I didn't have the energy to argue the point with her. But she was in the mood to tell me.

"Stories emerge from our deepest selves. One has to be very still to hear the stories that whisper, that nudge if one is quiet enough, and then blossom. The modern world is but a blur of frenzy, like the buzzing wings of a hummingbird as it drinks nectar from a flower."

When she left, I sighed with relief. Nobody can be quite comfortable with a mad woman around.

I sat up to drink water and tried to stand up. The almost bearable throb in my feet I had learned to ignore morphed into a shooting pain. Stubbornly, I took a step forward and grabbed the stick that Kamli had left for me to use as a crutch. The pain increased but I watched it as an observer from afar.

My right foot was bandaged; the big toe protruding was a blackish blue. The billowy pink and heavily embroidered loose trousers hid most of my foot. I was grateful for fainting when Gulraiz raised the wooden staff that he never failed to tell me he had inherited from his grandfather. Fascinating at first, it was now an instrument of torture and a legacy of cruelty. He enjoyed using it on me.

I limped to the clay water pitcher and poured some in a clay bowl. My tongue was a wooden pellet in my mouth. I could feel the sandpapery dryness of it all the way down my throat. I drank slowly to allow my parched mouth to hydrate.

I heard a footfall behind me. "You're awake, Janna?"

Janna was what they called me. It was not my name. Firdous was older than the rest of us, and as fierce as she could be gentle. She helped me back to the bed, a slab of stone. This would be my bed for as long as I was there. I didn't mind. I'd been there before and would be again.

"Janna, when will you stop angering that lion of ours, huh?" She looked at me as a mother would a child.

In the beginning I had raved at her. "Are you mad? He's a kidnapper and a rapist. You're a monster for helping him!"

I remained silent now. A lesson I had learned the hard way. Words can mean everything or nothing.

"Why do you keep trying to escape? He loves you. He hates hurting you. He has been worried about you and didn't go hunting with his friends as he'd planned. He hasn't been eating properly. Half the dishes come back full. And he's been asking after you."

I smiled. She relaxed. I had learned another language. I had been a proud polyglot all my life. I held onto little things, memories and accomplishments until…one day. One day, when I would escape and make new ones.

Gulraiz didn't see me during the times I was convalescing. Each time I was grateful at first. When I would return to the hut and even the women stopped coming, I thought I'd go mad. The brown mud walls of the room seemed to shrink. I'd trace the patterns of hay and dry grass mixed into the mud to insulate the walls. But the silence and stillness began to eat me at me. They left the food just inside the door they kept locked. I'd be taken to the water spring with them twice a day. But they were not permitted to talk to me or even look my way. I had been erased from existence, as part of the punishment. By the end of a few weeks, months, I do not remember, I would pretend to have learned my lesson.

When Gulraiz returned with gifts, I discerned in myself a surge of emotion akin to joy. I cried at my own symbolic death. The person I had been had died. I had become someone new. I swore then I was not going to be a victim.

Some months into my capture and my broken bones had healed more or less, at least they hurt less now that winter was over. Spring brought hope with it, even to prisoners. That evening when he came, I greeted him with a smile. I had brushed my hair for the first time in weeks, prepared myself for his pleasure. I had conformed finally, and he was happy to see the change.

"You seem in a good mood today," he said.

"Yes, I am. I was hoping to go on a walk with you." I wanted to trick him into taking me out so I could escape. My heart carried the secret fires of hope and rebellion.

Kamli had said that Trickster is in element on the road, on pathways, thresholds and at crossings. These can also be inward and are often more dangerous. When a Trickster lies, it is to open doors of opportunity.

I wanted to be Trickster.

"Ready to declare your loyalty to me and to the tribe?" Gulraiz was delighted. "I like it. Let's go. Wear the burqa Firdous got you."

It was an elaborate garment for a new bride, heavy and colourfully embroidered. The perfect disguise for Trickster. I was bold, hopeful and strong. My time was here at last. Enough with the victimhood.

"We will walk through the village to the hills," he said when we were outside.

The village was the settlement of perhaps twenty huts, the one I had crossed months ago with my colleagues. A lifetime had passed since then. I had no money, no passport, none of that mattered to me. I would run. Getting out of his clutches was all that mattered. My heart beat so fast I was afraid he would hear it.

He walked slowly and leisurely, speaking of the beauty of the full moon as it began to rise in the early spring evening, and how the moon was a recurring theme in Pashtun poetry because of its chaste beauty, like that of a good woman. I made appropriate sounds. Then we were in the hills. My shoes were not so sturdy. I might trip on them. I stumbled on purpose and I left one behind a small jutting of a rock. The other, under a small bush.

The ground was still hard and cold. We were climbing up. Then we were close to reaching the summit of the hill. I stepped forward faster. He didn't stop me. He slowed down. I was so high on adrenaline. So desperate to escape, I reached the summit, swivelled around and pushed him. He staggered. I did not wait to see him fall. I ran.

I tried to throw off the burqa as I ran. I stumbled and fell, scrambled to my feet and ran on blindly, finally throwing off the voluminous cloak. My heart was in my mouth and my feet swift on the slopes of these unknown hills that were dry as dust and burnt brown by the sun, even in spring. It was still early evening but as I ran, the deepening dusk turned the hills into shadowy silhouettes in the distance. My bare feet made soft thunking noise as they landed hard on the ground. Sometimes they cut on the small rocks and pebbles. But I kept going. My heart soared. I don't how long I'd been running. The air was now cooler on my face. The moon gave me some light.

From a jutting edge above me, I heard a sound and saw a cluster of men charging towards me from behind. I tried to increase my speed but they were too many and too fast for me. Someone grabbed my hair from behind. I fell back and hit my head hard. Darkness descended and then splintered into colourful lights. A point of pain at the back of my head expanded to every pore in my head. I screamed and the sound ricocheted back to me.

Gulraiz loomed over me, holding the burqa in one hand. "You really thought it would be this easy? You think me a fool, don't you? A barbarian? You probably think I rape you every night. Understand foolish woman that it is my conjugal right. You thought a smile from you would fool me? I know you women very well. I was raised by one. I understand your petty wiles and tricks."

On the ground, gasping and staring around for ways to escape, praying for wings to fly away, I sobbed for air, for a way out.

"You will not escape. You cannot go anywhere because it is not what I want. I am a man and you are a weak woman. This is the end of your story. Accept it. It is a happy ending. Soon you will bear me sons. When you are a mother, you will settle down. You tried to trick me and for that you need to be taught your lesson. You need to be taught your place." He swung his staff. It landed on my right ankle, and I heard a dull crack. I screamed. The pain spread like fire. I lost consciousness then.

FIVE

The early morning light was faint and grey. I was in the cave again on a stone slab. The pain in my foot was intense, like a burning boulder weighing it down. I was a prisoner. There was no denying it. I recalled the stories my grandmother had told me when I was a child many long years ago. My father too.

I used to love Aesop, *Arabian Nights*, and fantasy stories of all kinds of magic. It was a surprise to many that I became a journalist, following war and politics, and did not instead pursue writing fiction. But it was because I loved travelling and meeting new people and because I treasured these stories and sought new ones, even if there was no magic in them.

I began to tell those old tales of fantasy and magic to myself as hot tears fell.

There was once a princess who was captured by a Djinn. She soon discovered the Djinn had a secret. His life-force was attached to his beloved parrot. The parrot's golden cage hung high above the reach of anyone, near the ceiling of the tower in which she was imprisoned. A prince came to rescue her. She helped herself by telling him the secret of the parrot so he could wring its neck and rescue her.

That was the story of a princess. But not mine.

No one was coming for me. I was on my own. Hot tears gathered at the corners of my eyes, pooled on the side of my nose and slipped down the sides. They made their own path as water does on any surface. My tightly bandaged foot rested on a makeshift cushion, probably a bundled-up shawl. And who was there to wipe my tears as they slipped down my cheeks? Who would watch them gather and trickle to pool in the tiny crevice of my mouth, whose heart would contract at my pain?

I had thought I was Trickster. I had believed I would escape the trap.

Jackal was the original Trickster. Jackal however had to learn to be one because he was born in the land of the tiger and the cobra. He wasn't born a trickster but was destined to be one. He had to learn by trial and error. There was a time when Jackal was tricked. It was when he considered himself to be trickster but had not yet achieved the necessary strength and wisdom.

The stories tumbled into my head.

Once there was Sloth Bear who came to a field of papaya. In the field was a scarecrow brushed with tree gum. As Sloth Bear munched his papaya, he hit the scarecrow with his leg. His foot got stuck to the gum. Angry, he tried to pull away using his front paws but his paws got stuck as well. As he tried to free himself Jackal wandered into the field in search of food.

What are you doing there, Sloth Bear? Jackal laughed at the sight.

Sloth Bear, a gentle creature until riled, made a big show of how bored he was. "The farmer who owns this papaya field was angry because I wouldn't eat chicken with him. He has stuck me here as punishment. But this is nothing. There is worse. He said he will make me eat a chicken. He has gone to get it now!"

Jackal laughed.

"You are a stupid Sloth Bear. I will take your place and eat the delicious chicken."

"Are you sure?" said Sloth Bear.

"Off you go," said Jackal.

He pulled Sloth-Bear free and got stuck in the gum trap. The farmer found him the next day and shot him full of holes.

I knuckled away my tears. Tricksters had no time to cry. Victims cried. People with no hope cried. I was no trickster yet, not unlike Jackal of the story. Tears were useless, they meant self-pity. Jackal had to become a hunter and a trickster to survive. Jackal fell into a trap only as a novice trickster.

A true Trickster lay her trap carefully and so elaborately, even the wily predator did not see the trap, and one day walked right into it.

SIX

The next time I was in the healing cave, Kamli's cheerful song reached my ears before she entered with her dozen cats in tow. I hated her at the time for being free, for being a woman old enough to be undesirable to men. I wanted that boon of age and invisibility. I was ignorant then about what an insult that was and how much I had yet to learn even about being a true woman.

I could smell the pungent salves she carried with her, the smell of herbs and ointments. Everything about her was foreign to me.

"Let me tell you a story." She arranged the oils and potions close to me. "This happened long, long ago and my grandmother's grandmother told her the story. They lived in the same village as a girl called Fatima. Her parents arranged her marriage when she was sixteen. The marriage was to take place after the month of Ramadan which was approaching. Fatima asked permission to go into isolation and pray for the last ten days of the month, a common practice in the holy month and a superior form of worship. She was granted permission. When the ten days of prayer and fasting were over and the family gathered to welcome her from her isolation in her room, they saw that her beautiful long black hair had turned white."

Kamli opened a container with an unguent and sniffed it with her eyes closed. If this was a deliberate ploy for drama—it was to good effect. "People said she could do things...heal people; find things that were lost, and she could tell when someone was about to die even in another village." She closed the container and put it gently back with the others. "She never married." Kamli said this last triumphantly as if it proved something significant.

It was a haunting tale. I was moved but had a sense of foreboding. "Who was the girl?"

"No one knows."

"Is this your story?"

She rearranged the containers with her healing herbs and spices. Her silence was answer enough. Beginning a story with, "my grandmother told me" or "my grandmother's grandmother told me", was the same as "once upon a time". Once upon a time was a trope. It could be a story of yesterday but when we heard the words, once upon a time, we were already filled with magical expectation. These phrases were what storytellers used to invoke a certain atmosphere. I was quite certain Kamli had just told me her own story.

I learned much from Kamli and her stories, especially about subterfuge within women's tales. How women used silence and invisibility to get their way because they were often prisoners. Their cleverness was then used to brand them names—witches, liars, cheats, and all too often it was forgotten that they were tricksters.

Soon, lies became second nature to me.

Gulraiz wanted to come across as a compassionate jailor and I took advantage of his weakness, his desire to impress me. I lied about my period to keep him away. I asked for a bird as a pet. He brought me a pretty pair of tiny yellow parrots. The only respite I had from the daily rape was when I had my period. I would tell him my cycle was irregular. When it was true, he would find out anyway, but when I wasn't actually bleeding, he needed proof.

When the time came, I killed one of the birds with my bare hands. I wrung its little neck. There was a small sound like a knuckle cracking and it echoed in the house—my one room house. I plucked a fistful of feathers then slit the bird open with a piece of broken clay and cut the still warm dead body for its blood. I had broken a pitcher the previous day and spirited away a shard large enough to hold and small enough to hide.

I let the bird bleed on a piece of cloth Firdous had given me as sanitary protection. I mixed some sticky clay from the mud on the walls around the house with the bird's blood to show as evidence of my menstruation to Gulraiz. He asked only once, as I knew he would. I made the piece of folded cloth as bloody, clotty and repellent as possible. He didn't ask for proof again. I buried the remains of the bird in one of the caves when I went bathing with the women.

When Gulraiz asked where the birds were, I blamed a cat for their disappearance and showed him what was left of them, the few feathers I had kept, and I cried genuine tears. After all the hills were full of stray cats and stray dogs. I put the empty cage behind an old trunk that had been abandoned, in what I now called my house.

I kept the birdcage for rats. I caught one with my bare hands. Hands that now killed birds and animals with ease. Gulraiz had raped me and left. Late that night as I sat staring into the darkness, I heard a squeak. I just had to wait. It would come to me. I had a piece of flatbread in my hand. I could see its eyes shining in the dark. It could see me too. It waited. I didn't move. When it was close, I pounced. It squeaked and thrashed and tried to bite me. I kept it in the cage and slaughtered it when I needed blood.

I knew I could only use this excuse sparingly. But I tried very hard to not get pregnant. When you're a prisoner, your own body is alien. It is used. It betrays you. It accepts the invader's semen like a blind, ungrateful monster you've been feeding unknowingly. It starts to make a baby inside you. It begins to change and grow and your tears, screams, your attempts at killing this traitor fail. You are nothing more than a vessel to carry the enemy's heir to term.

SEVEN

I was allowed to go with my sister-wives to bathe in one of the caves which had a fresh spring. The cave was dank in winter but in the long summer it smelled of grass and tasted of stone. The walls and floor were moss-green and clay-brown with mould and it was beautiful in a way. To enter a cave spring is to enter an imagined geography because you can never really map water. It always escapes.

Water is sacred. It is ancient, healing and cleansing. It washes away sins, toxins, even magic. It does not divulge its secrets, like the earth where footprints remain, or air which retains traces of odours. Even fire leaves ash. Water tells no tales. One can seek refuge in it.

I would want to go daily. Sometimes, they let me go alone and I familiarized myself with the topography of the cave, its dead ends and its narrow holes.

The lavatory-cave was larger with a small air-hole far above us, through which the sun and the flies came down. And sometimes, a small breeze, which was the worst of the three because all it did was to snatch the putrescent odours and stuff them in our lungs. The children sang or hummed as they defecated; the mothers chattered with each other, unembarrassed, and I tried to make myself small and invisible. If I ever found it empty, I thanked Circe. Or Hecate. Or God, depending on who I was worshipping that day, or that season. I didn't always stick with one god for a whole season. I was as fickle as the gods. They had yet to earn my loyalty.

As Gulraiz exulted in the success of taming me, I began to ask for things. I asked for many, so he would not know which mattered most. I asked for books. He refused. I asked for my earrings back. To look pretty for him, I said. He laughed but did not give them back to me immediately. Then I remembered old stories and I asked him again when he wanted to have sex.

"If you stop fighting me, I will give them back to you."

I stopped fighting. What good had it done me? It was two long months before he returned them to me.

There is energy in our actions. Old stories are full of wisdom but they don't always reveal the whys of what happens because it is important that seekers learn on their own. Giving in, harms the heroes. They are faced with a test that might destroy them. Only because they thought, what good is this intangible emotion doing to me, why should I hold on to it? What good is respecting myself when I am being raped daily? What good is abstaining from a sin when everyone around me is a sinner? What you cannot see is harder to hold on to and what you cannot measure seems trivial in importance. Saying no matters. Fighting back matters. Words matter. You realize too late that holding back was doing all the good. Good is intangible. Some tests we fail because we have to become stronger for bigger, bitter, bloodier battles ahead, and repeated failure prepares us better for such battles than usual success.

When I discovered I was pregnant, I tried to kill myself. At least the first time I did. I stole a useless blunt knife from the fruit basket Firdous brought. That was the best I could do. My rat killing shard had broken long ago.

As soon as the women left, I slit my wrist. The knife didn't cut as deeply as I wanted, it was a shallow cut. It hurt. Blood appeared only in tiny beads. It took me maybe five minutes to try again. I was just about to cut myself again when Firdous came charging back. She had checked for the knife and found it gone.

"She is with child," Kamli informed her.

Firdous looked at her sharply.

"Let me die," I cried. "I don't want this monster…"

Firdous told the other women to keep the whole thing quiet. "Don't let Gulraiz know about this. If he beats her, she will lose the child. It is her first."

I cried because I had failed. Kamli mistook my tears for physical pain. She patted my head and told the other women to go. She stayed with me.

Firdous lingered. "Why are you being cruel to yourself? Life is a gift. Will you take it from your child too?"

"What do you care?"

"I care for the child. Motherhood is the greatest gift from God. Motherhood is the greatest avatar of a woman."

Kamli whispered in my ear. "She covets the baby."

Something electric passed through me. I shivered. "How many children do you have?" I tried to understand what that new information might mean for me and my situation.

"I have four. Gulraiz tires of women too soon. He married Meherbano five years after my marriage to him. Then came the other two. I had four children. Three girls and a boy. My son will be the next chief. My children have gone from me. My daughters married, never to return. If I am lucky, I will see them once a year. If not, maybe once in two or three years. My sons, I see from afar. My oldest does not even acknowledge me. You will have this baby for at least ten years if he is a boy and twelve if she is a girl. Ten glorious years of being needed and loved. You wish to rob yourself of that?"

Kamli nudged me. When I looked at her, she nodded with a wicked little smile I thought I understood.

A plan began to take root in my mind. I had the biggest bargaining chip with Firdous, growing in my belly. This was her weakness—a baby.

"I will leave Kamli with you. Do not harm yourself now," she said in the gentlest voice she had ever used with me.

Kamli laughed and clapped her hands when she had left. "Now you will have power. Now you have embarked on the next phase of your journey. You will gain and you will lose, as all who seek must."

I paid no attention to her. Maybe I could barter this thing growing inside me for my freedom? Firdous coveted this baby. That gave me power.

I began to eat whatever Firdous brought me, I washed clothes, walked and cleaned with the rest of them, which she said was the exercise my body needed. I let her behave like I was the surrogate of her child.

"I will need you for this baby," I said one day. She should not forget it was mine to give.

Her eyes fluttered. She smiled enigmatically. I understood what it meant only much later. "Of course, Janna. Of course!"

I smiled too because I could use Firdous and this thing growing inside me to escape. I did not feel like a mother. I felt as if my body had been taken over by a parasite gnawing and eating away at my insides. There is no sudden miracle that changes a woman's body and makes her a mother. That is a myth perpetuated by patriarchal women.

My first was a daughter.

She had been nothing but a trick for me initially when she was just an idea growing inside me. I could rage at how my body was changing because of an alien seed inside me. My body had given enough; she had taken life's blood from me and that was enough. I had hoped for weeks it would die a foetus. I had called it a snake and hoped and prayed that it would die. That would hurt Gulraiz and Firdous. I had expected I would hate my daughter just as I hated her father.

The change came upon me so surreptitiously I didn't even notice. It happened when I had my second child. It was something that I had not anticipated, never thought possible. The alchemy of motherhood changed everything. I had birthed a human being. I made a human being inside me and understood a new personal power I would never have otherwise. The pain of birthing was nothing compared to the great alchemical wonder of birthing. Pain is but an essential element of life, is it not?

I could not help the love that grew inside me. I had thought of using my first baby. And then I did in other ways. I would say she was ill or cranky. I would find reprieve from the attentions of Gulraiz for a week or ten days. She was a tiny helpless little thing and needed me as no one ever had. I oscillated between mother, and the other, the one who hated her and wanted to escape.

But the second pregnancy I carried to term was different from the first. The life growing inside me began to finally change me. I had been relieved at losing the ones I had. But with the birth of my second child, the sacred connection I had with women who had nurtured life within them began to dawn on me, binding me with a long chain to a tradition, a secret. When a woman embraces motherhood willingly, the power of that transition multiplies manifold. Despite the unwillingness with which I had entered this sacred temple, I began to feel the enormity of the bounty that had come my way. My grandmother had told me many stories of divine motherhood and how maiden became mother. It was a rite of passage that I was going to pass unwillingly, and so I did not, could not, fully receive the inner growth it brought with it. But I could not help the change the second time I became mother. The life that grew within me was innocent and I had no control over the love that blossomed in my bruised heart.

"You have changed," Firdous had noticed too. "You feel it, don't you?"

A woman changes forever when she becomes a mother. It is an alchemical change says the old wisdom.

Change is a secret path, an internal path. People can see there is change, but what it is, few will see, sometimes not even those whose secret it is, that change, will see it for what it is. But I did. My change was iron courage, a will of steel. My enemy had made me stronger. I had morphed into the next stage of any woman's secret journey. As a mother now I sought freedom not just for myself, but for my children.

I vowed never to harm myself again. I vowed anew that I would break free. For my daughters.

The fierce woman inside me that had awakened was a stranger. The numen of motherhood was sacred but was it really mine, when I hadn't even wanted it?

EIGHT

I named my first baby Scheherazade too. Firdous was happy I had shown interest in choosing a name for my daughter.

"Do you want me to keep Nur in my house so you can sleep better?" she said one day,

"Her name is—"

"No. Her name is Nur," she said firmly.

When I complained to Gulraiz, he was dismissive. "Don't be petty. What is the difference between you and my other wives then? They are always complaining to me about each other. You are an American woman!"

I calmed my fluttering heart within the cage of my ribs, fluttering to escape, fluttering against the darkening of itself and the death of all hope. Some magicks require time to come to fruition. My trap was still being laid. It was elaborate, but I had bait.

When Firdous offered to look after Nur, I would often agree. Initially, it was because I feared I would harm the child in my fury. I would sometimes imagine strangling her to punish Firdous.

The dividends of her staying with Firdous were higher than Gulraiz staying away because he disregarded what I needed. Whenever I fell into the habit of accepting Gulraiz's behavior or caught myself making excuses for him, I would meditate to make my mind stronger and remind myself it was only a matter of time and that I would escape soon. I would revisit my plans and strengthen my resolve. But there is a long and uphill journey before the end. My journey, like Sisyphus's, was one that started anew every day.

One day I asked Firdous to leave Nur with me. She stared as if I had asked for her life. She lifted the toddler in her arms and left. I had lost two pregnancies in two years after I gave birth to her. I nearly lost my life too.

"Please bring her back. Gulraiz would not like me complaining," I wailed.

She did not look back. I had lost the advantage already. Putting yourself in other people's shoes makes you weak sometimes. Seeing their humanity and showing them your own gives them an advantage leaving you with none. You become their prisoner. They begin to see you as a lesser human. They must think me rather stupid or weak. To many people it is the same thing.

When Nur had been a year old, I was pregnant again. I was violently sick. And then I started getting fevers. My body seemed to be rejecting the foetus and my reality. How could this happen to me again? Why God? Why do I have to go through this again? When will I escape? Will I ever?

It was Kamli who put it in perspective from her endless repertoire of stories. A man cut down a tree one day. A Sufi saw the atrocity and said, "Look at this branch, still full of sap. It does not know it has been cut off from life. In its ignorance, it is still paying homage to life, thinking they are still linked. But it will know soon enough. Until then, there's no reasoning with it."

The branch full of sap inside me, the dead tree, did not know it would be born a prisoner. What is freedom, if not life?

I have glossed over many incidents because my suffering is just words on a page. We don't truly understand pain until we ourselves have experienced that particular brand of it.

I lay in bed for days after she took my two-year-old daughter from me forever. Not moving. Not eating. Three years gone by, and I had miscarried two times.

"Firdous tells me you are too sick to look after Nur." Gulraiz looked down at me as I lay unmoving on the bed. "I have requested Firdous to take the child to her own house. You need looking after."

That was how it had started. I did not stir. I had been right. The fierce power of motherhood had curdled into self-loathing and rage, and become feral. There is no power in self-loathing and self-blame. It is what drains innate power. It is what shoves your true power down its dark gullet and rots your essence.

I didn't see Firdous for several weeks. Kamli looked after me and she was very happy to do so. She would spend the whole day with me and her chatter covered me like a coat too warm for the season. She would tell me stories as she fed me pieces of fruit.

"Nuri Mojudi, a Sufi would sit in his teaching room and tell his students to fetch this or the other. One lazy student said to another, 'Our Master sits and does nothing, and we work like donkeys for him. Maybe he doesn't know as much as he pretends.'

"The Master said from behind them, 'The Sufi is one who does what others do—when it is necessary. He is one who does what others cannot do—when it is indicated.'"

Kamli handed me a slice of golden peach tinted crimson at its inner crescent inside.

"Do you know what that means?" The sweet tartness of the peach flooded my mouth and coated my tongue in its thick sweet juices.

"It means we have to be what we need to be. Time is our teacher," she responded.

"Do you know what you need to do?"

She shrugged. "Be. Live." She gave me another piece of fruit. "Get the next storyteller ready."

"How do you do it?" She lived with nothing. She had nothing. For her, her stories were everything, and to me for the longest time, they had merely been stories.

"I practice patience. This world means nothing to me. It is temporary. What interests me is the mystery of the afterlife. What a story that would be, huh? I prepare for that. And in pursuit of the knowledge, I gather magic stories. The Homa bird as white as moonlight and larger than a bargadh tree, flies without rest, till it is ready to die and then it bursts into white flames. It then emerges from its own ashes, as they fall from the sky, and begins its flight again as a fledgling bird. Whoever catches a glimpse of it will have the fortune of kings, and whoever it touches with a wing or a glance will have the fortune of ten kings." She smiled at me. "So, it is said."

I thought then that the woman was old and didn't know the difference between a phoenix and the bird she'd concocted. Years later, I would discover the phoenix was actually a later addition to an existing myth and the Homa bird from Persia was as old as the Mesopotamian Sea.

When I smiled, she beamed. She reminded me of an old picture book I'd had as a child, with Maryam, the mother of Jesus on its cover. Kamli was a tragic old woman. But maybe she was this too, a wise woman with a treasure trove of stories. People were not just one thing or another. They were a galaxy of stars. I looked at her with new eyes.

She acknowledged the change in me and with an approving nod and smile. "I will bring you the stories. They are very old. I will teach you."

I took a peach out of her basket and bit into its golden flesh.

When Firdous finally came to visit, she brought Nur with her. The child watched me shyly, suspiciously. I was afraid to touch her. She was three years old then. I opened my arms to hug her. Nur cried and turned away from me. She did not want me to touch her. I had already become a stranger. I had lost something precious.

I gave birth to another daughter later that year. I named her Scheherazade too. It was like a mantra of power for me. Just saying her name gave me strength. It was an invocation. It was a plea to the goddess of story, willing her to listen to mine and to bless it with the divine power of hers, and to free me. Scheherzade was the Saint of Tricksters, of magic, of survivors and of storytellers.

"This one seems to be full of girls. Will she ever give him a son?" Meherbano was scornful.

Firdous laughed. "What does it matter? Girls are wiser. They are the ones who manage men in secret."

Gulraiz brought me gifts sometimes. I used them to garner favors from other wives. Blank paper. Pens. Reprieve from him for a night. Sometimes, I would tell them stories to ingratiate myself with them. They had more power over Gulraiz than I did, if it could be called power. It was a way to survive. Sometimes, they could sway him in my favor.

I told them the tale of Jacob and Rachel to get that particular bargain. They didn't know any of the old tales.

"Who is Jacob?" Jamila was wife number three and was the youngest.

"Yaakov, the father of Yousaf."

"Oh yes, yes, Hazrat Yaqoob. Tell us the story, please."

"Yaakov fell in love with Rahil, also called Rachel. He made a pact with Rachel's father, Laban, that he would work as a shepherd on his lands for seven years and in return he would be allowed to marry Rachel. Seven years passed and Jacob worked hard for Laban, making him richer than ever.

When seven years were over, Laban didn't want Jacob to leave. If he got what he wanted he would leave and Laban knew his prosperity would diminish. So instead of marrying him to Rachel, Laban tricked Jacob and married him to Rachel's older sister, Leah. Leah of the "tender" eyes. Leah couldn't see very well, but neither could Jacob because he realized the deceit only in the morning. The woman he had consummated his marriage with was not Rachel."

The women tittered and rolled their eyes. We knew what men were, we said in our shared silence.

"When Jacob confronted Laban, he offered him Rachel as well, but only if he worked for another seven years. Jacob agreed. When the next seven years were over and Laban was even more rich and prosperous, he made Rachel promise they wouldn't leave after the wedding. Rachel agreed. And Jacob couldn't deny Rachel anything.

Jacob continued to work for Laban. Leah gave Jacob six sons. It is said that because Jacob loved Rachel and not Leah, God opened Leah's womb to compensate, so she would have the love of her children instead. One day Reuben, Leah's oldest found a mandrake when he and his brothers were harvesting the wheat fields. When Rachel saw it, she wanted it. It was supposed to make a woman fertile.

"Please, give me some of your son's mandrake," she entreated her sister. According to old lore and superstition, mandrakes made a woman fertile, and Rachel craved children,

Leah's resentment of years bubbled over. "Isn't it enough that you have Jacob's love? Must you take my son's gift to me as well?"

"If you give me your mandrakes, I will send him to you tonight."

"Oh, God! She said that? She sold her husband?" There were shrieks of laughter and the older women smiled knowingly.

"Yes, and Leah bought a night with her own husband. She sold her mandrakes."

This caused more laughter. "Oh, dear God! How could she?" Jamila's eyes were round with wonder.

"She loved him. They both did and wanted to share him, and he got what he wanted." I winked salaciously.

A few days later, I wore a shiny hair clip I knew Jamila admired. She touched it lovingly. I took it off and whispered. "You can keep this and Gulraiz for a week, hmm?"

"Strange bargain," she looked at me oddly. "But I understand. You are neither Leah nor Rachel. You are Jacob?"

I shook my head. "I am something else."

She had lost interest and was admiring the clip.

NINE

By the start of my sixth year of captivity, I knew Kamli's stories by heart. They were my escape before I could actually escape. I tried to erase myself to become invisible and therefore untouchable. I had spent these years listening and had learned a great deal. I could speak like them now. Gone was the hesitation when speaking Pushto. I could emulate a range of local accents too. One day, I was going to be able to use all of this to my advantage.

Firdous would take Scheherazade away often, to help me she said. Initially, I needed the breaks. Later, it became a contest and she usually won.

When both my daughters were with Firdous, I would sometimes explore the caves and the pathways to memorize them and to observe how I could use my surroundings for my benefit. The mountains were bare and hostile, a bleak landscape caging me in against a faded blue sky.

I was allowed to wander like this only when Gulraiz and the men had gone hunting. The old men and women did not care where I went as long as I didn't go too far and was visible. A couple of old men followed me sometimes to keep guard.

I would sit on a rock and see those—to me—ugly peaks staring back at me. Rising and peering at me over the shoulders of other mountains, falling away, as if turning away from me in disgust. Kamli accompanied me often, telling tales from *Gilgamesh*, *Hoshruba*, *Amir Hamza* or the *Shahnameh*.

"As the sun entered the constellation of Aries, and the world rejoiced in the beauty of spring, a champion of men by the name of Zal, as splendid as the sun, with hair and eyebrows as white as an old man's, was born to a nobleman. His parents, who had been ready to receive their child with rubies, carnelians, sapphires and emeralds, were in despair.

"His father ordered his huntsman to take the child Zal and leave him at the top of the gold-veined mountain where the Simorgh resided. No human dared go near it and the child would be food for the noble bird. But when the majestic Simorgh took flight from her nest and saw the baby crying, her heart swelled with love and pity for the infant. Zal grew up in the nest of the mighty Simorgh, who hunted the choicest morsels for him. He wore the skin of leopards and lions for he was a mighty hunter who drank the milk of lionesses and she-wolves. He had hunted his first wolf at the age of nine and first tiger by ten. Tall as a cypress and strong as an ox, his face shone like the moon, with the glow of divine sanction.

He had no enemy in the world except for Khazu, the arch devil, the source of all darkness in the world. The mighty Zal was destined to father Rustam, the greatest warrior in all the worlds. The arch devil devised a plan to kill him. And so, Zal had to die lest Rustam be born.

When an angel informed Zal's father of the danger to his son and his lineage, the father was moved to anger. He went to find his son, Zal, the white-haired princeling, the boundary- crosser with his young body and old-man's hair, who was a Trickster too. Trickster is the wise fool, the gray-haired baby, shunned by his human father and embraced by the mythical bird Simorgh. Trickster, you see, is a paradox; the embodiment of ambiguity and ambivalence, and Zal was one of the greatest.

When the great Rustam was born to Princess Rukhsana, he was groom to jinnia, and pari, and women, and he was so handsome, even a she-devil fell in love with him…"

I learnt much from Kamli's stories. Even love could have layers of violence, and stories were so good at translating such atmospheric violence that children were quickly colonized into its dark empire, and parents and caregivers could reap the benefits of the fear they'd sown into children. These old tales warned that parents could abandon children, and that they would have to hunt tigers and kill wolves to survive, and if they did all that, then any female who came across their path was theirs to claim. Wasn't that a poor message to give to little boys? Boys who became tribal chiefs. Yet it was true that one sometimes did have to live with wolves. As I had done.

I learned subconsciously, perhaps my intentions weren't as cruel as theirs, but the result was the same. I didn't turn out to be a good mother, after all. I give myself no quarter.

That winter, my sixth in those mountains, had been hard. I hated being cooped up in that tiny low-ceilinged room. I had tried to escape twice and had two broken feet to show for it. I was therefore not allowed to go out of the room after dark. I learned that nobody came out of their house after dark in winter, only a few young men with guns; and stragglers, who would be forced inside before midnight, because the cold was unforgiving, a killer.

I watched two falcons streak across the sky. Under different circumstances I would have seen the beauty of my surroundings, none of this would have appeared ugly to me. I would have described the mountains differently. The weather wouldn't be harsh and terrible but a whim of the seasons. How our circumstances change the environment around us because our eyes are slaves to our minds. They see what they are taught to see, what they fear and what the mind makes them see.

I had begun to unlearn the programs of my brain, developed a dual and then a multiple view of looking at my surroundings and people. I started listening to them with a more sympathetic ear than previously. It isn't easy to change how you look at other people, the enemy, but I had time, and I had the will. I learned to evaluate my picayune perspectives and decisions, and to see beyond the obvious.

TEN

A pair of eagles, brown and speckled like the mountains, looped and glided above my head. The sun would set soon. An inky stain began to creep across the sky. The eagles screamed suddenly and rose with flaps of their mighty wings and disappeared in the far horizon. Hooked to a mountain on my left, the moon became suddenly visible while the sun sank rapidly on my right. Palms open, I lifted my arms slowly. If I squinted to my right, the sun kissed my fingertips, and if I looked to the left, the moon caressed my fingertips.

The sun left its footprint in a smudge of fiery orange. It faded into purple and the navy, and I was left with the pearly iridescence of the moon that called to mind the tales of the moon goddess. Should I pray to you, Diana, Ishtar, White Goddess? Will you listen? Because the patriarchal God of Christians won't. The absent God of Jews won't either. The invisible God of Muslims? I think not.

The moonlight cast shadows on the undulating waves of the now silent mountains, silver like my dreams and dark like my hopes. There was no sign of life. I was alone in the world. A lovelorn chicore partridge screamed at the moon and shattered the illusion of peace.

My life before this imprisonment had had a veneer of freedom. A difference of opinion, an ability to walk away had implied freedom of thought. Freedom of speech had given the impression of development but had been sanctioned by state, law and normative traditions. The truth was that anything which didn't fit the already circumscribed notions of acceptability, logic, civilization, already defined by culture and history, those differences, those dissenting voices and choices, were rejected. Words themselves were prisoners. Language itself was enslaved. And although following the rules sometimes meant a sort of freedom, it was only a poor shadow of it. There was no true freedom anywhere. Not even where I had come from.

If I gave birth to a boy, I would have some semblance of power. Maybe Trickster needed help to spring the trap.

Nine months later, I gave birth to a boy, Hamza. Like magic, someone granted me a wish. This time Gulraiz celebrated the birth. It wasn't his first son, but he wanted to let everyone know that I had finally given him a boy and I knew exactly what would happen. I knew my position had changed in their eyes because I had given birth to a boy. That was why I had wanted one in the first place. The structures of my trap were all in place. The structures of the trap I planned to lay hinged on the birth of a son.

Becoming Trickster is a process of living, transforming, sintering into something else. The fires of pain break you down, and the cold touch of will reshapes you while the sharp blades of Truth carve you into who you are meant to be.

When Gulraiz visited, I pleaded to have my daughter back. I hadn't seen Scheherazade for almost a month. "Please, my love, my great chief, won't you grant me my daughter back. Isn't it enough that she has Nur? Must she take all of my children?"

Gulraiz was overjoyed at having fathered a son with me and so he seemed to listen. "Boys are harder to bear and to raise. I will give you time to get your strength back, and to feed my son with your mother's milk." He was almost shy when he said that.

"I don't want Firdous to take away my baby."

"She won't," he said.

"You have spoken to me after a long time. You barely speak to me now. But no matter. I think you are adjusting well to your new life although our daughters are usually with their other mothers. Firdous said they don't care to come to you."

That night I made love to the man I hated, like I loved him.

The next day, Firdous brought my daughter back. "You are very clever. You have learned how to manipulate Gulraiz."

"No. I didn't manipulate him at all. Why do you think that?" I looked at her with large innocent eyes.

"Hmm. I thought you said something. But you are a simpleton. Maybe he thinks you need the daughter so I can have the son. She was doing so well. She is strong. Are you sure you didn't use your womanly wiles on him?"

"Do I even have any?" I laughed self-deprecatingly.

Her eyes raked me with contempt.

"Why doesn't Jamila come with you anymore? I hardly see her."

"Well, now you have this one. I will send Jamila to help you."

I knew in that moment, if I hadn't fought for Scheherazade I would've lost her too, just as I had lost Nur, my eldest.

Six years had gone by and I had had three children. Would I ever be able to escape? I was beginning to doubt it. But I clung to hope and continued to prepare my children and myself for the eventuality. I planted aloe vera in a small pot-plant in my house, which I had seen growing near the caves, and began to show a partiality for tea infused with loose leaves and cardamom.

I didn't think of Nur as mine anymore, but didn't voice it. Escape was the single-minded focus. Had I woven too desperate a trap, one that could prove as much a trap for me as for him? Waiting is itself a trap, one that can snare the planner just as surely.

To become invisible, you need time and patience. You need to know your environment. You need to know your enemy. And I remembered the tale of Zal and the Simorgh. He had been hiding in the mountains, living under his father's nose all along, because no man dared go where the Simorgh lived. I just needed a place where no one would find us.

I put my plan in motion. I felt in my bones that finally the time was right.

We had all gone bathing to the spring inside the cave. I got out of the spring, dressed and hid in the hole that led to the cave. The women continued to frolic and chatter in the pool. When they noticed my absence about an hour later, I heard panic in their voices as they scrambled out calling for me.

"She has run away again. That stupid bitch!" Firdous said with hope in her voice.

"Why should we be responsible for that cow? I don't know what he sees in her any way."

"She is his prize cow," That brought laughter.

"I am so sick of babysitting that she-dog." Firdous wanted me gone. Did that mean I could trust her? Or not at all?

I climbed out and lay down in a corner when they had left. I knew the men would come as soon as they learned of my disappearance and the first place they would check was right here in this cave.

I heard their anger and called out before they could come in.

"What is this? Isn't this women's bathing time? Go away!"

They stopped and there was irritated muttering. "These stupid women. She is still inside."

"They must not have seen her."

Someone made a joke. Someone else shouted, "Be quick!"

I reassured them and they went away laughing at the stupidity of women.

I walked slowly back to the house making sure everyone saw me. Annoyed, the women frowned at me as I passed them. "Where were you?" asked Jamila. "We looked everywhere."

"All that swimming made me drowsy, and I dozed off near the rear wall of the cave."

ELEVEN

I had worn a mask to trick them all. But I had worn it for so long it had become a part of me. I resented and despised this woman I had become and wanted to kill her. One day I was given the perfect chance to escape and did not take it. Fear, the same fear that had been instilled in these women, had poisoned my blood as well. Familiarity had paralyzed rationality.

"Tomorrow we are going away for two days to the nearby village for a wedding. You will stay here with a few old men should you need anything," Firdous informed me.

My heart leaped. "All of you?"

"We are all related to the bride and groom," Firdous was happy to let me know I was an outsider among them.

Jamila came to show me her wedding splendor. She was beautiful and so happy to be going away for a few days. They all were, even Firdous. It was a break from the dreary monotony of their lives.

"Gulraiz said Nur should stay with you," Firdous looked disturbed.

Something had settled on my chest, and I couldn't shake it.

Nur was petulant and irritable when they left. I planned to escape when the old men and women had gone to sleep. I looked at the little bundle that was my son. Scheherazade was only eighteen months old. They were both so tiny and vulnerable. What if something happened to them while I was trying to escape?

I should wait. Did freedom mean more than my children's lives? The night passed in a dilemma. I cursed myself in the morning. Why hadn't I taken the opportunity? How could I have? It was winter. The cold was a killer. The day passed feeding the kids and waiting for the night to fall. I was horrified that I chose to sleep with my children safely tucked into warm blankets with me.

Before I knew it, the opportunity had slipped away. Firdous and the others were back soon, cheerful after their little sojourn.

"Well, he was right." Firdous looked at me with approval. "Gulraiz said you would not try to escape. I had my doubts, though."

I wanted to ask what she meant but she was crooning over Nur who did not look at me again. She was happy to be with Firdous. Firdous had become her mother.

"Thank God you didn't try to escape," Jamila whispered to me after Firdous had left with Nur. "Gulraiz had stationed two guards on the other side of the hills with orders to shoot if you had tried."

Drained, I slumped down against the cold wall. I was alive. But could this be called life? Was I only pretending to be weak and submissive? Was I really the woman I believed myself to be?

To become another, the woman who would be Trickster, the woman who would, like Clytemnestra, slaughter the oppressor in his own bathtub, in order to become a woman who could one day kill the man who had ruined her, I had to pretend to be meek, broken. But the stories we tell ourselves about us have a tendency to manifest themselves. I was no longer pretending. Abused for years I had indeed become timid and weak, even fearful.

My internal narrative had to be so pure, so strong, that the outer narrative of victim, and weak prisoner could not overwhelm it and swallow it whole, eat it all up. My internal story had to be so powerful that it would break and shatter the outer story. Kamli said that in Sufi stories there is an inner world that remains secret, unknown and inaccessible to the protagonist until a certain level of understanding is achieved by them. The character must reach a certain level of insight or knowledge to access this deeper layer. For the reader that demystification occurs when the outer and inner worlds collide. She said the inner story is the soul, without which the outer story would not exist nor be truly meaningful.

The threat was strong and perpetual that could so easily masticate my very being into an unrecognizable amorphous pulp with no shape or identity. Hadn't it already done so? No, I vowed. That day I learned two things. One, that whatever shape our journey wrings us into, we must become that person to be successful. Becoming weak had saved my life and that of my children. I had lived that day to die another day. My story could have ended mid-escape. Thinking like a mother had saved me. I understood that to enter the next phase of self-growth, we must become something else, something we may think is worse. Perhaps what I perceived as weakness was not that at all but an intuitive strength which had given me caution. Perhaps, I had become a poorer, more inferior version of myself. Perhaps I had become more intuitive. But whatever it was, it had saved me.

The second lesson I learned was that there had to be something, a ritual or a token that manifested what was on the inside, what was hidden from the world and gestating in secret, for Trickster to work on the outside. I needed a ritual for my inner truth to live on in secret within me so that one day I could shake off the mask to embrace my true self.

All of life is ritual. The rituals we practice daily without thought, without attaching any value to them, influence our lives deeply and make us who we are. They have an intangible power that seeps within us so gradually we don't ever get a sense of it. We become what our rituals have prepared us to be.

Showering in the morning prepares us to face what the day might bring. It is quick and hurried because the energy is reserved for the day ahead. Bathing at night is a longer, slower ritual. It is about cleansing, washing away the impurities of negativity and toxic encounters. Lighting a candle is an invocation and a luxury—of fragrance and of time and overt meditation. Cooking is therapeutic and for healing, bonding. Helping someone, friend or stranger, is an offering. Denying yourself, even if it is as small and insignificant a thing as a coffee, is sacrifice and sacrifice is pure energy, pure power.

Rituals are most powerful when there is clear intention behind them. We can change our lives if we prepare with clear intention. But even without intention rituals have some power. I had to find a balance between what was outside of me and what was within me, what was overt and what covert. I was still the woman who would be Trickster. I needed to start manifesting it.

*

Seven years had already passed. I should escape. If I didn't, I would be stuck here forever. Wasn't that how things worked in old stories? Numbers are important even if it is just three pomegranate seeds.

I would teach my younger children, now three and two, to read and write, to survive, to hide. They thought it a game as I bathed in the spring. They wrote in sand. They swam and learned to hold their breath under water. They learnt to hide for hours. Who knew what form or path my escape would take? So, I prepared them for every possibility. I began to keep the left-over tea leaves from the recent carefully inculcated habit of tea-drinking. I would soak them in water and rub the dark waters on my face and body so that slowly, over the next few months, my skin began to darken and wrinkle. When the skin dried too much and stretched uncomfortably, I would use the aloe vera that grew abundantly in my house, to moisturize and layer my skin again with tea stains.

Gulraiz liked his women fair skinned and youthful. And I was getting the face and body of a woman twice my age.

TWELVE

The subconscious is always learning. It is a deep well of the unknown. And it continues to gather, to absorb everything unendingly. That is where stories come from. They originate from the wild paths of the psyche; secret doors to the deep stories within us. Some clandestine word, secret and unknown to us, magically opens a door to memory. Or a fragrance becomes the catalyst, and a long-forgotten recollection blossoms in the mind and saves us from darkness. The magic land of psyche, like the fictional Koh-e-Qaaf, is out there; just not always accessible to us. Like Koh-e-Qaaf, it needs magic words, and a keen and brave heart to enter.

What are those magic words, you ask? Each one of us have our own.

We must have wisdom and knowledge to solve problems entwined with hope and gratitude in our hearts. The magic that exists in this world isn't fantastical, and it is accessible. Did I not find it in strange mountains and a sky full of stars?

I had been telling myself stories for so long, I had forgotten something important. Stories have rules. Sometimes, rules can be broken.

I planned to escape soon and Nur would be left behind, I knew. I wanted to say goodbye. When we gathered to bathe in the spring, I watched out for Nur. When she entered with Firdous, I dressed and went towards her.

"Firdous, let me help Nur today."

She was surprised but allowed it.

My eldest daughter, now six, didn't look at me as a child did her mother. I sat beside her. "You are my daughter, you do know that, hmm?"

She was unresponsive.

"Let me help you," I helped her undress and whispered. "I love you. Always remember that. Even when I am not here, even when you cannot see me…" Tears clogged my throat and I couldn't continue. She ran away to Firdous.

When Trickster is caught in a trap, when she is uninitiated in lore and traditions, she becomes feral. Her instincts lose clarity. She swallows poisoned bait.

That night, I heard two men being placed as guards outside my door. I opened the door.

"Go back, Bibi. We will be sleeping outside your door from tonight. Sleep now."

My fond farewell to my daughter had been overheard.

Sometimes, our stories are not what we want them to be. My story numbers were not fairytale numbers. My story wasn't a fairytale at all. Why had I started thinking like the mad Kamli? Was I mad to think like a mad woman? Her stupid stories had messed with my head. Seven was not a magic number. I had bought so deeply into the power of story I had forgotten the most important law of storytelling.

There are no rules in storytelling. Each story makes its own.

THIRTEEN

After that seven-year magic number myth that I had held as a talisman in my heart, my defeat turned to stone within me. The following two years are a blur. I was broken. Even Gulraiz's staff hadn't broken me the way the loss of hope had. The years crawled by at a snail-like pace. Time seemed to stand still. I would look for its passage in the changing colour of leaves and fauna around me. And I would forget whether the flowers had bloomed for the first time that year, or was that just memory?

Kamli had gone on a pilgrimage of Story and returned after months to find me transformed. She did not seem displeased. She watched me quietly and I did not disturb her silence with my chatter. I had a silence of my own now.

"I will be gone soon," she said one day. "Do not lose hope, dear one. Do not lose faith in yourself or in Story. Tell me what saved you while you were here?"

I did not respond. I could not. Did I need to? Kamli seemed to understand so much without words. Stillness is an ancient teacher and a wise guide for those who will listen. In the stillness of soul, you hear many things. And I had not listened initially. But then eventually silence crawled onto my tongue and made its home there.

"You will know who you truly are when the time is right. You are more than you know. You are my heir."

She brought out an old book bound in tattered leather. "This book will teach you many things."

It was heavy and thick with old pages.

"What saved you, dear one?"

I did not know what to say. My children? Hope? But even as I thought about it, I looked at her with dawning realization. It was Kamli's friendship that had saved me. She, who wasn't mad at all, in fact. The fool, wiser than us all.

She nodded as if she had read my thoughts.

"There is a reason for everything. You and I are linked. Remember that. Our link is important. One more story then. There was an old woman who lived in a cave and ate a spoonful of dirt a day. It kept the sorrows away. She said, being wise, it would cause one to live a long time. But what good is time if you don't know what to do with it? It is like dirt when there's nothing to bury."

I didn't know what to say to her. What was there to say to this woman who knew all?

"I am very old. I am tired." She curled up in a corner of my hut and went to sleep.

Kamli never woke up again. Jamila said that was the way saints go. She was buried in a graveyard in the mountainside. I visited there the day after she was buried because burial is men's domain and women are not allowed to be part of the last rites of even dear ones.

Grief is mercurial. In the early days, it became heavy or vanished from my mind altogether for a few minutes, then hours and days. I would think, when Kamli returns, I will ask her. And then recall she wouldn't return, and grief would settle like a rock on my chest.

Grief has its own laws. It is a different language. It is a different planet.

*

I had been a prisoner for nearly twelve years. My oldest daughter was eleven, Scheherazade seven and Hamza six. The guard outside my house had been removed finally, a month after Kamli passed. They could all see what a blow her loss was for me. Gulraiz was convinced that with three children well past their infancy, I was comfortable and settled into a life with him there in those lonely mountains.

In these times, when I was neither myself nor become what I had desired, Gulraiz would sense my withdrawal and punish me for it. He broke my arm, with his hands this time without needing his staff. I had no tears left. Dry eyed, I crumpled into a heap. But it was the last time he bothered. He was disgusted by old age that appeared like silver on my head.

The harsh mountain weather and my tea tricks had aged my skin faster than was normal. I had allowed the cold to dry me into a husk. Laughing, Jamila stroked my grey hair one day and commented at how old I looked. "You must have loved that old Kamli. Her death has aged you."

It was true. With Kamli's death something had shifted in me. I didn't know what it was and so didn't dwell on it. Silence had become an inherent part of me. It ran deep in my veins like gold ore in the depths of earth and sea.

The children I had been allowed to keep slept in one corner of the room. With these two little ones in my care, I couldn't make foolhardy attempts to escape as I had in the past. Twelve years had passed and all I had done since their birth was to teach Hamza and Scheherazade languages and tricks. I had told tales, taught them to swim, and showed them how to hide in the various holes in the caves for hours. When they cried, I quietened them with a look. They understood the language of silence and learned to read a body frozen with fear. They became less and less like children.

My body changed and weakened. Bones I didn't know existed began to ache. The walks I could take in half an hour took me an hour. If I ate too late, I would stay up all night as my body struggled to digest the food.

The day came when Gulraiz lost complete interest in me. He came to my house one day and I could tell he was shocked to see me. My silver hair was a tangled mess, my skin dry, chapped and wrinkled, my eyes devoid of hope or emotion. He left without a word.

And in my heart the firebird settled, satisfied.

Without Gulraiz's sexual interest in me I was nothing to them. Nobody cared. I got no special nut and jaggery powders to strengthen me. I hadn't in years. Gulraiz had found another new wife, a sixteen-year-old from another tribe. I was shifted into a smaller house on the edge of the village and closer to the caves with which I had an affinity. After all, I had spent more time there than I had anywhere else.

Caves were the earliest home of human beings, and yet they never really belong to us. There is something inherently sacred about them, a timeless aura of the ancient that guards the wisdom of the Earth within them. I had nothing but gratitude for this neglect.

I knew by heart the stories in the big book Kamli had given me. One of them was a story by the great Sufi Master, Idries Shah. There was once a wise man who taught his disciples from a thick tome. The sage was the only one with access to the book, but everyone knew the book was a repository of wisdom. When the great sage passed away, his disciples rushed to open the book. They were confused to find all the pages in the book were blank. Except the first on which was inscribed: When you understand the difference between the container and the content, you will have knowledge.

A wise man, who understood the lesson, put it in a book and sold it for two gold pieces. Those who understood came back as disciples and those who didn't, wanted their money back. Who would pay two gold pieces for a book with only one page of writing? The wise man would say to them: "I will return your money if your return to me that which you have learned by this transaction. Because what you seek is seeking you. If you were seeking knowledge, it would have found you."

The thickness of a book does not determine its value. Just as the value of the dwelling is in the dweller, the value of a book is in the knowledge imparted, not its volume. It was a lesson worth learning. Hamza, who was seven, loved stories. I had written them down for him on the paper I had collected over the years as a talisman of my identity. I made the book for him by sewing together the pages with red and black silk threads. For the cover I used some pieces of leather I had got from Jamila years ago and sewed it over the papers with a red silk thread. I had drawn a few illustrations with pencil and ink. I wrote each story in a different language in small, neat letters. I would make the children read them one at a time, so they'd remember the magic of languages. I added Kamli's book to the one I had written for my children and bound it with theirs. I put the book away in the secret stash of the cave so that the children would have that to entertain them when we hid in the cave.

I missed Kamli and, in my grief, I avoided being alone. I often kept Jamila's company.

I sat with the women in the shade of the thatched veranda in Firdous's house.

"Firdous, when are the women coming to see our Nur?" Jamila said

My hand stilled at the sewing. Nur would be eleven now. I hardly saw her now even in the spring cave, sticking to Firdous's side like a sullen shadow.

"She has bled already. I have sent the invitation. They will come in a week or so and fix the marriage date."

My hand trembled. Tears burned in my eyes but the silence I had worn as a cloak enveloped me in a snug embrace, rendering me still.

"She is young," said Jamila.

"She is that. But she will be the first wife of the chief's son who is already sixteen. We are lucky to have such a good family accept her in marriage. She is known as my daughter and so no one thinks of her as an outsider."

"Yes, that is true," Jamila said, "Still, I would ask the mother-in-law to not allow consummation for another few years. I think you should try to convince her. It was difficult for me even though I was sixteen."

"I will," promised Firdous.

FOURTEEN

Once upon a long time ago, there was a fisherman who captured a woman. He had secretly seen her bathing in the river one night. She failed to escape his net and was caught.

"I have caught you to be my wife, to palliate my loneliness and my dark thoughts," The man said.

"No, please, let me go. I cannot."

The fisherman pulled out the sealskin he had hidden.

"How will you go without this?"

"No!" she cried. "Don't be cruel."

"Marry me and I will return this to you."

She was afraid for the first time in her life. "I will be your wife."

In time they had a child. She loved the child. She did not ask for her seal skin. In time her skin began to dry. It flaked and peeled. Her long lustrous hair began to fall and her plump tight skin became withered. Her eyesight darkened.

One night his mother's crying woke the child.

"Give me my skin that I am made of," she implored his father.

"You will leave me if I do," he boomed.

The next day the boy followed his father when as usual he climbed up the rocky mountain away from where they lived. He saw his father go into a cave and water something in there. When his father left, the child went inside and saw his mother's skin. He knew it was hers because it smelled like her, and purred at his touch.

The child took the skin to his mother. She hugged him and together they ran to the water. There she pulled her skin on, and they slipped into the water.

Would I be able slip away? Would my children?

I vowed not to doom Scheherazade to the same fate as her sister. I had forbidden her from speaking about what we did in the caves. Consequently, she hardly spoke at all. What else did I do but tell her stories about being invisible and being brave?

"Sherry," said Firdous. "What is your real name?"

She stared back at them solemnly and silently. They laughed at her and mocked me.

"This one takes after you. Silent as a snake," said Firdous.

Raising Nur and spoiling Hamza had given Firdous a new lease of life. In the end it was Firdous, his first wife, whose opinion really mattered to Gulraiz. His hair was silver at the temples now but he was still spry and energetic. Firdous was the only one from all of us who truly loved him.

Hamza was stuck between two worlds, mine and Gulraiz's. I tried to bring him back to me but the attractions of the world of men were too many and I had nothing but old tales to enchant him.

My plans had changed so many times. One more wouldn't hurt me and that was why I waited. I loved my son. He had been my hostage-child but he was my flesh and blood and I loved him. And because I did, I allowed him to play with Firdous and the others. He loved them all and they adored him. He was everyone's favourite. A precocious seven-year-old now who joked and sassed as their equal, and Firdous paid special attention to him. She made him his favourite dishes.

"Are you sure you are only seven, Hamza?" asked Jamila lovingly.

"No, I am seventeen," his childish wit and laughter made them laugh with him. "You are all my slaves," he would declare.

"Yes, we are," they would chorus.

Sometimes, I looked at my own children as if they were strangers. Even I had become a stranger to myself.

I requested a meeting with Gulraiz. "I wish to speak about Nur," I told him. "I heard Firdous and the others."

"What are you saying?"

"She is a child. You cannot—"

He got up, enraged, "Cannot? I cannot? I can and I will! I am her father. She will marry according to our customs."

I pleaded. I argued. Then I attacked. I went at him screaming and lunged at his face with my nails.

He pushed me away and warned, "Woman, you still have the two younger children to look after. Do you want to lose them too?"

He stormed off and I lay on the floor, unmoving. Scheherazade lay beside me with her little arms giving the comfort she could. Hamza wiped my tears, "When I am chief, I will not beat you."

Firdous was presented as Nur's mother when it was time to discuss her nuptials. Dressed in richly embroidered brand-new clothes she beamed when she came to see me. "Hamza should be by his father's side during his sister's betrothal."

Hamza was excited to be given such an important role. I didn't see my little boy for several weeks. Scheherazade and I continued with our excursions to the caves, our storytelling and our silences.

One day Hamza came to me unexpectedly. "Are you really my mother or is Firdous Moor, my mother?" he asked in Pushto.

My silence broke without conscious thought. The words that came out as a plea, a whine, "I am."

He was turning out to be the spitting image of his father. Sometimes, I hated looking at him. Did he sense my ambivalent feelings? Hamza stared at me for a long time and then Firdous called him away.

I woke up from an uneasy slumber with a start one night, the acrid taste of fear in my mouth. Hamza was sitting in his father's lap and whispering in his ear. I wiped clammy hands on the bedding.

Hamza was only a child. What if he let something slip?

FIFTEEN

The fourteenth year of my capture dawned, and my oldest daughter was twelve, soon to be thirteen. Firdous informed me Nur was to be married when she turned fourteen in a few months.

My face hid behind unfamiliar wrinkles. I was forty-eight but looked older in the small cracked mirror I barely looked into any more. My hair was already more salt than pepper. Scheherazade and I went to the caves in silence and we spent hours there, and walked back to the house only when I knew the alarm had gone off announcing our absence.

I often bathed alone or with Scheherazade, who wrote alphabets in the sand and learned them in whispers. I no longer cared what they learned. But they did out of habit or because they thought I cared. My body felt unfamiliar when I rubbed lye on it. When did it become so thin, my skin so full of wrinkles and scars? The elasticity of skin I had been used to, taken for granted as fact and biology, was beginning to fade. I put my hand between my legs, and the coarse sparse hair like the spiky grass out on the mountain. Unfamiliar.

I could not touch my skin too long. When I drew my hand away, my heart calmed. The layers of skin sagged and hung like veils of worn velvet, washed and used so often they become thin and fine. It wasn't just age that had made a stranger of my body and I thanked that invisible being I had called God all my life except in the last thirteen years. I had given up on Him, as He had given up on me. Now I prayed to the moon, the falcon, the wind.

The black, red and white colours of alchemy are connected to the menstrual and reproductive cycle of women. Black represents the sloughed lining of the empty uterus, red the blood retained in the uterus that tells of pregnancy, and white the mother's milk that flows to feed new life. Red is also the colour of sexuality and black of asexuality, white of virgins. Asexuality or abstinence is black, the colour of the Guide because it is the most difficult to embrace. I had gone through all those stages and emerged a stranger to myself.

I came out of the spring pool and dressed. Scheherazade came at me and hugged me. I pushed her away.

"No, dear. We don't do that."

"Why not?" her puzzled eyes smote me. I looked into her honey-dark pupils, so full of trust. She was almost a little replica of my Spanish grandmother. It was uncanny. Scheherazade was nine then. She was a quiet, thoughtful child. I had passed on as much knowledge as I could—stories, languages, numbers, life-skills, survival skills, pain, oppression, neglect. Even if I died, she would know to escape. I'd bequeathed her everything I had.

She knew how to lie, how to hide and become invisible, how to scrounge for food, how to watch others and learn their secrets and their weaknesses. She was only a child, and had learned as much as a child of that age could. I had faith she would save herself.

"Did you learn all the words?" I asked to distract her.

She nodded.

"Did you rub them all out?"

Everything had to be a secret so nothing escaped their lips.

She nodded.

"Good. Let's go into the cove and play our game again."

We play the game only ever in this cave, but the one I have chosen as my getaway, the children had not seen. Even the locals didn't know of it. I had excavated it myself, every day for the last twelve years, from a little cove into a hiding place. A hole collapsed into another cave. I dug at it, the soft earth between the rocks, just wide enough for a person to scrape through, until I reached another small tunnel that led to the open mouth of the cave on the other side. Every day, I would scrape and dig. The mouth was hidden by bushes and plants it was just a small rabbit-hole to prying eyes. But I knew better.

The hole was small, barely enough for one person but it had another passage further in. What seemed like a dead end, wasn't, and I twisted my meagre body and slid into the next hole. Two more paces, twist, and into another small hole, and then I fell out into the small cave, which led out into the mountains.

No one knew of this cave. I had watched its mouth surreptitiously many times on my daily walks. Nobody used it. I sat for hours on the stone far above it watching the falcons. The mouth was covered with bushes and shrubs. Undisturbed. The caves were like a different realm. Anything was possible there. Broken limbs healed; rapists did not enter. It was like stepping into a different time, not just space. These were the sacred caves of ancient goddesses. I was protected here. I trusted the caves.

Outside, in the mountains, the acoustics were different. Sound was lost, the breath quickened and became laboured. Inside the caves, even the tiniest sound was amplified, breathing was a conversation between you and the cave.

One day, I took Scheherazade and hid in one of the secret caves. All day we listened to the yelling and shouting of the men. Scheherazade lay in my arms, quiet as a mouse. I sat with her in my arms watching the mouth of the cave through the hole from which we had climbed in. When they left, we came out and returned home. Gulraiz found us there and laughed at his men and made jokes about their foolishness. One of them said I did that on purpose. I had done it before. But everyone laughed at him too.

Seven times I stayed inside the cave with Scheherazade. Hamza would be with Firdous or his father at those times. We stayed for two days once before the alarm went off. We ate raw onions, almonds, jaggery and drank water that dripped from the ceiling. I gathered it in my palms and made my Scheherazade drink. I recalled then what happiness felt like. It had a name. It was called freedom.

I did not try it again for many weeks.

Then finally Nur's wedding was in two days. My plan was to sneak out that night when everyone was busy with the festivities. There was no hurry. Nothing would stop me that night. I did even not speak to Scheherazade about it. Everything that happened to me so far had led to this point.

I had a way out. But would I take it? Did I have the courage or even the desire left? Sometimes, I did not know.

SIXTEEN

The other women and I were in Firdous's house, embroidering the last few things for Nur's trousseau early autumn morning. Her wedding would be that day and the bridal party would leave the next morning.

I had asked Hamza and Scheherazade to meet me at the spring cave in an hour. When the women had all divided their chores for the day, the food, the guests, and the preparations, they began to leave in twos and threes.

Firdous got up and said, "I am going to rest now. Make sure these clothes get to Meherbano in an hour."

I waited for half an hour and took the clothes to Meherbano. She didn't even look at me. I slipped away to the cave. No one had paid any attention. I went up to the children and put my finger on my lips. They nodded.

"Follow me at ten paces," I whispered. "Hold hands. Don't let go."

I walked towards the punishment cave keeping a wary eye. I caught a man watching. I sat down on a nearby rock, my heart in my mouth, looking around as if I were taking a walk, and resting for a breather. What if he noticed the children? I turned my head. Scheherazade was showing Hamza something. It appeared as if they were playing. I glanced at the man surreptitiously. He had moved away. No one was looking. I got up and quickly vanished behind the jutting corner of the hill. The cave was only a foot away. The children were soon there.

I took Scheherazade's clothes off and told her to get inside the hole. I did the same with Hamza. They were only in their knickers. I took my voluminous trousers and burqa off and bundled them separately. Tied them all together and pulled them in behind me along with my small book. I pushed Scheherazade in, urging her to twist and turn when required.

Hamza was smaller and fit easily into the hole. The dark was suffocating, and the walls of the caves were so cold they burned.

I pushed them on with my voice and hands. Inch by inch we pushed ourselves onwards. My shoulder stuck, and I flattened my elbow, scraping it. The pain did not even register.

Finally, we were inside the deeper smaller cave. My body had cuts and bruises. I helped my children with their clothes and tucked them into the blankets I had left there hidden, weeks before. I dressed Hamza in Scheherazade's clothes. He protested hotly. But I quieted him. They wouldn't look for a woman with two little girls. I put on my own clothes and then, in a daze, lay down beside them, hugging them tight. Was this really happening? Was it just another drill?

The afternoon sun streamed into the cave through the thick shrubs and leaves at its mouth. But it stopped a long way away from us. The warmth did not touch us. We stayed tucked inside the dark heart of the mountain. We waited for two hours for sundown and for the night to envelop the world. The shouting woke the children. I calmed their fears, hugging them and whispering tales. Scheherazade and Hamza ate the plums I had stored there earlier along with the blankets.

It was Nur's wedding day. My heart lurched and sank.

The voices were sometimes close, and at times very far. The panic and the voices did not cease. We waited quietly. Hamza was getting restless.

"Ama, will I not attend the wedding?"

"No," I said.

Early in the morning, I took my burqa and rolled it in the dust. Then tore it from the edges. I took the children's clothes and did the same. I took handfuls of dust and put it in their hair, their faces and hands and their feet. We would all go bare foot.

When the fireworks and the gunshots of celebration started, we stepped out into the dense noise and the dark night on the other side of the cave. The cold bit into my eyes and my toes.

"Are you okay, my little ones?" I asked.

"It is cold," said Hamza.

"Let us run a race." I made a funny face and Hamza looked at me as if to question that unfamiliar expression on his mother's face. But he was a child and happy to play.

We ran out into the cold. Bullets were fired into the air every few minutes and we cowered every time, hugging each other.

Hamza wanted to go back. "Please, Ama, I'm tired," complained my poor child.

"No," I kept saying firmly. "No."

Scheherazade quickly pointed at curiosities to engage him. We just kept going. We stayed in the shadows.

On the other side of the hill behind us, men danced with their guns in their hands. Every now and then one of them would shoot randomly in the air. There was a large log-fire in the middle, around which they danced. We hid in the copse of fir and pine trees nearby.

The groom's party would soon pass from here with the bride. And we would join the posse of beggars who followed the bridal party, in hope of money and food at the groom's house. We waited for a long time, sitting against a tree on the stone-cold ground. The night was dark and thick with cold and fog.

The children were huddled inside my burqa, one child on each side of me. When the guns were silenced, we fell asleep. It was nearly dawn when I woke them.

There was laughter and trumpets as the wedding party came towards us. This was the only path they could take. There were no familiar faces as they began to pass.

None of the girls" relatives would be there. But Gulraiz would have sent some men, surely?

"Join the beggars when they come this way and if anyone asks, tell them it is just the two of you," I told Hamza and Scheherazade, "I will join the party separately."

"Why Ama? I don't want to go alone, I am scared," said Hamza.

"It's okay, brother, I will look after you," said Scheherazade. "They are looking for a woman with two children. They will not notice us if we go separately."

Hamza began to cry. Two streaks appeared on his cheeks.

I looked around. The beggars were mostly men, but a few women and children as well.

"Go now," I whispered.

Holding hands, they left, their little feet red with the cold. I noticed a man at the edge of the group look at them suspiciously. Then he looked away. I slipped into the group.

"Mara, where did you come from?" asked a beggar woman.

"I was sleeping in the woods, among the trees," I said.

She laughed salaciously, "Had a good night?"

I tittered and pinched her arm. She was also wearing a tattered burqa. But two of the women were not. They were probably dancers for the wedding. Could I ask them for help?

"Who are these women?" I whispered.

The woman's voice changed, "They are the mistresses of the Chief. They dance and do whatever he asks."

My hopes died.

The children kept looking back at me.

"Look at these poor children. Why don't we both get closer to them?"

"Hmm. Clever. We can sell them later when we reach the city."

My heart dipped.

"Hello kiddies, come with us," she said.

They quickly came. Hamza tried to hold my hand. I bent down and whispered, "Don't hold her hand or mine. She is a witch. Be careful."

They held each other's hands and did not speak to the woman at all. I smiled. This was going to work. We had been walking for hours it seemed. Our fear and adrenaline kept us energized because we barely stopped for a minute.

"I do not wish to go into the village," I said to the beggar woman when the wedding party turned towards their village. "Let us take the children and go where we can sell them for profit."

"You are right. That will surely pay better than a tired wedding party."

I whispered to the children to stay close and we began to edge away from the wedding party.

"Hey you," said a man. "Where are you going?"

It was Gulraiz's man.

"You talk. Tell him I am your daughter and these are your grandchildren."

"Why?"

"Please. Just do it. I'll pay you."

I showed her my diamond studs through a small tear in the burqa. Her eyes widened and she nodded.

The woman laughed and repeated what I had said, adding, "Why? Are you asking because you like me? You want to marry me?"

The man laughed and waved us away.

"We cannot stop," I told her. "Hurry."

"Why?" she asked.

"I will tell you when we reach a safe place."

"I have a small place close by. Come there."

I nodded.

"I am so tired, Ama," said Hamza in a small voice.

"Just a little more, my precious, just a little more," I coaxed.

"Did he call you Ama?" she asked suspiciously.

"I think they must call everyone that, don't you?"

She nodded. "Poor kiddies."

We staggered on for the longest time on the dirt roads. By mid-morning we were nearing a small village. I was double minded about going there. What if they knew about us? What if Gulraiz had sent word ahead? What if we were recaptured?

But we did not go into the village.

I was afraid of the woman, but I had come too far to give in to doubt and fear. We walked towards what looked like an unused old train depot. Several train carriages stood silent and rusty on the dead tracks. Morning was upon us and in the cold winter morning, the place looked eerie and haunted. I spied a rusty old carriage that looked as if it was inhabited.

The woman walked towards it and opened the sliding door. The clang was too loud to my ears. I looked around furtively. Had anyone heard? Had anyone followed?

There was no movement, not a sound.

"Come on in," she said.

We climbed inside and she closed the door behind us. It was almost completely empty, except for old blankets, woollen knits and old quilts, and it was warm. The woman took her burqa off. She was old and frail, but looked bright-eyed.

"I am so tired. I want to sleep. Why don't you two sleep here?" she said to the children, pointing to a corner which had a blanket. I settled the children and tried to make them as comfortable as I could.

She sat down on the charpoy, and patted the place next to her. "Come sit here. Tell me your story. Take off your burqa then."

Reluctantly, I did.

Her eyes widened. "Who are you?" she asked.

I took off my diamond earrings.

"I will give you these for three train tickets to Kabul."

She nodded. "They are yours?" she pointed at the kids.

My gaze found some old bread and my eyes pleaded with her. She handed me a box of dry fruit that I accepted gratefully. My little ones were hungry and took as many as they could in their little hands.

"I was a prostitute. I used to help women with abortion. The men of the village caught wind of it and banished me. I have lived here ever since. Nobody bothers me. I don't exist for them because they think their women are safe from me. But women are like water, they always find a way." She cackled.

Even though my secret cave had helped us escape more quickly than we might have, we had the advantage of only a few hours.

"Please we really need to hurry."

Her eyes bored into mine for a few seconds. "A few years ago, a gori and two goras disappeared in the hills. The two men were found beheaded two days later near the edge of the river on the north-east. The woman was never found."

I had wondered about Shawn and Cyril in the early days until the battle with Gulraiz began to consume me so completely. Knowing Gulraiz as I did now, it came as no surprise. Human life was expendable to a tribal chief. Obedience and loyalty were what mattered. Instant justice in the feudal way with a head separated from the body with a sharp knife was not cause for comment.

"The military looked for her. When they found the bodies of the men they gave up. They will keep you safe now."

She took the earrings and got up. "I will be back soon."

She left us in the small space. Scheherazade and Hamza had fallen asleep thankfully. The poor mites. I was too worried to sleep. I kept looking out for her through the gaps in the planks of her walls.

It was afternoon then.

I heard women talking. A raised voice. Firdous. My heart sank and I had to swallow a gag. I scrambled towards my children.

"You stay here. Do not move or speak of this to anyone? Do you understand?" Firdous sounded as bossy as she always did.

A man said, "Yes, Ama."

The door opened and the old, dishevelled beggar entered the abandoned trailer with Firdous.

SEVENTEEN

"Well, well," Firdous looked her over with an enigmatic smile. "You really are cleverer than I gave you credit for."

She opened her arms and Hamza ran to her.

"She found me at the shop." The beggar woman eyed me apologetically, "She was already there."

"I came just behind the wedding party. I know this area very well. This used to be my home, my village. I thought you would ask for help from there. Then I remembered your earrings. That was the only thing of value you had. I waited at the goldsmith's. Where else would you go? He is the only one here for miles."

The beggar woman said, "I bought some tea and cakes. The children must be hungry."

Firdous said to Hamza, "Is my son hungry?"

He nodded. She fed him. Scheherazade crept near me. I took the cake and tea offered and gave it to her. She ate hungrily. My eyes were on Firdous and Hamza.

"I don't blame you for running away. You have been here what thirteen years? You still don't consider this home. You never will. I know you will keep trying to escape till you die."

She smiled at Hamza and gave him another piece of cake.

"You must trust me." She said in a maternal tone, "If you want to run, I will help you."

"Why?" When had she ever been a friend?

"Because I want something from you too. I want you to run away. I want you to make your life. But I want something in return. I will help you but only one condition. You will leave Hamza here."

Hamza stopped eating and looked at me, his eyes wary, waiting.

"The authorities have been informed," The beggar said. "They will be here soon."

Firdous shrugged, "Make up your mind quickly. I too have sent someone who will bring Gulraiz here."

My chest began to heave, I couldn't breathe. My mouth opened to gasp air. Leave my son?

"You want Hamza?" I croaked.

"Yes. I want him. Nur has left, she is married. Now I'll have Hamza. You can keep your precious daughter. I never liked her. She is too much like you. And she looks like no one we know. We call her the devil child." She laughed. Scheherazade crept closer to me. I put my arm around her.

"Why?" Was there no end to what this woman wanted to take away from me? "Haven't you done enough?" Tears pricked my eyes. I never wanted to cry again. Even Firdous's eyes widened for a moment.

She waved a hand. "I am not an evil witch. I am merely offering help. I will take the boy anyway, whether you agree or not. Like this at least you get your freedom."

Gatekeepers in folktales always test the hero. They ask for something precious to see if the hero is worthy. If the hero gives away what is precious, they pass. Firdous, however, was no gatekeeper. She was just a sad old woman who had tasted happiness again with borrowed children. Mine.

"That's the deal. Take it or leave it. The boy stays here. You and your daughter could have the life you want." She was becoming impatient. "Why are you even thinking so much?"

Did she think it would be so easy for me to make such a heart-wrenching decision? Did she think I was heartless? As I stared at in shock, her expression gave her away. She did not think of me as human. My emotional attachments in her perception, were not the same as hers, therefore not equal.

"You don't need him. You will have more children if you are lucky. You think I don't know why you have been so neglectful of yourself? I don't care if you live or die. You die here, I will still take the children. Both of them. But Hamza is more mine than yours."

"Please Firdous. Have I not suffered enough at the hands of your husband?"

"Yours too."

"Only because you helped him become so."

The nightmare was unending. Why was I in this position again? Had I not planned and waited for years? Had I not followed the patterns and the signs?

"This time Gulraiz will not forgive you. He will starve you to death."

Yes. He would.

This was my last chance. I would not get another. Even if she sent men after me to kill me, I was willing to take the chance. I had been living a lie, a shadowy existence. No, I had not lived. Nur was a stranger. Hamza would be too.

Hamza watched me with an unblinking stare. His eyes pierced my soul.

It wasn't enough to stop me from making my pact with the devil. I nodded. "Alright."

Hamza screamed. He launched himself at me with his little fists. "I hate you. I hate you. Firdous Moor said you didn't love me! I did everything. You said you loved me! You are a liar!"

Firdous quickly came and took him in her arms away from me.

"Hamza, I do," I said. "I love you."

"Liar! Everything you said was a lie!" His sobs lanced my heart.

Firdous' was a victor's smile. She nodded at the beggar woman who came forward. Firdous gave her a bundle of money.

Scheherazade began to cry.

"Let's go home, Hamza," Firdous soothed his back as she turned towards the exit.

Hamza did not look at me again. Scheherazade tried to hug him but he pushed her away. "You don't love me," his childish voice had become low and dull.

"Let me hug him please." That wailing voice sounded alien to my ears.

"I love you." I whispered in Persian,

Hamza had already stopped crying. "Let us go, Firdous Moor," he didn't look back.

Scheherazade wiped the tears from my face. My body trembled as I clutched her to me, and soaked her little neck with my tears.

The beggar looked at me with pity. "At least you have your daughter," she said kindly,

I had been training Scheherazade and Hamza to escape all their lives. It had all been for nothing. My victory was like ashes in my mouth.

EIGHTEEN

"The authorities are on their way," the beggar said. She said authorities as if they were God. She meant the army. "The captain will take you to the station. He does not say so but I know he is military. He is not from here. You must go soon. Yes, soon."

"Thank you for helping us." My voice was dull. The little warm hand in mine was trying to soothe me. I tried to smile encouragingly at my daughter. She put her head in my lap.

The woman waved a hand. "I will go now and get the help we need. Don't worry. You will leave this place."

I combed my fingers through my daughter's dust filled hair.

The woman soon returned with a man who did indeed look like a military man.

"Madam, let's go. I will take you to your embassy."

I looked at him fearfully. Would this be another betrayal? I gathered my daughter close.

"I have got the tickets. We should go." He looked towards the door as if expecting someone to rush in, as if he'd have a battle on his hands before his mission was accomplished. "We don't want to attract trouble."

"Go now," said the woman.

Scheherazade held my hand. She was still and quiet just as I had taught her to be all these years. I was still in my burqa. We walked on the dusty narrow road across the village at the foot of the hills.

"How far?" I looked back to see how much we had covered since we left the trailer. And how far had Hamza gone with Firdous?

"You're safe now."

He was confident and should have been reassuring. But I could not believe it yet.

EIGHTEEN

That evening Scheherazade and I took the train to Kabul. On the platform, before we boarded, we mingled with the crowd. I pretended to be with the large groups of families. Wherever I found one I walked with one, or sat with one. The train journey was long. It took nearly two days to reach the city. No one had followed us. I would look over my shoulder constantly and at those around me. I found no sign of any familiar face that I had known for thirteen years. I searched the crowds at every station, every stop.

We were finally in a taxi to the American embassy. The military man with us spoke to the officials at the embassy. They got someone on the phone. When he handed the phone to me, I didn't know what to say. It was hard to say my name. I no longer identified as that woman. I said that unfamiliar name. I told them of my abduction years ago and of my imprisonment, I told them I had no money, no clothes.

The gates opened. Two Americans came towards me alert and suspicious. They took me inside. I told them my story again and then repeated it someone else. I told them about Shawn and Cyril who had been killed. I told them I needed to go home. I wanted to go home.

The details are hazy now. I was hospitalized for a few days but wouldn't let go of Scheherazade or she of me. We huddled together everywhere. We got new clothes and passports. We would fly home in a week they said, as soon as I was cleared by the doctors.

Those thirteen years had changed me. I could feel the warping, the breakage, the havoc, the chaos and it was all dark and rank. But as those behemoth mountains had grown smaller, as my legs carried me farther away, I began to feel, I could almost hear the chains breaking, the walls that had caged me came crashing down and set me free.

The woof and weft of my very being had been shredded and rewoven. All the old patterns had become alien, and I would have to unravel, reweave, and spin anew all the threads and patterns of the fabric of my being.

But my story wasn't done. I told them about the other children I had left behind. I hoped they would be rescued soon.

We flew to the U.S ten days later. A special agent took us on a plane and brought us to a house where we would feel safe. I knew the procedure. They wanted to make sure I hadn't been radicalized. The safe-house was just a nicer prison. They wanted to send me back as a spy. To put my daughter in a special school. I knew what that meant. They would train her to be a spy too.

I refused.

"Would you say you were a prime candidate for the psyche ward? Your child will go into the system. Is that what you want?"

Some journeys, some stories are circular and circles have no beginning and no end. They are unending for everyone except Trickster. All storytellers are not tricksters, but all tricksters are storytellers. Those who seek to entrap Trickster and bind her, thinking she is alone, will fail. Because Trickster is no longer alone.

"You will cooperate with us?"

Trickster relies on her prey to help her spring the traps she makes. I had to save my daughter. No matter what.

I nodded. Did I have a choice? Had I not exchanged one trap for another? One prison for another?

BOOK THREE

The End of the Beginning

ONE

Mira's voice faded into silence and Layla became aware of her surroundings once again. Her phone screen showed two missed calls from Khayyam. A text message from Reza. She had put her phone on vibration mode and heard nothing. She'd been held in thrall, captivated by the master storyteller. She turned her gaze away from Mira, blinking, as if awakening from a dream.

"I remember now. Some of it." She finally said.

She struggled to reconcile what she had heard with what she remembered.

"You've only given a partial account. I don't remember you loving us. Ever. I remember your pain, your urgency that I swim, learn the stories, and stay quiet. Do you know that I suffer from claustrophobia now?"

The strange grief that had so smote her earlier seemed to have dissipated when the story ended. Was that part of the magic of the storyteller? Layla felt nothing but exhaustion.

She said, "You have told your own story as a storyteller, but you've told a portion of the tale. You mention your children in passing, casually, as if we didn't matter. You've actually just told me the tale of what is most important to you—storytelling. You were never really a mother. And I had to find you for closure, to know why, after all that we went through, you abandoned me."

Abandonment was violence. She was reminded of Rustam and Sohrab's famous story. Sohrab's rage at the forced separation from his father became a cold dark winter in his heart. Enraged at his mother for having hidden his father Rustam's identity from him, Sohrab went looking for Rustam. And on his way, entered into battle with a warrior whose name he did not bother to ask. When the warrior mortally wounded him and Sohrab lay dying, each warrior admiring the other's honor and skill, Sohrab told his secret to Rustam. Tell my father the famed Rustam, of me, he gasped before death seized him. Rustam spent the rest of his days a mere shadow of his former self, having killed his own son.

She did not see a shadow of a self when she looked at Mira, but a fulfilled woman who had spent years doing what she loved. Layla's heart constricted. *She had wasted her life looking for a mother who'd never even wanted her.* She'd thrown her happiness away looking for someone who had not wanted to be found.

"I am sorry," Mira opened her palms in a gesture of surrender. "I have told my story. Your version of it will likely be different from mine. My children are part of me and my legacy. Even in the telling I could not separate them from me."

"But in life you did." They stood before each other now, as Primordial maiden and Primordial Mother. "Do you know how many times I wondered why? I would think that someone had found you. Abducted you. Killed you. Then I would think, no that would be terrible after all our suffering. I remembered the fear. I remembered that place and the constant dread and the snatches of a looming figure of a man. I didn't know his name, his face, but I knew the danger we were in. I have been running all my life away from that unnamed fear and danger and towards you.

But thinking you had willingly abandoned me was even worse. So, I fought that version of my story. I thought if I found you, I would be able to rewrite our story. A better version of it. A redemptive version. I never stopped looking for you. For twenty-three years I looked for you."

She hated her plangent tones. She hated that her eyes were full again with unshed tears. She hated what she had been reduced to in the last few hours.

Mira came forward a step.

"My life has been the poorer for the choice I made. You think it was an easy choice for me? That I did not suffer by cutting myself off from you?"

But Layla had not witnessed Mira's suffering, unlike Badura the half-human daughter of the Queen of Djinn, who felt her mother's sorrow seeping into the human world for all to see and to bear witness, as in the cold barrenness of winter, when even roots withered and died. The love of Badura's mother was exposed to the human world when she unveiled herself as the Queen of the invisible Djinn. It was left to Badura to save both worlds, human and Djinn, as well as her mother—from her own rage and grief. Badura, who had inherited both worlds—her father's human world, in the shape of a handsome Prince who would wed her, and her mother's world, as the heir to the Djinn world. The Djinn accepted her as Queen only after many trials. Nothing is ever easy when one belongs to multiple worlds. One has to prove oneself time and again.

Unlike Badura, Layla had no proof of Mira's pain, except her own admission. And she did not trust Mira or her propitiations.

"Did you though?" she asked. "You think I can be fooled with this story you've told me with all its gaps and ellipses?"

It felt as if they were in a parallel universe, where only she and her mother existed, their speech the only language and their wounds, the only bright pain in the world. The sounds of the police station had dimmed to nothing.

"No, not at all." Mira put a trembling hand on her heart. "It is because I know you cannot be fooled that I told you this version of the story. Story is dynamic. It is a way of being and living. It is the sacred ground where plurality of all kinds, even of selves, co-exists. It is the site where language soars, transmogrifies, transmutes into experience and action, and becomes an event. And this event of us uniting is also a moment of truth."

She leaned forward, her body taut as she tried to make her daughter understand, "I told my story with hope of forgiveness, but I do not expect it. You think of me only as Mother. I have just recounted my journey from Persephone, the maiden, the story of my rape and brutalization, humiliation and loneliness, all that I endured, and then became mother, like Demeter. And now, who am I to you but a hateful Hecate, an old barren woman with nothing but wisdom of age, with my solitude and strength? My threefold transformation, my cycle of Maiden,

Mother, Crone is complete for me but not you…you see me from the outside. You know nothing of my life or what it means to me from my inner landscape. How can you fully comprehend the suffering, the experience of all that agony that shredded my soul to smithereens? You had a different cross to bear."

"It is not my story…even though it is the same story," Layla said. "How can I see it as you do? How can you expect me to? All I see is betrayal."

The concatenation of their stories was awry. They did not fit.

Detective Lance paced outside. She could see him through the opaque glass on the door. Then he called someone by name. She didn't hear. Perhaps he made a phone-call. No one interrupted them. She so wished they would.

"Wait…You said something about the CIA?" she asked, suddenly alert, the overwhelming pain receded for a moment.

"I had to do as they asked. I had to let go of you to protect you."

"So, you worked for the CIA?"

Mira nodded.

"Still do?" Layla asked.

"No, not anymore," said Mira. 'What does it matter? What matters where I went? How many countries, and how many cities? I was not there for you. I had to abandon you. You are right to be angry."

The pain in her chest was back. "Surely you could have contacted me before this? Why did you wait so long?"

"It all seems so foolish now," Mira whispered, "I saw someone. I recognized his face. I may have been wrong…but soon after we escaped the CIA, I saw one of Gulraiz's men. That's when I went back to the CIA. I was scared. I thought the only way to protect you was to align myself with them. I told them I would serve them but only if they left my daughter alone. I did not want them grooming you to be a tool. Endangering you by making you go back if I didn't hide you from them. I did what I had to do. The only way to save you was to give you up. It seemed to me that Gulraiz was after us. I believed it was them. I don't know any more. I think…I am quite certain, I was wrong."

"So that's why," Layla nodded slowly and the tight constriction, the taut tension that was so much a part of her being seeped away finally leaving her almost light-headed. "You never wanted to return. Admit it."

Mira looked away. Layla waited, tense. She knew though. She knew what Mira would say.

Then Mira looked back at her and nodded. "Yes. I owe you honesty. I was free of my past and my trauma. I thought I saved you. But it was for me too. I finally lived for myself once I was too old to serve the CIA. But I was never really free. And I was never safe. Never felt it. Giving you up was a sacrifice but once it was done...I could not find the way back to you. Perhaps because I did not want to. I failed you as a mother."

Layla's heart, already a ruin, couldn't take much more of the demolition her mother was accomplishing so diligently. She wanted her to stop talking but didn't have the energy to say it. She had not wanted her at all.

They stared at each other, both haunted with pain, loss and grief: two women, dealing with the loss of each other, and the lives they could have lived.

Layla had survived the three stages of childhood—imprisonment, freedom, and abandonment—with the help of stories. Stories were like water. They filled the emptiness of anything. And she, a broken child at the time, abandoned and betrayed, had rebuilt herself from all the broken shards of life into something stronger, layered with stories, bolstered with rage and fear, and strengthened by deep knowledge. She had been honed and sharpened and now with her dark edges and smooth stone planes, she was someone not easily broken, nor easily moved.

"Layla," Mira said tentatively. "I know this is too much. We can solve our own issues later. If we don't work together there will be more murders. Lives are at stake. We can stop this. Together."

Was she serious? Layla blinked. She'd just confessed she was her mother who had willingly abandoned her after a life of trauma, and then she just asked for help solving murders?

"What is wrong with you?" Layla's voice sounded strangled even to her own ears.

Mira sighed. "I am sorry. I admit I should've handled it better. I was taken by surprise...I didn't think I'd have to do this so soon and like this, although I know this talk is long overdue. Circumstances have forced my hand."

Layla suppressed the urge to say mean, childish things to hurt Mira. But she was an adult. She had become one far sooner than was fair or normal. Having a mother suddenly should not reduce her to tumultuous childishness.

Mira could have come for her, but she hadn't. Somewhere in Layla's heart were the irritating realizations; hadn't she, Layla, also been afraid someone would come to kidnap her? Kill her? Had she not also been hiding in big cities, always cautious? The fear was real. She had been only a child, but Mira had faced it as an adult. Was it any wonder then that was how she had lived and come to terms with the haunting fear?

"Alright. Let's put our personal issues aside for now. How do you think we will be able to solve the murders?" she asked. "I am a professor of cultural and oral history of women. I know nothing about crime. You are a storyteller. What are you going to do? Tell them stories?" She bit her lip. That last was childish.

"The murderer has given us the clue," Was that relief in Mira's voice? Was she grateful for the clue the murderer had provided? "Stories. The answer is in the stories."

"Which stories?" Layla was agitated and trying to be reasonable, trying to be the adult, desperate to stop sliding back to the angry, abandoned nine-year-old.

"I have identified one already, haven't I? But we must see which story fits the other, the previous murder."

"There is no indication they are linked, except for my presence."

"True. And the note says Mira has the answers. All my answers come from stories. In fact, I often say in my talks that stories have many secret messages if you're ready to receive them. Plural. The note said the answer is stories. Your presence at both sites of murder is the other clue that they are linked.

We must look into the previous murder. I have requested the file from Detective Lance."

Layla said, "I am surprised you actually succeeded in solving those murders before. But since you have, you should be able to handle this by yourself. This is all too much for me."

Layla picked up her leather tote, ready to go.

"I think you do understand why I need you," said Mira. "You and I are not that different, Layla. But you want to avoid understanding the uncomfortable truths that are staring you in the face."

Layla swung around to face her, "I already did!" Her hands fisted at her sides, "My whole fucking life has been about uncomfortable truths! I'm not a hero. And my life is far from a fairytale. I'm only concerned with my life. Real, hardcore, fucked-up life. Heroes are lonely and sad, and I don't want to end up alone. This whole myth of the hero sucks!"

Mira nodded, "Yes, I know. I understand. You think going through a tough life makes us heroes? No, Layla. That is not what makes us heroes at all. Misery is only a catalyst. Our choice is the difference."

"Well, I guess, I do not choose," Layla's voice hitched on the last word.

"Liar." Mira smiled tenderly.

Layla clenched her teeth.

Mira's smile was wobbly now "You wanted to be a hero even when you were five years old. You never complained. Not once. I would put you in the spring pool and you would swim like a little tadpole not making a sound, just slipping away till you reached the other end. You could swim like a fish by the time you were five. By then you could rattle off stories. I told you the tales of Scheherazade. You loved the tales of Aladdin and Ali Baba the best. You disliked your name because you said—"

"The woman was not a hero because she remained imprisoned."

"Yes," Mira said with a small smile. "Sometimes, that is the only way. She was a Trickster, that Scheherazade. She changed everything and yet nothing, ostensibly."

"Maybe." Layla's voice was choked "But she bore his children and she gave away her body, her very essence. For what? Who did she save?"

Mira stepped around the chair and came closer to Layla, the air between them throbbed with emotions long suppressed "Her son became the next Sultan. Her daughters were strong women with voices and stories of their own."

"You sound defensive." Layla felt her lips curl. Her heart felt cold.

Mira nodded with resignation, "We will have many opportunities to talk and to discuss Scheherazade. And we will have many opportunities to discuss your grievances further. Right now, we must solve the murders and prevent others from happening."

"You just walk back into my life as if the last twenty-three years didn't happen." Her voice broke. She turned away to hide the hot tears. She sniffed and bit her trembling lower lip, trying to still the feral child fighting to surface in her mother's presence.

"No. I walk back into your life, knowing that you cannot know my story until I tell you. Memory is never truthful. What you may or may not remember is your meagre understanding of my story. You were so little then. How could you possibly have understood the full implications of what was happening around you?"

Layla wanted to say something, to rage and yell but she was exhausted. She just sat there.

Detective James Lance burst into the room.

He locked eyes with Mira.

"There's been another murder."

TWO

Detective Lance turned to Layla and said, "The body was found in your apartment."

"Oh my God." Layla sat down in a chair with a thud, as if her legs had given way. What was happening? *Why* was it happening!

"My apartment?" she asked.

Then she remembered Sultan.

"Oh my God! My cat? I left it at home. I have to go."

She got up flustered.

"Wait. I'll see to it. Your place has been sealed off. It'll be some time before you can return."

He left to speak to another officer who nodded and left. "If he was there someone will know and bring him here."

Layla nodded.

"Who is the victim?" asked Mira.

"Probably a woman who was reported missing a few days ago. Just like the last one."

"So this victim was also carried into the building, like the last one?'"

James Lance shrugged, "We don't know yet but seems likely. The door was left ajar. A passing neighbour saw someone on the floor and called nine-one-one."

Layla was too stunned to say anything.

"It's quite clear whoever is behind this wants to implicate you. Who'd you piss off, Professor?" Lance was unsmiling.

"This isn't funny, James," said Mira.

"Hardly." Detective Lance cleared his throat. "A third murder tied so specifically to you. It doesn't look good. You are not a suspect of course but obviously you are a person of interest."

"She has alibis for all three murders and there is no motive. But with serial killers there usually isn't, except that they are sociopaths," Mira voiced what they all knew. "She's been with us for hours now."

When he didn't respond immediately, she glanced at the building. "I'm sure the cameras will have captured us parked here or someone inside the station will have noticed us drinking coffee."

"I know that, Mira. I am looking to you for help on this. It is all weird shit."

"I don't understand." Layla felt the fear rise in her throat like smoke. "Why do I get the feeling this murderer doesn't really want to pin the murders on me?"

"Either he is an amateur, or this was a scare tactic. But you're right. When we looked closely you had alibis for the first two and now again, you've been here in clear sight. I will verify that, as will Mira. We know he isn't an amateur. He hid his identity very well with the first murder. Apparently, there was a boyfriend, only no-one had ever seen him. No pictures, no texts, no fingerprints. The only way we know there was one is because the victim told her friend about him. She said he was smart. He was charming. He didn't want to meet her friends because he was a genius and everyone else was too common."

"Sounds like a gem of a person," said Layla. "If the idea is not to pin the murders on me then…what's he doing? If he is so smart, and he is so careful, what is happening here?"

"We need to find that out," said Lance.

"This doesn't make any sense. I was so careful." said Mira. Layla got the feeling Mira was fraying at the edges.

"I have lived a simple and rather careful life. I don't understand either. This is so bizarre."

Mira touched Layla's arm gently, "Some stories…lives, are written by vindictive gods."

"You are right. Mine…ours certainly is written as a tragedy."

Mira added, "Or as Mullah Nasruddin says, hardship is the training ground for us to become our best selves."

Layla nodded and turned towards Lance.

"What should I do? I don't even know what to say."

"We don't know ourselves as well as we think we do, Layla," said Detective Lance.

"No," cried Layla. "I do. I am the only one I know well. I've only had myself ever or my books that have been my companions and my bread and butter. Why would anyone frame me for murder? Three murders? And murders that are about stories?"

"What's that?" asked Detective Lance, eyes darting from Layla to Mira.

Mira nodded, "I'm not sure yet, James, but it seems to me these women are dressed up and positioned to look like fairytale characters."

"Dressed up? They were both almost naked. And I haven't seen this new one yet but I'm quite certain that'll follow the pattern."

"You are right, when I said dressed up, I meant, posed, about how they were found. I did not say I was certain, just…almost certain. The nudity is part of an imposed pattern which we will get to in time. But the ash on the body, the red cloak, all point to stories."

"And the note?" asked Detective Lance.

"That's the heart of the matter," said Mira.

"The note mentioned Mira specifically," Layla pointed out in an attempt to drive home the point, "Yet, the trail of bodies has reached my house. Why?"

Layla herself answered her own question after a moment. "Another imposed pattern, perhaps. But the truth is my name is also associated with stories. Not at the same level as Mira's, but all of my training and formal education have been about stories. Someone knows me very well."

"Who? What do you mean?" Detective Lance was watching Mira.

"The attempt, I think is to link Layla and me or to attach us together through the murders." Mira spoke slowly and thoughtfully as she worked through the possible motives. She took a half-turn and put her shoulders back as if coming to a decision. "Layla is my daughter, James."

Before he could react, she said quickly, "It's a long story."

A kaleidoscope of stunned and disbelieving expressions crossed his face.

"I promise I'll tell you, but not right now, hmm?" Fear was stamped on Mira's face, distorting her beautiful features. "My intuition is warning me that my daughter is in danger. The murderer is taunting us and believes he will get away with this.

I fear she may be next on his list."

THREE

Her life had never been normal, but she had never in her wildest imagination thought that she would be framed for murder. Let alone three.

Three was magic for a reason. Three was the sides of a triangle. Three twice over was a pentangle, and was often used in witchcraft. Three was considered lucky by some and unlucky by others.

Three held importance even in science: time, space, causality.

In psychology: Id, ego, superego.

In folktales: heart, mind and body.

In fairytales: three wishes, three little pigs, three bears.

Threefold repetition in religion had the power of invocation.

In paganism, three goddesses: Maiden, Mother, Crone. In Christianity, the Father, the Son and the Holy Ghost made the Holy Trinity.

The power of three reigned supreme in religion, cultures, despite the passage of centuries. Action done threefold bound the seeker with power.

They were sitting in Mira's flat with Detective Lance. Sultan was missing. Nobody had seen him. They said he would be returned if he appeared near Layla's apartment. Layla had made a quick call to Khayyam and updated him. It had been difficult to resist his offers of coming to her but she had resisted. She needed to still unpack everything that happened so quickly over the last twelve hours. Mira had confessed to being her mother. The new murder. It was all too much. He said he would meet her tomorrow. As soon as she wanted. Her treacherous little heart was still able to feel joy at that.

She sat now with Mira and Detective Lance, coffees in hand, tossing theories about motives. Layla eyed the space where Mira lived. It was sparse but overtly feminine. Florals and pastels abounded. Books on pretty shelves, exotic scented candles perfumed the room and rich luxurious materials upholstered the place. Green brocade, plush purple velvet and red silk. Mira hid behind colour and luxury because she no longer found it necessary. Mira's life had been stripped to the bare bones. She'd learned to survive with nothing. Now, she surrounded herself with luxury to erase the memories of stark caves, rough mats and stone floors. This was a veneer. It reeked of inauthenticity.

Detective Lance and Mira had been to see the crime scene… her apartment, which was now out of bounds for her. She had called the Dean and shared her predicament. Dean Rossi's response was sympathetic, and she promised to arrange an apartment or a suitable room for her at the university. But Layla heard the twinge of discomfort in the Dean's voice which had made alarm bells go off. What if she lost her job?

Layla drew her attention back to what Mira's was saying, "You know, women like you and I are taking our stories back. That makes us dangerous."

Layla was confused and tired, "What are you saying? Someone wants to kill me because I tell stories?"

"Perhaps. Women are learning the sounds of their own voices because our voices have been interpolated into patriarchal constructs falsely and for misdirection. Some people find women and their speech unimportant or too much to bear. And now that's changing. All three were strangled. That's significant."

"Three murders already. Two within a month. This killer means business and I don't want to see what else he or she's got planned," said Detective Lance picking up his phone. He got up and wandered away, talking into the phone.

"Yes. But if this killer is following story rules, he should stop at three murders. In fairytales, such things go in threes. You are as well versed in the lore as I am, Layla, what is your opinion?"

Never in her wildest imagination could Layla have thought that she would find her mother and be framed for murder all in a day.

"Or sevens. Three is the commonest magic number but seven comes close," said Layla.

Detective Lance came back and sat down, looking disturbed. He turned towards Layla, "The new murder...the girl in your apartment has been identified. She isn't a missing person. It's someone you know."

Her heart sank. "I thought she had already been identified. You said she was a missing woman."

"I thought she was, because the first two were also women who'd been reported missing earlier. I assumed, with the pattern going as it was...but she'd been identified as one of your students. Gul Inayat Khan."

"No!" Layla sprang to her feet, her head in her hands. "No. Not Gul!"

Mira got up to comfort her.

"I'm sorry. I am so sorry."

"This, changes things," Detective James said. "You knew her. The victim is your student. He brought her to your apartment. He is obsessed with you."

"He is changing the pattern," whispered Layla. Her hands still cradling her head, as if it would explode otherwise. She sank into the chair. "He knows me. He knows who I am. You are right," she said looking at Mira, "I am next. He is going to go for seven."

Mira bent her head, looking thoughtful. "Then you won't be next. You'll be the last."

Layla nodded. "Yes. And people close to me aren't safe. Poor Gul! I cannot believe...Gul. Oh my God. Ma. I...I need to call Ma."

They called people Layla thought she should warn. Only the ones Detective Lance approved. Ma and Munia. She wasn't close to many people, thank God. Only women were being targeted and she had already talked to Khayyam.

Detective Lance let out a sigh and got up. "He has not gone out of this vicinity so I don't really think your Ma and her friend are in any real danger.so I wouldn't worry so much, if I were you. I'll be off then. Let me know if you think of anything. I'm sorry, Layla. You need to be very careful now. I'll call you for your statement tomorrow."

Layla rose too, "I think I should be going too."

"It's late," said Mira. "Please stay here for the night, Layla. Tomorrow you can go and find a room. You won't find one at this time in such a small town."

Lance nodded, "She's right. Stay here. You've had a shock."

Layla took a moment to think and then nodded her assent. Detective Lance left.

Mira touched Layla's hair. A tentative touch. "Are you alright?"

"No. Not at all. Gul was…special. She was bright and lovely. Full of life. She did not deserve this. I want to get him before he kills someone else."

"Hate. Anger. Rage. Powerful emotions, all of them, but detrimental to the one wielding them."

Layla clenched her teeth.

Mira said looking at her, "You look so much like my grandmother."

Layla nodded, tired and near breaking-point, "Thank you for letting me stay. I'll sleep on the couch. I don't want to talk."

Mira's face fell. "I'll get the bedding."

As they were making Layla's bed ready on the couch, Layla said, "It's all happening so fast. She is dead because of me."

"Actually," said Mira, "it started several months ago."

Layla noticed Mira didn't try to disabuse her of her notion that it was because of her that Gul had lost her life.

"Now, two murders within a month. It's almost as if they're making up for lost time. Why though? What's the goal?"

"For the murders? Who knows! For the haste? The only reason that comes to my mind is that they're not taking any chances."

That was the logical explanation and yet Layla knew that Mira was lying.

"You don't think the identity of the victims matters?" Layla asked.

"I don't know yet," Mira said. "If I am right, the murders are based on stories. The note mentions me because I am the storyteller. Your involvement then, must be because of your connection with the history of stories. The link is stories. If so, then the identity of the victims might not factor in the plans of the killer."

Layla tried to join the dots. "So, the murderer didn't include me in the note because you are the bigger name? Or because he was trying to pin the murders on me? Or because I am the last victim? But…framing someone for murder? That's pretty personal, don't you think? I can't believe someone would go to such lengths until and unless it was personal. With Gul…he has made it even more personal."

"True. You are important to this pattern. There is power in your words, in your stories. And there are many people who do not wish to hear that power speak. That is also personal. Obviously, Gul meant something to you…maybe she meant something to the pattern too."

Layla had a sudden flash of scenes from her childhood, from that past forgotten due to the lapse of time or buried as self-defence after the trauma of their escape and her abandonment. She felt dizzy. She remembered now some of what her mother had left out when she had told Layla her story. Hazy memories of that man, who was her father, resurrected. Among them the sight of him taking a knife to Mira's tongue ready to cut it off.

It had been Kamli who had saved Mira. "Stop!" she had thundered. "I say stop, as a qalandar, as a Kamli—a madwoman—you know God speaks through mad people, don't you, Gulraiz? I say stop."

The man had halted and stomped off in a huff.

It was peculiar how things were coming back to her now that Mira was there before her. Layla put a hand on Mira's arm.

"You are right. She was important," said Layla. She didn't know what else to say. She rubbed her arms, missing Sultan. She wished she could cuddle him. She thought of Gul, and shuddered.

"But it still doesn't explain why would they want to bring us together? Unless they know that we are related and want to hurt you, or me, or us both?"

"Good question. Who would know? Layla, have you talked with anyone about your suspicions? Or mine about the murders being linked to stories?"

Layla feared anew Mira suspected something that was frightening her, but she wasn't admitting or sharing it. Why would she? She had lived her life as someone else—a mother without a child, a fugitive and a chameleon. And like Layla, did not trust anyone anymore. Layla understood. She was the same.

Layla had spoken to Hasina about her suspicions. That meant Munia knew as well. But she couldn't bring herself to say it to her. Mira would think everything was suspicious. Or Detective Lance would. She did not need to bring them into this sordid affair and so Layla shook her head. "No," she said.

Mira was right. They would have to work together to find the underlying system of secret meaning and patterns that bound these three murders together. Especially now that her freedom was at stake. It seemed all her life she had been fighting for freedom, from one set of oppressors or another. But wasn't that the story of most women?

FOUR

Layla spent the night tossing and turning on Mira's couch. She spent the night thinking of the murdered women, marveling that she now had two mothers, and that her life-long search was over. Her whole life had been a search for her mother. What was she going to live for now? Life was peculiar. When one achieved one's wishes, life lost its very purpose. As if the object of the desire was no longer important but the absence of that desire, now that it had been gratified, suddenly diminished life itself by its very void. That was why fairy tales ended with happily ever after. Life ended when desire was gratified. There was nothing else until the next desire.

She had got her mother back.

But had she really?

She turned on her side. Where was poor Sultan? She couldn't stop worrying. There were three murdered women connected to storytelling and to her in some way. Connected to both Mira and her. Mira and Hasina. Two mothers. Almost like something out of a fairytale.

And the very next instant another, unfamiliar fear gripped her by the throat. She could be the next victim of an unknown assailant. If he was breaking his own patterns, why would he delay?

The first murder. Ash on the body and a walnut in her hand.

The second murder. A red cloak with a hidden message. And the library? Was that important? And if the red cloak meant Little Red Riding Hood, then the ash on the body of the first victim, surely meant Aschenputtel or Cinderella? And if the walnut in the first murder hinted at Sufi stories, what was the Sufi story clue in the second murder?

Layla counted at least three. The red cloak. The colour of alchemy, red sulphur. The note: ostensibly a message from beyond the grave. The library: a place of learning.

And now Gul. A scholar was itself a Sufi symbol and Gul was a student. Her student. But she had no further details. Surely there would be a reference to a fairy tale and also a secret symbol of Sufi stories?

She waited for the greyness of dawn and then Layla got up and left for her morning walk and for coffee. She was on high alert, her eyes taking in every other person out on the streets. She had to steel herself from not glancing backwards to check if someone was following her. The hustle and bustle of a normal world grated on her nerves. Her world had turned upside down so irrevocably. She resented the regular lives with regular problems around her. The murderer was playing a game with women's lives, and it was up to Layla and Mira to stop him.

There was a distinct phenomenology to walking in city streets. The impersonal quick pace and avoiding eye contact was an ironic comfort. The noise of phones ringing, disparate snatches of conversations, a soothing babble of nonsense. Strangers walking en masse towards an unknown destination for a few minutes together and then dispersing at traffic signals, crossroads, becoming part of another crowd, lost once again amongst the unfamiliar faces, and feeling a sense of belonging still.

She bought two coffees and started back; her mind clearer and her heart heavier than it had been last night. She couldn't stop thinking of Gul.

Mira was awake by the time she returned with the coffee. She put Mira's cup on the table.

"I've been thinking about your offer. I'll do it."

Mira nodded, "What made you accept?"

Even though she must have known the answer already.

Layla took a sip of the coffee, averted her eyes and then put the cup back carefully. "Gul."

Then she said, as the scholar she was, "The first murder, with ash smeared on the body is a hint at Cinderella. The original tale, Aschenputtel, has been retold into the much shorter and more glamorous version of Cinderella."

"Yes, I agree. Not quite Cinderella but almost. And this new one…I don't know. I will have to see more. Here, I took some pictures for you…at the time I didn't know it was Gul. But I don't know if you should see this?

Layla locked eyes with her. "I will look. Gul needs me."

Gul seemed so young in death. She lay on Layla's Turkish carpet. The kind of carpet she wanted to write her thesis on. Gul…so vivacious, curious, intelligent, lay so quiet, so still.

"I'm sorry. This must be hard for you."

Layla didn't say anything. Just recalled how Gul had laughed so often. Now her lips were colourless.

Pull yourself together. She needs you, Layla reminded herself. She looked at the picture then, and not at Gul.

"Is she… wearing an apron? And is that a book sticking out from the apron pocket? It is a dummy book! It isn't even real."

"Yes." Mira took a sip of the hot cinnamon coffee. "It is a symbol. Remind you of something?"

"Alice in Wonderland?"

"May be…But no. I don't think so. The other two are fairy tales, and so this one has to be too. But it is not Beauty and the Beast because the version of Belle who loves reading is a Disney invention. Could the book signify a magical device found in such stories? Something a mother gives a daughter or a father to a son. There are so many fairytales like that both from the East and the West about the deathbed gift—the cat in *Puss in Boots*, the doll in *Vasilisa*—wisdom imparted on the deathbed."

"Yes. True. And what better symbol of wisdom than a book? God is the First Author. Stories have sustained human being since before language was a thing."

Mira nodded, "Exactly. So this book in the apron is that symbol of gift to the hero. Only why would he use this symbol? He had already killed her. What is he saying? That she was no hero?"

"No. She was a hero," Layla said. "You are right about the gift of the deathbed. There are objects like that in fairytales… though never a book, as far as I know. At least not in any fairy tale. We have to identify the story. This is a type of fairy tale then, not a specific fairytale? He is toying with us. The murderer really has broken the pattern this time then. Everything has changed. There are thousands of stories like this one. Are we looking at tropes now? The murderer is confused, perhaps? Or wants us to think so? Or it is deliberate, and we are missing something."

Layla felt like her brain would explode. She was tired and scared and devastated at having to see Gul this way. But she had to help catch Gul's killer. She must. She owed her that much.

Mira said, "We will have to distil the essence of these stories and get to their bones, so to speak."

"I never thought that answers to murders could lie in the deep aquifers of story," Layla commented. "But now that it's Gul, I will go through each one if I have to find her killer. I have to get him. I will. For her."

She had to think. Compare the symbols and see the Sufi patterns too.

"Murder, ugliness of the heart and mind, darkness are all part of human nature. We cannot avoid them. We cannot run away from them, not even in stories."

"Especially not in stories," said Layla. "Stories are more truthful histories if you know how to look. Gul loved stories too."

"Things seem different when one is almost seventy years old." Mira put her arm around her daughter. Layla didn't resist and moved infinitesimally into the embrace. "It's different when one is sixty even. Some changes are forced upon the body and one is helpless, but the wisdom and understanding that opens the mind and heart are precious…much more precious. I did what I thought was right, what was best for you at the time. And yet, we ended up here still."

She tightened her arm around her daughter. Being held in a close embrace by her birth-mother was a new experience for Layla. She did not flinch or resist. She savoured the feeling. This is what it felt like to be held close to your mother's heart, to feel loved. How real was it though? How long would it last this time?

Mira stroked her cheek with gentle fingers. "I have turned the whole situation over and over many times in my mind. What else could I have done? I don't know what I could've changed. If I had known we would reach this point despite our sacrifices, I would never have let you go."

Her mother's scent had changed from what she remembered from her childhood. Back then it had been roses, earth, citrus. Now it was unscented soap.

"I'm sure you hate roses as much as I do," Layla wrinkled her nose with distaste at the memory.

"And turmeric." Mira said.

They shared a moment of understanding. Layla smiled but her lips soon wobbled, and her body shuddered with a sob. Her mother gathered her close, and repeated the three little words every child wants to hear from their mother, no matter how old they are.

Mira hugged her close. "Let me take you back in memory and I'll tell you a story, like I used to, and I will tell you a familiar story in a way that is unfamiliar to you."

FIVE

Cinderella is too familiar a tale, with too many versions. There are some readings of it, however, that may be unfamiliar but are important. Cinderella lived in a manor, on a large estate and lost her mother when she was very young. She was too young to remember her clearly. She did recall her mother giving her a seed to plant at her grave. The hazelnut tree that grew from it was tall and strong. She'd watered it copiously with her tears. A bird would often visit and sing its beautiful songs for the orphaned Cinderella.

Her father remarried a rich widow with two daughters, whom Cinderella looked forward to meeting. Sisters! She thought happily. But things are not always as we imagine. Her step-sisters did not treat Cinderella with fairness, let alone love.

Cinderella's mother had taught her to be obedient and compliant, desired traits in virtuous women. Virtues in men and women, she'd been taught, were different. A woman we would call brave was called brash, an opinionated one was shrill and difficult. For many years she lived by the values her mother had instilled in her because she had never known anything else. The only story she knew was that of the good girl who was rewarded because she looked after everyone but herself. When her stepsisters and stepmother did not reciprocate kindness or live by the values that Cinderella did, she was confused.

Self-denial was not rewarded. When her father went to trade, he asked his daughters what they would like. Her sisters asked for silks and brocade for gowns. She asked for a rose. Did her father praise her for her selfless and simple tastes? No. He just brought each daughter what they asked for.

Tragically, he died only two years into his new marriage. Cinderella was left with her stepmother and stepsisters and that is where this story usually begins. Cinderella doubled her efforts to please her sisters and her stepmother in the hope of receiving mere scraps of love from them. She never did. They had not heard the story of the good girl and of kindness. They had heard the story of girls who got ahead when they looked after themselves and did not lift anyone but themselves. That was the only story they knew.

Ecologies of violence taught by the stepmother and practiced by all three against Cinderella became a palpable darkness inside the house. The two stories clashed and warred inside their hearts and on their hearth. Violence isn't just physical. Cinderella lived with the poisonous violence of emotional and mental abuse, and the violence of oppression. And the violence of stories that were sterile.

Cinderella didn't complain. By living a life of self-denial and victimhood, she thought she was being good. She slept near the hearth to keep warm and was often smeared with cinders and this was when she began to be called Cinderella.

Cinderella siphoned off her own energies to feed the idea of goodness without realizing that enduring oppression was creating a taste for violence within her as well.

In folklore, change comes when the enemy within is defeated, not just the enemy without. The light-stealer may be outside but there is always one within who is in league with the light-stealer without, because there is a part of us that has been stolen by our social censors. Any toxic person in a woman's life siphons off her heart, mind and soul. The light-stealer within does the same. Cinderella had to get rid of the light-stealer within by following her own instincts, which she did eventually. But some part of the violence she had endured, because she had been tacitly complicit in the descent into darkness through negative behaviour, would always be attached to her soul.

Her sisters didn't ever stop to question their cruelty. The stepmother, with the shriveled heart of a twice-widowed woman, directed her anger and hate for the misfortunes of her own life towards Cinderella. She did not prompt her daughters to be kind and good, as had Cinderella's, and so the three together starved Cinderella of love and compassion. Did they not realize it was their own hearts they were starving? The mother taught her daughters to be cruel never imagining it was her own daughters she was punishing.

If Cinderella's stepmother and step-sisters had not been so abusive towards her, she may not have thought of the Prince as her rescuer and she might not have entered into another kind of slavery. It was because she was so used to being a slave that she entered into marriage as if it were a boon.

In the popular version of the story the sisters were punished through not getting love or a prince while Cinderella's reward was both. But who is to say these are just rewards? Some versions tell us Cinderella took her stepsisters and stepmother along to the palace with her, some, that she had their eyes gouged out. Others still, that she was no longer used to sleeping on a bed, eating sumptuous meals, and so the Prince often found her sleeping in front of the fireplace, and eating crumbs off the table rather than the feast.

What we allow and accept, becomes who we are, because what we tolerate is what we accept as truth. Cinderella had so long been subjected to abuse, she accepted it as normal and so when sometimes the prince yelled at her, or the King and Queen mistreated her, she accepted it as normal. She never thought she shouldn't be treated badly because she had been treated poorly all her life.

Fairytales have an innate code. And justice is one of them. Justice includes violence within it because the ability to do justice is power. And power is inherently violent. Truth and justice are both coded in violence. What kind of violence could the powerless Cinderella resort to? Would a powerful Cinderella, who had endured the bruising of her soul and a damaged heart for years not give in to the violence shored within that broken self?

SIX

"I like the cartoon version of the story so much better." Layla said, thinking, was she being unforgiving to her mother, who had had little choice in even giving birth to her? And who could not have helped some resentment towards her, surely?

Mira chuckled, "You're making the mistake of thinking this is the end of Cinderella's story, that this version is the only true version. But neither is true. This story is a part of the story, a version of the story, a facet of a personality. She does not remain the same version of herself forever. She grows and changes. She tells her daughters multiple stories."

"Even so," Layla looked at Mira with narrowed eyes. "Those who hear this version, read this bit of her story, won't they feel… disappointed?"

Layla understood her mother a little more than she had before. This was what had happened to her in captivity. She too had tried to construct herself from stories to be something other than what circumstances had made her. Layla's elbows were on the table, and she put her head in her hands. She was more like her mother than she knew, and that was another fear added to the existing bricolage of fear that comprised her.

"I have to hurry. I need to print out Sultan's picture for fliers. I'm worried about him. And I have to see if I can speak with someone from Gul's family."

"I understand. I'll help with the fliers."

Layla felt a little robbed. This woman, who had become a stranger, was slowly eroding the meagre memories she had of her birth mother. She was taking away even the magic of tales. And yet, now she was beginning to truly understand the woman of flesh and blood.

Mira's voice intruded. "I'll go with you. No story is complete and finite. We see characters at a certain time in their lives. We catch a glimpse not of a life, not forever after at all."

"But these stories," Layla persisted, "fairytales…do end with happily ever after." Because hadn't they given her hope in dark times? And hadn't those dark times lasted forever? Until now, when she seemed to have entered the realm of Story itself.

Mira sighed, "In the hands of adepts, they don't. Sometimes stories are deliberately changed. They become plastic, rather than organic. It happens when the transformation is forced to fit religious or patriarchal functions. I have reclaimed many such stories. I dig deep, deeper and deeper, till I find their roots. I compare the different versions. I examine the archetypes and excavate the lost patterns. Most damage has been done to stories that were medicinal, truth telling stories for women."

"So, what's the moral of the story? Fairy tales always have one, don't they? For without healing stories, the scorch marks of fear will always burn. Maybe that is what we should look at, to decipher the final hint?"

Fear rose dark and smoky in her lungs, cutting off breath. Three young women had been murdered! And she could be next.

"Yes. The moral of the story is that ugly thoughts about others make one ugly as well. That wanting to be good is not enough. That one should not punish oneself. It is not our job to punish ourselves or others. That is the very definition of hubris."

Hubris? That was all that had survived the changing times.

Layla muttered, "Stories spring our eyes open. They are the quickening of dead paths leading inwards. Stories are meant to soothe fears and to give intuitive wisdom."

They'd done that for her. But now her life was threatened. Would stories really save her? They hadn't saved Gul.

"Exactly," Mira beamed. "The hard truth of old tales and women's stories has long been lost. Our stories, our journeys, the many archetypes we wear and discard, all make us who we are. When we embrace that, when we embrace the pain, the hardship, the loss, the heartbreak, the transitions, the changes—for change and transition are not the same—only then do we grow into the altered state."

"But I did. You prepared me to be invisible, to hide, to escape. And I've been doing that all of my life. Every time someone came close, I escaped because that's all I'd learned. Yet, here I am facing a murderer."

"I understand your rage." Mira covered her hand as it rested on the table. "But I don't have the answers yet. I will though, I promise."

"Forgive me if your promises are of little comfort to me," Layla laughed. A cold and bitter sound that was familiar to them both.

Layla left to make fliers for Sultan. Alone.

SEVEN

Layla lay in bed in the new flat the university had allocated her, a small and serviceable one as promised. She'd shifted within the hour so that she didn't have to impose on Mira's hospitality any longer. One night was enough.

She was alone. The night was cold and silent. She had spoken to Gul's mother that day. She was heartbroken yet had the graciousness to tell her how much Layla had inspired Gul. Layla blinked away the hot tears. She hadn't allowed herself to cry. She wouldn't, not now. Gul needed more than some futile tears.

Layla turned on her side. She hadn't drawn the curtains. Swathes of pale moonlight filtered through the glass panes. She listened to the familiar sounds of her own heartbeat, her slow even breath and the rustle of cotton sheets when she moved.

Three murders were somehow linked to her. Three. Like three little pigs. Like three bears and Goldilocks. Like three wishes given to Aladdin by the Genie. Three women had been brutally murdered and she had been in the mind of the murderer all three times.

Why?

And who were those unlucky women? She felt an affinity with those unfortunate victims because they were women, because they were victims who didn't want to be classified as victims, and yet had become so by a twist of fate. They were unlucky. They had been at the wrong place at the wrong time. And Gul? And Layla knew she was probably next. Detective Lance had provided a police officer for security. He was somewhere in a car outside, probably thinking it was a waste of his time. But she felt a strange sense of security.

How would the murderer ensnare her?

What had his earlier prey felt when they'd realized they were going to be murdered? How had he lured Gul? Had he ambushed her in Layla's apartment? Had he talked to her, threatened her before he killed her?

What would he do to her? What would she feel? How would she die?

Her mind blanked. Panicked. She threw the covers off and got out of bed. She wrapped a shawl around her and sat down by the window that looked into a back alley. The cold glass seared her forehead as her eyes stared into the dark of the narrow alley. Her eyes snagged on a small red glow in the dark. A pin-point of a red glow. And then it was gone. Snuffed. A cigarette.

Someone was watching her.

Layla shrank back into the shadows away from the window and against the wall. Her heart raced. Should she call the policeman? She decided against it. What would she say? That there was someone enjoying a stroll out in the alley? But she had to see who it was and so she slid down against the wall. She crawled on all fours, so as not to show even her silhouette at the window and checked her door. Triple locked. She crawled back to the window and reaching out with her arm, without showing herself, checked the safety locks. Secure. She crouched low. Heart in her mouth. She had her back against the built-in wooden bench she had been sitting on when she'd espied the glow of the cigarette, next to the window.

She really was a target. Someone wanted her dead. Someone who was standing outside her window in the middle of the night. Was it happening now? Would someone force her door open and kidnap her? Slit her throat right here? Bash her head in?

She took a long, deep breath. No. No fight or flight anymore. That was her past.

Only it wasn't. Something nudged her brain but vanished almost instantly into the red blaring sirens of fear.

Layla carefully lifted herself up. She stared at the sunshine yellow print on her cushion seat mellowed to pale in moonlight. She loved the sunny yellow print covers of the window-seat. She reached up and peeped out. Her eyes barely above the lattice.

Her head would be visible to anyone looking in carefully, and she knew now that someone had been looking.

She peered out into the shadows at the far side of the alley, divided diagonally in two by shadows. Not neatly, but in squeezed wedged shapes. The one, a sliver of hoary geometric shape on pavement and cobbles, the other dark, thick with shadows. She caught the barest movement. She did not back away. Someone moved forward and looked up. She saw nothing but the shape of a tall man. He turned around in a sharp swift move and was gone.

EIGHT

To Layla it seemed that her life was now divided into two realities. One where she and Mira unraveled Story for hints of gruesome murders and the other, in which she, Layla, pretended to be a teacher and a friend, and a victim of a ghastly and strange incident where Gul's dead body had been found in her home. Why would the killer leave a dead body in her house? Why hadn't anyone seen anything in broad daylight? Was it someone familiar to the area and therefore did not stand out? Too many questions and not enough answers dogged her.

Layla waited for Khayyam. He had offered to help her put the fliers up for Sultan. Her cat still hadn't turned up. She was getting seriously worried. But everyone assured her he would turn up. But he'd never vanished before, she explained endlessly. Most people who had cats told her that it was time he did. All cats did at one time or another. She wanted to argue and tell them she knew her own cat. But only Khayyam was worried like her. He believed her. Khayyam knew her.

She'd never been one to look for a happy ending for herself. But now…things were different. She'd found Mira after twenty-three years.

And a murderer of women had found her.

Everyone deserved a happy ending. But Gul had not got one. Neither had those other women.

After their initial call, Khayyam had called her again that morning and offered his assistance in looking for Sultan. After all she had found her cat at his flat in Lahore ten years ago. He could claim some part of ownership even. She'd jumped at the chance to see him again when he'd called and asked to meet.

In her early twenties when she'd first met Khayyam, she had associated her womanhood with her sexuality—how she expressed it, how others, men especially, responded to her. That had marred her early relationship with Khayyam who had been so in love with her then. Now, ten years later, her sexuality was not the burden it had been; now there was no anxiety and no pressure. She hoped things would be different this time.

She straightened her back as she sighted Khayyam on the other side of the street, waiting to cross. Her own pursuit of her mother all these years had been about identity, after all. She was neither young, nor anxious about expressing her own sexuality. She was no longer unsure of her identity, nor was she waiting for a man to show up in her life and give it meaning. But she was glad Khayyam was here now.

"Still no sign of Sultan?" he asked holding her close. Then he kissed her. When he pulled back there was something in his eyes. A question. Worry?

"I might be next," she blurted. It was the kiss. It had been too warm and too promising. It invited unburdening of the heart.

"What?" he was stunned.

Her heart lifted. "Get coffee please. I need something to warm me as I tell you a cold-blooded tale."

She wrapped her hand around the mug when he brought it over and took a sip. Then she told him all that had transpired since their last meeting. She told him about Gul, about the other murders, about Mira, about the man the previous night. He was stunned. But she felt the undercurrent of something. He knew something he wasn't telling. But was it anything to do with her?

"I can't believe you found your mother. It's Mira Heshmat? Wow."

It was there again that feeling that he ought to be more surprised. Something was off. Why was his voice so high when he said the words, like a stage whisper? What was he hiding?

"She waltzed in and announced it to me so casually. Just because there are bodies falling all around us, it doesn't make the fact of our relationship and her abandonment any less important. She deserted me at an orphanage after nine years of training me to escape a hell hole, and then she just… forsook me. Do you think I will ever recover from that?"

Khayyam squeezed her hand. Why did that touch mean anything? But it did. She was relieved when she saw only warmth and concern in his eyes. He opened his mouth and closed it. What was he afraid to say?

He squeezed her hand. "I'm sorry you're still hurting, Layla."

"And you're not?" Layla looked at him with a hint of surprise.

"I haven't thought about the bastard in years."

What a lie. His expression told her that he knew his lie had been caught.

He shrugged, "This is a fucked-up world because children are abandoned, abused and traumatized by their own parents or caretakers. Write that on my gravestone."

Layla wrapped her hands around her mug of coffee and watched him. How well she knew him, and how little! How she wanted to wrap herself around him and have him cuddle her as he had ten years ago. There must be a reason she hadn't been able to forget.

"That's why stories for children aren't always happy ones. We first prepare children for a fucked-up world through stories. Murders, and murderous mothers included. No wonder abused children grow up to be monsters." A dark realization made her choke on her last word.

He offered her a bottle of water. She uncapped the bottle and drank slowly. Khayyam had come around here the same time as the murder had been committed. He had contacted her a around three weeks later. Who knew how long he'd been here? Khayyam knew about stories. He knew about everything, even her missing mother.

Her world stilled. Her mind raced.

He had contacted her soon after the murder. He had been in the USA six years ago without meeting her. He could have done the same earlier that year when the first murder had happened. She took a deep breath and smelled green cardamom. The spice of comfort.

No. Her heart contracted. Not Khayyam.

Was the sweet scent of cardamom designed to disguise a darker truth? How could that be? She had known him a long time…no, whispered her heart, a long time ago.

"I was reading about how tricksters are never what they seem to be," she said, her voice barely a decibel above a whisper. Her heart was cold and dark again.

Khayyam gave her a long look. "What a coincidence," he said with a smile. "I was reading about female tricksters and how they often use their sexuality to fool men. Men are fools, aren't they? In ancient cultures, old folktales, there is always a need, a space though for the wise fool, the disrupter of things because excess, even of order, can lead to chaos. A little bit of chaos keeps the balance."

Why had the perfectly innocuous line about chaos chilled her to the bone?

If a story does not open your eyes to a new understanding, it is not a Sufi story. A new understanding…

"And who's the wise fool?" Her heart beat a slow rhythmic drum in her ears. There were enough wise people in her life but a wise fool was one who appeared mad or foolish. But that too was a trick. Because it was a disguise. A disguise could be anything.

"You tell me," he said.

"A wise fool is like Sufi stories, which are not always literary. They are sometimes just silly jokes and so they stay under the radar of orthodoxy and censorship. Sufi stories can do the work they are meant to do—be spells of change as they are read, retold, recited and shared."

"Exactly," said Khayyam. "You know, my favorite stories were those that use tropes such as exile and immigration, or human beings changing into something else, or about ghosts and supernatural possession, because these stories reminded me that I too can be more, I too can change. That transformation is an inevitable part of life. Perhaps the magical part."

How much had he changed though? Or had she not known enough? What secrets had he kept from her?

Layla nodded, "I agree. Those stories were actually meant to encourage growth and transition in their readers, and for understanding of the transmutation of the soul. Sufi stories themselves are the magic that they use as a trope. Like the *Swan Princess, The Ugly Duckling, The Wizard of Oz, The Conference of Birds*, the *Shahnameh*. You change too, as you read the story"

"I think trickster stories about women are the best though," he said with that wolfish smile of his, eyes glinting, as if he were enjoying himself.

"Like Princess Rukhsar who made weaving a trick and became a trickster," Layla said. They were talking in code but each knew what the other was saying. Did he know what she was accusing him of?

She continued, "An ancient trope for women because women have always had a secret history, myth, and folklore, with which they have secured and hidden. Symbols, codes, a secret language for other women of knowledge to understand and to retell old tales in new ways and guard the true codex, scattered in various stories."

"True," said Khayyam. "So many female tricksters everywhere, in stories and in real life."

Why was he being so flippant?

"Not at all. Female tricksters were erased from stories. The erasure of female tricksters depleted the strength of the trickster canon. If it were not for Scheherazade, the female trickster would have ceased to exist. Male writers turned the female trickster into monsters. Secuba, witch, vampire."

He shifted in his seat, just a little, and half his face was in shadow, "I couldn't agree more. But I must play the devil's advocate here. I mean, Scheherazade's world was a ritualistic one with a sacred context, right? It was really the Sultan who gave her the power of story with his presence, and separation from her husband made her an ordinary woman, possibly a silent one. So, if you think about it, it wasn't really Scheherazade at all, was it?"

Layla thought of Reza and how he had spoken to her back in his office all those weeks ago. Khayyam's words reminded her of that.

Khayyam added before she could reply, "*The Swan Princess* is a trickster. *The Twelve Dancing Princesses* are tricksters. Tricksters are shifting, charming and they always have a trick up their sleeves, unless—"

"Unless?" she gripped her cup and found her coffee had gone cold.

"Unless they are betrayed," he said slowly. "And when they are betrayed or captured, they fight back like the devil."

His eyes bore into hers. Her heart hammered against her chest. What was he saying? Her mouth had gone dry. She lifted the cup to her lips. The coffee tasted like mud.

"And we know all about tricksters, don't we? You and I?" Khayyam said, "We were the ones who were tricked. You by your mother and I by my father."

She smiled and her heart squeezed with the effort. She was not a fool. Not by a long shot.

"A trickster can learn by example though," she said. No charming trickster was going to trap her. "You know, at some point in the telling and retelling of Scheherazade's story, the introduction to her character was included, that she had read and memorized many books from a library as if storytelling could not come naturally to a woman. That she had to have "taken" the stories. Those richly diverse, pluralistic tales of Sufi wisdom had to have been "stolen" from someone else, and by implication, someone who was male. But the curative powers of storytelling belonged to women first."

Khayyam shook his head. "What were we thinking back then?" Then without waiting for her response asked another question, "Ever get the feeling we wasted ten years?"

He was leaping away from their conversation. Why? What had he seen in her face?

"Nope. Never. Everything that is, is for a reason. We might not understand it or know it but I trust my journey."

Khayyam's eyes lit up with more than admiration, almost like satisfaction.

"What?" She said, but actually wanted to ask, did you come to my last university as well, looking for me?

"Nothing. I was just thinking, you and I, when we met, we were sort of…broken people."

"What about now?"

Khayyam leaned back so that his face was in complete shadow. "I'm still broken in bad ways. There are things I cannot forget. I'd often see my mother with her clients. There was one who would beat her. That was his thing. Once when I was about eleven, I saw him come in and I knew the screaming would start soon and I wasn't going to cower in fear. Sure enough, her screams started and I barged in on them. He was inside her, yelling and humping and beating her with his fists. I lunged towards them. I must have screamed. He froze. He turned towards me and there was shame in his eyes." The whispered memory was a dark miasma of misery. "My mother yelled at me to get out. Yelled at me to get out because I didn't bring in any money, not even for myself."

Layla's hand reached out towards his. He was right. They were both broken. But was he broken enough to commit murder?

He jerked his hand away. His voice was soft, almost pleasant. "Don't pity me. I love my pain. It's my pain that makes me such a good artist."

Layla gasped.

He laughed. He pointed an accusing finger at her. "You're not right, either. You just don't want to remember, or see yourself truly. Brokenness is always more normal Layla, but cultural hierarchies cannot be built if brokenness becomes the norm. False ideas of masculinities, powerful male bodies that don't feel pain, don't feel at all, had to be built to create margins, where those who could be ruled by this false premise could be pushed—women, children and all those atypical "others" from the false norm created by these hordes. But in reality, it is the latter who are the norm. We, all of us—the broken and battered of the world."

They sat in silence, neither one speaking, each busy with their own thoughts. Layla was troubled. She knew this Khayyam.

How could she have suspected him of such a heinous crime even in her thoughts? What was wrong with her?

"Let's go and get the fliers out."

Layla bit her lip. She was wont to do that when she felt guilty.

Khayyam smiled. "Sure."

NINE

Layla called Ma every day now to ask after her, to make sure her and Munia were safe. What if they never caught the real killer? She kept imagining the bodies. One of them in her house. The possibility that she could be next. She put her forehead against the cool wall. Took a few deep breaths and called Ma.

"Ma, how are you?"

Hasina asked, as soon as the pleasantries were out of the way. "You should come home. You are grieving. She was your student."

"You are right. I am grieving. She was a bright young woman. It isn't fair she had to die like this."

She might as well go all the way. "Ma, there's something else. They think I might be in danger."

It took all of a fraction of a nanosecond for Hasina to assimilate the implications. Her voice down the line was matter of fact and decisive. "I will be there as soon as we can."

"Ma, no, there's no need."

Hasina's voice was gentle, "This is not a discussion, my love."

The conversation played in her head all morning. It couldn't have gone any other way. Ma would have done what she wanted to do. That's the way she lived, without being beholden to anyone, always being true to herself, even if it meant being ostracized by family and society, as she had been early in her life.

There was a knock at the door.

She was still smiling when she opened the door. Still thinking of Hasina and her love for her. When she opened the door there was a box on the floor. A gift box. There was no one there. But the smell was so strong she gagged. She knew what was in it immediately. She called Detective Lance, trying hard not to cry. She called Mira, in tears though. She called Khayyam. She wanted to scream.

Mira came first. Layla ran into her arms sobbing.

"Why? Why would he do this? This crazy son-of-a-bitch killed Sultan. I knew he wouldn't disappear."

Detective Lance came with an officer. They took away the box without opening it. Later they confirmed her suspicions. He'd been dead a while. He'd been strangled. His neck was broken.

Khayyam and Mira sat with her for hours. It was Khayyam who suggested burying him. It gave her some closure, but it didn't take away the pain.

"He was with me for so long. I cannot bear the pain."

They stayed with her. But they had no words.

*

Layla waited for Hasina to arrive with intense gratitude and wished she was as brave as Hasina and Mira. Ma was travelling alone, and Detective Lance would bring her to Mira's apartment, where Layla had relocated.

"She must be worried since you told her everything," Mira was helping Layla arrange the dinner table. There was no hint of motherly admonishment. If anything, Mira treated Layla as an equal.

"Not everything. She doesn't know about Sultan. That will scare her, and it will be painful. And she would be worried of course. She is my mother," Layla heard the touch of embarrassment in her own voice. Who was she trying to convince?

Mira smiled in acknowledgement of Hasina's position in Layla's life. She accepted that Ma was more her mother than she ever could be. Layla picked up the salad bowl. Sultan's loss was still too sharp and hot in her chest.

"Ma won't like the salad. Or anything else. Fair warning."

Mira laughed, "Oh, I know. My Spanish grandmother was like that. She was very fastidious about everything, especially food."

Layla smiled as she remembered the tales she had heard as a child about the Spanish great-grandmother and how she wished she could be more like her, not just in looks either. And all the other times too, when her mother had used to vanish for days, till at last Layla learned to find her in the cave of punishments. Trauma could alter the brain and memory a great deal. She had known it theoretically and now she was living through it. Memories she didn't know she had, were re-surfacing.

Mira glanced at her; eyes crowded with worries. "Are you okay? Tsk, silly of me. Of course you're not okay."

Layla said, "It's fine. I'll be fine. I mean of course it hurts. I can't stop thinking about Sultan, and Gul…and the others. I know it isn't an arbitrary act. It is the same person. In fact, I'm surprised there is no connection between the other victims. Were they just random women? At the wrong place and the wrong time? What about Gul? Why her?"

Mira nodded. "Sultan was very personal. It has thrown me off. I feel confused."

Layla was setting the table and asked, "So was Gul. But…do you think Sultan took my place. That he died for me?"

"He was your family. You were together for years. You looked after each other. He was your protector."

Layla shuddered. So, Sultan had died for her. Her animal protector. Her animus.

"I have been thinking about the murders and the stories related to them. I just don't understand the third story? Could it really be *Alice in Wonderland*? Even though it's not a fairytale. Is Sultan connected to the story patterns? If so, how?"

"It could be." Mira said as she set the cutlery on the table. "But I don't think it is linked to a story. I think Sultan's death is a breaking of the pattern. There is no story. Just death and pain."

Layla put the glasses down and leaned back to survey the table, "We mustn't forget the other symbols though."

"What other symbols?" asked Mira, startled.

Layla looked at her surprised. She sat down in one of the chairs at the small table they'd laid for dinner. Mira sat down opposite her, waiting for her to respond.

"Sufi symbols. The walnut in the hand of the first woman murdered at Belmont, with ash on her body. The colour red on the second body, and now this book on the body of the third victim. They are all Sufi symbols. The fairytales are the outer story, the diegesis, but these hidden symbols are the real hints, the hypo-diegesis."

"Tell me what you see," Mira sounded a little breathless.

"I'm sure the same things you see," said Layla.

Mira frowned, waved a hand, "Tell me."

"Well, the inner sanctum of a Sufi story in not reachable by all and sundry, right? It has to be sought with a pure heart," said Layla. "So, that walnut which they found on the first body symbolizes Sufi wisdom and Sufi knowledge because the shell of a walnut is hard but contains the soft kernel with all the nutrients just like Sufi stories have an outer meaning and an inner meaning. One has to work to get to the meat of the nut, just like one has to work to get to the esoteric meaning in the Sufi stories. Therefore, the walnut is the actual hint, not the ash on her body. This double vision indicates that nothing is as it seems, just like in Sufi stories."

"The ash is a hint to Cinderella and that story is the outer casing."

"Yes. Every murder has that same double vision. The code the murderer is using isn't just fairy tales. It is also Sufi secret symbolism and they're layered. But both are linked. I don't know why."

Mira's eyes glazed over and she nodded, "Yes. Interesting… almost as if they knew."

"Knew what?"

Mira seemed to snap out of a trance and said, "Tell me about the second victim."

Layla continued, "The second murder was in the library. The note to you was important, and not just because of what it said and that it was by the killer. It was a message from beyond the grave, so to speak. The body was the messenger. The note about stories was sent in the sacred space for stories and books—the library. It wasn't just about Red Riding Hood. That story is just the outer layer. Therefore, the red cloak was also about the colour of the cloak and not just the fairytale. Red is the colour of blood, of womanhood and of alchemy, and alchemy has Sufi roots, and red is the colour of the red sulphur at the end of the alchemical cycle, when the base metal turns to gold. The stage of completion or transformation."

"Bravo, my girl." Mira was impressed by Layla's analysis. "Go on. We begin to see the patterns clearly."

"Gul…the third body is the fairytale and the Sufi Story combined, so that like *Alice in Wonderland* there is logic in the illogical. The book is a combined hint to fairy tale gifts on the deathbed of wisdom and the Sufi symbol of esoteric knowledge. But there is another more potent Sufi symbol there. That is the carpet on which G…the body was placed. The symbols on the carpet—the Homa bird or the phoenix or Simorgh, a woman, the flora and fauna of Paradise, the rose and the hoopoe. The carpet tells the story of women as nourishers and storytellers."

"So, in essence…the killer is someone who is familiar with Sufi lore as well as folklore?"

Layla nodded, "They are often the same, in many cultures. But who is it and why are they doing this? I'm not sure we're dealing with only one murderer. This could be the work of two people working together or more. And now this book…The book represents knowledge. Secret knowledge. Who is keeping secrets? Why? What is the secret?"

"Yes," said Mira thoughtfully. "The book as a metaphor. Do you know that Sufi story about a book?"

Layla turned to look at her mother. Was she distracting her? From the pain of Sultan's death? She'd thought of the murders all this time, and everything had fallen into place for her like little pieces of a puzzle she was familiar with and the carpet… that had been so obvious.

"There was once a king," Layla said, "who became very sick, and no one was able to cure him. Doctors, hakeems, witch-doctors tried to cure him and failed. Ultimately, it was an old beggar who succeeded. Pleased, the king rewarded him with lands and riches. His position became stronger than even that of the Grand Vizier, who became jealous and poisoned the king's mind against the doctor claiming the king was being fooled. The king, now convinced that all his troubles had been imaginary, because was he not now well? Where was the disease for which the doctor stayed and enjoyed such luxuries? The man must die for taking advantage of the king. 'If you kill me,' the doctor said, 'who will look after you?' The doctor begged the king to spare his life, to no avail. The doctor cursed the king, 'God will smite you for your cruelty.' Enraged at the threats, the king ordered the execution to be carried out in three days. The doctor was allowed three days to put his affairs in order.

"As decreed, he arrived for his execution on the third day flanked by the king's guards, carrying a book in his trembling hands. 'Read this book after I am dead. It holds the secrets to your health and to an eternal life. Keep my head with you in a bath of chemicals I have prepared and left with your Grand Vizier.' The doctor was executed, and his head placed in the bath of chemicals in a fish tank. The king placed it near him and opened the book. He turned the first page. It was blank. He licked his finger and turned the second page, the third, the fourth and so on. He continued to lick his finger to facilitate the turning of pages, but each page was blank. When he reached the middle of the book, he coughed blood on the blank pages.

"The severed head of the doctor spoke from the tank, 'God smote you, as I said He would. The pages of the book were smeared with poison. Every time you licked your finger to turn the pages, you licked poison. And now, I must also meet my God because all I did was try to help you and you killed me for it.'"

There was a brief thoughtful silence when Layla finished telling the story.

"A sad story but it gives us an important clue." Mira looked at Layla with obvious pride. "The book as power. The book as talisman. The book as more than what it seems."

"Layla, I kept thinking about the way the bodies had been found, the way they had been placed and dressed, laid out almost artfully. And now when you've added more insight, I cannot help but think about what you explain in your books about Sufi stories. How Sufi stories often question the reality of the characters, until the reader will believe anything can happen in the story. That is a technique to encourage the role of imagination and wonder in the reader, since it is imagination which is free of all constraints and censors. The murderer is using that principle against us."

Layla nodded, a slight thrill that Mira was so familiar with her work. "True. Even the double-vision of story-within-the-story mirrors the author-reader dimension. Such concentric circles of revelation bring about an altered state of mind. How every scene is posed, how it opens up the possibilities for readers after they've read the book…for example, of Alice. Without the strangeness of the Wonderland and the pleasures of Alice's perfectly logical reactions to magic and wonder, the transfiguring effects on the psyche would not be possible."

Mira winced, "So, the murders are a means to an end? The women were just…props?"

Layla sighed. "All the signs point to that conclusion."

"That's horrible. And horrifying."

Ma had arrived and was outside the apartment building. Layla went to get her. Mira and Hasina met a little awkwardly, almost formally. Layla felt a strange vibe but couldn't quite decode it. It was as if there was something between them… respect? She couldn't quite say. She chalked it up to her own acute awareness of having them both in the same vicinity and shrugged it off. They talked long into the night and Hasina, Mira and Layla tried to unknot the mystery of who the murderer could be until dawn. Hasina was heartbroken about Sultan; grateful her daughter was safe, and scared for her wellbeing. Detective Lance had again stationed someone outside.

"Something Mira said a few days ago has stayed with me," Layla said to Ma before turning to Mira, "You said your journey as Maiden, Mother and Crone was completed. Now we have three murdered women here. The one murdered first is older than the others. I think…if we…if you ask Detective Lance to check his files, Gul will be a virgin, the maiden. One of the women will be the oldest and so fit the Crone archetype, and the other may have children."

Mira stared at her daughter, "But why?"

Hasina said decidedly, "Call him now. Ask him. It's not so late."

Mira called James Lance and her face changed as she listened.

"You were right, Layla," Mira said when she disconnected. "Gul was a virgin, and the second had had a hysterectomy. And for a man perhaps a sign that she would be a Crone. The first victim was two weeks pregnant."

Hasina gasped. "So, he isn't just a murderer, he is a monster."

"So, the maiden, mother and Crone triad is important to him. But why?" asked Mira.

"Maybe three women in his life who symbolize that for him?"

Layla could not help but think of a certain young man, who perhaps like her was reared by an adopted mother, did not stop looking for a lost mother and a sister lost. Some stories were written by vindictive gods. And some heroes became villains to avenge the wrongs done to them.

TEN

Hasina had returned home the next day at the behest of Detective Lance. He had said it was foolish to risk her life and they had all agreed. Layla was relieved but also sad to see her go.

Mira's lecture at the university was going ahead as scheduled despite the lurid excitement the murders had elicited. The turnout was still decent. Layla got a few curious looks.

"Wasn't a dead body found in her flat?"

"One of her own students…"

"Yeah, that's what I've heard. Creepy."

Layla and Khayyam met outside the hall. When she saw Reza, she waved and went towards him. She had already drawn her own conclusions. And today she was going to play Trickster and lay a trap. She wasn't sure which one of them would fall into it? One, or both? But she was certain, someone would.

They managed to get seats together in the back row with Reza and Khayyam sitting together on her right. They greeted each other. They had all met briefly a day earlier.

Reza looked pale. He gave her a sympathetic look. A nod. He opened his mouth to say something but didn't get the chance.

"Listen now." Mira Heshmat called. "The ancients believed that the auditory nerve was divided into three pathways. They believed each pathway heard at a different level. One heard the mundane words, the chatter of everyday doings and nothings. The second heard the deeper sense of other words spoken rarely, or left unspoken, of silences, and the third could gain knowledge from the stories that were transmitted from generation to generation from mother to daughter since the time of Eve. The first storyteller was Adonai, said Eve. She heard the first stories from her Lord God."

Layla glanced around. Was the murderer who had been watching her a few nights ago, here in the auditorium?

"Later people talked about writing with heart, mind, or soul. Later still, it was Id, ego, and superego. It doesn't matter what names we give to our auditory senses. The truth is that there are layers to all stories and the meaning reveals itself to those who can recognize it, according to which ear they lend the story."

Layla shivered. What was that proverb? Someone walking over her grave? Mira and Layla's last conversation had left them both shaken. They hadn't talked since, but Layla had taken a few precautionary measures. If the killer was after a book, there was probably something inside it that he wanted. A book is only as important as its contents. But Mira was talking of patterns.

It was the pattern of threes again. Mira was obviously thinking of it as well.

"Some stories are medicinal. They have power. When we listen with our inner selves, still and attentive, when we listen with our hearts and minds open, these stories repair, reclaim and remedy what is broken, damaged and in need of healing. Stories engender questions, more stories and other creative arts. Stories bring to the surface what is secret and hidden, even from us."

Layla stared at Mira. The answer is stories, the note had said. Mira truly believed that stories could solve all problems, and so it appeared did the murderer. Layla heard her knuckles crack and felt the snap. She unclenched her hands. Slowly. If she was right and the note hinted at her book, then she knew why the killer wanted it.

Mira said something about madness and Layla had a clear flashback of an old woman, her hair dyed henna-red, smiling at her mischievously, and writing things in the book of stories Mira had made. Nonsense words she had never been able to understand and then had ignored for as long as she'd had the book, until she had put them together as an adult. Layla had been alone in the room that time with Kamli. Mira could not have seen what she wrote. But she may have realized something had been added. It would have been just before Kamli died.

"The pathways to story are numerous and all are precious. What are the pathways, you ask? One is the deep pain you carry in your heart. Another is that small scar on your chin, the wounds on your body. Your heart and your soul are pathways into story, into wisdom and learning. If you yearn for something, that is a door into a new—"

"You're saying only suffering is meaningful?" Reza called out angrily looking at Mira as one would at a snake. "You think human beings need pain to grow as people? Isn't that a little primitive?"

Reza's angry voice had shaken Layla out of her own thoughts and smack into the present. She had both been listening to Mira and thinking about her suspicions. She looked up at Reza as he stood next to her. Everyone had turned to look their way. She tried to hunker down. She did not like attention. There was silence in the hall. Then a few murmurs.

Mira looked at Reza from the stage. "No, of course not, but I do think that in most cases, suffering brings wisdom that happiness often does not. Pain is more complex than happiness, I'm afraid."

"These are tales women tell themselves to enliven their sad meagre lives. Old wives' tales," he said with scorn.

Layla was taken aback. This was a different Reza. One she had only glimpsed in his office with Gul when he'd asked her about Sufi stories.

"I know mine is an unpopular opinion." Mira said. "I offer my stories, my experiences for those who seek more, especially those who toil in harsh inner landscapes. Our souls flourish and prosper in myriad ways, but they all need the help of stories to grow fully and reach the depths they must to grow. Healing stories and healed souls have similar natures. They are naturally powerful. They follow their own rules. They serve others, not themselves."

People were shifting in their seats. They wanted to see a showdown, or hear the woman they'd come to hear. The Dean was watching too. Layla did not want to be embroiled in yet another scandal, however minor. Layla put a hand on Reza's arm. Reza growled; his expression fierce but he sat down after a moment.

"When you enter the realm of story, you climb into a world and when you leave, you do so as someone else entirely," Mira continued as if here had been no interruption, "Stories change us. Stories are the connective tissue between the past as we knew it and the past as we understand it now that we have walked through the realm of story."

Reza tried to smile at Layla when she looked at him but the bloated nerve at his neck told her he was still seething. Why was Reza so agitated? Was it because of Gul? She'd been his student as well. The lecture continued but Layla missed the rest of it. Everything and everyone seemed to be unravelling.

Mira was saying, "I also think old wives' tales are important. In fact, I stress their importance often. Being old isn't an insult. It shouldn't be an achievement either but in this cruel world that seems to be the case, doesn't it?"

The applause was loud and long.

Mira's gaze rested on Layla and her companions.

ELEVEN

Murder is essentially a story about predator and prey. If you tell the story from the point of view of the prey or the predator, it becomes clear that both become who they are because of where they are born, how they are raised, their choices and circumstances. But in the end, if the predator is just a predator and the prey is merely prey, there is no story.

Layla stepped alongside Reza and Khayyam as they moved out of the hall.

"Reza…I'm so sorry…about Gul. I'd forgotten she was your student too," Layla said.

Reza nodded, "I'm sorry too, Layla. She was such a bright student. She loved you, admired you. What a terrible loss."

She nodded, thanked him.

"Let's get a cup of tea?" she offered.

After all a cup of tea was the simplest forms of food. Shared food was a sacred and ancient rite, and bond. She felt the power of Judith in her bones. During Mira's lecture she'd faced a few hard truths of her own. She had to take responsibility. She had to rise to the occasion; if not for herself, then for Gul, and Sultan and the other two women. She knew what the murderer wanted. She knew it the way she often knew hidden patterns of stories. She knew who it was but they wore a mask, and she had to unmask them if she wanted justice for those women. And if she wanted to save Mira's life and her own, she had to be trickster and lay the trap.

"Reza, you're upset. Mira has that effect," she said, "and I don't think you should be alone right now. Khayyam, join us?"

"Sure. I'll walk you home later," he said.

They all trouped over to the café nearby. It wasn't a feast and a spectacle with witnesses, and she was no Salome, but it would do. It was food. Food was sacred, breaking bread was sacred and so was blood spilled. And now they'd have both. She had a plan.

"You must have written me off as a misogynistic dick after that office rant and now this," Reza did not look at Layla. He still looked a little red in the face. He looked contrite. "I don't know what came over me."

"Can you blame me if I did think you were a misogynistic dick?" Layla raised an eyebrow. Then smiling, to soften the retort, she added, "Oh come on. I'm just kidding. It could happen to anyone. Don't worry about it."

Reza chuckled, "Hardly."

"I think you articulated what many people feel. No need to beat yourself up about it," Khayyam said sounding very much like a peacekeeper.

"I'm not beating myself about it. I'm just…I don't know. What good does it do to air your feelings? The world doesn't spin on the strength of feelings, does it?" Reza said.

"Says who?" asked Khayyam, smiling.

Layla smiled too, "Cheer up. I'm glad you spoke up. Rattled everyone, didn't it?"

"Yeah, I guess," said Reza. "On another note, how long have you two known each other?"

He took a sip of his tea and Layla hid behind her cup too.

"Really don't know how to measure time with us," said Khayyam, almost breezily. "We met in Lahore about ten or eleven years ago. Layla was looking for someone…"

Layla knew Khayyam well enough to figure he was thinking while he responded. His voice changed when he did that. It became tight, as if he was straining to speak, and so it was slightly hoarse and slow, each word articulated with precision. What was he trying to hide with this careful choice of words?

She remained quiet, listening. Unnatural silences, profane and wicked silences, enforced silences…most often the silences of women in stories, silences that screamed. They were familiar. The long lineage of women with faint voices or none at all, silenced and gagged. Was she one of them then?

Reza chuckled. "I hope you found them."

"No. Not then. Khayyam's mother was known to Ma. At least that is what she said. Khayyam met us at the airport and took us around the fantastic old walled city of Lahore for the two weeks we were there.'"

"As simple as that?" asked Reza.

There was a fission in the air. She didn't know what it was, till Khayyam spoke.

"Yes. It really was unbelievably simple."

Layla looked at Khayyam, he held her gaze in his own, cool and steady.

She looked away and said smiling, "Yes, but sometimes we find what we want, and then we realize that it was better to not have found it."

Reza laughed. "Hear, hear!"

He seemed suddenly pleased. Too pleased.

Khayyam and Layla glanced at each other.

Reza said, 'So tell me something. You won't believe it but ten or eleven years ago, I visited Lahore too. And there was some sensational murder at the time. It was in the news a lot. I recall it was some rich thug from the Old Walled City of Lahore. Wasn't the dead body discovered in a mansion? I remember hearing something like that? In fact, there was mention of a young painter who had just become very famous and it was his mansion or something? Do you remember that?'

Layla stilled. Khayyam was watching her with a grim expression.

"'A dead body?'" she faltered. "'A famous painter and a mansion'? What a coincidence, Khayyam."

Khayyam didn't respond.

Reza said, "Oh don't tell me? It couldn't possibly be you, and your mansion?"

Reza looked shocked, disturbed. Again, Layla got the feeling that she was seeing a masquerade.

Then Khayyam said drily, "And you were in Lahore ten years ago? Another coincidence."

"We seemed to be swimming in those. Are you going to tell us about the murder?" Layla said.

"It was a thug. No loss to humanity, I assure you." Khayyam's voice was tight. He didn't want to talk about it. He concentrated on his cup of tea. A nerve ticked at his temple. That was new. She had never seen that.

Two weeks' worth of love, ten years ago. She knew nothing at all. She was a fool.

Layla recalled the little boy ten years ago. And the thug who had humiliated him. He must have become more powerful and more dangerous. Someone…such people had many enemies, must have killed him. Someone who hated powerful men who humiliated little boys.

Reza made a face, "It was a rich thug who was likely involved in human trafficking. I say whoever killed him is a hero." He slapped Khayyam on the back. "Hey, I don't know you very well but after hearing that story I feel like I do." Looking at Layla he said, "We met just yesterday and got along so well."

Truth like perfume, cannot be long hidden.

A murdered man ten years ago. And now three murdered women. Khayyam was not the only link but she couldn't shake off the feeling that if she called someone in Lahore, she would find what she was looking for…a pattern. And when patterns and coincidence merged, answers emerged.

"Why are you so quiet?" Khayyam asked her. His eyes were on her, hot and angry.

"Just thinking about my class tomorrow." She replied with a smile. Her heart though was another matter. It wept.

Reza put his hand on hers, "Haven't they told you, Layla? The Dean has suspended your classes because of the investigation. Students, parents and some pea-brained teachers complained. The Dean said she'd talk to you first. I thought she had because we all got the email today. I'm so sorry."

"What?" Layla asked for no reason. She had heard him. She just couldn't believe it. No one had told her.

There was pressure on her chest. She was in a tiny space, and someone was pushing, *"Go, Go. Keep moving."* And she knew she had to, she had to move, or they would all die.

"Are you okay?" Khayyam sounded concerned.

Layla smiled, or tried to. At least she could breathe now. Shallow breaths. One, two. Three. Deep breath.

The truth of stories would save her as always. The laws of story would save her. Fairytales ended with happily ever after and murder mysteries always ended with the killer caught and brought to justice. Story laws would play out, wouldn't they? But Layla knew some stories lived in liminal spaces and made their own rules by breaking old ones. Not all killers were caught. Not all women survived.

"Layla, you'll be fine," said Reza. "They'll catch whoever did this and you'll be back to teaching in no time. You'll see."

"Those women will still be dead though. Even if they find whoever did it. They will still be dead." Her voice sounded angry and bitter. She did not like that.

"There is comfort in justice, no?" asked Reza.

"Isn't violence inherent in justice? Justice is not enough," she said. Her voice shook, "Undoing is what we need. But in matters of life and death, there is no undoing. Mira said something like that just today."

"Ah, the famous Mira," he said. "She's a big fraud. All that melodrama. I don't trust her one bit."

"Me neither," said Layla, without thinking.

Khayyam raised an eyebrow. She shrugged.

Reza drummed his knuckles on the table and nodded. "Yeah, you're right not to…although I remember you saying you love stories and you've never missed a single one of her talks."

"I haven't. But that doesn't mean I have to trust her or even like her."

"True. I've only ever trusted one person in my life. She'd dead now. She died a long time ago." The sadness in Reza's voice was a musical note accompanying lyrics, a mournful, long, low note of the flute.

"I'm so sorry, Reza."

"Thank you. She was my mother. I was her world. I was her everything. But I hear mothers come in all sizes and shapes."

"Tell me about it," said Khayyam.

"I'm lucky to have Ma. I don't know what I'd do without her," Layla agreed.

The three of them sat in silence for a moment, each preoccupied with memories. Then Reza spoke.

"I'll tell you a story about my Moor. I had gone hiking in the mountains close to where I lived when I was in my teens. I fell and fractured my ankle," Reza said. "I was in pain, but didn't make a sound. An hour later, a search party led by my mother found me. She'd heard me screaming. My home was miles away. And I hadn't made a sound."

"You had a fractured ankle and you hadn't made a sound?" Khayyam looked incredulous.

"Certainly not the screams she heard at home miles away," Reza chortled. "She heard in here." He touched his chest.

Khayyam was impressed and a touch envious. "I wish I had such a story to tell."

"What about you, Layla?" Reza turned to her.

Layla smiled, "I have a story. There's this tattered old book of stories I loved. It's a treasured token of my childhood. Ma gave me a box made from sandalwood. It smells faintly like incense and the wood is very expensive and rare now. She gave it to me on my birthday when I was a teenager because the book belongs to an era of my life that is bitter-sweet, and she helped me move forward. She helped me grow. It was just putting a book away in a box, but it freed me. I've taken it with me every place I've moved to."

"How did I know your most precious possession would be a book," said Reza.

"And mine is a painting by a forgotten Master of the East," said Khayyam.

"I have nothing," said Reza.

Layla thought she heard the undertones of a great sadness.

She also found the opening she'd been looking for. "You never said if they caught the murderer, Khayyam. The thug they found in your mansion? Was the murderer caught?"

Khayyam's eyes were in shadow, his voice was grave, "I honestly don't know. I never asked. It wasn't my problem really.

I'd sold the mansion and only found out about the dead body as I was leaving."

Reza started to say something, then stopped, as if confused. Layla looked from one face to the other and did not know if she trusted either one. She got up and took her leave. She had set the trap. She had done what she had meant to do. They all got up after her. Reza turned towards his apartment then stopped and hugged her.

He whispered in her ear, "He's lying. He sold it after."

Khayyam fell in step with her. She clutched her keys in her hand, making a weapon out of them.

"So, we both have the ignominy of having a dead body turn up at our home."

Layla started. She hadn't quite made the connection until he said it. Yes, someone had left a dead body at her home, but had the same thing happened to him, or did he want her to think that? She didn't know what to say so she said nothing. Just before they reached his apartment, Khayyam squeezed her shoulder and planted a soft, comforting kiss on her mouth.

"Be careful. I don't… Reza. There's something wrong with him."

She nodded. He turned hesitantly, but in his silence and in his every move, Layla could not get rid of the sense of a great violence held in check.

TWELVE

So much had transpired so quickly in the past few weeks and changed life irrevocably. She walked around the university aimlessly for a while. Give them time. They would go to her new apartment to find the book. The old one was still out of bounds, and she had shifted into the new one fully. She didn't want to go back to that apartment, where Gul's life had been snuffed out. They would look for the book, but they would not find it there. She walked around. She had some thinking to do. *Maiden, Mother, Crone*. What did it mean?

Winter was upon them, and the first snow of the winter had fallen in October. It was cold and scary. She was fed up with feeling so afraid and cautious. She wanted to have an uneventful life. She wanted to exchange her seeing, knowing, knowledgeable eyes, for those that were unseeing, unknowing, and blissfully ignorant.

When she reached her new apartment after thirty minutes of aimless walking, the door was open, and the lock broken as if someone had kicked it in. Her clothes were strewn on the floor like the entrails of a gutted animal. Her books on the floor, torn and ripped away, and her bedding overturned. Her whole place had been ransacked. A deep shudder shook her slight frame.

She knew it would be so, yet she was shaken.

She didn't want to enter the flat. Her plan had worked. He'd taken the bait.

She called Mira.

"Can you please come over," she said unable to hide the tremor in her voice.

"What's wrong?" Mira's voice was sharp with concern.

"My apartment…my apartment's been broken into but I—"

"God!" Mira's indrawn breath was audible down the wire. "Stay there. I'm on my way. I'll call James."

Layla slid against the wall in the hall looking in at the chaos that was her home. She willed her mind to find refuge and the safety of Story. But she couldn't.

She called Ma and told her what had happened, her voice calmer than it had been when she made the first spontaneous call to Mira. She discussed a tentative plan trusting Ma to veto it if she didn't find merit in it.

"Should I come back?"

"Of course not, Ma. You just went back a day earlier. Don't worry, Mira is coming."

"Good," Ma said with relief. "Let her stay with you if she asks. Don't be alone tonight."

Layla promised she wouldn't, and she hung on to her cell phone even after disconnecting the call. Her back against the cold wall. Only two hours earlier she had told two people about the book of stories being in a box of sandalwood.

Which one of them had taken the bait? Both? Or at least one of them. They had come looking for it. Both had enough time. Khayyam had been rather offhanded about the murder in his old mansion. Layla rubbed her temple to ease the start of a headache. One of them had violated her space. One of them was a murderer.

Words were such horrible little tricksters. They shaped and altered known reality. Friend. Lover. Murderer.

How could he…Khayyam or Reza…how could he have killed all those people? It was one of them, but which one? She had begun to understand clearly why. Even who it was, behind the mask.

And just as she always understood life through stories, she thought of them again.

Sufi stories enshrined within them a secret doctrine or truth. Sufi stories were instruments of change. Sufi stories often depict people as products of their society, following established social behaviors. These characters typically didn't challenge unjust authority until they had a personal awakening. The purpose of such Sufi stories was to surprise the readers and stir the "inner hero" within them, helping them to discover their true selves. Layla was not sure if she was the one who would be surprised or one of the two men she had just trapped into revealing himself. Not that she needed any more surprises in her life, but destiny and fate seemed to be writing a story that was forcing her to open her eyes to new realities.

The murderer wanted vengeance. He wanted to change the cards life had dealt him. He wanted to shuffle the deck. Khayyam had had a miserable childhood. That had been the basis of a shared empathy. He would want to rewrite the rules but would murdering three women alter the past?

Reza was a mystery. She knew nothing about him. He could be anyone.

Murdering three women could be an instrument of change only for the worst dregs of humanity. Whatever his past, was killing them instrumental enough? Killing changed reality. Did he think he wouldn't be caught?

Her friendships were turning out to be sterile. Especially with men. She couldn't trust either of them, and she had known Khayyam for a decade. No. She had known him for a couple of weeks in that decade. Not for a decade. And Reza, only for a few weeks. She didn't know them at all. But she'd wanted to and she still hoped, prayed that she was wrong about them. Both of them.

"Layla." Mira and Detective Lance came in her line of vision. She rushed into Mira's arms. Mira's stunned response was of arrested movement for a second before she held her close.

"It's okay. It's going to be okay."

"You didn't touch anything?" asked Detective Lance.

Layla shook her head.

Detective Lance had called for backup and three officers joined him. They asked if anything was missing. She couldn't tell. Everything seemed accounted for. She knew why and she needed to talk to Mira about it.

"What do you think they were looking for?" Mira asked. "Since they've taken nothing, they must've been looking for something."

"I don't know," she lied. "I'm just glad they didn't leave another dead body." She wanted to run her theory by Mira before mentioning her suspicion to the detective. She hoped she was wrong.

"You have somewhere you can go?" asked Detective Lance.

Mira said quickly, "Yes. You could come stay with me till this is sorted?"

Layla nodded, still shaken but thoughtful now.

Mira took Layla to her own apartment.

As soon as they closed the door, Layla turned to Mira.

"What if…"

"Yes?" asked Mira.

Layla said slowly, "Sufi stories assume the reader to be a sophisticated one, someone who expects magic to have logic and one who, when faced with illogical magic will interrogate the text for cause because that is where the secret lies. A Sufi story is for a reader who thinks critically, logically and at times to reach the logic of the story illogically, as Alice does in Wonderland or Mullah Nasruddin does in all his stories. The true magic is the story itself."

"Yes…" Mira waited for Layla to gather her thoughts and continue.

"And so, let's consider all the symbols that came attached to the murdered bodies. The walnut is a symbol of the story-within-story, to tell us that the murders are in fact not just about fairytales but Sufi stories as well. The second murder strengthens that idea with the written message to you, saying it is all about stories. The last actually has a book, blank no less, on the murdered body."

"Yes, go on." Mira said as she began to make the connection Layla was leading her to.

"What if," said Layla, "it is about a book. They're looking for a specific book."

"The note said the answer is stories,' said Mira.

"Do you know which book?"

Mira looked drawn.

Layla whispered, "I know which book. He wants the storybook you wrote for your children." Layla spoke slowly, connecting the dots aloud. "The Book I've kept all these years. That's what he's after. There is only one person who'd want that book."

"But that makes no sense," Mira's distraught whisper ended on a sob.

"It makes perfect sense. Look at the signs. It all adds up."

Mira looked worried. "Kamli knew of it. Jamila knew of it. Who knows how many people they told?"

Layla felt sorry for Mira. She didn't want to admit to what was staring them in the face. She wanted to spare her mother. "It could be Gulraiz. Maybe Firdous knew and told him. Maybe he is here."

Mira looked at her, stunned and horrified of a spectre from their past.

"Yes, it could be him."

THIRTEEN

Death kept finding her. Death was the door out of the dimension of time into an unknown space of mystery and possibility. Death was the essential event which gave meaning to life. In Sufi lore, love, death and annihilation of the Self were synonymous. Death was the ultimate truth. Layla's breath came out in a shudder. Sufi literature depicted death as a tragedy for villains but as apotheosis for heroes.

She knew where death awaited her.

Anyone who knew her even a little bit would go to the library. The obvious place to find a book. That's where she would go. Where else to find answers? And answers she must find. Though she knew perfectly well who she would find there, she did not know which mask he wore to conceal his true identity.

It was almost midnight. Mira was asleep. Layla left her a note and slipped out. Night-time was still a trigger for her. She did not generally go out at night. She felt unsafe and insecure in the dark. And tonight, it was downright dangerous, but it had to be done. She kept an ear to every passer-by, as if he'd jump at her with a gun and attack her. She'd grown up with such fears. Strange then, that she felt no fear when she reached the library and saw the chaos there.

Books were strewn on the floor. Her desk had been emptied. Turned over. Someone was still searching in the archives. She could hear the shuffling feet, the panting breaths of frustration. She could hear the books being thrown on the floor, one by one.

A little knowledge was a dangerous thing, like misinterpretation. That was why Sufi wisdom was imparted in secret, in fairytales, in folktales, disguised as magic or children's stories because only the wise would be able to decode the messages. Hidden patterns that encouraged thinking in parts of the mind not reached ordinarily. Some Sufi stories were written in the scatter method; where material was arranged in a way that the effect on the reader occurred in tiny impactful doses which bypassed the conditioned consciousness.

She had enough information to bypass her usual censors.

"It's me, Scheherazade," she called out.

All movement ceased. Layla cleared her throat and said simply, "The book isn't here. If you had asked, I'd have given it to you. Why didn't you just ask?"

She heard someone coming towards her, and she felt fear again. She was deep inside the library by then. The only door was far behind her. They were almost in the centre of the room where a square of empty space was left with a table and a few stools for students and any researchers.

He hadn't harmed her yet. He hadn't even implicated her in the murders badly enough for her to be charged. Her father would have had no such compunctions. He had no love for stories ever. There was only one person who had suffered like her. One person who had loved stories like her. And one person who had gone on suffering like her.

Her little brother. Hamza.

She and Hamza had suffered together the tyranny of their mother's captive intelligence and spirit. Surely her brother wouldn't harm her? She stood near the table, waiting for him to show himself.

"I'm s...sorry for what happened. I'm sorry you got left behind. I've missed you." It was true. She had. She had felt a phantom pain all her life. For her lost mother and her memories. Including that of a brother.

The footsteps from the far right ahead of her seemed to pause at her words. As if a mention of affection got to him.

"Hamza?" she whispered again.

It was Reza Kemal who stepped from behind the shelves.

"It's you!" whispered Layla. "Hamza?" She choked on the question.

"Hamza," she said softly and covered her mouth with a hand.

"And who did you think it would be? Khayyam?" he scoffed. He stood there before her, just as he had so many times in the past few months. Her brother.

Of course. It had to be Reza. Unconsciously, she touched her hair, untimely grey like his.

"I'm disappointed you didn't know it was me. But how could you know? You haven't seen me in twenty-three years. I've missed you too, sister. I missed you so much I came looking for you. Why didn't you? You went all the way to Lahore looking for our mother? But not me. Why didn't you look for me? Are you lying about missing me?"

"Hamza—"

"Stop!" he yelled.

She shrank away from him.

"I'm sorry," he breathed heavily to calm himself. "I shouldn't have yelled…but that name…I'm sure you can understand the trauma attached to the names we were given by her. I'm glad you changed yours too." He came towards her and looked at her with a warm smile…a smile she'd become used to seeing on an almost-friend.

"I've read all your books. I've already told you that. I loved them all. The way you pick the stories all apart is sheer genius."

Layla stared and when he looked at her, frowning, she said quickly, "Thank you. I'm glad you think so. Your opinion matters."

He nodded and laughed appreciatively. "Your books helped me finalize my plans. I'd been following Mira for five years, keeping an eye on her, and on you. Then you found her too." He clicked his tongue against his teeth. He shook his finger at her, as a gentle father would reprimand his little girl. "I couldn't let you both be together again. I'd barely got to the point where I could find a place in your life. I wanted to be in your life. This time I wanted to take you away from Mother. The way she took you from me? It made me happy to know that you hadn't been with her. That meant you were not as corrupted as her. I could save you still."

There was an old proverb for when someone found it difficult to translate emotion into words—like an ox had sat upon the tongue. She understood that now.

He touched her face with his index finger, "Do you know I joined the Belmont University for you? But by the time I arrived, I found out you were leaving. That pissed me off."

The finger on her skin awakened her to his other face. A killer's hands. Tears pricked her eyes. She, who never cried, felt tears misting her vision, clogging her throat and nose. She had known Reza hated stories, and Khayyam who found a story in everything. How could she have confused the two? Stupid. Stupid.

"Who was she? The woman you killed in Belmont?" Layla asked him.

"What does it matter? It was your fault though. Why'd you have to leave Belmont for Mira? How many times are you going to leave me for her?"

Her heart was a little bird inside her ribcage, fluttering for freedom. "Did you know she was pregnant?"

"Yes, it was mine," he sounded like Gulraiz, the utter arrogance of a toxic male explicit in every word. "Why do you think I killed her? She was talking of going public and giving me grief over being secretive. Always nagging. She reminded me of Mother. Not every woman is supposed to become a mother. Ours shouldn't have been one."

"You killed your own child?" she whispered in horror.

"What does someone like me do with a child? Do you know what it means for a child to be abandoned? To be left behind? To be bartered?"

She let out a sound, a strangled noise of denial and grief.

"I guess you do." His words had taken them both back to the time they'd been together, to the miniscule portion of their lives they had shared, the pain and closeness that had been theirs. "Only a little. Not like me though."

"I suffered the same as you, Hamza—"

"No," his voice was a lash. "Don't. Just don't. You did not."

Layla suppressed the urge to cry. She nodded.

"Do you know, I tried to understand the murderer in the context of what I know so well? Sufi stories reconstitute the emphasis of stories as instruments of change, you know.

Stories which are not regenerative and which lack mystical depth are considered sterile. But…I arrived at an erroneous conclusion."

His smile vanished. "Doesn't surprise me at all. You're blind. You've always been. You always thought she loved us. But she didn't. You're foolish."

She understood then. Like a flash of illumination. Mother, Maiden, Crone. In his warped mind, Layla was the maiden, Mira was the Mother, and Firdous was the Crone. That's why he'd killed Gul. Gul had died in her place. Layla's fell to her knees, sobbing.

"Oh, Gul…I'm so sorry…"

Ignoring her, Reza said, "That's why I became an anthropologist. I wanted to understand the history of motherhood. You know what I'm going to do? I'm going to get that book and I'm going to kill Mira Heshmat."

There was nothing in his face that she remembered. There was no memory of voice, inflection, intonation, gesture. Nothing. How could she have remembered what she hadn't heard? They'd been children. She'd never heard his adult male voice. All she had was a name.

"But that will be against all the rules you laid out for yourself when you dressed the murders as fairytales. Things happen in threes. This would make it the fourth. That breaks the rules. There is no story attached to this one."

"No. You already know I have no respect for stories. That's why I'm breaking the pattern. But why do I hate stories so? And her? Because she abandoned me? Because I was dispensable for her? Is it really so simple?" he asked as if he was asking an academic question of a student.

"Because long ago, you loved stories just as much as I do," Layla murmured,

He smiled. A handsome face. Sad too. His smile was tinged with sadness. In retrospect there were so many hints. The hair, his constant seeking her out. The mention of Angkor and how he had stayed there for years. The academic world had been rocked by the disappearance of Dr Reza and then he had emerged into the spotlight suddenly. He had been a recluse before.

"That's true. Stories made me feel safe. Us. You and I felt it always. And then she took them with her."

"Reza…please let me help you. You've killed three innocent women. Who were the others? Do you understand what you've done? You killed Gul! And those other women. You killed my Sultan! You need help. Please let me help you."

"Help? Hmm. I wonder. I don't know if I am mad or sane. Do you remember that old witch with red hair who was always hovering around us? She used to tell us stories. I thought she was a madwoman. But I don't think I am mad, sister. I know what I am doing. Sometimes, I do it for the pleasure of it. You know, it's almost funny, I can understand what Gulraiz felt. I sort of get him. Remember how angry he would be if he found Mother with a book? He said books had made her mad. Made her think she was equal to men. I think he was right. Why do you think I want that book now? That is a thing of evil. It brought nothing but pain, even when we wanted it. I know it's just a symbolic act. Just like the murders of these other women. What I'd really like is to kill Mira and you. I am not sure about you, though. I'll see."

Layla hadn't been afraid to come here. She had been remembering little Hamza, who kept his treats to share with his sister and how they'd eat them while she told him stories. Ritual secrets had immense value. Sufi literature was often about the union of contradictions and about transformations. Madness was often used as a metaphor for enlightenment. He was right. He wasn't mad.

She tried another tactic, "Reza, I am so sorry for what happened."

He smiled, "Thank you, sister. So am I. I'm so sorry she abandoned you too. But we did well, didn't we? I'll tell you my story now. Did you never wonder what happened to me after Mother chose you and freedom and bartered me off to Firdous?"

He brought her a stool and she noticed his hands were big and fleshy. She flinched as he reached out to her. How had she missed noticing how thick his fingers were?

"Don't be afraid. I won't kill you yet. I might not kill you at all. But I don't know yet. Sit. Listen to my story now."

FOURTEEN

"Hear me sister, this is the tale of your lost brother Hamza and of how he became Reza. When I left with Firdous, I didn't eat all day. I slept in despair. I would wake up thinking I'd heard you call me. Or Mother had called me, but it never happened. It was always a dream.

"I was a child of seven and soon hunger and distractions claimed my attention. Firdous never left me alone in the first few days. But soon when I found her preoccupied, I went in search of the storybook mother had made for us. I looked everywhere for days. You see, even when I was coming back with Firdous without you and Mother, I had this hope that at least the book was still hidden at home. That I had our stories, and you did not. You had Mother and I had the book. Our book. Imagine my shock when I found it was gone.

"That's when it finally hit me that Mother never thought of me as her son. It was just as Firdous had always said. Firdous said I looked too much like my father. That you were too much like our mother and so she favoured you over me. I think it's true. She took everything from me that day. Even the power of that book."

Layla swallowed but there was a constriction in her throat. She'd lived every emotion he had. She wanted to tell him the book had been only a small comfort. A tangible proof of what they had suffered at a time when she'd suppressed most of it. The amnesia had been a cloak of protection against what her childish mind had wanted to keep out.

She opened her mouth to tell him, but Reza stalled her with his hand.

"Don't interrupt me with your futile sympathy that holds no sway over me, sister. Who am I now? Was Hamza the monster or is Reza? Was it always the monster who took different names? You are still the Quester, heroic, but what am I? I have long been Villain, long been Monster and long been all that is dark and rejected. Did she see something in me to reject me or did I become this because I was rejected? I think that's the question I'd like to ask Mother the most: Why did you leave me? What had I done wrong? Didn't I learn everything my sister did? Didn't I love her as you did? What do you think it was? I'd imagined myself to be Gilgamesh and Enkidu not Humbaba. I didn't think I'd be the monster everyone hated. When did I become one? But Gilgamesh and Enkidu grew with each other. The wild man became noble, and the tyrant became a hero. What would have happened if we had been allowed to grow up together? Don't you wonder?"

"But Humbaba wasn't all monster either. He cursed Gilgamesh and it came true. He had a tragic nobility."

For those who love stories and who fight battles on the page with heroes and superheroes, our own battles seem less insignificant, less painful. The usefulness of the passage of time, the kindness and cruelties of time, help us understand ourselves and others. Not all battles are equal and neither are all stories. Some are born in daylight and others in the dark. Layla wished her brother's hadn't been so dark and the seed of evil hadn't taken root in his heart.

"Yes," he looked delighted. "Thank you for saying that. You see me more clearly than anyone I've ever known, sister. I am grateful. Yes, Humbaba cursed the heroes, didn't he? Just like me."

Layla saw a movement from the corner of her eye. Reza seemed not to have noticed.

"Do you know I killed Gulraiz when I was sixteen? He had it coming. I bashed his head in with that long staff he used to carry everywhere. Surprisingly, it was Firdous who stood by me and proclaimed me Chief. I was the chief for two years and then she died. I had nothing left. So, I gathered what money I could and travelled around getting what education I could. Or at least moving in circles that got me what I wanted. It was in Turkey five years ago that I first caught a glimpse of you, Mother."

Layla turned. But she couldn't see anything.

"Do you appreciate the irony of Gulraiz's death, Mother?"

Layla heard a sob.

"Come on out, Mother. It's a family reunion after all."

Mira stepped forward looking haggard in the meagre light of the room. The only light came from the lamps in the far corners of the room so that there were swathes of light on their left and right and they sat in the shadows where the light dimmed. For the first time, Mira looked like a frail old woman. Where was the tall, strong woman, the storyteller?

"Hamza, my son!" she whispered. Her cheeks glistened as she moved. She was crying.

Reza laughed or keened; Layla wasn't sure what the sound was that came out of him.

"Come on Mother don't say things you don't mean. Let's just say I killed Gulraiz with seventy gashes or something. Actually, I didn't count. I sold the staff for a handsome amount. Come, have a seat, Mother."

He pulled out another stool for her next to Layla, who sat facing him. Mira sat down, looking at Reza as if searching for her little boy in the man in front of her, traces of innocence, tenderness of the little boy who would nestle instinctively against his mother when looking for comfort and cuddles.

"When you came to Turkey five years ago, Mother, I followed you. I invited you there. I had asked my colleagues to invite the great Storyteller. You came! By then I had already killed the man whose identity I took. He'd written a few books that were famous, but he was a sad recluse—no one had ever seen him. Once when it became known he was lost in Angkor, I too went there. I found him, killed him and took his identity. Later I used ghost writers to write more books from his bundles of notes and got them published. With this face, and my natural charm, everything fell into place. Reza Kemal as you know him now, was born. It was so easy. It was like fate. I played a few cards right and got a work-visa and a job here so I could keep track of your movements. I would not have to let you out of my sight ever again. It was not so difficult. By then I'd had another couple of ghost writers help me write books. I was famous.

"I followed you, Mother. I knew your every move. You were keeping an eye on Layla Rashid and so I did too. That's how I found you, sister. She always knew where you were. She is evil, this one. Gulraiz hated me, Mother, because I was a reminder of his failure. Firdous saved me a few beatings, but not all. He hated your guts. He would scream and rant and shoot. I think you broke him. And then you left me with him."

"Won't you let me ask for forgiveness?" Mira's eyes pleaded. "And ask for it in return?"

Layla touched the book she carried hidden in her tunic. Sometimes even love created monsters. She would have to make Mira understand that to help absolve her of guilt. And herself.

"No. Because you won't find it here. Where is the book? I want to burn it before your eyes. Maybe I'll burn you with it."

"So, you came to get a book written on scraps of paper? Why would you commit so many murders for that? It doesn't make sense." Mira seemed have controlled herself now, as if a switch had gone on. "Why is that book so important to you when you hate me?"

In a Sufi story, when the different layers are revealed, the reader's sense of her conscious, perceived reality becomes unstable. There is an outward explosion of sorts, a point of realisation for both the character and the reader when they come face to face with the hidden truth of the story, a kind of knowledge they did not have before. That point of experience which is also illumination, is called fana or annihilation."

"He wants it because for us as children that book was a symbol. It was a symbol of you. He wants it because books are a talisman. They are the key to knowledge and wisdom. Books hold secrets, codes," Layla couldn't help speaking the truth of the matter.

"What were the secrets in this book?" Reza hissed. "How to be a good mother? Guess our dear mother never unlocked that secret, huh?" He laughed looking at Layla. Sharing the joke with her.

Layla looked away towards Mira.

"It's okay," said Mira. "Do not worry. The laws of story have taken over. How often do truth and fiction collide? Why are so many readers wary of lessons in fiction?" she looked at Reza and added, "Because they are uncomfortable with knowing truth."

Reza jumped up and struck Mira across the face. Layla gasped.

"Did you see the truth then?" Reza mocked. "Did you? What good did it do?"

Mira was here, James would be coming soon. Mira must have informed him. Maybe Khayyam would come too. Maybe she'd see him one more time, before she died.

Layla vied for Reza's attention, "We both started our search more or less at the same time, Reza. You wanted to attract Mira's attention with that first murder. I was still supposed to be living in the building where the dead body was found. You know a lot about stories for someone who hates stories."

"Very good, sister. Continue please," he said with a smirk. "Or maybe I can help. You will probably say that men have always culled the stories of women. Killed them. Abused them, raped and plundered them. Yadda, yadda, yadda."

"Yes. It is an old story…the one you chose to tell. Killing women. It won't shock anyone." Layla replied.

"But this isn't about you. Or women. It is about me. Now be quiet. We practiced it often enough as children."

Ashamed that she could understand her brother so well, that she knew exactly why he had done every terrible thing he had, she bit her lip trying not to cry out in pain. He had done it all only to find his family. He only wanted to hurt the people who had hurt him. His mother who had left him behind and the sister who got to go away with the mother. Layla was sad for the little lost boy who had been her brother. But the man who stood before her, had become a killer of women. He had become the very thing she had vowed to fight.

Could he not have just asked her for the book? Could he not have shared his pain and tried to imagine hers as well like she was doing now? The book wasn't what he wanted really. It was merely a symbol for him. A symbol of love betrayed. A symbol of stories he'd been robbed of and perhaps even a symbol of the mother, who to his mind, had rejected him. And wasn't it true that they were all three guilty, that Reza had reason to feel as he did, although the killing hand had been his alone?

"But I was telling you the missing parts of your story," said Layla. "You see, no one knew that I had already moved out, and that I was leaving the next day. It was so sudden. It was only by chance that I'd found out about Mira being in this town, being a visiting faculty member here, so, I'd made my decision quickly. I'd resigned and was to leave the next day, but only the Dean knew. I had been planning on leaving. The Dean and I didn't quite get along. He accepted my resignation very happily."

Reza's smile as he watched her was almost affectionate. Could ties of blood ever be severed?

"You could always keep a secret. So that is why you left so quickly. Because of her!"

Layla continued briskly, "It must have taken you some time to realize I was gone. But you found me again, quickly enough. You found me and got a position here. Your journey and mine are almost identical, save for the murders. We have both been looking for our mother. We both entered the world of academia and stories which would help us find her."

"I don't do stories," Reza said, with a slight inflection that hinted at a dark emotion. "I am a historian and anthropologist. Our stories are not identical at all."

Layla attempted a smile, "History and anthropology are the closest you could have come to stories."

Reza looked away.

And she found the courage to ask, "Why did you have to murder those women? And Gul? Why her? Why did you have to kill at all? If you wanted that old book, you could have just asked."

"But I did. Sort of," he said with an odd, constricted laugh. "This was the way. Blood and sacrifice have power. This binds us forever now, when even our own shared blood could not. You will always remember that these murders were committed because of you two and your actions. You were there with me."

Mira's low moan of despair was a sound too familiar.

"Yes," Reza smiled with relish. "That Gul loved you and admired you so. It was annoying. You know what, I enjoyed killing her in a way I didn't enjoy the others. The others were just work. This one was...pleasure. I knew it would hurt you."

Layla sobbed, "Yes. You are right. It does hurt me." Then she went on blindly, trying to engage his attention, "I began to suspect you after you murdered Gul. It was the carpet. I had told you about it in your office. And then other things began to fall into place. Your hatred of stories. Your rage at Mira.

"I told you about the book on purpose, and my apartment was ransacked. When you didn't find it, the only other possible place was the library. You knew I'd come, didn't you? And I knew you'd come here. I had to know, and that's why I lay the trap of telling you about the book. I suspected but I wasn't sure till the apartment was ransacked."

"Of course, you suspected. But you suspected that fool Khayyam too," he said. His eyes had a strange glitter. "You are a seeker. You are a Quester. Already perhaps a Hero, too? There is a reason you hid the book away, Layla. What is that reason? Did you find something? Did you find something you don't want to share?"

How could he have known? Did he remember so well then?

She stared back at him, "You killed because you wanted to prove Mira a liar. She betrayed us both. You killed women because they represented us. I understand your rage because it was mine too, for the longest time. But I'd never hurt an innocent person."

"You know nothing about my rage." His words were low, as if heavy with a burden, so that his voice couldn't quite carry it and struggled under its weight. "You hurt me. You went with her. You never looked for me. You forgot me. I was innocent then. I was not a murderer then. You both made me a murderer. So don't flatter yourself. You've sinned too."

"Yes, you're right," said Layla. "That's why I understand Mira better now. Because I understand the limitations of our good intentions. Mira did what she could. She tried. We cannot know her truth even though we lived part of it. We could only see and understand a part of what she endured alone." Her words of defence for Mira sounded strange even to her own ears.

"As did I! She should've been the one to die, don't you think, sister? Not those women I had to kill. I used them to send you a message. I wanted you to be afraid. I wanted you to suffer. I wanted you to feel the fear of a sword hanging over your head never knowing when it might fall. I wanted Mira to die. I will kill her. I promise you that."

Layla squirmed, "What if I give you the book? Will you still kill her?'

"Do you have it here?" he asked. His eyes gleamed. "It's on you, isn't it?"

He leaped at her and though she flinched, she didn't try to run.

"I have it. I'll give it to you," she said, her hands before her face in defence.

Reza stopped, held his hand out. Layla brought it out of her tunic folds. When Reza saw it, he smiled.

"Just like that," he marvelled. "It looks exactly as I remember it. Just a tad smaller. Was it always this small?"

He held it for a few moments, with love and regret etched on his face.

"It's a pity," he said as he put it on the table. He turned his face towards her.

He was so handsome. Yet she couldn't bear to look at his face.

"What do you mean?" she asked.

"You don't know anything." Reza's laughter was merry as he stared at his mother, "All rules are malleable. Gulraiz trained me to kill you. But I killed him first. But not for you. I killed him for me. After Moor died, after that tragedy, I ran away. I joined one group of killers after another, trying to find you, trying to live with the fact that my mother had left me behind to save my sister. You. I wanted to punish you both but didn't know how." Then he looked at the book, "Maybe now I do."

"I did not choose to leave you." Mira whispered.

"Yes, you did!" shouted Reza. "You chose her!" He surged to his feet looming over Mira, pointing at Layla. "You chose her over me and you left me with the man you hated, in the place you hated, because you hated me too. Because I looked like Gulraiz. You hated me for a fault that wasn't mine."

Mira protested but he looked away and faced his sister. His smile was pleasant, but his eyes glittered with menace. "You, like your mother, are a trickster. Now you just hand me this book after all this time. Why, I wonder?" He turned to the book and turned a few pages, then he put it back and glanced at her. "I don't understand. It's just like the way you left Belmont. I couldn't make head or tail of that. I had to make quick decisions. Providence, I think you'd call it in a story."

He picked up the book again, opened it and turned a few pages. He was emotionally erratic obviously. How had he fooled them all for so long? Then she recalled the prejudice-laden words in his office and the scene in the auditorium. What about now? Would he flip out? Would he regret? She couldn't tell.

He closed the book with a sigh and said, "But I wanted to pin the murder on you, to teach you a lesson, initially. To separate you from Mother forever. I carried her in the cold darkness of late night all the way to your house. When someone saw me, a drunk student I think, I made a joke about a drunken girlfriend and a devoted boyfriend. It was so late, and it was freezing that night. It was right after new year's, wasn't it? The walnut was an afterthought. But it was so clever. I had just finished your books for the third time. Your books became for me what our story book was to us as children. And all this? I was so pleased with my work. I enjoyed setting up the game for you. I worked in the dark and put the ash on her and all the rest of it. It was very tiring, especially because I had to wear a coverall, gloves and a mask and do it all quickly. I was filthy by the time I finished. It took me two hours, but it was so late no one saw me. Even if they did, they must have thought I was a worker. And after all that effort, you left!"

Disgust was written on his face. His hands tightened on the book. The knuckles whitened. "Can you imagine the problems that created? I nearly killed you when I found you here, I was so angry. But I didn't waste any more time after that first experience. It was such a great game too. I wanted to play it with you. It was all quite thrilling, seeing you falling for the trap I'd laid out for you so carefully layering the fairytales with Sufi symbols, and the women archetypes? You aren't as clever as you think, Mother. But Layla was quick. You soon saw the Sufi hints. Too soon. I would've liked to go for seven. Makes more of an impact than three."

"Why didn't you implicate me fully?" asked Layla. "Why did I always have an alibi?"

Reza's eyes shifted away from her. He fidgeted with something in his coat pocket. Was it a gun? Layla snuck a look at Mira. But she was watching her son with a mixture of love and despair.

"Tell me? Why?" she insisted.

"Because I couldn't, okay!" he shouted. "I couldn't make up my mind. I didn't want to lose you again. I wanted to punish her more than I wanted you punished. She is the one who made the choice, not you. I remember," his voice dropped, "you ran after me, you tried to hug me, you cried. You loved me, you used to tell me stories. You used to give me baths, although you were only a year older. I remembered you loved me. Also, if you'd been implicated who'd have played the game with me then? No one understands stories like you do. Not even Mother."

The silence in the library was so acute its presence was suddenly oppressive.

"Hamza," she said, "I'm so sorry for all the pain you must have gone through. I understand. And I am sorry."

Reza shrugged, "Too late, Layla. Hamza is gone forever now. Reza Kemal knows nothing but the bitter taste of abandonment and betrayal. And I will exact vengeance upon you and your mother." Then he picked up the book again. "Why did you just give this to me? You've taken all the fun out of it. Are you tricking me?"

"No, of course not. What's the trick? I just want you to have it. That's what you wanted, isn't it?"

"Not like this. Don't be ridiculous, Layla," he put the book back. He frowned and paced and then turned towards them again, with a gun in his hand, "I must kill you both."

Layla would have screamed but Khayyam stood at the door with his hands up in surrender.

FIFTEEN

"Oh, hello Khayyam," Reza said. The gun was pointing at Mira.

Khayyam hesitated.

"Come on in," Reza said with a smile. "Join us. You know how these things go."

Khayyam glanced at Layla. He walked in slowly.

"Good," said Reza. "Have a seat."

Khayyam pulled a low stool next to Layla. "Are you hurt? You okay?"

"Yes, how did you—"

"Mira called me. And I called Detective Lance. He'll be here soo—"

"Oh, pish, pash. Let's not waste time. I'll be long gone before he comes." Reza interjected.

"Why'd you murder those women, Reza? Why do you have your sister and mother at gunpoint?"

"Don't be such an ignoramus. Look at him, Mother, asking questions the wrong way. You have to ask questions in the right order, so the story makes sense." He turned to Layla, "I wanted you to find me." Then he turned back to Khayyam, "You have to appreciate the aesthetic of it all. It was very artistic. Did you get the subtleties of fairytales being Sufi stories? No, I doubt that you did."

"That was very clever," said Layla. "Especially because you went around telling everyone how much you hated stories. It was a very effective alibi."

Reza laughed. "Exactly. But I do hate stories. I also happen to understand them very well."

"But even you don't know the whole truth. The truth behind the truth," said Mira.

"What? Mother?" Reza glanced at Mira with a frown. "What are you saying?"

His voice had undertones of panic. He must always be afraid of falling short. With an adversary like Mira, in the arena of stories. He'd put the book on the table. Now he placed a hand on it. Stories were strength.

"You must first understand who we are, and who Layla is destined to become." Mira continued.

Reza shifted his weight from his left foot to his right, "Be very careful, Mother. Your life depends on it. You're making me angry again."

The air tasted of fear. Reza made a sound of impatience.

"Then hear me Layla," said Mira. "There is and always has been a circle of storytellers," Mira continued. "It is known by many names, the Axis Mundi, the Pole and the Pillars, the Mandala, and so on. When you first saw the pictures, the dead girl, Gul, on your carpet, with the book in her apron, the carpet caught your eye. The code was obvious to you, the signs were there—flowers and animals, the roebuck, the hoopoe, the rose. In Sufi tradition they're known as secret keepers."

"What does she mean, Layla? Tell me!" ordered Reza. The gun was not steady in his hand. It was now pointed at Layla.

"The h-hoopoe is the crowned bird, who hides her eggs most cleverly from predators and other harm. Eggs are a symbol of hidden truth. The hoopoe is known in Sufi literature as the symbol of the wise." Layla said in a low voice.

"What else?" said Reza.

"A-a story was woven into the carpet about a princess and a firebird in a secret garden," she added. "The firebird symbolizes truth."

Layla had loved the imagery. She'd loved the hues and patterns as well as the paradisiacal birds and flowers of the carpet. Sometimes when the nights had been unusually dark, she'd wished it was a magic flying carpet that would carry her far away.

Khayyam added, "Repetition of pattern indicates a short message, a geometric pattern means that numbers are involved, and a floral design specifies a scriptural reference as flowers are indicative of the Garden of Eden. Only the most knowledgeable of ancient storytellers can read those symbols and messages woven into carpets."

Reza looked at them with mock surprise, "I could read it! I knew. I have read all your books. Why'd you think I chose to put the girl there? Bet you couldn't see the link, Khayyam."

Layla's heart sank. She was beginning to see what Mira was getting at. The ability to understand the secret wisdom, though rare and valuable, was not enough on its own. One had to then practice the knowledge received. One had to live the life, make every choice in the light of that wisdom, that knowledge, and choose to be the hero in one's own and in other people's lives. It wasn't easy being a hero when no one was watching, when the right thing to do was to stay silent, to forgive, to let go, to not be seen. It wasn't easy having power and not using it.

Stories were the luminous landmarks that identified such heroes. Stories were the evidence that women of knowledge and power, who could be everything, had existed over the long passage of time.

"There was a seeker," Layla said. "He asked his Master to reveal to him the secret name of God. Hadn't he dedicated his life long to the Path, he asked. The Master took him to the city centre where the poor and the wretched lived. The city police beat up an old man for passing too close to them. Little children ate from the refuse. The seeker bowed his head and meditated for another year. Then he asked his Master again and the same thing happened. Again, they saw the wretched old man being beaten, the children living in squalor and neglect. When the third time the seeker asked and the Master took him to the slums, she pointed to the old man and said, "That is the man who taught me the secret name of God."

Reza scoffed, "What's the lesson, sister? Don't be a fool like the old man?"

"No," whispered Layla, "the lesson is having power does not translate into usage. The lesson is, having knowledge, you must use it at times to conceal the very knowledge you have, to protect it from being used for wrong reasons by the wrong people."

Reza looked bemused. "Power and knowledge have long been confused. Knowledge is power only when you know how and when to use it."

Mira said softly, "Power without knowledge is tyranny. In Islamic mysticism, the hoopoe is mentioned as the keeper of Solomon's secrets. The hoopoe is known to disguise secrets, to keep wisdom and knowledge safe till it is time to reveal it. It is the leader of the birds in *The Conference of the Birds* by Attar."

Layla whispered, "The roebuck is another secret symbol of the mystics because it is itself hardly ever seen. It is a difficult animal to hunt, and it is a king without being a predator."

"And the rose is a symbol of love and of fragrance, and perfume denotes truth because like perfume, truth cannot be hidden." Reza's voice had become strained. His gaze a little off-kilter. He didn't know what it was perhaps, but he knew something was up. Mira and she, both hated the fragrance of roses. Did Reza hate it too?

"The symbols of the secret lore of Sufi storytelling," Layla summed up.

"Sometimes," Mira said, "carpets can hold a whole story in a two-inch space, or a clue, to those in the know of emblems, of mythical birds, even paradisiacal plants and herbs never seen on earth."

Never seen on Earth...

Layla recalled the nonsense words Kamli had written in her mother's story book. She didn't say anything; she couldn't because right then, something was happening. An initiation. And Layla was afraid that it was hers. Reza didn't know it yet.

"What does any of this have to do with me? Why did you say I have to understand? I know all this, and I understand," Reza said.

"As in a Sufi story," said Mira, her voice low and foreboding, "carpets have multiple weaves. Some cut against others, some mesh, and others stand out to mark change. You could have been a storyteller too. But you cut against the weave. You could have been a Pillar, but you chose to be a murderer instead. You chose another path. You chose destruction instead of healing and serving. You sought to destroy the very thing that you should have protected—the first stories you heard and loved. You wanted the book to hurt me, and Layla. You wanted to destroy the book and us. You betrayed stories and your true calling."

Some endings were too final. Some stories like threads, remained loose. Reza's planning had been deliberate, meticulous. He had cut at the deepest symbols of women and stories by placing the dead body on the carpet.

Reza's laugh was manic, "Such fairytales. Axis Mundi! Rubbish!"

Layla felt her heart sink like a stone in a still pond. Whenever a tale was shared, there was the warmth of fire between the storyteller and the recipient of the tale. In the telling of the tale, sometimes the fire might dim, and cold seep into the bones of the recipient. At times, the fire burned too bright, blinding the recipient, and the recipient would come to the secret of the tale later. Perhaps, too late.

Sometimes, it was too late.

Reza glanced at Khayyam, who watched back steadily.

"How do you know who they are? These Pillars and poles, storytellers. How do they become pillars and poles?" asked Reza.

"One Pole and four Pillars. That is how it's always been. Those who are drawn to the work of Storytelling choose themselves for the job. No one asks them. No one forces them. They are drawn to it. Their lives are what they are and so they become the storytellers and the Pillars. And the Pole rises in rank from among them to the position because of the quality of their work, the longevity of their work and the influence of their stories and their person." Mira stated.

Reza glanced at Khayyam again.

Khayyam said. "It is true. The Sufi story is a rite of passage. A journey that changes the heart. All Sufi stories have the watermark of truth woven into them for the discerning eye to see."

The stories of Prophets—Abraham, Isaac, Ishmael, Jacob, Joseph, Moses, Jesus, Mohammad. They had all experienced the hero's journey as Joseph Campbell described. Mothers lost or denied; homes lost or denied; oppression, the call, doubt, answering the call, hardships, regression and finally, victory.

Reza's eyes narrowed; he sucked his teeth. Khayyam was pissing him off.

Layla said, "Sufis and storytellers aren't usually kings and queens, although there have been those as well. They have been prophets too. Solomon was the most famous and all three, a king, a Sufi storyteller and prophet, a bridge between East and West. And Mary is another such bridge across the three monotheistic religions, revered by all. Mary is the quintessential Mother."

"Not everyone can hear the Call," Reza said. "Not everyone gets the opportunity to be a hero."

The wistful undertones wrenched Layla's heart. She could so easily have taken his path. Perhaps not the murdering rampage, but the hate and the rage certainly could so easily have destroyed her and then, no stories would have healed her. She would tell no healing stories, no empowering stories, and she would unearth no secret stories, nor forgotten ones. What a sad and empty life that would have been.

A shadow passed over his handsome face. "You're one of them aren't you, Layla? You're part of the Axis Mundi? That is what she said? She is initiating you right in front of me."

Mira turned towards Layla then, once again the Storyteller. The famed Mira Heshmat. Her voice held the power of Story.

"Your initiation started a long time ago. Don't think it's a random raffle, Layla," said Mira gently. "We who have suffered pain, and sacrifice and lived with it understand these are the sacred rites. Dedication to learning, to knowledge, combined with your suffering, grief and loss are what make you a true storyteller...We're chosen so we work in secret, in the margins, under cover, never claiming victory at having righted a voice wronged in a story or in life, that has been oppressed so long people have forgotten there was one. We are meant t—"

Reza turned and shot Mira.

SIXTEEEN

The gun shot resounded in the high-ceilinged old room.

Mira toppled down from her stool on Layla's left.

Layla heard screaming. She slid to the floor and cradled Mira's head in her lap. Her vision blurred. Her hands shook and she felt cold. Khayyam, who had been sitting to her right, was now down on his knees looking at Mira's wound. Someone was still screaming.

"Stop!" Reza yelled in her ear. The screaming stopped. He remained standing before them just as he had been earlier.

"God, the noise! Why are women so shrill?" He walked back and forth before them.

Her body was shaking. It was she who'd been screaming, she realized.

Reza stood over them with bloodshot eyes. "Suffering? Loss? I suffered!" he shouted. "Where is my reward?"

Mira was bleeding out on the floor of her library. Layla held her. She made no sound. The world still resounded with the discharge of the gunshot. Khayyam scrambled out of his jacket and pressed it on the wound on Mira's stomach.

"You're okay. She's okay."

Mira's face was losing colour and was turning ghostly pale. When Layla looked up at Khayyam's face, he looked back, grim-faced and helpless.

"Press here," he said, putting Layla's hands on the jacket, which was darkening under her hands, the blood sticky. Her vision blurred.

"It's okay," said Mira. "Don't cry."

"Please…please," Layla choked. Who was she begging? Why? It was already too late.

"Is this true then?" Reza demanded. "What she says is true? The book is useless. That's why you gave it to me. You lied!"

Reza threw the book at them and turned away. Khayyam made a movement, but Reza sensed it. He turned and pointed the gun at him and jerked his head to the stool. Khayyam, glaring in impotent rage, sat down again. His hands were bloody.

Reza pushed his face into hers and then Khayyam's, "Feel any different? Do you feel powerful? Do you feel important?"

There was an edge to his voice.

Khayyam said, "Something you wouldn't understand, Reza. Storytelling, but especially Sufi Storytelling, is not about power, but service."

"So, it is true," Reza said softly.

"It isn't all true," Layla said. She caressed her mother's cold cheek. "There isn't just one way to Story. Suffering is not the only way. But one does have to choose the Path of story. I chose it. Intention is all that matters. Love, joy, loneliness are all paths to story."

Mira had chosen it too. But that Mira didn't know everything, surprised Layla. How could Mira, the famous storyteller not understand that suffering was not the only way? An immense grief settled on her heart. It was heavy. It made breathing difficult. Suffering had been her way and she had thought it was the only way.

"The telling of a tale is a debt, a gift, a responsibility." Layla whispered, as much for herself as for Reza. Her vision misty, her cheeks wet. "The storyteller must pass on the story so that it does not die with them. That is the debt. Shared with the wrong person, or at the wrong time even with the right person, it is useless. It is a dead thing then. That is the responsibility–to share the story at the right time, with the right person."

It was no accident that she had been adopted by Hasina. Mira had known all along where she was and with whom. Her mother had stayed away to protect her from the dangers of Gulraiz and Hamza, and she'd been right. But Hamza had found them, hadn't he? And now Mira was dying in her arms. But in the story, it wasn't Rustam who died. It was Sohrab. This was wrong. She had just been getting used to the grief of the reality and not the perfection of imagination of finding her mother, and now she would have to live with the pain of losing her forever.

Reza was at her shoulder, asking something. She didn't understand.

"Please don't die," she whispered. Mira's frail hand on hers was so cold. Khayyam had been pushed back in one of the seats by Reza. He sat there, rigid and tense.

Reza's face was close to hers, "Is Khayyam one of the Pillars too?" he turned to him. "Are you?"

Mira grunted, "Yes." Her eyes turned upwards, trying to see Layla, "He met you in Lahore to be initiated by Hasina."

"Let me call an ambulance. She is so pale," she said. Death was the last act. Then there was silence.

Reza shook his head. "What does it mean to be the Pole?"

Layla answered, "It means she is the leader. Storytellers guard the accurate stories long hidden, so that women always have someone to remind them of their truth, their agency and their secrets.'

Mira's wobbly smile faltered. "For…now. But soon…"

All her rage at her mother dissolved into regret. Stories followed their own laws. And she must follow them too.

Layla turned to Reza, "Burning the book won't accomplish anything. There is a secret in it you must know. It won't do you any good though. And I am glad of it. You don't deserve stories or their legacy. Your heart is sterile."

"Tell me the secret," Reza hissed.

"Kamli wrote in the book, a word here, a word there. Because I read the book so frequently, I know the words by heart. Then one day they fell into place. I know what the words meant. They were just a few lines.

"*'Eve brought the Book of Signs with her from which stems all knowledge. She brought it with her from Paradise and entrusted her daughter with it. The Book has been bequeathed from daughter to daughter.'*"

"What nonsense!" he asked. He cocked his head, looking at Mira, then Layla. "I don't understand?"

"Stories are alive, like us. Stories grow. Stories reproduce. Stories die. And Sufi stories tend to come to those in need of them. The best stories, the strongest stories, the ones that last and have an impact, are tended with love and blood. Passed on. They are nurtured in the habitat of soul and instinct. One such story, a secret story, is that Eve brought the Book of Names with her from the Garden of Eden. She instructed the Book be passed from daughter to daughter."

"Some would call that fantasy," said Khayyam.

"So, what's this? What do you believe?" demanded Reza.

Layla said, "Well, I believe there was Eve and Paradise and there's God. I believe in all of that because I have lived and breathed Sufi stories and their inherent laws for too long to not see the Divine patterns. I believe. But I don't believe that there is a Book that Eve brought with her. Or Adam. Least of all him. I believe that having eaten the fruit of the tree of knowledge first, Eve *was* the Book of knowledge. She passed on the knowledge to her daughters through storytelling. I believe that knowledge is never a secret. It is always available for those that seek it."

"You must think I am mad, or stupid?" said Reza.

"It's just a parable. There is no such book. There was no secret. Knowledge is within us, isn't it?" Layla said.

"What is this?" Reza turned to Mira, "What is she saying? All books are just a symbol then? What are you saying?"

Mira tried to say something, but she was not audible.

Was it sirens Layla could hear? Had detective Lance called for back-up before he'd come? He must have. Could Reza hear? Or was he too distracted by her apotheosis to Storyteller to hear. Then there was nothing. Had she imagined the sirens?

She looked squarely at Reza, engaging his attention, "Stories impart the immense knowledge Eve suffered so much to get. She ate of the fruit first and became more than she could have imagined, because she had shaken off the oppression of being secondary, not just second. She became first when she ate the fruit and became wiser and learnt the secret knowledge of the universe."

Mira squeezed her hand. There was no pressure at all. But she knew Mira wanted to speak and so she looked at her. Reza did too.

"Reza…still time…return." Mira wheezed. Layla feared she would lose consciousness soon. She'd lost too much blood.

Reza's expression turned speculative. "Will I become a Pillar?"

Mira's breath came out in a wheeze.

There was no response.

He nodded, "So, she gets to be your Pillar and I don't? She gets to be a part of your legacy and I don't? Again."

"Reza—"

"Shut up!" he yelled. "Do you see what she does?" He pointed the gun now at Mira, now at Layla, as he talked and gestured standing over them. "Do you see? Manipulative bitch! She learned from the best. That bastard Gulraiz said he'd make me Chief if I got him your heads. He would say I was the best. And then he'd make his guards beat me to a pulp."

Mira's breath was shallow.

"Wake up, you old hag! You witch!" Reza yelled. "Firdous Moor was right. You don't deserve to live."

"Please," Layla begged, her mother's frail body in her lap. "I just found you. Reza…haven't we all suffered enough?"

"Reza, listen to your sister," Khayyam was watching Mira, gravely.

"Put your hands in the air where we can see them…"

The shadows were moving. A red dot appeared on Reza's chest. He had been too busy yelling at them to notice the movement at the door. A uniformed officer approached pointing a gun at him from one end of the library. Others appeared behind him and soon surrounded Reza. He turned towards Layla, as if to shoot. Detective James pushed forward and snatched the gun away from him.

Too late. They'd come too late.

"This isn't over, Layla. I'll find you no matter where you go," Reza said as two officers pulled his arms behind him. Reza's eyes were on Mira. Layla wanted to comfort him, and she wanted to shut her eyes and never see him again. But it was Reza who looked away. It was always he who turned away from her.

Paramedics were already seeing to Mira but she was suddenly heavy in Layla's arms. Khayyam put his arm around Layla's shoulders.

Layla heard the words they said. She'd lost too much blood. But Layla couldn't let go of her body. Mira had just come back into her life to initiate her into the art of storytelling and the Path of the Axis Mundi. That was all that Mira cared about. That was all Mira's life had been.

Layla finally understood her mother. And in understanding her, she feared her own future. There was an old Asian saying. Blessed are parents who are buried by their children. What about those who are killed by their own children?

Layla picked up her beloved book from the table and handed it to Detective Lance, "Please, give this to him. It might give him some peace."

She didn't need it anymore, and it might help him. She hoped it would.

"I called Hasina. She will be here in the morning," said Khayyam. He did not leave her side. "Let me take you home."

Khayyam's eyes were crowded with worries.

She nodded. Her world had never been safe or whole. It was already time to bury her birth mother, the fount of stories. The mother who had followed the pull of stories into danger, and finally death. For countless others, stories were still the precious shelter from the storms of life. They were still a sanctuary for the lost and abandoned, the misunderstood and the seekers of truth, and she was entrusted with the task to make sure they remained so. That was her life's work, to ensure that stories remained true psychic maps and that she would be one of the makers of such true maps. It was sacred work.

Khayyam took her hand. And she held on tight.

But was she willing to make that sacrifice? She wasn't sure. Stories were the only constant in her life but now she was afraid of their power. And, as she knew so well, grieving wasn't done in a day. She wasn't sure she'd be mourning just the death of Mira, and the betrayal of Hamza alone.

She was going to mourn the death of her soul if she did not answer the Call, and the death of freedom as she knew it if she did.

ACKNOWLEDGEMENTS

Every time I get to this point, I marvel at my blessings. Alhamdolillah.

Thank you, Archna Sharma, for believing in this story. Without Archna's meticulous editing there would be many a mistake in timeline calculations and I would have missed many a finer point. My thanks to Sofia Rehman who first acquired this book for Neem Tree Press. A huge thanks to everyone at Neem Tree Press, for making this book a reality. Special thank you to the UK cover designer Anna Morrison who made this stunning cover.

Thank you, Archana Nathan, my editor at Penguin India for your faith in this book and for bringing it out into the world. Thank you also, to Shubhi Surana and the whole team at Penguin for bringing this book to life. My heartfelt thanks to Tarini Uppal at Penguin India who first acquired *The Sufi Storyteller*.

Annette Crossland, you are the best agent anyone could ask for. Thank you for your patience, support and for always cheering me on. Thank you for your hard work and for always listening. Thank you to everyone at A for Authors.

Libraries everywhere have a bit of my heart, but perhaps a few libraries have a bigger chunk of it, like the Senate House Library, where I wrote most of the first draft of this novel. Libraries and books are my happy place and I want to thank libraries and librarians everywhere.

Thank you, Jazz Singh for reading the fledgling drafts of this story and for your feedback and late-night phone calls.

Thank you Falguni Kothari, Shandana Minhas, NN Jehangir for reading the secondary drafts and giving me some hard truths. My writer friends, Awais Khan and Naima Rashid, thank you for your support always. Thank you to Dr Waseem Anwar and Dr Claire Chambers for your support always.

There are some debts that are beyond words. This book would never have been written if twenty-five years ago I had not come across Idries Shah's books, especially *The Sufis*. That book was the trigger that sent me on a quest to find out more about Sufi storytelling. I owe a huge debt to Idries Shah. Dr Clarissa Pinkola Estes's work has long sustained and shaped my imagination. In fact, Mira is my tribute to Dr Estes. I must also mention Fariddudin Attar, Marina Warner, Maria Tater, Lewis Hyde, Robert Graves, James Fraser, Joseph Campbell, Toni Morrison and Ferdowsi, whose body of work has informed and stimulated my creativity.

My deepest gratitude to the Idries Shah Foundation. Not only did the Foundation very kindly allow me to use a quote by Idries Shah, the team there has, on several occasions, sent me his books; one which I had sadly lost and some I did not have in the first place. Sincerest thanks to Tahir Shah, who is the illustrious scion of Idries Shah, for giving me such a fabulous quote for this book.

Lastly and most importantly, a huge thank you to my beloved husband, and my sons, who make my world colourful and joyous and who support me always. I love you all so much.

ABOUT THE AUTHOR

Faiqa Mansab is a Pakistani writer. She holds an MPhil in English Literature, an MFA in creative writing with a high distinction from Kingston University London, and an MA in Gender and Cultural Studies from Birkbeck University London. She has written and continues to write for numerous publications both local and international.

Her debut novel *This House of Clay and Water* was published to much critical acclaim by Penguin India in 2017. It was longlisted for Getz Pharma Fiction Prize and the German Consulate Peace Prize at the Karachi Literature Festival 2018. It has since been optioned for screen and been published in Turkish by Dedalus Press. Blackstone Publishing USA released the audio book of *This House of Clay and Water* in 2022.

Faiqa lives in Lahore with her family.